Curiouser and

fucking Curiouser.

MW01147035

BOOKS by C.M. STUNICH

Romance Novels

HARD ROCK ROOTS SERIES
Real Ugly
Get Bent
Tough Luck
Bad Day
Born Wrong
Hard Rock Roots Box Set (1-5)
Dead Serious
Doll Face
Heart Broke
Get Hitched
Screw Up

TASTING NEVER SERIES
Tasting Never
Finding Never
Keeping Never
Tasting, Finding, Keeping: The Story of Never Box Set (1-3)
Never Can Tell
Never Let Go
Never Did Say
Never Have I

ROCK-HARD BEAUTIFUL
Groupie
Roadie
Moxie

THE BAD NANNY TRILOGY
Bad Nanny
Good Boyfriend
Great Husband

TRIPLE M SERIES
Losing Me, Finding You
Loving Me, Trusting You
Needing Me, Wanting You
Craving Me, Desiring You

A DUET
Paint Me Beautiful
Color Me Pretty

FIVE FORGOTTEN SOULS
Beautiful Survivors
Alluring Outcasts

MAFIA QUEEN
Lure
Lavish
Luxe

DEATH BY DAYBREAK MC
I Was Born Ruined

STAND-ALONE NOVELS
Baby Girl
All for 1
Blizzards and Bastards (originally featured in the Snow and Seduction Anthology)
Fuck Valentine's Day (A Short Story)
Broken Pasts
Crushing Summer
Taboo Unchained
Taming Her Boss
Kicked

Violet Blaze Novels

(MY PEN NAME)

BAD BOYS MC TRILOGY
Raw and Dirty
Risky and Wild
Savage and Racy

HERS TO KEEP TRILOGY
Biker Rockstar Billionaire CEO Alpha
Biker Rockstar Billionaire CEO Dom
Biker Rockstar Billionaire CEO Boss

BOOKS by C.M. STUNICH

STAND-ALONE

Football Dick
Stepbrother Thief
Stepbrother Inked
Glacier

Fantasy Novels

THE SEVEN MATES OF ZARA WOLF

Pack Ebon Red
Pack Violet Shadow
Pack Obsidian Gold
Pack Ivory Emerald
Pack Amber Ash
Pack Azure Frost
Pack Crimson Dusk

ACADEMY OF SPIRITS AND SHADOWS

Spirited
Haunted
Shadowed

HAREM OF HEARTS

Allison's Adventures in Underland
Allison and the Torrid Tea Party
Allison Shatters the Looking Glass

SIRENS OF A SINFUL SEA TRILOGY

Under the Wild Waves

THE SEVEN WICKED SERIES

Seven Wicked Creatures
Six Wicked Beasts
Five Wicked Monsters
Four Wicked Fiends

HOWLING HOLIDAYS SHORT STORIES

A Werewolf Christmas
A Werewolf New Year's
A Werewolf Valentine's
A Werewolf St. Patrick's Day
A Werewolf Spring Break
A Werewolf Mother's Day

OTHER FANTASY NOVELS

Stiltz
Gray and Graves
Indigo & Iris
She Lies Twisted
Hell Inc.
DeadBorn
Chryer's Crest

Co-Written

(With Tate James)

HIJINKS HAREM

Elements of Mischief
Elements of Ruin
Elements of Desire

THE WILD HUNT MOTORCYCLE CLUB

Dark Glitter
Cruel Glamour

FOXFIRE BURNING

The Nine
Tail Game

OTHER

And Today I Die

Allison and the Torrid Tea Party

Copyright © 2018 C.M. Stunich

ISBN-10: 1 726815064 (pbk.)
ISBN-13: 978-1-726815062 (pbk.)

All rights reserved. No part of this book may be used or reproduced in any manner whatsoever without written permission except in the case of brief quotations embodied in critical articles or reviews.

For information address:
Sarian Royal, 89365 Old Mohawk Road, Springfield, OR 97478

Contact the author at
www.cmstunich.com

Cover art © 2017 Amanda Rose Carroll
The characters and events portrayed in this book are fictitious. Any similarity to real persons, living or dead, businesses, or locales is coincidental and is not intended by the authors.

Dedication

Generally, when I write a dedication it will be a sentence or two at most. But this book hit me at a strange time in my life, and it really made me pick apart who I was inside, and try to figure out how to put it all back together.

I have never received so much love mail or *hate mail for any series in my six-year career. Many people seemed to love the book, but others were upset at the wait for book two—understandably so—as well as my promises that it was* coming soon. *So, I just want to say that I apologize for that. I've been told by one of my PAs, and my best writing friend in the whole world not to promise release days until after I'm done; I just get so excited sometimes and can't seem to contain myself. I always think I can get more done than is humanly possible. LOL*

Some of the hate mail was horrible, some of it made me cry, but you know what? It also made me push harder than I ever have before. I think this book is one of my absolute best, and I couldn't be prouder. And for those who sent inspiring, positive messages, I just want you to know that you literally changed my world when I got to open and read them.

This book is therefore dedicated to the kind souls who cheered me up with their own words: I hope I can cheer you up with mine!

Also, huge thanks to:

Tate James, for being the best co-writer a person could ever ask for.

Bailey Lynne Hewlett for always being my positivity co-pilot.

Sara Vermillion for kicking my ass when it's needed most.

CoraLee June and G. Bailey for being warm, wonderful, and supportive.

Amanda Rose for loving the croquet scene.

And all the haters, because without you, I might not have pushed myself to the limit. Rock on, and here's a little love from me to you!

Allison and the Torrid Tea Party

harem of hearts

2

C.M. STUNICH
INTERNATIONAL BESTSELLING AUTHOR

Alice of violent wild magic
And loyal men who follow!
Though time be fleet, and truly tragic
The future is not hollow.
Thy mighty power will soon prevail
Turn nightmares into fairy-tales.

Underland soaked in haunting pain,
Topside goes burning after:
No other Alice sheds these chains
Spurred by her carnal rapture—
Blood shall spill when devils burn bright
Winning her the fucking fight.

A tale begun in other days,
When magic girls were glowing—
A simple time, that served divine
Before the Riving went a'sowing—
Dark echoes live in memory, yes,
Though greedy bastards say "forget".

Come, hearken then, ere voice of dead,
The Anti-Alice haven,
Shall summon to unwelcome dread
A melancholy maiden!
We are but wily soldiers, friend,
Who fret to find our homeland's end.

Without the magic, blinding power,
The storm-wind's moody madness—
Within Torrid Tea Party's tower,
A nest of lust and heat, true madness.
These magic words shall save us last:
All must love their warring badass.

And, through the shadow of a sigh
Her men push through the story,
For 'happy future days' come high,
And vanish'd bloody glory—
They shall not touch, with hands of hate,
The pleasance of our Heart'd gate.

1

An Even Madder Tea Party

He's going to die, isn't he?

I sit in the back of a carriage made of fucking *porcelain* and stare at North's comatose form, blood leaking from his head at an alarming rate. In a way, that's a good sign, I guess, because if he's bleeding then that means his heart is still pumping, so he's still alive.

Dead things don't bleed.

"If you don't give him medical attention, he'll die before you make it to wherever it is that we're going," I say, staring up at the three men sitting in the back of the carriage with me. They're all situated on the floor in a semi-circle, sipping *tea.* Like, laced-with-drugs, seriously-going-to-mess-them-up tea. And then what?

North will lie there and bleed to death, and I'll sit here, shackled to the wood floor, forced to watch.

"Oh, well, wouldn't that be a shame," the Mad Hatter says, his hat lilting to one side, this disheveled dishabille that he wears so well. And those eyes, the color of marmalade, this honeyed orange shade that I've never seen before. But hell, why should *that* surprise me? After everything I've seen in Underland so far, it's hardly the weirdest.

The man holds his teacup in hands dripping with ink, tattoos crawling out from beneath the black jacket he's wearing, over his knuckles, along his fingers. He's so dainty about it, too, like he's actually got some manners in that crazy head of his.

"You don't care if he dies then?" I continue as the three of them continue to lounge in the back of the jostling carriage. It's a big round, white thing that looks like a fucking teapot on the outside. The driver's sitting on a platform perched on the top of the spout, and the handle was used to open the massive door I was shoved through; there's not a single window in the whole damn thing, but I can see flashes of lightning through a circle in the roof, where I'm assuming there's some sort of 'lid'.

The screech of a jabberwock echoes outside the carriage, but nobody inside of it seems bothered except for me. Leaning back against the wall, I put my hands over my ears as the three men pass around a pot of tea like it's a bottle of whiskey. Only difference here is they pour it into a teacup before they sling it back like a shot.

"We're going to drop him off close to a musking female jabberwock nest and see what happens," the March Hare says, twitching his velveteen ears and crossing his legs at the ankle. The look he gives me is downright lascivious, but I think, rather than checking *me* out, he's fantasizing about North being ripped apart by an angry dragon.

"What the fuck does musking mean?" I ask, adjusting myself slightly and listening to the awful clank of my chains. We've been in this carriage for the better part of an hour and frankly, I haven't been able to brainstorm a way out of this one. Some part of me wonders if the twins'll come for me, but I'm also not into the whole *being-saved-by-a-prince* routine. Err, prince*s* in this case, I suppose. But still. I have to just assume that I'm alone here and try to find some way out of this mess.

"Musking," the Mad Hatter replies with this awful curve of a smile transforming his face. "That's just a dirty science word for *horny as hell*." He takes another sip of his tea and then tosses the cup aside, letting it shatter against the back wall of the carriage before crawling toward me, his honey-orange eyes bright, his skin as pale as moonlight. When he smiles, doves cry.

That's how scary this motherfucker is. "We're going to leave him out there, helpless and prone, and see if there're any takers."

"You're sick in the head," I snap back at him as he reaches out and curls some of my blonde hair around his fingers, pulling it to his face for a sniff. Seriously? What a pervert. When I jerk back, all I end up doing is yanking my hair painfully; the Mad Hatter does *not* let go. "What's the point of all that anyway, taking a hostage only to watch him die? What purpose does that serve?!"

"Who says it serves a purpose," the Mad Hatter—Raiden Walker, I guess, is his name—purrs, using the handful of my hair to pull me toward his face. "The Duke of Northumbria is a supporter of the King of Hearts—and a hefty giver of tithes to the crown—so we figured, we came all the way out here to nab *you*, why not grab him at the same time?"

"Cruelty for cruelty's sake," I retort, but the pale—and admittedly handsome—man in front of me just grins bigger and snaps his fingers. *Bingo,* I guess, *I've figured it all out.* He lets go of my hair and then sits back, propping one knee and throwing his arm casually across it. The strangely beautiful color of his eyes drifts down to my neck, watching my pulse hum and throb beneath my skin.

"Cruelty is in the eye of the beholder," he says, just as vague and weird as everyone else that lives here. They can blame all their strangeness on the Riving if they want, but I blame it on testosterone poisoning. Clearly, with a ratio of ten men to one woman, that must be it. The air is thick with it. My guess? The Duke and this guy, Raiden, they have some sort of pissing war going on. "Tell you what?" he says after a minute, just when my eyes begin to stray over to the March Hare and the Dormouse. I turn my attention back to him and our gazes lock. "Answer me a riddle and I'll let the Duke go."

"Ask me a riddle and if I get it right, you give him medical attention and keep him *alive*. You don't even have to let him go; he can stay with me." The Mad Hatter raises two dark brows, his black hair curling out from under his hat in a defiant sort of way. I figure beggars can't be choosers and it'd be better if North were alive and being held prisoner than lying half-dead and free in the middle of the forest.

"You're an interesting one, aren't you?" Raiden glances over his shoulder at the March Hare, still slowly sipping his tea and watching us with eyes the color of dark chocolate, bitter and sweet at the same time. On his other side, the massive hulk of the Dormouse is sprawled and sleeping, teacup clenched in his huge hand.

"Smart, too," I quip, crossing my arms over my chest and hating the feel of the cold chains against my skin. I'm still wearing my dressing gown, and really, it doesn't provide a lot of coverage. In the darkest depths of my mind, I realize what could so easily happen to a girl like me, dressed in a nightie and kidnapped like this. The awful, awful fate I avoided that night at the hands of Liam and his friends—the salvation that cost my brother his *life* and my mother her freedom—that could all be revisited on me here.

But these men, they seem … well, *mad.* And if I can just keep them talking, maybe I can hold them off from trying anything else, buy myself time to escape. The Vorpal Blade is still there, resting against my thigh. I can practically *feel* it pulsing against my skin, begging me to spill blood. Or maybe that's just because I'm pissed off and hating these guys right about now?

A bit of crimson warmth from North's head wound soaks into the edge of my nightgown and I glance down, touching my fingertips to it and holding them up in a quick flash of lightning that briefly illuminates the dark interior of the carriage.

My blue eyes lift up to the Mad Hatter's orange ones.

"Ask me the damn riddle," I growl, dropping my hand into my lap. I'd scoot out of the way of the blood, but there's nowhere for me to go. I'm chained down; North is chained down. I can't even put his head in my lap or stroke the side of his face with my fingers. Seeing him like this, I wish I'd gone all the way during training and had sex with him.

What if he dies? What if I'm sitting here and he takes

one, last shuddering breath? The thought makes my insides churn with anxiety, like a swarm of moths pulling apart an old blanket, leaving it riddled with holes. I can feel their tiny mouths nibbling away at me as I sit there and stare my captor down.

"Okay then," he starts, his voice this ice-cold lilt that somehow has me leaning forward to listen as he taps a tattooed finger against his lips. In my heart of hearts, I'm hoping that *this* time, life stays true to the prophecy, to the original book. Because if so, I've got an answer for the riddle I so desperately want him to ask. "Why … is a raven like a writing-desk?"

Fuck. Yes.

I try not to smile too much when I hear those words, the riddle from the classic novel *and* the same one used in the Disney adaption with Johnny Depp.

Oh, come on, this is almost too easy!

"Assuming you have no real answer in mind," I begin, because Lewis Carroll was once quoted as saying that it was originally intended that the Hatter's riddle had no answer. Later on though, about thirty years after the book was published, he made one up. "I'll give you one: because it can produce a few notes, though they are very flat; and it is nev*a*r"—I spell this part out because the word *never* is intentionally misspelled to read *raven* backwards—"put with the wrong end in front."

I sit back against the wall of the carriage and wait while the man stares at me for some time and then gives me this *slow* ass fucking smile that flashes me two sharp white canines in his mouth. Not like a cat, not like Chesh, but like … a *vampire*. The dude looks like a fucking bloodsucker.

"You're a clever little Alice, aren't you?" he asks and then tosses me a key. "Go ahead," he continues, reaching up to adjust the hat on his head. It's huge, at least a foot and a half tall, and slightly wider on the top than the bottom. "Free yourself, and him."

Even though I'm skeptical as fuck, I unlock the chains, my eyes drifting back to the March Hare as he sits there, stoic and unblinking, bathed in shadows. I have no idea what to make of him, but as long as he doesn't move, I'm okay with his creepy weirdness.

"North," I whisper, unlocking the chains and praying that maybe, just maybe, the man is playing dead. You know, like an exit strategy or something. But he doesn't move as I unshackle him. How could he? With hole in the side of his head like that.

Raiden leans over next to me and grabs North by the horn, yanking him across the carriage and into his lap. My entire body goes stiff as the Mad Hatter flicks his orange gaze up to mine and smirks. He's fucking terrifying, this guy, and how the hell do I know he's going to help the Duke and not just slit his throat? I answered a riddle, so what?

Bad guys never keep their promises, right?

"I do love riddles. I'll have to come up with another. Maybe if you answer the next one, I'll let you go?"

I snort.

"And why would you do that?" I ask as he lifts his wrist to his mouth … and *bites* it. Blood wells around his teeth, staining his tattooed skin before dripping onto North's pallid face. The poor jabberwock man is completely out, his pulse so light that I can't make it out, not even in a flash of lightning. He seriously looks like he's dead, like I'll never see those golden eyes again, feel that tail wrap around my ankle …

You just met this guy, so who cares? I try to tell myself, but it doesn't matter. I just met him, but I like him. A lot. He's charismatic and interesting, took the time to teach me, gave me the Vorpal Blade. He didn't *have* to do any of those things.

"Because," Raiden continues, pulling his mouth away from his arm and then placing his wrist at the Duke's pale lips. "I'm a mercenary. I do whatever I want, whenever I want. The King of Clubs paid me to kidnap you … but, for example, if I decide I like you, I just keep you for myself."

He presses his wrist against North's mouth, but the man is so out of it that blood just puddles on his tongue and spills out the sides. Raiden lowers his gaze to the comatose guy in his lap, removes his wrist, and then places it at his *own* mouth, sucking out the blood until his mouth is full.

With his lips pressed tight, he leans down again and places his mouth to North's, parting the Duke's lips with his tongue and *kissing* him, forcing him to drink all of that blood. My cheeks heat, and I can't decide whether to be pissed off, turned on, or … what.

"What are you doing?" I manage to choke out, but the Mad Hatter just lifts his orange eyes to mine and locks our gazes. He continues to kiss North until the Duke is shifting and groaning, dressed in a pair of cream silk pajama pants and nothing else. They're stained with blood, just like his golden hair and sun-kissed chest.

The Mad Hatter ignores me until North is shoving him back and surging up with a gasping, choking sound, almost bumping his head against our captor's forehead.

"What in the bloody fuck?" the Savage Duke growls, and my heart swells with relief. *Holy fucking shit.* I hadn't even realized until that moment how goddamn stressed I was. Without giving myself even a second to question my luck, I throw my arms around North's neck and … *kiss him?!*

Oh, well, whatever.

I tongued him in the training room and that was just pure lust.

This is so much more important than that … And even

though it takes me a moment to remember that he just sucked down some dude's blood, I don't care. I pull back and put my forehead against his, my skin erupting in little goose bumps as he clamps his hands on my hips and squeezes *tight*, claws digging into the thin silk as he lets out this animalistic snarl and curls his tail around my ankle.

"Welcome back to the world of the living," Raiden says as North's gold eyes light on my face and then flick over my shoulder to look at the … well, actual fucking vampire dude?! I don't bother to turn around, reaching up and spreading North's hair to look for the missing chunk of skull and flesh that I saw earlier.

It's gone.

All closed up. Just smooth skin and gold hair and hard bone underneath it all.

"What on earth are you up to, Hatter?" North asks in that crisp British-but-can't-be-British accent of his. He pulls me even closer against him, squashing my breasts to his chest. There's not a lot of fabric between us, and I'm not wearing underwear so … I wish we weren't being kidnapped by a maniacal vampire mercenary.

"Oh, you know me, my loyalty goes out to the highest bidder," Raiden says from behind us, his voice casual despite the fact that both North and I are now free. He's not worried about being attacked? If he really is that powerful, we're fucked. If he's just that cocky, we might be okay. "Nothing personal, really."

"Please," North says, curling his arms around me and holding me so close I feel like I might choke. But he's so damn warm, and I'm so glad to see him alive. Plus, I'm riding the high of being shackled and then set free. "You've never liked me." The smirk that crawls over his face morphs rapidly into a wide grin, his teeth white in his bronze, bloodied face. "Especially not now that I have the love of the Alice."

"Love?" I ask, but it's hard to want to argue, trapped in the back of the carriage like this. I push back from North, but he only lets me go enough to turn around and sit on his lap, my back to his front. Does not make the position any less sexual. Between my legs, a throbbing starts up that I do my absolute best to quell. Now is hardly the time for thoughts of thick cocks and wet cunts and all that nonsense.

The Mad Hatter leans forward as I swipe some long, blonde tendrils out of my face.

"Your hair wants cutting," he remarks, those orange eyes glowing in a flash of lightning. Between bouts, it's almost pitch-dark in here, just a few stray shafts of moonlight cutting through the ice-cold drops of rain leaking in through the ceiling.

"You should learn not to make personal remarks," I snap, narrowing my eyes at him and tucking my hair behind my ears. "It's fucking rude."

He just smiles at me and then pauses when the carriage comes to a stop.

"And here we were planning on leaving you out for the female jabberwocky to pick apart," Raiden says with a small sigh, nodding his head to indicate something to the March Hare. The other man taps his palm against the wall twice and the carriage begins to rattle onward. "I was hoping they'd rape you, steal your seed, and leave a corpse."

My jaw drops open, but the Mad Hatter is already turning around and crawling back over to the teapot that's on the floor near the March Hare. There's not a lot of standing room back here, so he leaves himself completely open and vulnerable as he moves back to his original spot.

Turning my head into North's arm, I whisper as quietly as I can, "I have the Vorpal Blade with me." He tightens up, but it's too late. I've already made a mistake. As soon as Raiden turns around and slumps back against the wall next to his companions, he's smiling.

"You think I'm stupid enough to miss a blade? Also, I should warn you, having been bitten and turned into one of the undead has given me *spectacular* hearing. If I were you, I'd keep all my secrets to myself."

He picks up the teapot and pours himself a new cup.

So far, I haven't noticed the Mad Hatter showing any signs of that light, ethereal nonsense I experienced when I was high on tea, but maybe he's just a heavyweight? A little patience might be called for in this scenario.

"Don't attack him," North tells me, his arms wrapped tight around my middle, just under my breasts. "Not with magic, not with the Blade. Just let it be." He squeezes me a little harder and I grunt. "And thank you for saving me."

"I'm not even sure how you're alive right now," I whisper back, but, of course, Raiden Walker, Vampire Extraordinaire, hears me and decides to comment.

"Vampire blood has incredible healing properties, doesn't it, North?"

"You may call me the Duke of Northumbria, my right and proper bloody title." The Duke leans back against the wall, taking me with him. I'm sitting there wondering why he isn't shifting and tearing this place apart when I feel his pulse thundering against my back, his breath coming in short, sharp bursts. He's physically healed from his wound, but his body is still recovering, damn it.

Still, shouldn't a massive black dragon be more than enough to bring down this house of cards, so to speak?

But the rules of this game, of Underland, they're all still a mystery to me. I'll just have to follow North's lead and hope he knows what he's doing. He seems pretty interested in not only delivering me to the king, but also becoming one of my … *gulp* … husbands. Anyway, I figure I can safely assume he's on my side.

"Well, *Duke of Northumbria,*" Raiden drawls, tapping his fingers against his knees and smiling at us with his long, thin, beautiful mouth. I couldn't get that image of him French kissing North out of my brain if I tried—and I don't much want to try. "I was going to kill you, but seeing as the Alice answered my riddle fair and square, I figure we can bargain instead. How much to take you both safely to the King of Hearts?"

"What?" I ask, blinking stupidly in his direction. "Are you trying to *buy* your way out of a contract you already signed?"

"We don't sign contracts," the March Hare says, speaking up for the first time in a while. He leans forward, his dark brown eyes the perfect match for his brown ears and brown skin. But all three parts of him are different shades, giving him this earthy sort of look. He'd be hot if he wasn't kidnapping me, but what's new? Basically every man in Underland is hot as fuck. "People give us money and pray that they're not outbid. Think of it … like a silent auction or something." He glances down at the Dormouse and then both he and the Mad Hatter reach down and pinch the big man from both sides at once. "Wake up, Dor!"

The Dormouse slowly opens his eyes.

"I wasn't asleep," he says in a hoarse, feeble voice, "I heard every word you fellows were saying."

March snorts and gives the hulking man a scathing look.

"Bullshit," he says with a curl of his full, generous mouth. "You narcoleptic fuck."

"Ten thousand coins," North inserts as I watch the Dormouse sit up and stretch his tree trunk-sized arms over his head. He's just as attractive as his companions, but in a different way, not my style or type. He's got that bulky bodybuilder look that's a tad too much for me. And his face is a little Neanderthal, like *I-drag-you-to-cave-by-hair* alpha male-esque.

"Oh, please," the Mad Hatter says with a roll of his eyes, pouring himself another cup of tea and then turning his attention in my direction, an earnest sort of look on his face. "Take some more tea, Alice?"

"I've had nothing yet," I reply in an offended tone: "so I can't take more."

"Ah, you mean you can't take *less*," says the Hatter: "it's very easy to take *more* than nothing."

"Nobody asked *your* fucking opinion," I snap back, and he smiles at me in a way that makes me wonder how dark and how brutal this negotiation is heading. He doesn't just want money, does he?

"Who's making personal remarks now?" Raiden quips triumphantly.

"Thirty thousand," the Duke says, his voice this low, humming growl that vibrates through his body and straight into mine. It feels so good that I have to resist the urge to wiggle on his lap. Not here, not in front of these three assholes. "And you *know* the King will match whatever I spend."

"I quite imagine the King wants the Alice far more than he values sixty thousand measly coins," Raiden continues, glancing across Dor's lap and over to March. "Don't you think our friend here would've gladly *paid* sixty thousand coins to see the Savage Duke raped by jabberwocky?"

"One hundred thousand," North snarls, uncurling his tail from around me and slamming the long, black scaled length against the floor in frustration, quite like my cat Dinah does when she's having a fit.

"Let me bash his head in again, sir," the Dormouse growls right back, leaning his massive form toward us. In a flash of lightning, I catch the ragged stripes of scars across his face, and the small round ears sticking up from his tousled brown hair. "I'll give you my wages for the next ten years to take the privilege."

"You're starting to annoy Dor," March says, his voice crisp with a 'British' accent similar to North's. But there's something else to it, too, like maybe a bit of Irish? *Fuck, this guy looks* and *sounds like Rob Evans!* The sexual selection happening in Underland is seriously *insane*, like there are so many men they have to be hot as hell to have any chance of finding a mate. Makes sense from a scientific level, right? "And if you're starting to annoy Dor, then you're starting to annoy me, too."

"Five hundred thousand," the Duke spits, his arms tightening around my waist. "You bloody twat. Crook. Fearmonger."

"Five hundred thousand, doubled by the King of Hearts," the Mad Hatter continues, sipping his tea. "I like that. Oh, and also, I want to marry the Alice. Political power suits me, don't you think? I'd make a fine husband."

"Marry you?!" I blurt and then let out the most caustic, scathing laugh imaginable. "I don't think—"

"Then you shouldn't talk," the Mad Hatter inserts, causing me to grit my teeth and clench my fists in anger.

"If I get out of here, I'm going to make it my personal life mission to dump your body down a well," I snap back at him and he grins, flashing me those vampire fangs of his.

"A water-well or a treacle-well?" he purrs, and both men beside him let out these deep belly laughs, like that's the greatest joke they've ever heard. Me, I don't get it. I know treacle is like, syrup or molasses or something, but a well of it? I guess this world *is* weird enough for something like that. Still …

"Where would they draw the treacle from?" I snap back

at him, even though I know it's totally stupid and a complete waste of my time. These idiots are obviously talking in riddles—like Tee and Dee—so why am I justifying their stupidity?

"You can draw water out of a water-well," says the piece of shit Hatter, "so I should think you could draw treacle out of a treacle-well—eh, stupid?"

I surge forward, intending to tackle this back talking a-hole, but North holds me still, his muscular arms like bands of steel around my waist.

"A million coins," he grinds out, but the Mad Hatter and the March Hare just exchange a look across the lap of the Dormouse.

"Five hundred thousand from you, and five hundred thousand from the king, and this girl's hand in marriage," Raiden continues, staring me straight in the face. "Or else we take you to the King of Clubs, as planned. *He* has already promised me a spot as one of your husbands, Alice."

"Alli*son*," I correct, but really, why bother? The people in this place are clearly deranged; they can barely seem to keep their heads on straight, so how on earth can I expect them to listen when I tell them my name. "So what you're saying is, accept this offer and pretend I'm making my own choice about taking you as a husband or else you'll sell me to the next highest bidder and then, what, rape me in our marital bed after the forced wedding?"

"Whoever said I needed to have sex with you to gain the political prestige of being married to the Alice?" he asks with a tilt of his head, his top hat falling to one side but still managing to stay atop his head of dark, wavy hair. "Let's make a deal: the promised coins, your hand in marriage, but I won't fuck you until you beg."

"Oh, please," I snort, with a sneer worthy of my little sister, Edy. "You're fucking delusional."

"Delusions are just illusions without any truth behind them," Raiden says, and it's such a stupid, useless riddle that I just count my lucky stars that he really *did* follow along with the prophecy and use the raven/writing-desk one in our bargain. If not, who the fuck knows what would've happened to North?

"Fine," I say before the dragon … err, jabberwock … behind me can protest. "It's a deal."

The Mad Hatter reaches out and grabs my hand in a tight shake before the Duke can stop us, squeezing my hand tight and then lifting his knuckles to my lips for a kiss that's too hot, too intriguing for a villain.

"Excellent," he murmurs as March smirks at me and the Dormouse scowls. But the way he stretches out those three syllables … it feels like the mark of a dark promise.

What the hell have I just gotten myself into?!

A few hours later, after dozing in the protective circle of North's arms, the carriage stops.

The sudden lack of movement churns my stomach, and I realize as I crack open my eyes how goddamn hungry I really am. There's a brief moment there where I don't *want* to wake up, where I want to sit with my nose pressed to North's bare skin, breathing in that sweet, musky masculine scent of his.

But then I realize that the back door of the carriage is open and there's sunlight streaming through. Outside, I see puddles reflecting back a blue sky dotted with shrunken gray clouds, like the rain's reminding us it's still there, that it's only taking a quick break to recharge.

With a groan, I sit up and stretch my arms above my head, wishing I could've been kidnapped in something besides a purple silk nightgown with lace accents. Leather boots, breeches, a jacket, now *that* is proper kidnapping material. At least the Duke is shirtless and in blood-soaked pj pants, so I'm not the only person here who looks a hot mess.

"You weren't kidding about the Hatter, were you?" I whisper to North as I sit up, adjusting myself so that I'm straddling his lap. He meets my eyes with his gold ones, dark horns curving out of his blonde hair. "He's fucking *insane*."

"Yes, well," the Duke breathes with a sigh, "I can only offer my sincerest apologies, Miss Liddell, and admit my surprise at being attacked *in my own home*." His voice drops down to an animalistic growl that rumbles us both. "But I can't say I'm not at all shocked at this turn of events. As soon as the Hatter found out the Alice was in Underland, he was bound to seek your company—whatever the price."

"Can't you just go jabberwock on his ass?" I ask as North scoots me off his lap and sits up, getting onto all fours and stretching like a cat, bowing the front part of his body low and lifting his tight, hard butt up into the air for me to stare at, his tail twitching all the while.

"There's no guarantee that I'd win a fight with Raiden Walker," the Duke says, scooting over to the edge of the carriage and dropping into a puddle, sunlit gold water splashing as he lands. He turns and lifts his chin, ever the picture of royalty, sophistication, and bestial beauty all wrapped in one. North offers me his hand and I take it, hopping down beside him and wondering what the *fuck* this Raiden guy must really be like if he has a goddamn *dragon* nervous to face-off against him.

"Good morning," March says, leaning against a tree and carving an apple with a knife. He braces his muscular shoulder against the rough bark, his fingers handling the blade with a precision that makes me wonder what else those hands can do. I mean, not to me, I'm not interested. I just mean in *general.* His brown eyes are flecked through with red and orange, like an autumn skyline, and his mouth is full and luscious, even as he wears it in a stupid, little smirk. The red apple peel comes off in one, perfect strip and then falls to the ground near his feet. In an instant, there are a half-dozen little flies dropping down to feast on it, their wings a shimmering iridescent turquoise, their bodies … in the shape of wooden rocking horses.

Fucking rocking-horse flies.

Fantastic.

I blink a few times and shake my head to clear it, putting my fingers to my temples.

"Good morning," North replies with a civil coolness, his tail splashing through puddles as he swishes it in frustration. "Shall we get on then? What's the delay?"

"No delay," the Mad Hatter says, appearing out of the trees with the Dormouse on his heels. They're carrying large chunks of soft, spongy flesh—*mushroom* flesh. That reminds me … I have a bit of the mushroom meat tucked in my sheath along with the Vorpal Blade! Well, fudge on a fucking stick. If I'd just remembered that a few hours ago, maybe I could've gone house-sized and kicked this son of a bitch's ass?! "I'll call Twinkle, and we'll be on our way."

"Twinkle?" I ask as Raiden adjusts his top hat, decorated with a little white slip under the orange-red ribbon that reads *In This Style 10/6*. He catches me looking at it and points up at his head. "Are you interested in this, darling? Because for my future bride, no price is too high for a hat." He pulls it off his head and underneath, there's *another* friggin' top hat, this one white with a black ribbon. Raiden moves over to me and reaches out to put the first hat on my head, but I slap his hand away.

"What does the tag mean anyway?" I ask as he smirks and drops it back over his head, covering up the white hat underneath once again.

"Costs ten and one sixth coins," he explains as I roll my eyes and the man puts two fingers up to his lips, letting out a shrill whistle that echoes through the towering forest of trees and mushrooms. I thought the King of Hearts literally killed people who fucked with his mushrooms? But none of the three assholes here seem to care as the Dormouse shoves the massive hunks of multi-colored mushroom meat into the back of the carriage, slams the door shut, and slaps his palm against the side of the oversized teapot.

The carriage takes off, the horses' hooves splashing rainwater as they gallop off. I remember North telling me that in a wild magic storm, a horse is as likely to be a pumpkin as it is an equine. But the Mad Hatter's horses are all wearing raincoats, little hats, and boots, and they seem just fine. Huh. Glancing down, I realize that my legs are now wet with this supposedly horrid magic rainwater.

"The wild magic moved on hours ago," North tells me as Raiden continues to whistle, "and the regular rain washed most of the power away. Don't worry." He reaches down and takes my hand in his, squeezing me so hard that his talons dig into my skin, these shiny black hooks of claw that I actually find sort of … sexy?

The Mad Hatter pauses in his whistling to sing a ridiculous little doozy of a tune, his voice this low, icy creepy sound that both fascinates and frustrates me to no end. His accent—because supposedly, he's from my world, right?—is definitely a West Coast USA sort of sound, but heightened, elevated, like he's a bit older than I think he is.

"*Twinkle, Twinkle, little bat! How I wonder what you're at? Up above the world you fly, like a tea-tray in the sky. Twinkle, Twinkle—*"

When he sings, I get chills. When he stops singing, cut off by the sudden sound of flapping wings above us, I feel the blood drain from my face.

What. The. *Fuck.* Is. That?!

My mouth hangs open as a massive bat swoops down low and drops two long ropes from its hooked back feet. With a skip and a hop, Raiden Walker steps onto a metal bar attached to the rope and then curls his arm around my waist, snatching me from North's grip. Dor does the same, taking hold of the March Hare and the second rope at the same moment.

The dinosaur-sized fucking bat changes course on a dime, rising into the sky with huge, long flaps of its leathery wings. As dumbfounded as I am by the size and sudden appearance of yet *another* weird ass creature, I don't miss the fact that we've just left North behind.

"Wait!" I scream as the air rushes past me and the ground … gets farther and farther away. My stomach lurches and like, I have a fucking *thing* about heights. Remember that *C* I got in gym because I refused to climb the damn rope? Well, now I'm on a rope with nothing to cling to except a vampire/mercenary asshole who wants to marry me.

And the ground … the ground is so very far away.

Turning my head, I bury my face in the hollow of Raiden's throat and throw my arms around his neck. I even wrap my legs around him and hang on for dear life, my heart thundering in my throat, my eyes closed so tight they hurt. I bet the view is amazing. Hell, I'm sure it's *spectacular.* I just don't want to see it.

A roar sounds from behind us, this bone-shattering, eardrum-bursting screech that I somehow recognize as being North's. Well, at least that answers that. He's shifted and is following us via jabberwock wing. Good for him. Hope no horny females pop out of the trees and attack. How ironic, is it, that in this world, it's the *men* who have to live with a low-grade anxiety at all times, wondering if a woman might pop out of nowhere and sexually assault them?

All those stories Tee and Dee told me about the Riving, and about my world—Topside—affecting Underland make so much sense when I think about it from North's point of view. He's living the life of a human woman … as an Underland male.

"I'm going to puke all the hell over you and this bat thing that's carrying us," I choke out, but the Mad Hatter just chuckles and wraps his arms around me, holding me tight. We move through cool, misty morning air, beams of yellow sunshine warming our icy skin. My dressing gown sticks to my body like plastic wrap, whipping in the wind along with my hair.

Fortunately, the ride only lasts maybe an hour, but to me, it feels like *weeks*. Weeks in the goddamn sky, hanging above a forest made of old-growth trees and mushrooms. By the time we land, I'm shaking, brimming with adrenaline, and the last person in either world anyone should mess with.

The bat drops us off in a copse of trees, undistinguishable from the rest of the forest, and then flaps patiently above us as March and Raiden re-tie the ropes around its feet. Looking up at it, it doesn't look any different from the bats back home. Same piggish little nose and giant ears, leathery wings, black fur, hooked claws. Just … all in *gargantuan* proportions. Of course, it only looks that way until North lands behind it, a sinuous curve of black scales and horns and claws.

He hisses at the bat creature, and it hisses right back at him.

"Best control your male before he makes a fool out of himself," Dor barks, but I'm not in the mood to take shit.

"Maybe you best control *yourself* because you're already acting a damn fool!" I snap, storming over to the massive form of the black goddamn dragon sharing the copse with us. He's a jabberwock, fine, okay, but he *looks* like a dragon to me, this lizard/cat/dog hybrid with big webbed wings, claws, and a long sinuous tail cutting ruts into the undergrowth. He smashes mushrooms and wildflowers that explode with poofs of bright dust and glitter.

Hope none of that's poisonous because it sure as fuck looks it.

"Hey," I say, putting my hands on one of his massive front feet. "Shift back for me, would you? I could use someone to talk—" Before I can even finish speaking, North's wrapped me up in his massive tail and lifted me off my feet. He's so large that even though it's just the tip—get it?—that he's using, I'm completely wrapped up in thick muscle and smooth, black scales.

The Duke's eyes flash gold as he pushes his way through

the trees and over to a spot of dewy nine-leaf clovers. I wasn't even *aware* there were such things as nine-leaf clovers, but he lays me down in them, still holding me with his tail, and proceeds to *sniff* me from head to toe. His breath is hot as he snorts from his massive nostrils and then slowly, shrinks back down to size.

That sun-kissed bronze body is now hovering above me, every muscle taut, cock swollen and erect, horns curved and deadly. The wings are the last things to go, shifting off of his back as his tail unwinds from around my waist. The smell of man, musk, and arousal is unmistakable in the air.

The Savage Duke indeed, I think, as he pins my arms down and sniffs the side of my neck again. I wiggle, bringing my silken nightie riding up my thighs.

"Mate with me?" North asks, his voice barely above the level of a growl. My heart is racing, and I so desperately want to fuck this guy, take the beast out of him, and bring him down to a more manageable level. What's hotter than that? Taking a wild animal like the Duke and making him feel human again. Something about that appeals to me.

We're both basically naked, so the question of condoms is out; clearly he doesn't have any.

"I don't want a baby *or* a disease," I choke out, even though it's the hardest thing in the world for me to say.

There's nothing more I want to do right now than have sex with the Duke of Northumbria.

"Jabberwock," he snaps out at me, dropping his forehead to mine and then *nuzzling* the side of my face and neck with this rumbling growl that does all the right things to my body. My core is already slick and throbbing, my nipples pebbled and tight. "No diseases. Can't get a human pregnant." His teeth are clenched tight and he looks about two seconds away from tearing out of here and destroying everything in sight.

Putting my hand to North's chest, I try to use my magic to invade his mind the way I did Dee. Doesn't work though. All it does is encourage him to press closer, running his tongue up the side of my neck. He pushes his pelvis into me, the only thing separating us the thin layer of my silken nightgown. But I can feel the hard tip of him push into my body, just a little.

My breath rushes out and I arch my back, dragging that nightgown out of the way just enough that there's now *nothing* between us anymore. North drives into me and I groan, wrapping my legs around him as he fills up every empty part of me. My body contracts, gripping him tight, and he makes this *sound* in my ear that isn't at all human.

His tail, that stupid tail that I've been fighting off for days, wraps around the top of my nightgown and yanks the lace out of the way, curling around my breast and squeezing it tight, the tip flicking across the hard pink point of my nipple.

My fingers dig into North's hair, threading through the silken gold strands and then taking firm hold of both curved, wicked horns, holding on tight to him as he fucks me into the dewy clovers. My back is all wet from the foliage, and my *core* is all wet from my arousal and the Duke's deep, wild thrusts.

Our mating is a little … well, like a *mating* and not much like any other sex I've had. It's fast and wild and quick, but the Duke knows exactly what to do, dropping his tail between us and teasing my clit with the very tip. He keeps us going until my body locks around him and holds tight, my spine bowing in an intense, animalistic little orgasm. I claw at the Duke's hair, yank his head close to me, and kiss him with tongue and teeth until I feel him tense up, exploding inside of me with a snarl that catches between our joined lips.

When I collapse back into the clovers, the Duke collapses onto *me* and just lies there, panting hard, breathing frantic. His tail twitches absently against the wet leaves of the plants.

"So much easier to come down from my other form with a mate," he grumbles, and then pushes up, looking down at me with gold eyes and a satisfied smirk that both excites and infuriates me at the same time. I shove him off and sit up, the Vorpal Blade still strapped to my thigh, my heart thundering faster than the bread-and-butterfly's wings as it sits on a flower not ten feet from me.

I know what the damn thing is because I remember reading about it, an insect with wings of bread and butter, the body of crust, and the head a lump of sugar. Mostly, it looks like its head is actually made up of two multi-faceted pearl-white eyes, similar to what a dragonfly's back home would be. But I only stare at it for a moment because all three of our captors are coming through the trees, and I'm tugging my nightgown back down my thighs.

"Excellent," Raiden Walker says, adjusting his hat as he grins at me with two sharp canines. The March Hare is still lazily eating his apple, cutting slices from it with his knife and then stabbing them. He sucks the bit of fruit right off the end of the blade. The Dormouse, on the other hand, just glares at North and me like he's fantasizing about bashing both our heads in this time. "You've soothed the jabberwock, and now we see the king."

He removes a small, golden key from the front pocket of his jacket, steps over to a large tree and bends down, unlocking a tiny little door.

"For the future Queen of Hearts," March says, reaching into *his* jacket and pulling out a pair of bottles, both labelled *FUCKING DRINK ME!* I take them both, my heart contracting at the thought of the twins and what they might be thinking about my sudden disappearance. Without looking at the Duke, I pass over one of the bottles, our fingers tangling together and sending warm little thrills through my body.

Oh, what the hell? I can't help myself. I flick my gaze his way and pop the cork on my bottle. He does the same, and we toast each other.

"Bottoms up," I murmur, and then chug the sweet liquid in a single gulp.

2

The King's Croquet-Ground

There are simple rules in life that everyone knows: such as, always smoke pot first and binge on booze after, the pullout method doesn't really work, and if you drink from a bottle marked 'poison', it's almost certain to disagree with you, sooner or later.

However, this bottle's marked FUCKING DRINK ME so like, I'm pretty sure it's not arsenic. Anyway, it's bubbly and reminds me of champagne. It has, in fact, a sort of mixed flavor profile. And by mixed flavor profile, I mean this is some effed up Willy Wonka type shit. The taste on my tongue morphs from cherry-tart to custard, from pineapple to toffee, and then cycles through roasted freaking turkey and hot buttered toast. It takes me all of one gulp to finish it off, downed like a shot of vodka.

"What a ... *curious* feeling," I grind out, blinking as my head swims and the Duke reaches out to steady me with a hand on my elbow. I can feel the whorls of his fingertips pressing against my skin, and a warm flutter takes over my tummy. Either I have a massive crush on him (hard enough to make *diamonds*) or this drink is not sitting well with me.

"Are you alright?" North growls, his tail curling around my ankle as I blink furiously through a flood of adrenaline. It sends my heart racing as I stumble into his big, beautiful bronze body. My fingers curl around his shoulders as an earthquake starts up beneath our feet, and I let out a high-pitched squeak.

"What the hell is going on?" I choke as the ground roils and the trees sway in a supernatural breeze. Or ... wait. Am I the one moving and they're all standing still? I squeeze my eyes shut as my stomach lurches up and into my throat. You know that first hill on a roller coaster, the one you roll up with an ominous *click-click-click* sound from the tracks? And then you hit the top and there's one peaceful moment before all hell breaks loose?

Yeah, well, there's no peace here, just that horrific feeling of my stomach being left behind while the rest of my body hurdles through space.

When I flick my eyes open, I'm standing in front of

the little door that's not so little anymore. And when I turn back to look at the trees … they make the sequoias back home look like playthings. My brain swims as I blink frantically and try to make all of this strangeness work within the confines of my logicality.

There's a leaf next to me that's bigger than my ex's fucking car. That’s a hard pill to swallow.

"What happens if I drink more of that while I'm this small?" I ask, and the Duke cocks a golden brow.

"Most certainly," he says in that crisp accent of his, looking down at me with serious bedroom eyes, "you'd go out altogether, like a candle. I wonder what you should be like then? What is the flame of a candle like after it's been blown out? Simply smoke, I'd say."

Carefully, I extract myself from North's grip, trying not to let what just happened between us take over my thoughts completely.

But oh, we're close. So close. I’ve got giddy girl thoughts for *days*.

Eep! Just look at him! My lady parts sing, staring at his chiseled muscles, wide shoulders, and … well, his entire package is still on full-display. Now, that, that is a *man*.

Crinkling up my nose, I turn back to the Mad Hatter as he lifts his hat and draws out a decorative black cane from underneath it. It shouldn’t rightfully fit in there, but of course, it magically does anyway. As soon as North sees

Raiden's new toy, he curls the edge of his lip up in a snarl, claws extending from his fingers.

It's made of the same material as the hilt of my Vorpal Blade … so, jabberwock horn? No wonder North is pissed.

"Shall we?" Raiden purrs, smirking at us before swinging his cane in a circle and taking off through the now open door and into bright-ass sunshine. Wherever we're headed is a hell of a lot less cloudy than the forest.

"I thought there was only one door into the king's garden?" I ask. "Or rather, one door that leads anywhere close to the castle-grounds at all." See, I do sometimes listen when Tee and Dee talk. *Tee and Dee ... I bet they're freaking all the way out right now.* If I'd woken up and found them gone, I know I would be.

"There *is* only one permanent door," the March Hare says, smoothing his hands down the front of his black trench coat. Yeah, did I mention that yet? That he's gone total villain cliché with a trench, a *velvet* trench at that? Looks stupid good on him though, the bastard. "We just made this. Now, if you'd kindly step through before Dor gets fussy, that would be highly advisable."

March blinks big, brown eyes in my direction, and the ears on the top of his head swivel to listen to a distant sound, the cracking of a twig and the rustling of leaves.

Uh.

It sounds like something's stalking us.

I don't need to be told twice. I might not like taking orders, but I also don't like being hunted and eaten by things with names I can barely pronounce. Can you imagine, being masticated by a *mome rath*? Now try putting that on a headstone: *Allison Liddell, eighteen years of age, gobbled up by mome raths.*

Reaching down, I snatch North's hand and drag him through the door. Maybe I just want an excuse to touch him again? Maybe I just need to hold onto something that feels strong and solid? I have no idea. But he squeezes my hand with his just hard enough to pierce me with his claws. Doesn't hurt really. I almost like it.

No, no, I *do* like it. I should start being honest with myself. Then again, I often give myself pretty good fucking advice although I very seldom follow it. Probably why I've gotten into so much damn trouble in my short eighteen-year span on earth and … well, Underland.

A large rose-tree stands near the entrance of the garden; the roses growing on it are white, but there are three gardeners at it, busily painting them red. *Curiouser and fucking curiouser,* I think as we step through the small door into the royal grounds I saw on my very first day here.

Everything—including the flowers—towers above us, masking for just a split-second the rancid scent of blood in the air. My gaze drifts back to the gardeners, and I realize with a start that their red *paint* is actually blood.

"Jabberwock, bandersnatch, jubjub, and so on and so forth," North whispers, naked and standing too close to me. I can feel his heat, clenching my thighs tight and trying not to think so much about how wet I am between them. "That's their blood, mixed up and painted around the gardens to keep them away from the castle. It's *nauseating*." He wrinkles up his nose with a wicked little growl, sending a sharp surge of adrenaline through my body.

"Makes some sort of perverted sense," I say as Raiden Walker strides down a small dirt path that winds through a path of daffodils, as bright and cheerful as the morning sunshine. "But aren't we going to, uh, nibble some *FUCKING EAT ME* cakes and get big again?" I can't help it; my eyes find the gardeners again, as large to me now as North was to me in his jabberwock form.

"Not until we get into the castle," March tells me, tossing his apple core onto the ground … and then receiving a middle finger from one of the *flowers*. He flips it off right back as my mouth hangs open and I stick close to the Duke's side. I figure if someone comes close to stepping on us, he could shift into his jabberwock form and he'd be at least the size of a small dog, right? "If any of the guards see us here now, they'll probably stick us all full of arrows before we get a chance to explain."

"Oh, well, *that* makes me feel better," I snarl as Dor takes up the rear and we trudge on through the garden. At this rate, it feels like it'll take *days* to get to the castle. Shit, it probably will. And my thighs are wet, and I'm wearing a flimsy, damp nightgown. The Duke is naked, and neither of us is wearing shoes.

"You'll see, when you meet the King," North says, drawing my attention over to him. "Becoming the Queen of Hearts, that'll heal all of Underland." I narrow my eyes on him, trying not to think *too* hard about the wild, angry mating session we just had. That's a problem for later. Right now, I just want to get into the castle, shower, and put some damn clothes on.

I don't bother to tell the Duke that first chance I get, I'm bailing through the Looking-Glass. And not just because I'm afraid he'll try to stop me. No, it's more than that. I don't even *know* if I want to go back anymore. I make a rough, low sound in my throat and put my hands up to my face.

The Duke doesn't say anything else for a while, but he *does* curl his tail around my ankle. I let him do it, too, even though I grit my teeth. I guess seeing him comatose with a hunk lopped off the side of his head endeared the asshole to me more than I care to admit.

We walk like that for several hours, beneath the lush jungle-like folds of … a well-manicured flower garden. But from down here, it all seems so wild and untamed, so dangerous. The rocking-horse flies and bread-and-butterflies look like fucking monsters. They don't seem interested in us though, and North stays fairly calm as we walk, so I decide to relax my shoulders a bit and just marvel at the idea that I *am* this tiny. How cool is that? Besides, if I really need to, I have that mushroom meat stuffed in the Vorpal Blade sheath. I can pull it out at any time and return to my normal size.

For the next few hours, we walk in silence, the sunshine filtering through the leaves.

Occasionally, I hear Dor mumble something rude and violent behind us, but I ignore him. Seems like Raiden and March have him on a pretty short leash anyway.

Sometime later, just before we reach the edge of a white gravel pathway—a full-sized one that looks like a hundred mile stretch of white desert at this height—I hear the thundering of footsteps. It's like a herd of elephants barreling down on us, and I shrink back, unintentionally putting myself against the Duke's naked front. He's half-hard, too, and stabbing me in the lower back with his dick.

First come ten soldiers carrying swords; they're all dressed in red, black, and white livery decorated with hearts, their faces severe, mouths in tight, thin lines. Next, ten courtiers: they're all ornamented in dresses and jewels and fine shoes, cloaks billowing out behind them.

I've never even seen such a prissy, spoiled looking group of people.

Oh. Wait.

An old memory of Ellie Arkley—showing up to the first day of school in a stretch Hummer limo, dressed in a pair of ten thousand dollar shoes and an outfit that could purchase a homeless family a decent place to live—springs to mind like a weed. I remember her glittering diamond earrings, plastic surgery smile, and eight hundred dollar haircut, and almost puke.

Yep.

That's what these people remind me of, privilege and unchecked wealth and greed.

I'll see when I meet the King, huh? Yeah right. If these are just the courtiers, then I'm sure the King is a nightmare. And how could I *ever* like a man who treats the twins the way he does? No, no matter what happens with the Looking-Glass and the prophecy and my staying here … this King and I are *never* going to get along.

After that horrid procession moves by, I finally catch sight of him.

The King of Hearts … *and* beside him, the White Rabbit.

"Rab!" I shout, tearing from North's arms and stumbling out onto the white gravel. He doesn't seem to notice *or* hear me, so I shove the silken folds of my dressing gown out of the way, flip open the small leather pouch on the side of the sheath and take out a bit of mushroom meat. I used my fingernail to carve a 'B' into one and an 'S' into the other —for big and small.

Taking a small nibble from the 'B' side—I learned a lot from reading the original Alice books, and I know not to take too much, too fast—I feel myself rise up into the air, like I'm on the rope dangling from Twinkle the Bat's massive hooked claws. My stomach lurches, and I almost scream, but then everything is snapping into place and I'm staring into Rab's red eyes.

"Miss Alice," he whispers, his ears twitching on his head.

I don't even get a moment to breathe before the *King* is putting a blade to my neck with so much force that I feel a drop of hot, red blood leak down my throat and chest.

"Your Majesty," Rab growls, putting up his white-gloved hands in a placating gesture. "Please, calm yourself. This is *the* Alice."

"My name is Alli*son*, so please Your Majesty," I snarl out between clenched teeth, my eyes meeting the dark irises of the King of Hearts. His hair is blood-red, his scar ragged and white in the sunlight. I've never *seen* such a handsome face, but my God, what a complete and total prick. Even though his advisor is standing right there, telling him who I am—the girl he *supposedly* wants to marry—he holds his blade in place for so long that I start to sweat, beads of moisture mixing with the blood leaking from my throat.

When he finally pulls back, he turns his mouth into this disgustingly triumphant smirk, sheathing his blade at his waist and planting his hands on his hips. He gives me a very slow, very unnecessary once-over and then nods, like I'm a bit of horseflesh that's met his stern and calculating approval.

This guy … he can go fuck himself with his royal scepter for all I care, shove it right up his ass to join the stick that's already clearly wedged there.

"The Alice," the King breathes, ignoring my previous proclamation. Eh, so what's new? Not a single person here has listened to me about my name … except for Tee.

Speaking of … Behind the King and Rab, just off to the right and down another white gravel path, a set of double doors swings open and there they are, my twins.

My twins?

Uh-oh.

"Allison-who-isn't-Alice!" Dee shouts, taking off across the gravel and grabbing me before I can take two steps toward *him*. He wraps his arms around me and squeezes me so tight and close that my feet come right off the ground. His wings are nowhere in sight—they couldn't possibly be, since I wasn't around to free them—but he's smiling so big and wide that I can't help but smile back. "Oh, you gave us quite the scare."

"Quite the scare," Tee chokes out from beside his brother, his amethyst eyes locked on mine, the sun catching on his purple-streaked black hair. His brother kisses me before I can get another word out, burying his tongue in my mouth and making me groan. He isn't shy about his hands either, groping my ass in two tight handfuls. I encourage it by leaning into him, rubbing up against his body and lifting my nightie a bit on the process. *Enjoy* that *show, you assholes,* I think, smirking as I continue my kiss with the angel prince.

I don't think Dee's intention is to break the curse—his kiss is too pure—but that's what happens anyway. In two brilliant bursts of sapphire light, Dee's wings explode from his back, pushing up his trench coat and tearing through his black and white striped shirt. There's a collective gasp from the courtiers waiting up ahead on the path, hiding like the little blue-blooded bitches they are behind a row of guards.

Oh. They don't like seeing how princely and perfect their slave really is, do they? Too damn bad.

I pretend not to notice the genteel gasps and mutters, pulling away from the kiss with a laugh dancing in my heart and tingling on my lips. I even take a moment to brush some blue and black strands of hair from Dee's forehead. The tension is thick enough to cut with a knife, but I make sure I look him in the eyes to let him know that to me, he matters. His expression is equal parts worry and fear, but he still manages a smile.

"You son of a bitch," I breathe, pushing him back a little, so I can get some air. He lets me go, and then his brother and I stand there awkwardly for a moment before I embrace Tee, too. It surprises me how happy I am to see him, and I find myself rubbing my cheek against his chest as he curls his fingers around the back of my head and pulls me close.

"I'm glad you're safe, Allison," he whispers, pressing a kiss to the crown of my head. His hot breath stirs my hair, and I shiver slightly. "And I'm sorry that we failed to keep you safe …"

"Oh, cheer up, would you?" an ice-cold voice says from behind me, and I whirl around to see the Mad Hatter rising up from the edge of the flowerbed. The King goes to put his sword to the man's throat, same way he did me, but Raiden just laughs and knocks it aside, throwing up some sort of magic shield to catch a good two-dozen arrows aimed for his back.

Soldiers rush up and surround him as I dive forward and just narrowly manage to protect the Duke from being trampled. My reward is to get kicked in the face, have my leg stepped on, and end up almost getting killed myself when a jumpy soldier shoots an arrow at *my* back.

"Enough!" the King screams, throwing his arm wide and sending the soldiers scurrying back. Most of them drop to one knee. All of them except one, tall, blonde woman with a serious fucking attitude problem. Her eyes catch mine for just the *briefest* of moments before I hear Raiden Walker chuckling behind me.

I glance back over my shoulder and find that it was him who snatched the projectile that was aimed for my back out of mid-air, his other hand help up and brimming with a magic shield to keep Rab and the twins back.

"Relax, relax, everyone," he purrs as I scoop the Duke into my hand and leave the March Hare and Dormouse on the ground. I also inadvertently saved them, too, but North is the only one I care about. I tuck him to my chest and then offer up the bit of mushroom flesh still clutched in my left hand. I forgot I was holding it, and it's a bit squished now, but it works. "You see, *the* Alice, why I didn't want to make such a fuss? Now you've ruined my grand entrance."

The Duke of Northumbria gives the mushroom a lick, and then he's toppling into me, knocking me onto my back and giving me a very vivid reminder of the sex we just had. We exchange a long, languid look before he finally stands up and pulls me along with him.

"What the fuck are you doing here?" Tee snaps before the King gives him a look. Tee curls his lip up in a snarl, but he steps back … even though his eyes go straight to mine and his hand hovers at the knife on his hip. I feel a little guilty, having had sex with North. I should tell Tee and Dee, first chance I get.

"Me?" Raiden says with a smirk and a cocky little head tilt. "I'm just delivering both the Alice *and* your precious Duke." A moment later, the March Hare and Dormouse sprout to life behind the Mad Hatter's shield. In fact, all five of us are trapped inside of it.

"Explain yourselves," the King says in a surprisingly level voice. His dark eyes are as cool and even as granite, his shoulders relaxed. While everyone else looks like they're about to turn this into a brawl, he looks like he's about to take tea. Well, maybe not boosted tea, but like tea back home. Normal fucking tea. "What do you want Hatter?"

"Your pet Duke here," Raiden begins, letting his marmalade orange gaze slide over to North. "He guaranteed me you'd match his generous donation of say … five hundred thousand coins, *and* the Alice here—*the* Alice, mind you—has also promised me her hand in marriage." He turns back to the King, but there's still no emotion brewing in the man's eyes.

"Bargains made under duress are no bargain at all," Tee snaps as Dee curls his lip in agreement, reaching up to adjust the peaked cap on his head. His wings cast beautiful shadows on the pavement in front of his feet.

"No bargain at all," he agrees, his sapphire eyes lighting on mine. I don't know what the hell this magic shield is that's separating us, but nobody seems willing to approach it, so I don't either. Instead, I hang back and wait to see how these politics play themselves out.

No chance in fucking fuck that I'm going to marry the Mad Hatter, but I'm also not going to tell *him* that while I'm standing inside some magic spell he's just cast.

"I can leave right now?" Raiden asks, pulling off one top hat, and then another, and then *another*. He tousles his dark wavy hair with his fingers, but just keeps smiling, like he knows he's already got this one in the bag. "Leave the Duke with a musking jabberwock, and turn the Alice into the King of Clubs like I'd originally planned."

"Stand down," the King says, lifting a gloved hand in the air. It's covered in rings that sparkle with an unnatural light, like there's so much more going on here than first appears. I feel a sigh come over the courtyard as the courtiers stop tittering, and the soldiers rise to their feet to put their bows away. A quick glance up at the walls and the turrets shows me dozens of other soldiers relaxing their postures—pretty much all of them are women, by the way.

The monarch licks his lips and then flicks his eyes

down my front before turning back to Raiden.

"I'll have a page show you to a guest room. Clean up. Have something to eat. Join me on the lawn for croquet—*both* of you. Duke, with me, if you please."

The King gives me one last look, his dark eyes meeting my blue ones, before he spins away in a sea of red and black robes, Rab catching my attention before he moves off after him, dressed in a waistcoat and pinstripe slacks.

The shield around us comes down, and nobody tries to stop North and me when we move out of that bubble and over to the twins. Dee puts his arm around my waist in a semi-possessive but also comforting sort of way.

"Let's get you some food," he says as my tummy rumbles, and I put a palm over the front of my nightgown. Dee rubs his coat sleeve against my throat to clean off the blood from the King's knife as I glance briefly at North, still gloriously naked and not giving two flying fucks about any of it. He meets my eyes, and I find myself biting my lower lip in a flirtatious sort of way. Gross. Edith would make so much fun of me if she could see me in my current state—panty-less and making come-hither faces at a dragon.

"I suppose I should tend to the King," North says, but the way he looks at me makes me think he'd rather be tending to *me*. I shiver and Dee cocks a dark eyebrow in my direction. Ah. Clearly I have some explaining to do. "Take your time and fetch yourself a pair of knickers." He flashes a sharp grin at me as my cheeks heat and I narrow my eyes on him. "I'll keep the wanker occupied and be waiting for you when you come down." He reaches out with the long, muscular length of his tail, tucking my hair behind my ear with the tip before he turns and moves down the path in the direction of some rolling green lawns.

"Something's changed between you," Tee says, drawing my attention back to him. He doesn't sound upset though, just … curious. And relieved. God, if I could bottle up his relief and sell it, I'd be a millionaire back home.

The thought makes me smile.

"Food sounds good," I say, finally responding to Dee's statement, "but I'd prefer a shower and some fresh clothes first, if you've got any."

"Your wish is my command," Dee says, keeping his arm around me but affecting a little half-bow as he sweeps his hat off his head. The feathers of his wing brush against my bare back and make me shiver as he stands up straight and folds them tightly together.

As we walk away, I look back and see the Mad Hatter, watching me with a smirk on his face and a wink at the ready.

He gives it to me nice and slow, theatrical, and then we turn the corner to head inside and he disappears from view.

"I was so fucking worried about you," Dee says, hugging me close and making me go all warm and fuzzy inside. The feel of his hard muscles pressing against the thin fabric of my nightie is nice in so many ways. I missed him, weird as that sounds. I mean, we were only separated for a day. Not even, really. But it feels like an eternity. I guess the thought that I might be raped and killed has sort of … *shifted* my priorities.

"*We* were so fucking worried about you," Tee says, standing straight and tall and proud on my other side. He's looking dead ahead, toward a set of double wood doors that are standing wide open. On the outside, he's all calm, quiet strength; on the inside, I can see him fuming. When he flicks his aubergine eyes in my direction, I can tell he's scared shitless, too—or *was*.

For me.

Tee was scared for me.

"Worried, anxious, distraught, broken, twisted …" Dee pauses and adjusts his hat with his left hand, shifting his wings around in the process. Before I can think better of it, I reach out and ruffle the feathers, making him shiver. He casts me a lascivious little wink and tosses a smile my way that's only slightly tainted by worry. My disappearance really messed with their heads, didn't it? *Just like you're starting to care about them, they're starting to care about you,* I think and then shake my head to clear it.

How can I really care about someone I just met? How can they care about me? And yet … I study Dee's blue military jacket, the silver heart buttons, the tight black denim jeans, and the leather belt with his knife hanging off it. His mouth is pinched just a little too much, his eyes are just a tad too hooded.

Yep.

For whatever reason, he cared that I was gone; he cared a whole fucking lot.

"Were you really?" I ask, feeling my heart thunder in my chest. Just before we head inside, I glance out at the lawn once more and see North standing next to the King, gazing after me with heavy-lidded eyes. He blinks them twice then smiles. Guess he's not worried about this whole effed-up situation. He is, after all, a 'hefty giver of tithes to the crown' anyway. These dudes all seem pretty serious about this prophecy thing, and about dating me, so maybe the Duke'll keep me safe against the King?

If he can.

I give North a wave, he salaciously rubs his hand up one of his horns, and then I turn back around just in time to see the black and white checkered marble floors of the palace. We're not two feet into the place before things start to get weird.

The arched ceilings are covered in faceted mirrors, lending this eerie funhouse quality to the ostentatious beauty of the palace. There are intricate gold arches sweeping above us, a match to the gilded frames on the walls featuring various members of the royal family in frilly gowns or furred cloaks—essentially all of them are female.

"I take it there aren't often kings that aren't attached to queens?" I ask, and Tee makes a slight, soft sound in his throat. Almost a scoff, but not quite. His amethyst eyes are focused straight ahead, but I direct my stare toward him, let it burn until he finally flicks them my way and blinks like he's coming out of a coma.

"It's your world, reversed. So no, there aren't many unattached kings." Tee rubs his hands down his face, flashing some of the tattooed skin on the backs of his arms, and sighs again, like he's exhaling the stress of the last twenty-four hours. "The court expects him to be married as soon as possible."

"As soon as possible," Dee repeats, his voice a much more chipper version of his brother's. "To you, of course." He fluffs his wings, almost like he's just checking to make sure they're still there. I see Tee's eyes go straight to them, and I'm tempted to free his, too, right here where any asshole could see. And yet, there's something about the idea of kissing Tee that makes my cheeks go bright-red. I think it's his intensity. While Dee is light and fluffy and fun, like a beam of sunshine on the skin, Tee is as fleeting and rare as moonlight.

"I'm not marrying the King," I say, and those aren't empty words. My brother died because he was protecting my right to decide what to do with my own body. He shouldn't have had to, but he did. And I bet marriage in this world carries similar expectations to that in mine. If you're not catching my drift here, I'm talking about sex. "I'm not fucking that prick of a king," I say aloud, grinding my teeth. "If I have to, I'll make a run for it, straight through the damn Looking-Glass."

Tee turns me suddenly toward him, cups my face in his hands, and kisses the ever-loving shit out of me. His tongue slides against mine in this passionate, frenzied tangle. There's fear in that kiss, or maybe panic, I'm not sure. Either way, his wings burst from his back, rending his shirt, and spreading like rain clouds across a desert sun, bringing shadow and wetness where there was none. I feel *drenched*, and I mean metaphorically speaking, not just between my thighs.

"Don't talk about it," Tee whispers, his lips pressed close to mine. I open my eyes and all I can see is him. His face is too close to my own, there are too many shades of purple in his irises, and his mouth is too full and beautiful. My knees start to quiver, and if he didn't have his hands on my waist, I might've hit the floor. "Not here."

"Won't the King flip out if he hears you were tonguing his future bride?" I whisper, my hands trembling and curling into unconscious fists in my nightie. I can feel a single bead of sweat working its way down my spine, a warm heat blossoming low in my belly.

"We belong to you," Tee says curtly, releasing me and stepping back. But I don't miss that last, lingering look he gives me, his eyes as purple as summer grapes. Dee makes a sound from behind me, and we all pause as a pair of *playing cards* with arms and legs scurry past us. They're the size of small children with faces printed on their fronts, frozen in expressions of terror, like they died screaming.

And they're fucking terrifying.

"What the hell are those?" I ask, stumbling back and slamming into Tee's broad chest. He puts his hands on my shoulders and squeezes as the pair of animated cards walks past with silver trays on their outstretched palms. The creepiest part is how human their appendages are, with skin tones in shades of cream and cocoa. Not to mention they each have scabs and scars and *hair* decorating their limbs.

"House servants," Dee says, snapping his fingers. One of the cards, the one with a female face, makes her way over to us, a pair of black Mary Janes on her feet and little frilly white socks poofing around her ankles. "Can we get three meals brought up to the Penthouse Suit, please?"

"Penthouse *Suite*," I correct, but Dee just raises a dark eyebrow at me.

"Not Suite, although it is very *sweet*, but Suit. Penthouse Suit, like Suit of Cards. Although it's just the difference of a single 'e', now isn't it?"

"Make that *four* meals, you crooked little tidbit of dark magic, you," a voice purrs—quite literally—in my ear. In the span of an instant, I've got a heavy weight on my left shoulder, and a fucking cat rubbing against my cheek. "I'm quite *fur-amished.*" I narrow my eyes at the admittedly terrible pun, and reach up to give Chesh a small scratch on the head. There is a distinct possibility he's looking down my top, so I should probably punch him, but I'm too much of a crazy cat lady at heart. Even lecherous pussies deserve love.

"Are you even allowed to be here?" Tee asks, crossing his arms and lifting his chin in the direction of the guards posed against the opposite wall. These, at least, are human, even if their red suits of armor are a bit strange. They reek of blood, too, this coppery scent that stings my nostrils and makes my eyes water. If the blood is supposed to repel things like jabberwocky, then how is North putting up with it?

"Can a person really be allowed or disallowed from being in a certain place or time?" Chesh slides off my shoulder, shifting as he goes, like a cloud of smoke moving from one place to the next. When he materializes, he's dressed in tight, leather pants, a silver chain belt, and nothing else. It's hot as hell, especially when he licks his tattooed right arm and slides it over his head, crushing one of his striped ears against his dark hair as he cleans himself. "Only gods have the right to do that, and gods do not exist." Chesh flicks his tail and narrows his gray eyes on the three of us. "How was your date with the Hatter?"

"Maybe we should head up to the room before we discuss this?" Tee snaps, and Chesh lifts his gaze lazily up in the twin's direction. He looks downright bored—like most cats. I still can't figure out his position in all of this. There's the King, the King's servants, the King's bloody Duke, and the King's, uh, spiritual advisor, as well as the King's enemy-plus-sidekick, and then there's … this guy. With no relation to the King whatsoever. I'd been guessing he was the Duke's servant, yet he seems a tad … removed from the situation.

But standing here under a mirrored ceiling, with fucking playing cards sweeping past us with their creepy little legs and silently screaming faces, is not really the place to get into it.

"I could use a bath," I say, feeling a slight heat suffuse my cheeks. There's still *evidence* down there of my rumble with North. And yeah, by evidence, I mean cum—his and mine. "And a dress that doesn't show my nipples."

Dee snorts as Chesh smirks lazily at me, his mouth stretching wider than it rightfully should, all sharp, white teeth and sass.

"I like a dress that shows your nipples," he says, disappearing from view until there's nothing left but that smile.

“Mind your manners,” Tee snaps, brushing strands of hair from his forehead as Dee gives him a quizzical sort of look. I think Tee carries more stress on his shoulders than his brother realizes. I’m starting to wonder what time they realized I was missing last night, and if they got any real sleep. Tee has dark purple bags under his eyes. “You may come *only* if Allison gives you permission.”

“Allison, is it?” Chesh purrs, his eyes and striped cat ears fading back into view. “Oh, he calls her *Allison*. How charming. But her cat—and we all know there’s no higher authority on Topside above or Underland below that’s more prudent—calls her *The Midnight Knicker Dancer*.” I choke on my own spit and Dee has to pat my back to help me breathe again.

“What the hell did you just say?” I ask, feeling my cheeks go beet red as I think about dancing in my panties at home in front of my little black cat, Dinah.

“Your *pussy*,” Chesh purrs, reappearing fully and then

rubbing his whole damn body against mine, "calls you The Midnight Knicker Dancer. It's written all over your face and ankles." He pauses in front of me and points to my head and then my feet with a sharp-nailed finger before leaning in and rubbing his cheek against mine. "Cats have scent marking glands in their face, didn't you know?"

"Yeah, I *did* know," I say, pushing him away from me as Tee scoffs and Dee raises both eyebrows. "What does that have to do with a stupid nickname you just made up?"

"Made up?" Chesh asks, putting one hand on his bare chest and drawing my attention to his myriad black and gray tattoos. "If I were going to make up a nickname for you, it most certainly wouldn't be *that*." He licks his lips, his two little feline fangs sticking out in the most adorable way. "Your cat left it written in your scent, as bright as the fireworks on coronation night. She quite literally *rubbed* you the wrong way, didn't she?"

"You learned all that by smelling me?" I ask, getting sassy and cocking a hip out as I cross my arms over my chest. As soon as the question leaves my lips, I regret it. *Oh God, my tumble with the Savage Duke!*

"That's not *all* I smell," Chesh purrs as Tee shoves him to the side and grabs my arm.

"Let's head upstairs. You don't want your first meeting with the King to be when he's in a mood." Tee scowls, tossing a glance over his shoulder that's pure poison. I'm not sure yet if he hates the Mad Hatter or the King of Hearts more.

"*Head* is right," Dee says with a small grimace, drawing a line across his throat with his finger, reminding me of the King's scar. "Because heads *will* roll if we piss him off." Dee takes up a position on my other side as Chesh shifts again and hops into my arms. I grab him out of habit, but give out a little growl of my own when his head gets too close to my boob.

If he 'scent-marks' that with his cheek, there'll be hell to pay.

"Lead on," I tell the twins, and they do, away from Raiden Walker and the King of Hearts and all of their bullshit.

At least … for now.

But peace, true peace, doesn't last long in Underland.

The Penthouse Suit of Hearts is basically an entire floor that encompasses a bedroom, sitting room, library, and bathroom all in one. Only downside is that the bathroom has no door, just a sheer curtain on a circular metal loop that I can pull closed. I decide I don't care enough for modesty to be bothered by it, and sink into the hot water. It was piped in here, just like it was at Rab's. This world is both medieval and modern. Total fucking mind trip.

"So what happened?" Tee asks, just outside the curtain, leaning against one of the curved, white walls with his boots crossed at the ankles. It's like he's afraid to walk away from me, like I might disappear if he does. Hell, maybe I would? In this place, it's hard to find anything that's an impossibility.

"You mean when I was kidnapped?" I ask, feeling the deliciously scalding water surge over me, cupping the sweet soreness between my thighs, buoying my breasts. Have you ever noticed that? That breasts float? Like … sexy pool toys or something. "Because I was about to ask you the same thing. You said I was safe on the Duke's estate."

"I thought you were," Tee chokes, his voice much rougher than it was before. I think he feels like he failed me. Not in my book though. I get the idea that the Mad Hatter and Company are pretty badass. He's a fucking vampire for Christ's sake. "Although that doesn't excuse our behavior."

"Off with our heads," Dee quips playfully, trying to lighten the mood as he lounges on my new heart-shaped bed. There's a knock at the door, and I watch as his shadow rises to its feet and makes its way over to answer it. Guess our food is here. And it's been delivered by creepy little card people with macabre expressions of torture and terror etched into their fronts. I'm sure dinner will be downright goddamn delectable.

"Did the king order you beheaded?" I ask, narrowing my

eyes. I've read the book; I've seen the movie. Isn't that what the Queen of Hearts always says? Off with their heads?

"He said it, but he doesn't mean it," Tee growls as Dee wheels in a cart and heels the door closed with his boot. "He likes our pain and suffering too much to end it."

"Well, if North was captured by the Mad Hatter and the March Hare, there wasn't really much hope for me, was there?" I say, picking up a red bar of soap. It's, unsurprisingly, also in the shape of a heart. They're really big about themes around here. I lather up and start soaping my armpits. Hate to admit it, but I could really use a razor. "They were waiting downstairs with North's head bashed in. I had the Vorpal Blade, but no chance to use it."

Running the soap down both arms, I take a surreptitious glance at the decorative table next to the tub. It's plied with all sorts of different toiletries, but I've only got my eye out for one thing. I spot a straight razor next to a bottle of glowing perfume that says *FUCKING SPRAY ME!* which is like, never going to happen. If EAT MEs turn me into a house and DRINK MEs shrink me into a mouse, what the crap does that thing do?! Grow me some slimy green tentacle arms?! I snatch the razor up, flip it open, and try to figure out how to shave my pits without filleting all my skin off.

Yes, I am a very classy girl. Cue eye roll.

"How on earth did the Duke manage to survive that particular encounter?" Chesh purrs, curled up on the massive continent they call a bed. Clearly, it was made for like … hmm, let's say *ten people.* Yeah, I really could fit nine suitors into that thing. Huh. They really do take that fucking prophecy seriously. "It's no secret that the Hatter and the Hare are not exactly fans of the Heart."

"I made a bet and won it," I say, letting my mind wander to that glorious kiss between Raiden and North. Now, that made the whole experience almost worth it. Almost. I mean, other than the threat of being sold to the King of Clubs, forced marriage, and/or death. "Raiden gave him some blood and voila, he was healed."

"Raiden gave North blood? Because of a bet?" Tee pauses and exhales. "Sounds about right. He's fucking insane."

"Mad really," Dee says, pushing aside the curtain and making me squeak. I'm covered in bubbles, but still, the invasion of privacy annoys me. Sure, we had sex, but that doesn't mean I want him watching me shave my armpits with a too-sharp razor. My anger is mollified though when he hands me a chocolate cupcake with sparkly heart candies on the top. "Can I get you a towel, Allison-who-isn't-Alice? Or a kiss? A hand job perhaps?"

Never mind. My anger is not mollified. I'm still irritated,

but also … I think he's cute, too. Damn my girlish hormones.

"A towel, yes. The rest: not a fucking chance," I say, tearing the wrapper off the cupcake and shoving half of the dessert in my mouth. Dee complies, fetching a red towel and robe from the cabinet and draping it over the little side table. He slides the gauzy red curtain back into place, giving me that extra second I need to finish shaving.

And why are you so concerned with shaving, Allison? I think as I examine my calves for any stray hairs. *Because you plan on rubbing up naked against a pair of fallen angel princes?* With a sigh, I drop my leg back into the water and realize that I've sort of given up on fighting this whole Underland experience. It's happening; I'm here; I'm going to make the most of it.

"The King was serious about us joining him downstairs?" I ask as I splash my face with water and fight off a crippling wave of fatigue. When my head finally does hit those (obviously heart-shaped) pillows, I'm a goner. "Because I could really use a nap."

"A cat nap?" Chesh purrs, but I ignore him.

"The King is always serious," Tee says, and the melancholy in his voice makes me want to wrap him up in a hug. It was the current king's father who sent soldiers after the twins' people, right? I can't be bothered remembering the whole history of Underland; I'll ask questions later, when Chesh isn't around to eavesdrop. Speaking of the prior king … those soldiers in Dee's memory, they looked like cards, too, didn't they? What's up with that? "The Duke will keep him occupied for a while, but we shouldn't push our luck."

"Speaking of the Duke," I start, wishing I could sink into this bathtub and drown my embarrassment, "we sort of … mated."

Hearts above, why did I just use the m-word?! What the crap is wrong with me?!

"With that arrogant look on his face," Dee muses, rooting around on the food cart, "there was no doubt." All I can see through the curtain is shadow, but his voice sounds light enough. There's not even a hint of jealousy in there.

"No doubt, nohow," Tee repeats softly, and I wish fervently that I could see *his* face. I pop a soap bubble with my finger. "And no surprise: there's not a soul in Underland who didn't think the Alice would fall in love with the Savage Duke."

"I'm not in love with him," I blurt, but does it really matter? I slept with him; I like him. I guess that makes him one of their supposed nine? "But, uh, aren't I supposed to ask the primary if he can … join the harem?"

"Oh, harem, I like that word," Dee says licking something off the tip of his finger. It's hot, even if all I can see is his shadow.

"Can I join your harem then?" Chesh asks, tail flicking anxiously. "Because I didn't just bring you mice —I brought you *rats*. That's a worthy gift, don't you think?"

"Make Tee the primary," Dee says, ignoring the cat. His voice is still all light and fluffy, but I can see right through him. He cares about his brother, and he's trying to make him happy. My heart grows three sizes like the damn Grinch's, and I shift in the bathtub, my bare butt cheeks squeaking against the porcelain. "And ask him."

"I don't need to be the primary, Dee," Tee says, and his brother snorts, turning and leaning against the food cart. I need to get out of this damn bath, so I can see facial expressions.

"Contrariwise," Dee snorts as I stand up and dry off (well, in a half-assed sort of way—there's still some bubble bath in my crack). "You're the older twin, so you should be the primary. Technically, *you* were the crown prince back home." I wrap the fluffy white robe around myself and step out of the bathroom, trailing bubbles behind me. Both twins and Chesh turn to look at me with varying expressions on their handsome faces. "Don't argue with me: you know I always win."

"Fine," Tee says, giving in surprisingly easy. My guess? He didn't *want* to win this particular argument.

"Then I accept the Duke, but not you."

"Ouch," Dee hisses, cringing and then winking at me as I pause next to the smorgasbord of … totally weird shit. It *looks* like food, but who knows for sure? I drop the cupcake wrapper off and trade it out for, well, I *think* it's a sandwich. There's a dark brown roll (did you guess that it was heart-shaped? if not, you fail, because it is) that smells like sourdough, and it's piled high with meat and veggies. What sort of meat, I just don't want to know at this point. Probably freaking jubjub bird again. "So awfully cruel, brother."

"And what about the *cat*?" Chesh insists, pulling out a pack of cigarettes and lighting up. "Or has he not courted Midnight Knicker Dancer for long enough?"

"If you call me Midnight Knicker Dancer again, not only will you not be welcome in my harem, you won't be welcome in my room, or even my good graces." I sit down heavily on the edge of the bed with my food and try not to sigh with bliss. It's beyond soft. The King of Hearts really knows how to live. It takes every ounce of willpower I have to resist the urge to lie down and go to sleep. Back home, it's my favorite activity. In this world, it's a rare treat. I rub my hand down my face. "Let's pick up this discussion later, when I'm running on more than just fumes. What do I wear to this croquet thing anyway?" My lids are heavy, and my lashes feel as if they're coated in sandpaper and sitting heavy on my cheeks. "And do I really have to play the game with a flamingo as a mallet and a hedgehog as a ball?"

"Even more proof that you *are* the Alice," Dee says, swinging back a heavy red velvet curtain on one wall and revealing a hidden closet. It's about, I'd say, three to four times the size of my bedroom at home. There's a crooked chaise lounge, no less beautiful because of its wonky shape, and a chandelier made out of skulls that are just a bit too human for my liking. The clothes inside, however, are exquisite: velvet, furs, brocade, leather, embroidery, silk, and more jewels than one girl could wear in a lifetime.

I miss jeans and t-shirts.

"How is that proof that I'm the Alice?" I ask, taking a bite of my sandwich and sighing with relief when it actually tastes good. I force my tired body off the bed with a groan and move to stand in the entrance to the closet. It's too big, too grand; I don't know what to do with it. As nice as it is, it can't last. Nothing good ever really does. "I'm too tired for riddles."

"You just know the prophecy oh so well," Dee says, hip-bumping me out of the way and moving across the thick white rugs piled high on the closet floor. He opens one of the cabinet drawers on the far wall, digs around a bit, and pulls out a pair of black suede slacks, a peaked cap similar to his own, red leather riding boots, and a black and white checkered blouse. "You've even got it memorized."

"So … there are flamingos and hedgehogs then?" I ask as Dee presents me with the clothes, and cocks his head to one side.

"What's a hedgehog?" he asks, but my brain is too tired to deal with nonsense. I just push him out the closet door and kick it closed, so I can change in peace. I keep telling myself that in this castle somewhere is the Looking-Glass, my ticket home. I'll get to see my dad and my sister again, my cat, Dinah. Somehow none of that provides me much motivation, not when I know the fate I'd be leaving Tee and Dee to. And then there's North … and *his* cat. Fucking Cheshire Puss.

Ugh.

This is why I don't sleep with guys on a first date. Things get complicated; things are *already* complicated.

"How do I look?" I ask after I slip out of the robe and into my new outfit, throwing the closet door open with a dramatic flourish. Dee ruffles up his hair with long fingers and gives me a slow, calculating once-over.

"Like a queen," he says, and then I'm sorry I even asked. How can I be a queen of anything when I can barely take care of my own life? Back home, all I do is read, sleep, and eat. Rinse, repeat. That's my entire life; I can't be expected to run anyone else's.

"You look beautiful," Tee adds as I exhale and pick my

robe up off the floor. Maybe there are servants who do that sort of thing here, but having morbid little card creatures doing my laundry is not an idea that appeals to me.

“Good enough to *eat*,” Chesh purrs, arching his back and digging his nails into the bedspread. He hops off the bed and swaggers his leather-pant-wearing ass over to a tall, carpeted sculpture in the corner.

Oh. It’s a cat tree, as in a play structure made specifically for cats.

"Who are you anyway?" I ask, glaring at Chesh as he climbs up and then lounges on said cat tree—in full human form, I might add. His leather pants are too low slung, and there's a tantalizing trail of dark hair below his belly button. Normally, I'd try not to stare, but this is Underland, and I'm tired, and there's a vampire and a king waiting downstairs for me. So I just look at him until he reaches down, unzips his leather pants, and then — "Please don't lick your crotch while I'm in the same room as you."

"Would you rather lick it for me?" Chesh growls, mouth spreading into a cat's grin. I flip him off and take a red wool military jacket from Dee's hands, our fingers brushing together for a moment. He purposely tangles his with mine and pulls my hand close, giving my knuckles a long, lingering kiss with his hot mouth.

"I'm glad you're safe," he whispers, going down to one knee in front of me. Our eyes lock, and I feel this little quiver of excitement sizzle through me. I can't forget the feel of his wings on my skin, the warm slide of his body inside of mine. "I'm really glad." Dee gives my hand a kiss and a squeeze, and stands up, stepping back to give me some room. Tee hands over the thigh-sheath with the Vorpal Blade in it next, *and* the Queenmaker tucked in a gorgeous red leather waist holster with tooled black hearts.

“Thanks,” I say, licking my lips and glancing down at the black hearts on the toes of my new boots for a moment. There’s an awkward silence that follows that I’m so desperate to fill, I turn back to Chesh again. "Anyway, you ignored my question: who *are* you?" I repeat, focusing on the asshole’s pierced septum and wondering if I sound too much like Lar. Speaking of, where is that cheeky butterfly?

"Why, I'm the cat," Chesh purrs, sweeping his black and white tail around in a curious little wave. "The *Cheshire Cat.*"

"I'm well-aware," I say, struggling and failing to put the new belt around my waist. Tee steps close to help, his body heat seeping into mine, his serious stare a welcome bit of steel in this crumbling world of rainbow madness. "What I meant was, who are you in relation to the hierarchy here? Are you the Duke's servant?"

Chesh blinks huge, gray eyes at me, and then yawns,

flashing his bright pink tongue.

"Servant? You know as well as I that a cat serves no one but himself." Chesh sits up and leans over, his beautiful stomach muscles bunching up, my eyes drawn right back to that line of dark hair all over again. "I'm the Duke's friend. Don't you have any friends, Alice?"

"Alli*son*," I say out of habit, sweeping back wet strands of hair from my forehead. "And that's it? You're just a friend?"

"Just a friend?" Chesh asks, cocking one triangular ear back. "Friends are rarer than diamonds and twice as precious. Are you quite mad?"

"Apparently," I say, shrugging into the wool coat and taking a deep breath. *I'm about to play croquet with a bunch of mentally insane psychopaths; this is a new low, even for me.* I hadn't had much of a plan before I got to the palace, and I'm starting to feel like I'm even more out of my league than I first realized. "We're all mad here. I'm mad, you're mad …" I trail off as Chesh howls with laughter, run my suddenly sweaty palms down the front of my new jacket, and get ready to face off against the King of Hearts.

♦ ♠ ♣ ♥ ♣ ♠ ♦

The March Hare is waiting just outside the gargantuan double doors that lead from the palace to the royal gardens. He's got a carrot in his hand which should be funny, considering his brown rabbit ears and all, but really, it's almost sexual the way he eats it. He sucks the tip into his mouth, swirls his tongue around the orange flesh, and then gives me this easy, one-sided smirk.

"The Boss wants me to keep a close eye on you," he says, his voice laced through with an English accent. It's much less formal than North's, but it has this quiet, lilting quality, like I'm hearing his words inside of a dream.

"Does he now?" Tee snaps, his teeth clenched tight. "Seems to me that your *boss* best defer to the King when it comes to the Alice."

"Oh?" March asks, tipping his top hat forward to shade the velvet brown color of his eyes. "You think the King of Hearts has any influence over the Hatter? That's a unique perspective."

"You think one mercenary asshole has the power to topple an entire kingdom?" Tee asks, stepping forward and putting the toes of his boots against March's. It gives me a little thrill, watching him stand up for me like that. Not that I can't stand up for myself, but it's always nice to have allies.

The look on the March Hare's face is demented. Deliciously demented, but still, it gives me pause. He runs his fingers along his chin and twitches one brown ear.

"Ask the Queen of Clubs," he drawls, and then sets off toward the grassy area on our left. I've never seen such a curious croquet-ground in all my life. Hell, I'm not sure that I've *ever* seen a croquet-ground in my life. It's all ridges and furrows; the croquet balls look like ivory lumps, and the mallets shimmer in the sun like bone.

The wickets are made up of the little card people, their grotesque faces twisted into silent screams. Just looking at them, with their human legs and arms bent into unnatural positions, makes me want to puke. Sure, the garden is beautiful, and the flowers smell like honey and sugar, but there's a tension in the air that I don't like. It snaps against my face with each gust of wind, stinging my lips and tangling my white-blonde hair into snarls.

It also brings with it the metallic scent of blood.

"What the fuck is that?" I ask, but I'm well-aware of what I'm looking it, shimmering in the sunlight across the courtyard.

It's a guillotine.

Not sure how I missed it before.

It's impossible to miss now, considering the fact that it's spattered with blood, and there's a guard dragging a body away. For a moment there, my chest fills with panic when I see a pair of limp, butterfly wings on the back of the dead man. But then Lar is standing right beside me with a deep-set frown etched into his face. Relief pours over me in a wave.

"What's going on here?" I ask him as he studies me

with eyes like chips of ice, his pale blonde hair tinted with the slightest drop of blue. It goes well with his pale skin and provides a nice contrast against the vibrant sweep of his blue, black, and gold wings. He has the most mild of expressions on his face, too, like nothing in the world bothers him. His hands though, I can see them curling into loose fists.

“It’s nice to see you’re still alive, Sunshine,” he says, eyes going half-lidded as he smiles at me. The wind picks up strands of his shoulder-length hair and sends his sapphire earrings dancing. Light refracts through them and casts a blue glow on the white squares of my checkered top. When he finally lifts his head to look in the direction of the guillotine, his smiles fades to a thin line. "The King likes to kill decoys to vent his anger, when he can't be bothered to rid himself of the real thing."

"He's killing a decoy of you?" I ask, studying Lar's white jacket, tossed casually over his shoulders. I still can't get over how similar he is to the character of Howl from the movie *Howl's Moving Castle.* Kills me every time. I find myself subconsciously running my tongue over my lower lip. Hard to maintain a flirty moment though, knowing some innocent dude was killed because he *looks* like the Caterpillar. "Why?!"

"We failed the king by losing you," Tee whispers, voice low and dark. He won't look at me now, especially not when he sees my gaze swing over to the trail of blood that mars the perfection of the white gravel pathway. At the end of it, there's a whole sea of familiar corpses, wearing hats that match the twins, one with a tail that matches the Duke's.

I know then and there that I am always, *always,* going to hate the King of Hearts.

"We failed the King, but he fails himself if he loses us," Dee riddles, adjusting his hat to protect his eyes from the sun. I notice that most everyone out on the croquet-ground is wearing a peaked cap of some kind. Guess it's in fashion around here. Even the King—can't miss that handsome face, not even from a hundred yards away—is now wearing slacks, a jacket, and a hat, too.

"Oh, but he'd kill *me* if he could," Chesh says, curling his furry little cat body around Dee's neck and staring at me from eyes like two full moons in his black and white striped face. "You'll see no by-proxy murder of this pussycat. The King hates me with a violent passion. Not a cat person, but I suppose there's no accounting for taste." Chesh waves his tail across his body and disappears behind it, like he's erasing himself from existence. The only sign that he's still there is the faintest whisper of a purr.

"This can't be happening," I whisper as I shake myself out and rub at my temples with two fingers.

There's no one actively being shoved onto the guillotine, but I'll be damned if I stand by and watch an innocent person die. "I can't let this happen."

"Tread with care, Sunshine," Lar whispers, tugging on one of his sapphire earrings and giving the twins' angel wings a slow once-over. "The King is already displeased with the lot of us."

"Yeah? Well I'm displeased at his execution factory over here," I grind out, gesturing wildly in the direction of the bodies. There are multi-colored crows pecking at the corpses, their feathers a sea of rainbow colors that reminds me of the dyed strands in my own hair. Just over the castle wall, perching in a tree, is a row of vultures with eyes like shards of obsidian.

I shiver and straighten my coat out, starting across the too-green grass with my metaphorical hackles raised, the men trailing along behind me. The March Hare is waiting along the way, falling into step beside us, but I ignore him, cutting a path straight to the King, the Duke, and the Hatter. I do not, however, miss the mischievous little smile March tosses my way. He's eating again—a big ripe peach this time. I wonder if he ever stops?

"Well, well, so lovely to see you again," Raiden says, the orange-color of his eyes obscured by heavy lids and thick lashes. There are two card servants nearby, holding up frilly parasols covered in hearts. They shade Raiden's pale skin from the relentless rays of the late afternoon sun. "And so soon."

The Duke snarls under his breath, claws curling from his fingertips as he whaps his tail against the lawn, creating little divots. He's dressed in a loose white top, fully unbuttoned and flashing bronzed skin, as well as tight brown leather pants and black boots with red hearts on the toes. His gold eyes glare daggers at the Mad Hatter before sweeping my way with a heat that's twice as powerful as the sun's rays. Now I feel like *I* might need a parasol.

"You're dressing people up like your servants and then having them slaughtered?" I blurt as the King turns slowly toward me, his face drawn into this expression of intentional neutrality that scares the crap out of me. He's not scared of anyone, not intimidated by anything—not the Duke, not the Hatter, and most especially not me. "The great wonder is, that there's anyone left alive."

Glancing around, I notice that the entire entourage that was parading through the garden earlier is seated and watching … and they're all fucking staring at me.

"Here," says the King, his dark eyes sparkling in the sun. He passes over a mallet which, unsurprisingly, is a petrified skeleton. It looks like a flamingo, you know, except for the sharp teeth in the fossilized little beak. "Take a mallet, hit a ball, Alice."

"It's Allison," I correct, watching the dark shadows flit over the King's face—both physically and metaphorically.

"Well, *Alice*," he says, purposely putting emphasis on the name and tapping the skull of his mallet against the soft ground. He's tall, towering over me and enjoying looking down his perfect nose, I bet. It really is a perfect nose, too. It offsets his full mouth beautifully, the scar just barely noticeable on the right corner of his lips, trailing down his chin, and slicing across his throat. His blood-red hair ruffles in the breeze, and I'd almost find him handsome if he wasn't such a horrible human being. Or … is he human? I don't even know. "Why don't you play a game with me? Winner can decide when the killing stops." He lifts his hand and the human guards in their red and white suits of armor drag one of the card people over to the guillotine, cutting the creature in half with the wicked metal blade before I can even think to utter a protest.

Blood sprays everywhere, and the scream that spills from its dying throat will haunt my nightmares for years to come. My hand drops to the Queenmaker, and I have to fight really goddamn hard not to blow this arrogant asshole's head right off.

"Careful, Miss Alice," an icy voice whispers in my ear, just before Rab appears on my right side, holding out a mallet and a ball. His red eyes meet mine, and he raises his brows as if to say *you have no idea what you're messing with here.* “The King is as vindictive as he is handsome.”

I snatch the equipment from Rab as the King smirks and twists his white-gloved hand around the base of his mallet. The way he’s looking at me makes my blood boil, like he’s a farmer inspecting his cattle and finding one of his beasts sorely lacking. My nostrils flare as I struggle to hold in my temper and do my best not to think about all the eyes on me. I've never been much for public displays; I'd rather sit in a corner and read.

"You're on," I say, dropping my ball to the grass and putting my foot on it. It takes me a moment to realize it’s a *skull.* Yet another fossil in this maelstrom of hell. Not sure if this one’s human or not. If it is, it must’ve belonged to a child. Bile rises in my throat as my stomach roils. "I win, and you stop beheading people without my permission."

"Your permission?" the King asks, his voice low and dangerous, like the whistle of a far-off wind, one that promises future storms. "How interesting. It's a deal then: you beat me in a game of croquet, and I'll let you stay my executions." His mouth curves up into a cruel smile, pulling at the ragged scar etched into his skin.

I take a deep breath and shrug my shoulders, loosening my joints.

No fucking way I'm losing this match.

“And if I win,” the King continues, moving closer to

me. When he glances over at Rab, the rabbit-eared man takes several steps back. I meet the Duke's narrowed eyes over the monarch's shoulder and at least get the feeling that he'd fight to defend me if needed. That doesn't do much to comfort me though because I'm not at all certain he could take the King down. "You'll kiss me in front of the entire court."

"Are you insane?" I ask, but the arrogant male triumph on his says he most definitely is *not.* Piece of shit. "Fine, bring it on, bitch." The King raises his brows at my name-calling, but tosses his skull into the air and then rolls it onto the grass next to a red and white stake.

Oh, wait. It's not a stake—it's a bone with blood spatter on it.

"How intriguing," says the Hatter, adjusting his black top hat and grinning with two sharp canines. "Mind if I excuse myself to make some bets? Where there's a challenge, there's always money to be made." He moves off to join the March Hare near the white lawn chairs where the audience sits, and starts to smoke a cigarette in a gold holder with lazy drags.

My eyes lock onto the King's dark ones, but they're impossible to read. I've never seen someone so closed-off before. It's terrifying. Kissing this guy must be like swallowing a mouthful of ash and hate. *You're only thinking that because you're disturbingly intrigued by him,* my mind whispers, but I ignore it.

"So, what are the rules?" I ask, because like, I've clearly never played fucking croquet before. Even if I had, I doubt the rules in Underland would be anything like they are back home. “Who goes first?”

"The blood-spattered ball *always* goes first,” the King says, turning his skull ball with his foot so I can see the red stains on the front. “And the rules … are exactly what I want them to be." He lines up a shot with his macabre mallet while the grotesque little card creatures shiver and shake, their painted faces twisted into expressions of horror. Without even bothering to aim for the wickets, the King knocks his bloody ball into the fray, and the cards shuffle to accommodate him. "Four points," he calls out after the ball passes underneath several arches. "And four extra swings.” I watch as he works his way around the heart-shaped court. I think in traditional croquet, the wickets and stakes are supposed to be in a double diamond shape. But, of course, there’s nothing traditional about Underland. “Your turn, Alice," he mocks as the nick on my neck throbs and smarts. I won't forget that he held a blade to my throat anytime soon.

"Son of a bitch," I snarl as I kick my own ball into place, trying to ignore the entourage behind me. Tee, Dee, Lar, and … I have no idea where Chesh went, maybe rubbing his invisible self against the Duke's legs. Rab is standing off to the side, arms crossed in front of him, one of his white ears twitching. It's impossible to miss the grimace that crosses his face.

He turns one of his arms over and shows me the watch tattooed there, ticking down to something ominous, no doubt. Probably my inevitable loss in this game.

As I ready my shot—because I have to at least try—I notice something strange shimmering in the air near the slave-card wickets. It weirds me the fuck out until I realize that what I'm looking at is a grin.

"How are you getting on?" says the cat, as soon as there's enough mouth for him to speak with. It's no use talking to him until his ears are there, or at least one of them. In less than a minute, there's a cat's head floating in the air not six feet in front of my face.

"I don't think they play at all fairly," I growl, gritting my teeth and glancing back over at the King. He's staring at the cat with a mixture of rage and frustration. Oh. I like that. So there *is* something that can shake the unshakeable. Good to know. "There don't seem to be any rules in particular; at least, if there are, nobody fucking attends to them."

"How do you like the King?" says the cat in a low voice. Clearly, he's trying to pick a fight. Not sure how smart of an idea that is. The rest of the guys seem pretty freaked-out by the King of Hearts. Understandably so, considering he kills random strangers to vent his anger.

"Not at all," I say. "He's so extremely"—I pause when I notice how close the King is behind me—"likely to win, that it's hardly worthwhile finishing the game."

The King smiles, but it's not a very pretty expression.

"I see you're back again," he says, resting his hands on the end of his mallet, the skull dug firmly into the grassy earth near his boots. "After last time, I'd think to find you more intelligent than all that." Chesh smiles, his eyes twinkling, a disembodied tail fluffing around behind him. "I don't like the look of you at all. However, you may kiss my hand if you like."

"I'd rather not," the cat remarks, and just like that, all of that cool, easy calm leaves the King in a violent flood. I can see the muscles in his jaw ticking with rage.

"I'd fetch the executioner myself," he growls out, "if you had a body that I could remove your head from."

"What a pity, what a *shaaaame*," the cat purrs, its head twisting around until it's looking at us upside down. "So there *is* something the precocious King of Hearts can't attend to?"

"Whatever am I going to do with you?" the King grinds out as Chesh tosses me a little wink, licks his lips, and promptly disappears from view.

"He belongs to the Duke; you'd better ask him about it." And then I crack my mallet on the ugly little skull and send it flying. The card wickets try to shuffle out of my way, but a little shimmer and a swipe of some nearly invisible claws keeps them in just the right place for my ball to fly right on through.

"*Five* points," I mock as I stand up straight and give the King a triumphant look that, had these idiots not completely bought into the prophecy thing, probably would've gotten *my* head lopped off.

The King's gloved hands squeak as he tightens them around the handle of his mallet.

"Very well then," he says, curling the edge of his lip up and meeting my eyes dead-on. The crown perched atop his head slides to one side, this lazy little dip that's too sexy for words. But it doesn't fall off, like it's defying gravity just for him. "I'll play you fair, Alice." The King stands up and spins his mallet in a circle, cracking the skull side against the ground before he takes off to meet his ball, the empty eyes of the hollow skull staring up at a blue, blue sky.

"Don't even *try* to win, Allison," Tee whispers, grabbing my arm. I glance back at him, and whatever he sees on my face must convince him that I'm doing this whether he likes it or not. “Fuck, you’re going to get yourself killed.” With a growl and clenched teeth, he releases me, watching as I follow along after the King.

The asshole’s next shot is damn near perfect, and even without cheating, he manages to knock his ball through three more wickets. Not sure how many of those arches are *supposed* to be in the game, but here in Underland, there are hundreds, maybe thousands. It almost looks like a graveyard, all these silent faces staring up at an unyielding sky.

"I've got your baaaack, so to say," Chesh purrs in my ear. I can't see him, but at least when I hit my ball, all the cards stay in place. I miss the next wicket and don't get any points, while on the King's next turn, he hits my ball with his own, calls a 'roquet', and then smashes my ball into kingdom come with his next swing. I finger the Queenmaker as I grind my teeth. *Bet this baby could turn the dickhead to mush,* I think as I stretch my neck and give a deep sigh.

The audience may as well be made up of corpses for all the noise they make, sitting quiet and still as a storm cloud rolls in, covering up the sun and casting strange shadows on the field.

"You should know better," the King says, his voice even-keeled and wicked all over again. The way he looks at me, I just want to turn and run, stumble through the castle until I find the Looking-Glass and forget I was ever here. There's something in his stare that promises I might do things I never thought I'd do—and that I might *like it.* "Challenging me."

"I've seen bigger bullies than you," I snort. If I hadn't

met the Mad Hatter all of say, oh, twenty-four hours ago, that might not be the case. I can't help but glance over at the man in question, wondering not only how he came to be in this world, but also how he became a vampire. "Now if it will please Your Majesty …" I can't help an eyeroll to punctuate my words as I gesture at the King with my mallet. He glances down at the lump of bone near his feet, folds his arms across his chest, and stays put. With a small snarl, I stalk over to him and stand far too close for comfort.

He smells just as good as his garden, but with a solid note of thyme and rosemary that hits the back of my tongue when I breathe in, something savory to balance out all the sweet.

"You know what *would* please his majesty," he whispers, his breath far too near my ear for comfort.

"No," I say firmly, cracking my ball and managing to just barely sneak it through the right wicket. "And I don't think I want to know."

"I will have you, Alice," he says, his dark eyes glittering like a starry sky. "You've always been destined to be mine."

"I'd rather marry the Mad Hatter," I grind out, and the King's full mouth twists into a severe frown.

"That's part of the arrangement. At first, I was upset. But I've decided this can only bring prosperity to the Kingdom of Hearts. If the most powerful mercenary on the continent is tied to the crown, think of the possibilities."

"I think that my heart and my vagina aren't bargaining tools," I snap as the King purposely brushes past me, his fingers curling around my wrist. When I glance up, I get caught in his eyes. Fuck, I practically fall into them. It's like I'm tumbling down the Rabbit-Hole all over again, getting twisted up in glitter and bones.

"And *I* think that your fate is to belong to me." The King grabs my chin in tight fingers, but my reaction commands are on point. I smack his hand away and stumble back, stepping on one of the poor cards by accident. The sound it makes … it's like I've taken all its breath away. A gasping choke tears from the poor creature's throat as I jerk back, tripping over and crushing my ball before falling right on my ass.

The card person thrashes and chokes, sitting up and turning its silent screaming face toward me. It reaches its too-human hands up and claws at its neck, like it's choking. I back away, even though I know I shouldn't, even though I know I should feel pity and sympathy instead of horror and fear.

"It's a curse they brought on themselves," the King says, smashing the end of his mallet into the card's face. A tear of blood escapes its frozen eye before it collapses to the ground, shudders … and dies. "You're wasting your sympathy."

I look up at him with this expression of horror

plastered across my face. When he sees the way I'm staring at him, something flickers in his gaze that I can't quite read, like a shooting star cutting across all that darkness. But he turns away too quickly for me to get a good read on it.

"Your Majesty," Rab is saying, his red eyes flickering briefly to me and then back to the King's. "The Mocking Turtle and the Gryphon … they're at the gates."

I wish I could explain the expression of rage that crosses the King's face then … and the look of terror.

3

The Mocking Turtle's... Scary As Fuck

"Who won the game?" I ask North as we follow the King's entourage through the palace, trying my hardest not to think about the dead card servant that was just dragged across the lawn outside. If I think too much about what just happened, I'll get dizzy and this fatigue headache I've been nursing will finally win over and knock me on my ass. The Duke's long, black tail slashes across the checkered floor like a scythe, but the expression in his gold eyes is pure, unadulterated *excitement*.

And I think that excitement might be for me.

Oops.

I wonder if mating with him really was a good idea? Or maybe his lack of mating was what made him savage in the first place?

"Clearly, the bloody King," he says, and despite his expression, his words are a bit clipped, gold gaze swinging over to the grand front entrance of Castle Heart. We come to a stop in an area that's roughly five times the size of my school's gymnasium—and this, this is apparently the *foyer*. "Although I suspect he'll wait awhile to collect on his prize." North flicks his attention back to me and smiles lasciviously. "I doubt he wants to share your first kiss the same day you experienced the most wonderful lovemak—"

"Ooookay," I say, interrupting him before he can get started regaling the others about our tryst in the woods. If the twins really want to know, I'll tell them later. Right now, I want answers. Well, I would if the Duke's shirt weren't unbuttoned, a stretch of bronze chest exposed. I can see all the hard lines of his muscles as he turns toward me and leans in, breath hot against my ear.

"You're thinking about something, my dear, and that makes you forget to talk." North nibbles the edge of my earlobe, and I slap him away, coming to like I've been splashed with cold water. I really need to figure out how to function with hot guys swarming around my hormone-addled body all the time. "I dare say you're wondering why I don't put my arm around your waist?"

I decide to ignore the Duke and focus on Lar instead. He looks like an intelligent enough man. And those eyes, they're like soft blue sea glass. They pierce straight through me.

"Who are the Mocking Turtle and the Gryphon, and why did everyone shit their pants when their names were mentioned?" I ask, my cheeks warming slightly as Lar smiles at me and reaches out to push a few loose rainbow strands of hair back from my face. I feel like Tee notices my barely-there blush, but that's not a surprise: Tee notices everything.

"I have an unfortunate inkling that you'll soon find out for yourself," Lar says, holding his jacket over one shoulder, his ice-blue shirt unbuttoned just enough that I can see the keys pierced through his nipples. As I watch, he reaches inside his top and unhooks one, passing it over to that blonde woman I saw this morning, the one with the nasty frown who keeps *staring* at me like she expects me to sprout a second head.

She's tall, thin, and that sort of dangerous pretty that makes grown men weep. I'm surprised *she* doesn't have an entourage of dudes drooling after her. Dressed in a full suit of white armor and carrying a lance, she looks like she could take on a jabberwock. That is, until she trips over a potted plant and lands face-first on the rug in front of the gilded gold doors.

"Take those nonsensical things off and answer the damn door," the Duke calls out as the woman finds her feet and whips around to glare at him, smacking him in the face with her waist-length hair in the process. At first I'm not sure what the hell he's talking about, but then I notice the strange metal fins feathering around her feet. Ah, no wonder she tripped. I was too busy being jealous of her boobs to notice her weird shoes.

"These are *ankle shields* to guard against the bites of sharks—it's an invention of my own. I don't see *you* inventing anything new." The woman sniffs and lifts her chin haughtily, clutching Lar's key in one hand, and flicking her lavender eyes over to mine. She stares at me a moment, taking in my state of dress, and then sighs. "You'll hardly be able to defend against these assholes wearing this."

I'm still wondering why the hell she thinks she needs to guard against sharks on dry land when she reaches up and flicks two buckles open, one on either shoulder. Her white breastplate comes right off and she moves over to fasten it on me.

"This, it's an invention of my own," she tells me as I sag underneath the metal armor. How the fuck am I supposed to stand up while wearing this?! It weighs about a million pounds. "I don't have a name for it yet, but I will."

"Do spare my mate the idiocy of your inventions," the Duke says with a little growl, his gaze focused only on me.

It's like he doesn't even *see* the gorgeous blonde standing beside me. And I like that. And I also feel a bit like a misogynistic prick for thinking that way.

"He might bite," Chesh says, appearing out of thin air on my left, still dressed in leather pants and nothing else. "Either you or the Alice, I'm not sure." North weaves his arm through my right while the Cheshire Cat does the same to my left. "But if he bites you, White Knight, it won't be for pleasure."

"My job is to protect the Kingdom of Hearts, and that includes keeping the Alice safe. Stand down and let me do my job." She turns on her heel and heads back to the throng of guards near the front gate, unlocking the double doors, and gesturing for the card servants to open them with long ropes.

"I do quite like a little nibble every now and again," the Duke growls, tightening his grip on my arm as Tee rolls his eyes and Dee grins. But in the next minute, all their faces fall, Lar's included, and I glance up to find the King standing there in front of us, arms folded, frowning like a thunderstorm. Rab's standing just behind and to the right of him, one tattooed hand holding a cigarette, the other swinging a pocket watch around on a gold chain. He smirks at me when he sees me looking, and I flip him off.

"A fine day, Your Majesty," the Duke says, his voice

high and threaded through with a growl. He sounds annoyed, but I'm not sure if it's with the King or with the Mocking Turtle and the Gryphon, whoever the fuck they are. All I know about them is what I read in the original story; they scared the shit out of me in those old Tenniel drawings. Gross. "How can we be of service?"

"They want to meet the Alice," the King says, lifting his cell phone and reminding me that they *do* in fact have phones here. That they never use because their network is 'compromised'. I guess when you're talking to the enemy anyway, it doesn't matter if they've tapped the phone lines. I notice Tee and Dee exchange a worried look.

"They want to rape and kill the Alice," Dee growls out, surprising me. He's generally a jovial person. To see him so angry is disconcerting. I *really* don't like it—especially when he reaches out and puts his fingers on my hip, just above the Queenmaker, like he's reminding me it's still there. Nobody here seems concerned about giving me a gun in the presence of a king I already hate. I can't decide if it just means the Castle Heart security is poor, or if the King is such a badass that me having a weapon in my hands doesn't matter much.

My bet's on the latter.

"Tell them no and send them on their way. Better yet, carve their flesh like a holiday ham and mail their corpses back to the Walrus and the Carpenter," the Duke says, curling the corner of his lip up in a snarl, curved horns catching the light above us. I'm sure as soon as I have a moment to myself, I'll start thinking about our wild rut in the woods in graphic detail, probably masturbating to it, too. For now, I sort of need to compartmentalize it.

Did I just hear rape and kill?

"If I could, I most certainly would," the King says, tilting his head to one side. The gold crown he wears catches the light as he narrows his eyes on me. "But they're Recitations, obviously. We could obliterate them, but what good would that do? We may as well get as much information from them as we can."

"What's a Recitation?" I ask, scrubbing my hands down my face. I don't even want to *speak* with the King, particularly after watching him kill the card servant earlier, but I also need to know who—or *what*—is trying to kill me. I mean, rule one of survival: know your enemies.

"A Recitation is a copy of a person's image, with no person waiting behind it." Lar pulls—no joke—a glass pipe from the pocket of his white slacks, and lights up. Clearly, he's not smoking tobacco. Is it too much to hope that there's a little pot in there? Rab flicks his cigarette butt on the floor, and a card servant promptly cleans it up. The two men each take a drag on the pipe before Rab finishes Lar's thought.

"It's a mirage," he says, smoothing his hand down one of his ears and smiling at me in a way that I can only describe as half horror movie/half romantic comedy. Looking at his ears makes me think of the March Hare and the Mad Hatter. They disappeared at the mention of the Gryphon and the Mocking Turtle, and I haven't seen them since. Coincidence, much?

"A mirage that can spy and report back to the Walrus and the Carpenter." A shiver chases down my spine when Tee says those two names. They should be ridiculous—I mean the *Mocking Turtle* for fuck's sake—but there's something eerily ominous about them, and I can't help but think of the prophecy. Just what do these guys have to do with all the bullshit befalling Underland? When Tee murmurs another stanza under his breath, I get this horrific sense of déjà vu, like I've been here, done this all before.

"The eldest angel sneered at them,
And many a word he said:
The stubborn monarch closed his eyes,
And said she won't be dead—
They had to let the Alice think
Else his Queen would soon bleed red."

The King lets him finish and then turns to me with his ebon eyes as Dee whistles under his breath.

"You have to admit, Highness, that's hardly coincidental. Lar?" Dee glances over at the Caterpillar, but all he does is tug on one of his earrings and shrug his shoulders in a noncommittal sort of way before taking his pipe back from Rab.

"I deliver prophecy—I don't interpret it." Lar folds his wings together behind his back at the same moment Dee drops his feathered appendages to the floor, and Tee curls his protectively around his shoulders. I notice the King of Hearts keeps his gaze entirely focused on me.

"Well?" he asks, and there's this challenge in his voice that just gets me. He thinks I'm going to say no. He must, the way he's quietly smirking at me. But then, he doesn't know Allison Pleasance Liddell, does he? I never back down from a challenge.

"I want to see them," I say, feeling the muscles in my lower belly tighten. The King tosses some red hair off his forehead … arrogantly. How one can toss hair arrogantly is beyond me, but he manages to pull it off without looking like a total twat. "Where are they?"

"Come," the asshole says, turning in a billow of his heavy white and red coat. Without waiting to see if I'll follow, he moves with long strides across the checkered marble floor, Rab and a female guard flanking either side of him, and soldiers trailing in two lines behind. With both North's and Chesh's arms tucked in mine, I move to stand behind him and notice that the large, gilded gold doors have opened up to reveal … two wooden doors that are painted red.

When the King waves his hand, these, too, are opened. And behind door number two? More fucking doors. As the servants continue to open them, I notice that the entrance is getting smaller and smaller. On the ceiling above, there are remnants of all the previous doors in layers, like a fucking cake.

"I don't suppose that disappearing act of yours is contagious?" I ask the cat as he rubs his cheek against my shoulder. He seems almost above all this hierarchal bullshit. Which, of course, makes complete sense if you know anything at all about cats.

"Perhaps it's sexually transmitted?" he purrs, flashing me a bit of canine. "Maybe we should test the theory?"

"Don't be crude," North drawls, but he's hardly paying attention to my exchange with his pussycat. No, his gaze is focused on a small set of metal doors no bigger than my front doors back home. They're silver and inlaid with a massive anatomical heart. It splits in half in a crooked, jagged shape, like a broken heart in a child's drawing, revealing a long, dark stone walkway … that leads to nowhere.

It protrudes past a cliff's edge, over a vast valley shadowed by the clouds overhead. For miles, all I can see are trees and mushrooms and the blue snakes of raging rivers. There's no discernible way for a person to get up here, other than the pair of red doors on a floating island at the end of the path.

Another portal then?

"I'll be here if you need me," the White Knight says, moving to stand beside Rab and the King. She taps her chest with a gloved fist, like she's trying to remind me that I've got her breastplate on. I suppose it helps boost my courage a *little*, although it is heavy as hell.

"And I won't be," Lar says, flapping his wings softly. They glow a gentle blue-gold as he gifts me with the briefest of smiles and tugs on one of his earrings again. "Can't risk stumbling into any visions or prophecies with that lot around. Good luck, Sunshine." With another flap of his wings and a puff of glitter and dust … the Caterpillar is gone and there's a butterfly drifting lazily through the air in his place.

Um. The hell did I just witness?!

I blink a few times and then turn to North, but he's focused on that walkway and whatever's at the end of it. One glance and I can already tell what's caught his attention: there are two men waiting just in front of the red doors. My nostrils flare and this … this *feeling* shoots through me, like a shooting star made of acid, burning its way into the depths of my soul. The Vorpal Blade on my thigh tingles, and the Queenmaker just begs me to wrap my fingers around the grip and fire.

They might look like men, but the creatures I'm staring at are fucking monsters.

Without meaning to, I step outside and then pause on the stone walkway, sliding my arms out of Chesh's and North's grips. The Duke immediately curls his tail around my ankle, but I'm too focused to care. The only time in my life I've ever felt this way about another person was when I was damn close to being raped. Those boys that attacked me, that subsequently killed my brother, they had the same aura as these men. Now, I'm not sure if I believe in such basic concepts as good and evil, but there are checks and balances in every facet of nature. On one end of the spectrum, there are cuddly kittens and puppies licking faces and batting balls of yarn … on the other end, are these guys.

Pure pond scum.

"What fun!" says the man on the right, the one with a massive pair of eagle wings protruding from his back. They should be pretty, like Tee's or Dee's, but instead, they're scraggly and scarred, casting strange shadows over the man's beak-like nose and too-full lips. He's 'handsome' enough, I suppose, following the unwritten rules of this world that every dude needs to be attractive, but there's a slimy quality to him that puts me immediately on edge.

"What *is* the fun?" I grind out as the King steps aside, his entourage parting like the Red Sea. He crosses his arms over his chest and looks right at me with eyes as dark as a starless night. His lashes are so goddamn long though, sweeping up and framing his expression of disdain with just the right amount of pretty.

"Why, *he* is," says the winged guy who I'm guessing must be the Gryphon. He nods his pointed chin in the direction of the King of Hearts. "It's all his fancy that: he never executes nobody worth executing, you know. Come on, have a stroll down here so we can have a look at you."

"Everybody says 'come on' here," I growl as I plant my feet firmly on the walkway and mimic the King's pose, crossing my arms under my breasts and lifting my chin in defiance. No way in hell I'm taking a single step closer to these men. "I never was so ordered about before in all my fucking life." Scowling, I spit and try not to look too closely at the other man. If the Gryphon scares the piss outta me, the Mocking Turtle is what makes up *his* personal nightmares. "Never. And I'm not about to start obeying orders now."

The Gryphon smirks, running his hand over his slicked-back brunette hair. It reminds me of John Travolta in *Grease*, just … way less attractive. Disturbing, really. It's hard to explain, but it's the very mundane blandness of this man that's scaring me. He's so unremarkable as to be remarkable, like a sterile white waiting room in a hospital with squeaky clean floors and the scent of iodine. Only, beneath it all, you can still smell the blood.

"Don't let them pull you in," Tee whispers from behind me, his calm, inner strength seeping into me when he puts a firm hand on one of my shoulders. "Don't let them get to you; that's what they're here to do."

"I can see why the guy on the right is called the Gryphon, but where did the name *Mocking Turtle* come from?" I whisper as Dee rests his chin on my right shoulder. The twins' clean mountain air scent wraps around me like a shield, calming my frantic heartbeat just a tad.

"Legend goes that he can bring any person to tears with a single word, and send them to the grave with a short story. He quite literally *mocks* his enemies to death." I'd laugh at Dee's words if I wasn't already starting to wonder if they were true. Turtle-Dick hasn't said a word yet, and I've already got the chills. *Click, click, click* go his fingernails as he clacks the pointed black tips together.

"And the Turtle part?" I breathe, just before I finally catch sight of his face and see the hooked shape of his upper lip. He smacks his jaws at me with a disturbing amount of force, and I notice that he hasn't got any damn teeth.

"Legend goes," Dee starts again, standing back up and putting his palm on my lower back for comfort, "that he bites like a snapping turtle."

"Oh? Is that all? Fantastic," I grind out as the two men start forward in disturbingly perfect unison, pausing only when Rab moves to cut them off. But they're close enough that I can *smell* them. There's the sharp, bitter scent of fresh soap with the underlying choke of rot, like roadkill left in the hot, hot sun. It makes me gag, which of course only makes them both smile.

When the Gryphon smiles, doves cry. When the Mocking Turtle smiles … angels die.

He looks at me with large eyes, as dark as the King's but without a hint of soul in them. There's just nothing there, like an endless void that leads to nowhere. Just staring into them makes me sick to my stomach, like I'm falling down that Rabbit-Hole all over again, only I'll never find a place to land. I step forward and put one of my hands on Rab's tattooed muscular forearm, remembering the feel of him catching me when I fell. Maybe, metaphorically, he's doing the same thing now? When he glances down at me and I see that ironclad calm, I know I'm in good hands. I guess I might forgive him for shooting Brandon. Maybe.

"This here young lady," says the Gryphon, glancing over at his bald-headed companion, "she wants to know your bloody history, I believe."

"I'll tell it to her," the Mocking Turtle replies in a

deep, hollow tone, “so long as she doesn’t speak a word till I’ve finished.” He licks his gross lips with a thick, slimy tongue. “*Frederick*.”

“Fuck you,” I growl out, putting my hand on the Queenmaker. I saw what it did to the jubjub bird. I bet it could blow these men to bacon bits. How *dare* he bring up my brother’s name. Even bigger question: how did he know it in the first place?!

“They’re not really here,” North says, squeezing my ankle even tighter with his muscular tail. I thought I hated the feel of it on me before, but now I think I’m starting to like it. That’s what a surge of sex hormones will do to a person, I guess. “They’re Recitations, just ghosts of their true selves.”

“Well, I’d still like to blow them to queendom come,” I say, whipping the pistol off my belt and using a flick of my right arm to open the chamber. With my left hand, I open one of the leather pouches on my belt and remove a fuse, metal ball, and a couple of fresh matches. One of these I strike, just so I can see it burn, smell the scent of sulfur. The other, I tuck behind my ear before I load the weapon and snap it closed. "I don't care about your bullshit; I just want to know what you're after."

"Hold your tongue," snarls the Gryphon, before I can finish telling him to fuck off. "Clearly you've missed a few classes at finishing school. When a person talks, it’s only polite to listen. Can't you see he has a story to tell?"

"Now where was I?" the Mocking Turtle asks, glancing over at his companion. "Was I discussing Tweedledum and Tweedledee's dead family?" Both Dee and Tee stiffen up behind me, but they don't say anything. Good on them. I could practically spit I'm so fucking mad.

"No, I don't believe so," the Gryphon continues, rubbing at his chin thoughtfully. "Were you talking about that time the *former* King of Hearts tried to kill his own son? Or that *other* time the former King of Hearts cut up the White Rabbit's pet mouse and fed it to him?" My eyes dart over to the men in question, but neither of them reacts. Rab, actually, looks quite happy smoking a fresh cigarette.

The Mocking Turtle snaps his fingers as I grit my teeth in anger. There are so many revelations running through my mind right now, but I have to pick them apart later. Now is not the time.

"Oh, *that's* right," the Mocking Turtle says, turning to glance up at the very last bit of sun showing above the navy mountains. Very soon, it'll be full dark. At least there are two moons here, right? More silver moonbeams to cut through the horror of this meeting. "I was discussing her dead brother Frederick and how he had to die because the Alice is a whore."

“You son of a bitch,” I snarl, snatching the match from behind my ear. I’d have lit it, too, if Rab hadn’t curled his gloved fingers around my own. “Say that again and we’ll see how well the Vorpal Blade can perform a castration.”

“No, she’s certainly never been to finishing school, a crude cunt like her,” the Mocking Turtle says, adjusting his tie. Yes, he’s wearing a suit. Both of these crazy men are. Unlike the Gryphon, I don’t suppose the Mocking Turtle would be considered handsome by anyone. He’s tall and muscular, but almost *too* muscular, like some kind of pre-human caveman species. That, and he has the most grotesque mouth I’ve ever seen with those hooked lips, toothless gums, and thick grimy tongue. “I'd like to put her into a class at the school of Reeling and Writhing, and then run her through the different branches of arithmetic: Addiction, Dissection, Mutilation, and Derision."

I remember this play on words in the original Lewis Carroll book, the Mock Turtle’s strange twist on *addition, subtraction, multiplication, and division.* Only … you know, it wasn’t so macabre. And compared to *this* turtle, that one wasn’t so scary after all. Their lyrical nonsense doesn’t frighten me though, no way, no how.

"Stop with the riddles and the bullshit. What do you want, and why do you give two shits about me?" My men—err, the hot Underland dudes I’ve been hanging out with—wait quietly behind me, providing a wall of support at my back.

"You *are* a simpleton, aren't you?" the Gryphon mocks, lifting his wings high up on his back. I wonder what species he is, as he's the only person I've seen with feathered wings other than Tee and Dee. But they were very clear: they're the only angels left alive in Underland. So what is this guy?

"If you insult the Alice again," North snarls, his accent clipped and sharp. Black, scaled wings explode from his shoulders, and his tail tightens around my ankle, squeezing to the point of pain. "Well, *nobody* insults a jabberwock's mate and lives to tell the tale."

"Shut your mouth," the Gryphon says, and I have to hold North back by grabbing his tail *tight* in my fist. "The last thing we need is the opinion of another useless, cursed male. We're here to speak to that slut of an Alice." The Duke crouches low and punches his fist into the stone walkway, leaving a crack and a mini crater in his wake. I'd try to comfort him, but I'm too busy watching the way the Gryphon and the Mocking Turtle watch *me*, like they're soaking me up, like they have sponges for eyes. My stomach twists in my gut, and bile rises in my throat.

Maybe Tee was right and this wasn't such a good idea?

"The Alice is like the sun that blasts away the

shadows," the Turtle says, twisting his hand in a small half-circle. He summons darkness to his fingers, just like that. "But there's always an eclipse to look forward to, isn't there?"

"Eat shit," I say, whipping another match from the pouch on my belt, striking it, and lighting the pistol's fuse. The Turtle begins to laugh, head tilted back, his Adam's apple bobbing with the chortle. The Queenmaker launches my little cannonball into the air, and sends it right through the Turtle's apparition. It falls over the edge of the cliff, and explodes in a sea of fire that reaches the sky. "If you didn't come here to talk, then what is it that you want?"

"To state our intentions," the Turtle says. Just like I thought originally, he's clearly the leader of the two. "And let you know that there's only one future queen of Underland." His mouth stretches wide, flashing swathes of empty pink gums.

"There's a future queen of *Wonderland*," the King of Hearts says, but almost like he's bored. Apparently, their intimidation tactics don't work for shit on diagnosed socio or psychopaths. Oddly enough, I'd almost like the guy if I hadn't seen him murder one of the poor card servants earlier. "Underland won't last long."

The Mocking Turtle—let's call him M.T.—stretches his mouth into a grin, and I watch as he bends down and picks something up in his hand. I can't see anything until his fingers are curled around the creature. Only then do I realize he's holding a lobster, an animal unfortunate enough to actually be in the same plane as that nutjob which, in turn, makes me really glad that I'm *not*. I will take a Recitation any day, thank you.

The lobster's clearly still alive, claws waving around as the Turtle lifts it up to his face, opens his mouth so wide it looks like his jaw is coming unhinged, and then bites the thing's head clean off.

It might 'just' be a lobster, but I get the idea that M.T. would enjoy it just as much—or more—if it were a kitten or a puppy … or a human baby.

"Tastes like the sweet flesh of an angel infant," he says, licking his fingers as the Gryphon crows with laughter. Both Tee and Dee move around me, tearing their knives from their belts. But this meeting is done; we all know it.

"Get the fuck out of my kingdom," the King says, his voice like a sonic boom, just as powerful as the blast of the Queenmaker. With a snap of his fingers, he dismisses the two Recitations like fog in the wind. Their see-through visages shimmer and fade, ripped back through those red doors on the floating island. They slam shut, forming the shape of a heart and leaving nothing but the scent of rot and blood in their wake.

When the King turns back to look at me, bloodred

hair dripping onto his forehead, I feel like I can see the hint of a cruel smile on his face.

"How do you feel about staying in Underland now, Alice?" he mocks, before waving his hand for Rab, the White Knight, and the soldiers to follow after him. The King of Hearts disappears inside the castle, and me, I disappear all the way up to my room.

"You have no idea how good it feels to lie down," I say, turning my head slightly to the right to look at Dee. His blue and black hair is rumpled, and his smile is sweet, but there's a shadow lingering across his face that mimics the darkness eating away at his brother's.

"We're only going to get a second alone," Tee says, pacing at the end of the bed, his boots shuffling against the shaggy white carpet. It's a very similar, err, rug to the one that Rab had in his house: white with purple spots—i.e., something's *skin*. Tee lifts his amethyst eyes to mine, sending a small shock through me. He's just so damn pretty, this fallen angel prince. "Whatever you do, don't mention the Looking-Glass. If we get a chance … no … *when* we get a chance, I'll take you through it. Allison, I'll take you home."

"Give me a few more days," Dee pleads, sitting up all of

a sudden and running his fingers through his hair. "Give me a chance to show you what you can *do* here, all the changes you can make. Allison-who-isn't-Alice, you can turn Underland into Wonderland again, undo a hundred plus years of pain and suffering. You can fix it *all*."

Dee wiggles closer to me, sliding one of his wings underneath my body and making me shiver. What he doesn't know is that I've already sort of, kind of decided to stay. The night Tee and I first made love, he looked at me like I was changing his mind about Underland, too. How can I throw that away? And how can I possibly leave this place in the hands of the Red King, the Mad Hatter, and that freaking Turtle-Dick? What kind of person would I be? It'd be worse than handing Underland over to Trump. An uncontrollable shudder overtakes me.

Tee and I exchange a glance, and I swear, it's like he's reading my mind. His mouth twitches up at one corner.

"Who's this queen those assholes were talking about?" I ask, running my hands down my face. It's been … what? … a week and a half since I got here? And yet it feels like months. Years, even. But not in a terribly bad way. I mean, the Gryphon and the Mocking Turtle weren't particularly pleasant, but all they've really done is incentivize me to fight back.

"The Alice is the one, true queen of Wonderland," Tee says, his voice pitching low. From the look on his face, I can see right away that this isn't a subject he particularly wants to talk about. And yet … why? He's been nothing but forthright the entire time I've been here. What's so bad about this chick? "But if you liked the status quo … no, if you wanted things to get *worse*, how would you fight against a queen?" Tee blinks his dark-lined eyes nice and slow. "Only a queen can battle a queen."

"It's like a game of chess," Dee says, opening his azure eyes to look at me. "The king wants to be protected by a queen because in all reality, he's worthless." I prop my head up on a hand, breathing in nice and deep, past the sweet smell of sun-dried linens and soap, and pulling in two deep lungfuls of the twins' shared scent. "So the other three kings, they'll want to go toe-to-toe with us."

"The other kings?" I ask as Dee sits up and takes his shirt off, getting it tangled in his wings and then simply *tearing* the fabric off like some romance novel MMA fighter. My heart starts beating like crazy because I just *know* that I'll have to free his wings for him again tonight. In fact, I've been fantasizing about what *else* that magic kiss might lead to since I saw the twins in the garden this morning. "I thought those two psychos worked for the Walrus and the Carpenter?"

"The Carpenter and the Walrus," Tee growls, reversing my order, "aka the King of Clubs and his brother." He's scowling so violently his face looks like it might split in half. "The Carpenter currently wears the crown. But don't worry: I'm sure they'll take over the Kingdom of Diamonds or the Kingdom of Spades next, and then they'll *both* wear jewels on their filthy heads."

"Did somebody say jewels?" a voice asks, just before a bag appears out of thin air, turning over and spilling a sea of diamonds onto the carpet. "Because I've brought more presents." The Cheshire Cat's kitty head appears upside down, grinning wildly at me. "I've made all of this, you know. With just my love for you."

"You're not in love with me," I say, crossing my arms over my breasts, and over the silky soft perfection of my new sleeping gown. I was going to go all modern and wear a tank and panties—because they do have that shit here—but hot damn. How could any girl resist a nightie like this? Edith drools over crap like this in the Frederick's of Hollywood window all the time. Wait, though. Does that make this lingerie? Am I wearing lingerie right now?!

"Am so," the cat says, spinning his head around. His body appears next, like an ink drawing being traced into the warm air of the room. Outside, storm clouds have rolled over the castle grounds, and there's that same electric charge in the air from the other night. Wild magic, free magic, tainting and eating away at the landscape. I can't help but think how all of that power used to reside in the bodies of this world's women. Now, it's just a plague, like acid rain rolling across the landscape and poisoning everything in its path.

Is it any wonder that this whole world's gone mad?

"You are not," I say, throwing my feet over the edge of the bed and tucking them into fuzzy slippers with hearts on the toes. The King certainly has a thing for branding; all of his soldiers have sleeves of heart tattoos. Yeah. Not *one* heart tattoo, whole sleeves of red and black and gray. Or so Dee says. Hard to tell with all of that armor they wear. "And put those diamonds back where they came from. The last thing I want is to have my head lopped off for harboring stolen goods."

"Oh, the King would never lop *your* head off. Perhaps a stand-in dressed in blue and white. But never you, oh beautiful Alice." Chesh shifts in mid-air into his human form, and lands barefooted and quiet as a pussycat on the carpet. The look Tee throws him is one of supreme annoyance, but not outright hatred the way he looks at the King. Good sign, right?

“He may very well take *your* head then,” I say, wondering if the cat is checking out my nipples again, and debating how hard I may or may not want to punch him in the nuts.

"Have you ever heard of taking a head when there's nothing but a head to take?" Chesh's body disappears for a moment before flickering back into place. "It just simply doesn't make sense."

"Do you just exist outside of this whole hierarchy then?" I ask, moving over to a small table near the door. There are tiny cakes and pies, a pot of hot water, and plenty of tea. There's a small part of me that considers drinking it, but then I remember where I am and what's at stake.

Somewhere in this castle, there's a Looking-Glass that leads to home. To Edith, to Dad, to … sort of Mom. And on the other side of these walls, there's a pair of mercenaries-for-hire and a mad king who wants to marry me. Either way, getting high on boosted tea is not a good idea. I pull open the door to a tiny cabinet that sits on the back of the table and find it full of FUCKING DRINK ME bottles and FUCKING EAT ME cakes. Hmm. I push it closed again and leave the small key in the lock where I found it.

"You mean why am I such an insolent little prick?" Chesh asks, coming up behind me and taking a bit of my hair in his hand. He sniffs it, and I reach back to slap him away. As soon as our skin brushes though … ugh, I'm done for. I can feel the chemistry between us brewing like a witch's cauldron. If I drank that shit, I'd probably turn into a frog. "The answer to that is simple, Alice."

"Is it now?" I ask, piling a plate high with sweets. I'll

go on a diet when I get back home. Or not. Turning around, I eye the tall, lanky frame of the cat with a discerning gaze. I'm desperately trying to find *something* wrong with him. Like, if he had a huge, bulbous red nose with tons of pores and pimples then maybe I could pretend I don't find him attractive. But he doesn't. No, of course he has a small, triangular nose above his full, wide mouth. His striped ears twitch in his ebon dark hair, and his silver piercings catch the dancing flames from the fireplace. He's got a piercing in the center of his nose—a *septum* piercing—as well as one on either side of his lips, and hoops lining both his cat *and* human ears. "So what is the answer to your stupid riddle?"

"I'm a cat, of course." Chesh shrugs his muscular shoulders and then scratches at the line of dark hair below his belly button with long inked fingers tipped in pointed black nails. He swishes his tail as he grins at me, and I roll my eyes. I figure he followed the Duke here: he seems pretty overprotective of North. So why then is he in *my* room?

The doors to my bedroom fly open and in struts North, still dressed to the nines in his stupidly tight leather pants. His white shirt is still unbuttoned and flashing bronze skin, and his golden hair is shiny and straight, highlighting the wicked darkness of his horns. He flicks his tail and smashes it into the wall, rolling up his shirtsleeves as he does.

And right behind him is the Mad Hatter, the March Hare,

and the Dormouse.

"This is a ridiculous violation of my rights," the Duke says, and he sounds *savage* all over again. My skin heats up, and his eyes whip over to mine, the corner of his mouth raising up in a small snarl. He thrashes his tail again, knocking a sugar dish to the floor and breaking it, then crosses his arms over his chest. "This bloodsucking demon is demanding a room in the Suit of Hearts—one of the *Suit*or's Rooms, to be specific."

"You're telling me," the Mad Hatter starts, tilting his lazy top hat in my direction, "that I'm asking too much? The Alice *is* my future bride, after all." His orange eyes flash as he smirks at me, taking in my nightgown with a very discerning edge. There's no doubt that *he* is checking out a whole lot more than just my nipples.

"You're a real piece of work, aren't you?" I ask as March helps himself to a heap of pink heart cookies from my table. He nibbles one and twitches a single brown ear in my direction, his dark eyes flicking to each of the twins and then over to the cat. I get the idea that the Mad Hatter is the brain of this operation, the Dormouse is the muscle, and the March Hare is the eyes, ears, and nose. He twitches his like he's scenting for something. "Like I didn't notice you disappeared the *second* the Gryphon and the Mocking Turtle showed up?"

"Calm down and have some wine, Alice," March

says, blinking big brown eyes at me.

I grit my teeth and curl my hands into fists.

"I don't see any wine," I choke out as March tilts his head to one side.

"There isn't any," he says as Raiden chuckles. The Mad Hatter pulls his cane out from beneath his hat, tapping it on the floor as he makes his way over to one of the leaded glass windows next to my bed. He stops to gaze out at the pouring rain like it has all the answers.

"Then it wasn't very civil of you to offer it," I snap, raking my fingers through my tangled hair. It's time for bed —like *way* past time—and here I am with an entire harem of men in my room.

"It wasn't very civil of you to accept the Hatter's hand in marriage if you weren't going to let him stay in your Suit. A Suitor does belong in a Suit, after all, you must agree," March drawls lazily, snapping a heart cookie in half. The Dormouse grunts from behind him, and I see this quick flash of annoyance on March's face as he turns to look at the much bigger man. Dor has a Neanderthal's thick head, and arms that are hairier than the Cheshire Cat's fluffy tail. Gross.

"This girl don't look like much to me," Dor grumbles, shaking his head and ruffling up his brown hair with thick fingers. "Don't see why we're even bothering. Let's kill her and the jabberwock and be done with it."

"You are most certainly not qualified to comment on muchness," March growls with a dramatic roll of his eyes, finishing his last cookie and taking up a cupcake next. "You're not much in the way of muchness, yourself." Dor narrows his eyes like this is the worst insult he's ever heard in his life while I'm standing there trying to puzzle out what their fucking conversation is even about.

"Certainly it's standard for a Suitor to live in the Suit," North interrupts, digging his dragon nails into his palm and making himself bleed. I start to move over to stop him when Chesh rubs his cheek against the Duke's shoulder and lets out a fierce purr. After a moment, the Duke of Northumbria stops and gives Chesh a scratch behind the ears, visibly less upset than he was a moment ago. "But Miss Liddell has only just arrived, and it's custom for the primary to assign each man his Suit."

"Tee is my primary," I blurt, and all the men turn to look in the twin's direction.

"The King is the primary, surely," North starts, but I'm already shaking my head and waving my arms.

"No, no, nope. No fucking way. You tell that asshole if he wants to play ball" —I pause because that reference is clearly lost on these guys— "metaphorical croquet with me, he'll listen to my demands. The first is that Tee and Dee stay with me at all times." My throat clogs up, and I have to force the next words past my lips. "And the Duke."

Oh, and the look he gives me … it's so savage.

"Well, then," March says, drawing a key out of the front pocket of his velvet trench, "you'll be wanting this then."

"The Queen's Key," Dee chokes out, and he looks like he's about to have a heart attack. "Where did you get that?!"

"I pinched it, of course. The King should take better care of his things, don't you think?" He flicks the key in my direction, and I just barely manage to snatch it out of the air, uncurling my fingers to find a gold key with a heart on both ends, one big and one small. When I look up, March gives me this slow, dangerous little smile before pointing over to one of the paintings on the wall.

I follow along and glance over at the framed art piece. It's an intricately rendered oil painting based on John Tenniel's—the original illustrator of the Alice books—illustrations. Or … is it the other way around? This particular painting is of the Mad Hatter, mouth open as he sings *Twinkle, Twinkle Little Bat* to Alice. The only difference between this piece of art and the original, is the small gold lock in the center of the Hatter's bow tie.

"Oh for fuck's sake," I whisper as I shuffle across the carpet, the men's eyes following my every move. As soon as I lift up the key and touch it to the painting, it slides into the lock and turns. The entire frame swings forward as I step back and find myself looking into a long stone hallway dotted with torches in the shape of top hats.

My eyes narrow as I turn to look at Raiden Walker, vampire-mercenary extraordinaire.

"Remember when I agreed not to leave the Duke naked in jabberwocky territory?" the Mad Hatter asks, twisting his hat around on his head. It keeps spinning long after it should've stopped. "This is all I asked for in currency. Well, this and a million coins." He flashes a vampire grin, strides up to me, and leans down to whisper in my ear. “Remember: not until you *beg*.” He stands up and just laughs when I punch him as hard as I can in the arm.

“You can sleep in there with the door *locked*,” I grind out, pausing to glance over my shoulder at the March Hare and the Dormouse. “But they have to go.” The look Dor throws me in that moment is pure hatred. If the Hatter let him off his leash, he’d probably tear me into little pieces and lap up the blood.

“Dor will go; March stays.” Raiden turns to go and then pauses, nose twitching as he glances back at the twins. He studies them for a long, agonizing moment, and then smiles. It’s not a very nice fucking smile, I must say. “I thought I smelled angels. Interesting.” With an exaggerated wink, he saunters down the red runner that covers the hallway’s stone floor.

"Boss!" the Dormouse calls out, but March is already chucking his cupcake wrapper in the big man's face.

"Stay, *pet*," he drawls with a sneer, pausing to turn and bow for me. *Technically*, he's being respectful, but I sense this nibble of mischief eating its way into his smile as he stands up, steals a few small pies from my table, and heads for the hallway.

Tee shoves the painting closed behind him, and I hear the very distinct click of a lock sliding into place.

"You know where the exit is," he snaps at the Dormouse, and it looks like the big man is seconds away from tearing Tee's wings off his back. As if on cue, the grandfather clock in the corner of my room chimes, and the twins' wings fold back into their body with the sound of clanging chains. The look of anguish on Tee's face makes Dor grin.

"Cursed fuck," he grumbles, putting his meaty hand on the doorknob and turning it.

"Woman-less prick," Dee calls out, and I see Dor's shoulders tightens as he rips the door open, storms out, and slams it closed behind him. Some of the tension clears from the air as I finger the gold key in my hand.

"Why would Raiden be interested in angels?" I ask, because it feels like I might be missing something here. That statement, it wasn't at all random.

"Angel blood sends vampires into Frenzies," Chesh says, pouring himself some cream in a chipped tea cup. He doesn't actually add any tea, just licks the cream out and purrs again. It's kind of hot, actually—probably because the hand holding the tea cup is covered in tattoos.

"Frenzies?" I ask as Tee scowls and takes his cap off, reaching out to drop it on a hook near the door. As he extends his arm, the gold hook stretches out and takes the hat from him. It's fucking creepy as hell. *Note to self: have that shit removed in the morning.*

"Doesn't matter," Tee says as he starts to unbutton his coat. "There are only two angels left in Underland, and he won't be drinking from either of them."

"Either of *us*," Dee says with a roll of his blue eyes. "Only crazy people talk about themselves in the third person."

"Contrariwise," Tee says as he shrugs out of his military jacket *and* his shirt. I try my best not to drool. "I'm the only sane person here besides Allison; I make the rules." Dee grins and slumps back into the pillows, watching me carefully as I pick up and nibble on a pink star cookie with little sprinkles in the shape, size, and color of pearls.

"So, are there nine suites … I mean *Suits* in here?"

"Sure are," Dee says, fluffing his pillow and snuggling into it. It doesn't look like he has any intention of moving off my bed. "*Nine big cocks.*"

"They didn't all have to be big, you know. The Alice

is bound to get exhausted. A few medium-sized ones would've been appreciated." Chesh and Dee both laugh, Tee's cheeks look a tad pink, and North's eyes sweep me in my nightgown appreciatively.

"Sorry I can't help with that last request," he growls out, and I grind my teeth.

"So … what happened between you two anyway? I mean, other than sex," Dee asks, and he doesn't sound at all upset by that. What a weird change from back home. In my world, these two guys would be beating the shit out of each other, squirting testosterone all over the damn room. Gross. I like this better.

"I had to tame the beast," I say with a loose shrug of my shoulders. "It was a stressful morning." Just *thinking* about that giant bat is giving me the heebie-jeebies. Not because of the bat though, just the height. Ugh. Next time, I'm riding North.

Heh.

Riding North. Get it?

"Thank fuck for that," Chesh says, sliding his tongue in a circle around his full mouth to clean off the cream. His tongue is longer than a normal person's. Can't decide if it creeps me out … or if I'm sort of curious to see what he could do with it. "It's been quite a long time since the Savage Duke has had anyone in his bed. I should know; I usually sleep at the end of it."

He flashes a fang when the Duke reaches out and absently scratches Chesh on the top of the head.

"Are you two lovers or something?" I ask, tilting my head to one side, white-blonde hair sliding over my shoulder. The rainbow streaks are still there. If anything, they seem even brighter than when I left. Not the weirdest thing I've seen since I got here, so who gives a shit?

"Lovers?!" North asks, completely and utterly aghast. He even puffs out his chest in indignation. At first I think he's about to go on an anti-gay rant, and I get my feathers all ruffled. "Are you quite serious? The Cheshire Cat is my *pet*."

"Meow," Chesh says with a grin, curling his hand into a little paw and then teasing me with it, like a cat batting at some yarn. "You hear that: his *pet*."

"Where are the rest of your people?" I ask, because he can't possibly be the only cat person in the entire world.

Wrong question to ask apparently.

Chesh shuts down and looks away at the same time Tee sighs. We exchange a look and the expression on his face tells me all I need to know.

Maybe Chesh *is* the last of his people?

"How did you two meet?" I ask as Chesh moves over to my bed and crawls onto the end of it, stretching the full length of his body out on the red comforter. His tail twitches lazily and his right ear swivels in my direction to listen.

"He showed up bloody and soaked to the bone on my doorstep," North says, looking at me with a very serious expression in his gold eyes. "How else does one acquire a *pussy*?" This last part just oozes out of his mouth, dripping with carnal decadence.

Getting a straight answer out of these people is damn near impossible.

There's another knock on the door, and I sigh, reaching out to open it. I'm fearing the worst, expecting the King of Hearts and his ostentatious entourage. Instead, it's Rab and Lar, waiting with torches in hand.

"I thought we'd never get out of there," Rab says, his white ears twitching on the top of his head. He blinks red-red eyes at me and then tilts his head to the side. "Well, aren't you going to invite us in?"

With another sigh, I step back and welcome the two men into the room.

We've got a full house in here now, but I don't really mind. I'll be going home eventually and … then I'll be all alone again. See? Doesn't it make more sense for me to stay here? I'm starting to truly believe it does.

Sucking in a sharp breath, I run my hand down my face. I'm no idiot. It's pretty clear all *these* idiots think they're sleeping in here tonight. Not sure why. Even if I *were* inclined to take nine lovers, it'd be nice if I got some say in the matter.

Lar unfurls his butterfly wings, that blue and gold shimmer reflecting the light from the fire. I wonder if he's got another prophecy? If he does, I'm not sure if I want to see it. If I'm going to get eaten by a giant bird tonight, I'd at least like to sleep first. But all he does is relax his wings until they're dragging on the floor.

"The King likes to work us until we can't stand up anymore," Rab says with a sigh, sitting down hard in an upholstered chair and letting his head fall back. "Prick." He crosses his legs at the ankle, his feet bare, like he's already dressed for bed. The long-sleeved black nightshirt and black and white striped sweats add to the ambiance of comfort. I doubt he was assassinating people for the King of Hearts dressed in that.

"These walls do talk," Lar says, playing with the gold bracelets on his arm. He lets his ice-blue eyes slide over to mine, catching my gaze. There's so much emotion packed in there, I can't even begin to unwrap it, so I look away. "Even in the Alice's room."

"No," Rab says, lifting his head for a moment. His voice is like the howl of the winter wind, chilling and intriguing all at once. "The King certainly isn't *that* stupid, bugging little Sonny over here? Does he know what a praying mantis does after it mates?"

"Are you insinuating that I'm going to fuck the King or that I'm going to eat his face off … or both? I'm not sure which of those things is more offensive." I take my plate of sweets and my tea over to the bed. It says it's chamomile. I've changed my mind about drinking it; I figure even if it's boosted, it oughta put me to sleep, right?

"All I'm saying is that you have the power to kill the King." Rab shrugs, and then smiles, the expression making it painfully obvious that he is, indeed, a psychopath. Only a true crazy person can smile like that, like a knife cutting its way across the face. I half-expect to see blood spill. "I'm glad to see you alive though. Quite the surprising treat."

"Why, thank you," I quip as Lar shrugs out of his jacket. Tee watches him for a moment before heading to one of the dressers and pulling out a pair of pajamas for both himself and his brother. Doesn't surprise me that their pj's are already in 'my' room. This is what the King's been expecting this whole time, for me to show up here. "I'm also quite glad to be alive."

Rolling my eyes, I settle into the pillows again and start to deconstruct one of the fancy little toadstool cupcakes. The top is covered in some sort of red modeling chocolate with little white spots. It really does look like a mushroom. Underneath the cap though, there's a creamy fudge filling that tastes a bit like hazelnuts.

"My prophecies tonight …" Lar starts, making up a cup

of tea. "They were quite disturbing." I notice his shoulder-length hair dancing in a magical breeze. It teases the strands and stirs the white fabric of his shirt, but it doesn't touch anything else. He's brimming with power; I can practically smell it. I'd hate to see what happens when the Caterpillar gets pissed.

"Flames and blood, the stench of death. It was like the post-Riving all over again." Rab accepts the cup from Lar's long, pale fingers, and takes a sip, closing his eyes with a small groan. "The Walrus and the Carpenter were unmistakably present."

"They want to put their own queen on the throne," I repeat, staring into my own tea cup. I remember Lar saying he could read tea leaves. I'd like to see that sometime. That is some straight-up *Harry Potter* shit right there. "And then do what?"

"Dismantle the four kingdoms, make them one again," Lar says as Tee disappears behind the bathroom curtain and starts to strip. I can't help but watch his shadow as he undresses. Crap. What am I going to do with these guys? I've got to take them home with me, right? I mean that's what Tee wants. Dee, I'm not so sure about. If I did leave, and I took his brother with me, would he come or would he stay? "Except, they don't want to restore order; they want to maintain ironclad control. They're both sociopaths, the Walrus and the Carpenter. Lewis Carroll used to be their soothsayer, you know?"

"How is that possible?" I ask, putting my tea cup down on the saucer so loudly that the clink makes me cringe. "That'd make them both over a hundred and fifty years old."

"Time is relative to some," Rab says, lifting up his shirt to show off the ticking clock in the center of his chest. "They're both—*relatively*—immortal."

"If they're immortal, then how am I supposed to kill them?" I ask, lifting an eyebrow.

"I said immortal, not invincible," Rab replies, his voice like an icy breeze on the back of my neck. It makes all the hairs on my arms stand on end … and heats up a warm pool in my lower belly. Told ya I was attracted to crazy people. I must be damaged, but I suppose that's okay—I'm pretty sure everyone else here is, too. "They can still be killed; that's your job, Sonny."

"Marry the King. Kill the bad guys. Save the world." I keep my gaze focused on my tea for a moment, and then chug the rest of it in a single sip. "Sounds easy enough." Just a few days ago, I would've taken this shit in stride because I wouldn't have planned on doing any of it. Hell no. I was ready to run home like a rabbit down its hole.

But not anymore.

Now I'm freaked the fuck out.

Because I'm pretty sure I'm *not* going home until I make some positive change here in Underland.

"Now get the fuck out of my room, so I can go to sleep." I poke the Cheshire Cat with my toe as North moves over to stand beside me. My heart starts to pump, and I can't help but lift my head to look up at him. He smells like sandalwood and musk, and it's making me feel a little dizzy.

"I have my own wing here," he says, bending down next to me and taking a knee. His gold hair feathers across his forehead, and I have the strangest urge to brush it away with my fingertips. Instead, I bite my lip and pretend my nipples aren't so hard they hurt. "But I'd be honored if you'd give me access to one of your Suits. After all, as your future husband, it only makes sense."

"Listen buddy," I start, but he's got such a sincere look in his gold eyes … plus, you know, that bloody beautiful accent. I just shrug and gesture at the other paintings on the wall. There are nine, now that I think to count them. "Be my guest."

"Wonderful," North declares, rising to his booted feet before leaning down and capturing my lips with his. My first response is to stiffen up and punch him in the nuts. Instead, I end up groaning and leaning into the kiss, enjoying the feel of his tongue sliding against mine. He tastes like a good chai latte, nice and spicy and sweet all at the same time. When he pulls away, I'm breathless and wanting, a boat adrift without an anchor. I almost reach for him, but end up curling both hands into fists. "The moral of the story is: if you need me, you have but to call." He steps back and gives me this hungry, half-lidded look that undoes me completely. "*Oh, 'tis love, 'tis love, that makes the world go round!*"

North sings this last bit as he rises to his feet and snaps his fingers. With a growl, the Cheshire Cat shifts back into furry form and lets the Duke pick him up, stroking his back with long, sure fingers.

"I will see you in the morning for practice," he says with a sharp nod. "It wouldn't do to have an Alice who can't fight."

North pulls a ring of keys from his pocket, removes one, and leaves the rest on the bench at the end of the bed. He approaches another painting, this one of a jabberwock, and uses the key to unlock the door that the giant black dragon's just busted through. With a salute, he passes inside and closes it behind him.

"You may as well help yourself to some keys," I say, gesturing at Lar and Rab. "Because I get the feeling you're not going to leave me alone until I give you each one." Setting my food aside, I crawl into the blankets to wait them out. Maybe if I pretend to be asleep, I'll be left alone? I'm just *so fucking tired* right now.

Besides, I figure after Rab and Lar leave, I'll kiss the twins to free their wings. And maybe … something else, too.

I'm asleep before Tee finishes tucking me in.

The night is as dark as velvet when I wake next, studded with stars that twinkle like fine diamonds. Both Tee and Dee are asleep on either side of me, but they look exhausted, so I do my best not to wake them up. I feel bad that I conked out before I could free their wings, but I suppose there's time for that later. Instead, I kick the covers back and slide carefully off the edge of the mattress. Tee stirs and blinks his eyes open for a moment, but when he sees me slip behind the bathroom curtain, he closes them again.

I make sure to pee before I try anything else; I have a feeling Tee and Dee are going to be more cautious with me from now on. Last time I snuck out, I was kidnapped by the Mad Hatter. Maybe not the best idea in the world to sneak out again, but I want to see a bit of the castle without an entourage. I could wake the twins and ask them to show me the place, but I need a minute alone to think. But only a minute. Alone and lonely are two entirely different things, but back home, I was alone so much that I *became* lonely. I really do prefer the company of these men—even if they're all mad.

Slipping on a furred crimson robe, I tiptoe to the door and let myself out into the hallway. The stones are cold beneath my feet, but the torches on the walls seem to give off an unnatural amount of heat and light.

This place is huge, at least four or five times the size of the Duke's place and that was a fucking palace to me. Padding softly across the stone floors of the upper level, I just start checking doors. Most of them are locked which frustrates the hell out of me. Of *course* they're locked. The few that open lead to empty bedrooms or sitting rooms. I feel like Belle, exploring the Beast's castle, looking for the forbidden wing. Now, if the furniture starts talking, I'll have really seen it all.

"If you're in search of the Looking-Glass," a voice says from the shadows, "then rest assured: it's well-guarded. The Walrus will never find his way into your world."

"It's not the Walrus I'm worried about," I say, curling my hands into fists as the King steps out of the shadows. He's dressed in a *suit* this time. Yes, a suit. A black suit with a black undershirt, well-pressed slacks, and shiny white loafers with hearts on the toes. His tie is even covered in hearts.

He moves forward to stand beside me, looking even older than he did outside on the croquet-ground, like he's in his late twenties, possibly early thirties. Or maybe it's just the suit?

"It's me. I need to be able to go home when I'm ready." I cross my arms over my chest. Even if I was just caught snooping, I'll remain obstinate. It's one of my better traits.

"Home? You are home, Alice. Your bloodline descends from Wonderland." The King pushes gloved fingers through his bloodred hair as I examine the scar on his neck. It reminds me of his guillotine, and the pile of headless bodies bleeding next to it. The Gryphon mentioned something about the former King of Hearts trying to kill his own son; is the King's scar related to that? My guess would be *yes*. No wonder the guy's a cranky asshole.

"Yeah, but *I* don't. I'm not from here. And I have a sister, a dad … and a mother back home that need me." There's not a single doubt in my mind that that's true. They all might treat me like I don't exist, like I'm not important, like I don't matter. But they all lost Fred, and I know that if they lost me, too, then his death would seem like it was for nothing at all. I can't do that to them, even if the more selfish parts of me would rather stay here in Underland forever. I'll stay *awhile*, and then I'll go home. That makes sense, right?

"There's an entire world that needs you here," the King says, his voice full of quiet, commanding strength. "Stop being so selfish." His lips turn down in a frown as his ebon eyes sweep over me. He exhales a long, tired sigh and shakes his head. "I've never put that much faith in the prophecy *or* the Alice, but really, you're still a disappointment."

My blood boils, and I step forward, into a shaft of silver moonlight. I can feel that strange tingling in my fingertips again, the power collecting in my hands. Guess beheading would be a real possibility if I accidentally, like, zapped the King, right?

"You're one to talk," I snap, feeling anger overtake me in a crimson wave. "You killed that poor card for no reason." When I close my eyes, I can still see its silently screaming face. And all that blood …

The King just smirks at me, a perfect twist of the lips that would have any girl swooning.

But I'm not just any girl—I'm a cynical asshole. We're a special breed.

"Good. Just continue to deny your destiny. It'll give me more fodder when I put you on trial and have you deported. Oh, you'll get to home for sure—but on my terms. Trust me Alice: getting rid of you is now my number one priority." The King turns to leave, but I stop him with a hand on his arm. I half-expect to have my ass handed to me by the palace guards, but there don't seem to be any around right now.

We're well and truly alone.

"Why did you bring me here if you're just planning on sending me home anyway?" I ask, hearing my voice crack with frustration. If I didn't know better … I'd say I hurt the prick's feelings? But no, that can't possibly be it. The King's hair glints in the moonlight, as red as fresh blood from an open wound.

"I will have you, Alice. You've always been destined to be mine." Why did he say that if he wanted to get rid of me all along anyway? It doesn't make any sense. No, I smell a bruised ego. I bet he thought I'd stumble into the castle, fall all over him, simper my undying love … Ew.

"There are still idiots who believe in the prophecy," he says, looking down at me. No, he towers over me, *lords* over me like he owns the fucking place. I mean, I guess technically he does, but I've always had a problem with authority, so screw him. "Like Tweedledee for example. And if I can't appease the simpletons, I could very well have a riot on my hands. But won't worry, Alice. All I needed was for you to fail, and you're doing an excellent job at that already."

The King starts moving as my fingers loosen on his arm, his footsteps loud as he heads down the dark hallway in the opposite direction from my room. I wait until he's out of sight and then lean my back against the stone wall, sinking to the floor with my robe and nightgown billowing around me.

I never asked for any of this.

So why the hell do I feel so goddamn bad about it all?

It's not my responsibility. What should I care if the King makes a fool of me before he sends me home? It's what I want anyway. I should be *happy* about it.

And yet … I'm not.

Not at all.

I feel like crying, like the original Alice from the storybook, shedding so many tears that I flood the entire castle. But I don't cry anymore, remember?

Brushing a small bit of liquid off my face, I stand up and shake the feelings off before I make a liar out of myself.

Instead of crying, or running away … I'll just have to prove the King of Hearts *wrong*.

4

Lost in a Quintrille

"Rise and shine, Allison-who-isn't-Alice," Dee says, stroking a finger down the length of my nose. "We've got a busy day today. Breakfast with the King, training with the Duke, and your dress fitting for the ball."

"A ball?" I ask with a groan, pushing Dee's hand away from my face. "How cliché is this place?"

"Clichés are simply repeated patterns," Dee says, grabbing the pillow I've just chucked over my face and prying it from my sleepy fingers. "They couldn't even be clichés unless we repeated them. A princess arrives at the castle, and we have a ball. It all fits the story, you see."

"All I want to see are the backs of my own eyelids," I

say, but my blankets are being thrown off and onto the floor. Dee is already dressed in his usual outfit: painted on black denim jeans, a button-up shirt, and his blue and black military coat. He's even got his peaked cap nestled onto his blue-streaked black hair.

"Breakfast is always served in the garden," he says, setting a stack of clothes on the bed next to me. I recognize Edith's dress right away and my heart catches in my chest. When I'm home, I hate her. Now that I'm here, I miss her terribly. "And lunch today will be served in the solarium. Training with the Duke will take place in the athletic facility between meals, and your fitting will be later this afternoon."

"Where's Tee?" I ask groggily, rubbing at my face as Dee brings over a cup of tea and carefully places it on the intricately carved nightstand next to the bed. The top is made out of a piece of red quartz in the shape of a heart. Back home, I'd have flipped my lid to own furniture even half this nice—or this cool. No boring oak shit here. No, everything I look at is a piece of art, something different. Sometimes it's kooky, sometimes it's ugly, but it's always interesting.

Can't say that about home.

"He's with the King; they all are," Dee says, nodding his head at the paintings on the wall. "But he shouldn't be long. We're yours now. We'll be spending all our time with you." Dee lifts his chin in the direction of my tea. "Drink up. It has a light energy boost in it, that's it. It won't fuck you up." He winks at me, claps his heavy steel-toed boots together, and offers up a salute. "Soldier's honor, miss."

"Can I wear something else?" I ask, rubbing the white apron of the dress between my fingers. This dress represents the conundrum inside my head and heart; I don't want to wear it right now.

"You can wear whatever you like," Dee says, opening the closet door and moving over to a row with dozens … maybe *hundreds* of outfits in glittering high-def.

Jesus.

Edith would shit her pants for this. Maybe she should've been the Alice? We were at the same party after all. In fact, she had to *beg* me to go. What if this is all some sort of mistake, and I'm stealing my little sister's destiny? I watch Dee walk back toward me, thinking that maybe he should've been hers.

That thought *infuriates* me.

I push the stack of clothes aside and stand up suddenly, throwing my arms around Dee's neck and pressing my lips to his. As soon as I do, I feel it, that power exchange between us. The air smells fresh and crisp, a mountain high that swirls around us. Dee's jacket explodes outward to make room for his wings, the fabric billowing in the rush of magic.

We have a bright citrus-y kiss, like spring and

lemonade. I smell flowers and an easy breeze, my tongue tangling with Dee's as he wraps his arms around me and lifts me off my feet. Only my toes are touching now, and just barely. The fingers of my right hand tangle in his hair, while I use my left to shove the chains from his wings.

They hit the floor in a clanging heap, echoing around the circular bedroom.

"The King will be furious," Dee whispers against my mouth after a moment. But I don't care. If the twins are supposed to belong to me, then I'll damn well do with them what I want. And what I want are their wings, free and clear. Not that I mind kissing them every day, but I want to find the witch that cursed them and get rid of this spell. Whoever she is, she's going to be sorry when I get my hands on her.

Dee wraps his wings around us like a cocoon, cutting us off from the outside world. I love that, feeling safe inside his feathers. His breath stirs my hair as I look up into his sapphire eyes, sliding my hands over his shoulders to tickle his feathers.

You just met this dude, my brain continues, ever the persistent optimist. And yet, I can't bring myself to care. I *like* being around Dee, more than I ever liked being around Brandon or … Liam. Especially Liam. And the sex is better, too. If Liam weren't already dead, I'd go back home with the Vorpal Blade and the Queenmaker, and I'd kill him myself.

"You let me worry about the King," I say, stepping back

and enjoying the soft brush of Dee's feathers against my bare arms and shoulders. After last night, I'm more determined than ever to piss the asshole monarch off. After all, who was the focus of the prophecy? Not him. *I* am the one who's supposed to save Underland, so who the fuck does he think he is? You know, besides the ruler of an entire country.

It's virtually impossible for me to leave an asshole that smug, that arrogant alone. Nah, it's my job in life to bring him down a notch or two.

"By the way," I start, making my way over to the row of clothes and putting my hands on my hips. "What's the King's name?"

"It's Brennin," Dee says, pausing next to me and reaching out to finger an outfit that's eerily similar to his own that's hanging on the rack next to the one with all the dresses. "Brennin Red."

"Red, huh?" I ask, grabbing the outfit Dee's touching off the rack and taking it from the hanger. The jacket and button-up are basically identical to his, save the color which, of course, is *red*. There are no jeans though, just a pleated red skirt. I like it though. Boots and pleated skirts are sort of my thing. Drives Edith nuts. "You people like to keep things themed, huh?" I move over to one of the stands in the center of the room, the top encased in glass with a black velvet cushion beneath, laden with jewels.

There are drawers down the side of it where undergarments are kept. Shocker: all the panties are white with red hearts on them. Bras, too.

I drop my nightgown to the ground and glance over my shoulder to find Dee watching me, his eyes half-lidded and burning. When he flicks his gaze up from my ass to my face, a slow smile takes over his mouth.

"The King likes to keep things branded," he says, his voice husky as I turn away with a chuckle and get dressed, slipping into the skirt which hits at mid-thigh, my new bra, and the button-up shirt. I leave the panties for last and then decide to tuck them into the front pocket of Dee's jacket instead. The look he gives me is freaking priceless. He cups his palm over the pocket and smiles lasciviously. "He's a very controlling individual, as if you couldn't tell."

"Well then." I shrug into the red and black military coat, sweep my hair out from under the collar, and step into a pair of boots before turning around to throw a feisty smirk Dee's way. "Let's go get breakfast with Brennin *Red* then. If that piece of shit thinks I'm going to call him *Your Majesty,* then he's got another thing coming."

♦ ♠ ♣ ♥ ♣ ♠ ♦

As soon as we step into the back garden, I start to hear voices.

Panic surges through me and for the briefest of moments, I wonder if I really am crazy, if I've dreamt this whole thing up. They say schizophrenia sets in during puberty, right? I mean, I'm way past puberty—I started my period at age twelve—but there's still a chance, isn't there?

"I can see right up your skirt, and you're not wearing any skivvies," a matronly voice says from near my right ankle. With a squeak, I jump and slap my hands over my ass, glancing back to glare at Dee. I'm expecting a servant—maybe a human one this time—but instead, I don't see anything but the handsome man with the azure eyes looking at me curiously. "And if you're not going to wear skivvies, could you at least have manicured down there?" the voice continues from somewhere in the cluster of daffodils.

On closer inspection … I realize that the voice isn't coming from inside the cluster. No, the daffodils are fucking talking.

I did not see any of this shit when I was mini and creeping through the small garden door. Think I would've noticed if the local flora had nasty, judgmental attitudes.

"What the fuck …?" I start as the flower scoffs at me. "You can talk?!"

"We *can* talk—provided there's anyone worth talking to," replies a tiger-lily from the next garden bed. They're laid out in color coordinated rows, creating a beautiful waving rainbow effect from where we stand, all the way out to the exterior walls where the roses drip with blood. I can smell it from here, the metallic copper bite mixed with the sweet cloying smell of rot.

"Soon as I saw you," the daffodil continues, tugging at the lace of my boot with one of her leaves, "I said to the others, 'Her face has got *some* sense in it, though it's not a clever one!'"

The flowers chortle in unison, waving in the breeze.

"If you don't hold your tongues, I'll pick you," Dee says, putting his boot dreadfully close to the face of the bitchy daffodil. When I bend down and squint, I can just make out her tiny eyes. She's most definitely glaring at me. And then, as we stand there, she lifts her leaves up and makes a gesture that I'm pretty sure is meant to convey a staunch *fuck off* message.

"Talking flowers," I say to Dee as I stand up. "I never thought of that before."

"It's *my* opinion that you never think *at all*," the red rose says.

"I never saw anybody that looked stupider," a violet chimes in, just before Dee bends down and plucks several of the flowers up by their stems. My mouth hangs open in shock as he lifts up the bouquet—now containing a daffodil, tiger-lily, rose, and violet—and hands it over to me. Blood drips from the stems, and I feel bile rise in my throat.

"What have you done?" I choke out as I feel leaves pummeling my calves.

"He's just plucked my prettiest blossom," the matronly voice says, coming from a different daffodil. "What a foul, lazy, useless beast. It's no wonder that his people went extinct!"

Dee plucks another daffodil and adds it to the bunch.

"The flowers are inhabited by pixie spirits," Dee says, pushing the bouquet closer to me. The blood has mostly stopped dripping, though there are spatters of it all across the white gravel. "If you pick one flower, they just move onto another."

"Eat shit," one of the roses says, ruffling up its petals. I carefully extract the bouquet from Dee's hand, feeling our fingers brush together in the process. Heat suffuses my cheeks, and I try to pretend that I don't see the majority of the men sitting at a table under a gazebo, watching us.

Dee lifts his wings for a moment, shading my face from the sun before he leans in and puts his lips close to my ear.

"I'm afraid," he says, but I just turn my face and kiss him again, lifting up my right hand to push his wing out of the way so that everyone can see. *Fuck you, Brennin Red. You might be* a *king, but you're not* my *king*. I'm an

American, goddamn it. We don't respond well to authority.

"Don't be; I've got you."

I turn and follow the winding path through the garden over to the table where the King sits front and center, his arms crossed over his chest, his ebon eyes sliding over my shoulder to glare at Dee.

But … he doesn't say anything.

Lucky him.

When Brennin looks back at me, I can see the smallest hint of a smile on his face. It's not a pleasant expression though, not even close.

"Good morning, *Alice*," he says, putting such a strong emphasis on my name that I know it's on purpose. He gestures for me to take a seat opposite him, opposite all the men really. On the opposite side of this table, there are nine seats.

And just me on this side.

Dee makes his way around me and sits on the far end, opposite his brother. I can feel Tee watching him, watching me, taking in the situation. His wings are next, preferably if I can kiss him in front of both the King and the Hatter.

Just taking in the row of male specimens, I can sense it: two supreme alpha assholes.

"Well, well, aren't we looking lovely this morning?" Raiden Walker oozes, his purple velvet top hat sliding forward on his head, the brim casting the most perfect of shadows across his marmalade colored eyes.

"Eat shit, asshole," I say, turning to the King. "This man tried to kill your Duke, tried to sell me to the King of Clubs, and blackmailed his way into the castle. And you're going to sit here and have breakfast with this piece of crap?"

The Mad Hatter throws his head back and laughs at me, flashing fang.

"You're one very brave woman," Raiden says as the King's mouth lifts up at the edge again. He's wearing the same suit from last night. Would not have surprised me if he wore it all night and never slept. Do villains really need to sleep? Or do they just run off evil batteries? He probably charges them by kicking puppies and burning books.

"Not really," I say with a sneer, sitting down and popping my bloody bouquet into a glass of ice water. "I just don't like you." I tap my nails on the table and let my gaze drift to North, sitting on the King's left. Chesh is next, then Lar, with Dee on the end. On the opposite side, the Hatter sits next to March, Rab, and Tee. Behind Raiden and March, there's a host of palace guards … and Dor.

I really, really, really don't like Dor.

The way he's looking at the back of North's head is scaring the skirt off me. The dragon … err, jabberwock

… seems to know he's being hunted though. His tail is thrashing violently against the white and red stone patio, and he keeps looking over his shoulder. I wonder how Dor caught him off guard in the first place? He's not a man easily taken advantage of.

"You don't like me?" the Hatter asks, taking off his purple hat and revealing a marmalade colored one underneath that matches his eyes. Instead of *In the Style of 10/6* on the tag, this one reads *In The Spirit of 10.* It's probably a reference to the nine men in the prophecy, plus me. See, I'm not stupid. What I am is frustrated. "But we had such a lovely trip together?"

"You are not part of my nine," I say with a snarl. Maybe I'm getting too involved in this prophecy shit, but I can't help it. "None of you are unless I say it." I pause and wet my lower lip. I've always been a fan of the underdog … "And Tee and Dee most certainly are."

One of Rab's white ears swivels in my direction and he smiles. It's almost pleasant. Almost. If his smile wasn't as icy as his voice, I might think he was enjoying the moment.

"And …" *I feel like I might regret this later.* "North." My voice catches in my throat, and I stuff a scone in my mouth to cut off the sound. Pretty sure I got lucky with my choice of food though. As I chew, I notice that the breakfast assortment this morning is, how should I say, *eclectic*. Some of the boys have colored drinks with crickets for garnishes.

I'm pretty sure Tee is drinking out of a large blue flower —a real one.

"Quite bloody right," North says, giving me a look across the table. His gold eyes meet mine just before he snakes his tail underneath and wraps my ankle. I even let it go this time.

"I thought just last night you told me you wanted to go home?" the King asks loudly, loudly enough that I'm sure all the guards and a couple dozen bitchy flowers probably heard him. There are human servants tending to our table. Maybe even old Red finds the silent, screaming cards creepy?

"If I'm the Alice, I can claim nine men, and I'm claiming those three." I pick through the crumbs of my scone, checking for insects. Fortunately, there aren't any. There *is* a candied honey bee on the cupcake I grab next though. I carefully pluck it off and set it aside. "Does it matter what I said or didn't say last night? Because if I did say it, I certainly didn't mean it. And if I didn't say it, then I'm most certainly not at fault, am I?"

Look asswads, I can riddle, too!

"Cute," drawls Brennin, but I'm pretty sure I just pissed him off. "But to answer your previous question: these men are here because you brought them. There are no package deals here. Only the Alice knows who the true nine are." The King taps his fingers on the table while somewhere off in the distance, there's that horrible whistling sound of the guillotine. When I glance over, I see a body with two big angel wings, twitching while blood spills across the pavement.

Cold chills break over my body, and I find it suddenly hard to swallow. It's obvious even from here that the wings are fake, but the gesture has its intended effect. Both Tee and Dee pale, and I can feel my heart thundering wildly.

Brennin Red just smiles.

"Listen *Brennin,*" I say, putting a huge amount of emphasis on the prick's name. "If you don't stop executing people left and right, we're going to have problems."

"Are we now?" the King asks. He puts his head on one white-gloved hand and leans his elbow on the table like he's bored. "And what, exactly, are you going to do about it?" I squeeze my hands into fists on my thighs as anger roils hot and wild inside of me. What am I going to do about it? Against the King and his million guards? All I have is a knife, a gun, and a few loyal allies. But would the Duke really stand up against the King for me? I wouldn't want to test that theory.

Brennin waves his hand in the direction of the guillotine. I glance over my shoulder just in time to see a girl in a blue and white dress being dragged toward the bloody red edge of the blade.

"What the fuck?!" I snarl as I stand up, knocking my

chair over in the process. "Don't you dare." Now I'm shaking, my fingers curling into fists on the white tablecloth. "Don't." This last word is whispered, my eyes locked onto the King's ebony ones.

The way he smirks at me … I know I'm in for some trouble.

He gives a slight nod of his head, and the girl is brought forward, shoved to her knees, her neck put on the wooden part of the guillotine.

"I said *don't,*" I repeat, feeling that strange energy spiral up and through me. Magic. *My* magic. And I'm not afraid to use it—even on a King. Lar's blue eyes widen, his earrings and hair dancing in the breeze, while the March Hare raises one arched brow at me. They're the only ones who seem to notice that's something going really wrong inside of me.

"Or what?" Brennin taunts, standing up from the table. He stares me down for a long moment before tilting his head just slightly. The guards pull the rope and the menacing blade of the guillotine rushes down toward the girl's neck.

Something wild floods through me, like electricity coming from inside my heart, trying its best to find a way out. Without thinking, I fling my arm up in the direction of the execution, and energy shoots through me, tearing across my chest and making me scream. It feels like I'm being ripped to pieces from the inside.

"Allison, don't!" Tee screams, shoving up from his seat and leaping the table in a single vault. He's at my side, grabbing me before I can hit the ground. My body spasms like I'm having a seizure, but even with all of that, I don't miss the fact that the guillotine explodes into a million pieces. Even the blade shatters, sending shards like knives throughout the garden. "Allison!" Tee shouts, putting his fingers into my mouth.

I don't realize how hard I'm biting my tongue until he gives me relief from it. Pain explodes like starbursts behind my eyes as I bite down on his fingers instead. He grits his teeth, but doesn't pull back, keeping my airway clear as the power finishes its wild ride through my body.

"It's okay, Allison-who-isn't-Alice," Dee whispers, kneeling on my other side. He spreads his wings and then dips one underneath me. Tee lets his brother pull me up and into an embrace, taking his fingers from my mouth only when he's certain I won't choke on my tongue … or bite it off.

I'm panting now, eyes rolling back into my head.

"Well now," the King says, pausing beside Tee in his stupid suit. The Hatter stands next to him, his decorative cane held underneath two carefully folded hands, tapping gently against the stones beneath his feet. "That sure was stupid, wasn't it?"

North slides between us, tail smashing the stones beneath his feet.

"You know I'll do whatever it takes to protect my mate," he snarls, and the King nods.

"At least now I know she's not entirely useless," Brennin says, looking down at me like a tool he's just found a use for. "So the magic *does* still sleep inside of you?" The King smiles and leans down, getting in my face. “By the way, I prefer to be called *Red*, rather than Brennin. Maybe I’ll call you Allison instead of Alice if you return the favor?” The King stands up with that awful smirk still on his face, and then saunters off in the direction of the castle. I can hear the flowers chuckling at me from their beds. *Butt waffles.*

"Are you alright?" Dee whispers as I shake and shiver in his arms. I can't even describe what I'm experiencing; it's too intense. My thoughts feel like electric sparks pinging around inside my skull. I don't even feel human right now. All I can think about is the Riving. If my weak-ass magic just fucked me up that bad, then what was it like to be torn apart by it? To be changed into a man and stripped of all that power?

Because even though I feel like it just killed me, I want it back.

No, not just back.

I want more of it.

As much as I can fucking get.

The Duke sits on the end of my bed, the long black lengths of his talons digging into his pants. I can see tiny of beads of blood welling up through the pierced leather breeches. That's nice, and very prophetic—the first thing I see when waking up from my short nap is blood. I reach out and grab the pocket watch that's sitting on my nightstand—pretty sure it belongs to Rab—and check the time.

"No training today?" I manage to choke out. Three hours and a nap later, and I've just now gotten my voice back. Sort of. I sound like a frog with strep throat.

"Are you taking the piss with me?" North asks, looking over his shoulder and blinking big gold eyes. He *did* stand up for me out there, didn't he? The thought warms my heart, and I lick my lips as I struggle to sit up. "I've already cancelled lunch and dinner; our meals will be sent up to the room."

The Cheshire Cat stands up—in cat form—and stretches his front paws out in a little bow, kneading at my sheets and snagging the fine fabric. He doesn't seem to give two shits, and neither do I. I hope he fucks up all the King's nicest linens *and* pisses on his pillows. Because that's what cats do when they're mad: they pee all over your favorite stuff.

"The King was going to execute that girl," I cough, picking up the strange pink drink on my nightstand. My hands shake, and I end up sloshing half of it onto the bed. But when Dee approaches to help, I wave him away. I've got this. Even if the drink is glittery and has gold sparkles around the rim of the glass, I'm too thirsty to care. "Because she looks like me."

"Miss Liddell," North starts, and then pauses. He turns more fully to face me, tail swishing gently as Chesh bumps his furry head against my elbow. "That girl is dead anyway."

"No," I say, starting to shake my head, but that doesn't change reality, does it? I screamed and cried and wished and prayed away my brother's death, my mother's incarceration. It didn't change anything. No, I lost my family to toxic masculinity and nothing can bring them back, no matter how hard I protest.

"The King only kills convicted criminals," Tee says softly, but with a voice laden with anger. I don't think he's trying to defend Brennin; he's trying to protect me. "He just wanted to hurt you, make you think it was your … *our* fault. But it's not. He just dresses them up like that to screw with our heads. Those people are all murderers —or worse."

"Underland is not a pretty place," Dee adds, crawling onto the opposite side of the bed and making his way over to me. There's more than enough room for his wings, at least, on a bed this big. "I promise you, if they were innocent, we wouldn't let the King execute them like that."

"It's still fucked up," I say, scrubbing at my face with one hand while I hold my drink with the other. It tastes like strawberries and sunshine. Honestly, it tastes a little bit like Dee himself, like I'm kissing him every time I take a sip. I take three more. "Psychological torture. And how do you *know* they're guilty?"

"A simple curseworker incantation can turn a person's hands red if they're guilty of murder," Tee says, reminding me of the King's gloves. He's *always* wearing gloves. Why is that, I wonder?

"Discussions of capital punishment aside," I begin, sipping the sweet glittery drink. Despite the dead butterfly garnishment on the side of my glass, it's actually pretty miraculous. With every sip, I feel the fiery pain in my throat easing a little. "What the hell happened out there?"

"You called on the magic," North says, lifting his head up, like he's scenting the air. He pauses after a moment and looks back at me. "The Alice is special because she isn't limited to the power inside of her; she can draw on the world's energy like it's on tap. *That*, my dear mate, is why the world either wants you … or wants you dead. There's no one you can't defeat, if you learn how to use that skill."

"Except for the anti-Alice," Chesh says, shifting back

into place with his head on my lap. Dirty, sneaky little trick. I shove him off, but I can't resist pinching and rubbing one of those fuzzy little ears first. He bats at me with his fist curled up like a paw.

"What's the anti-Alice?" I ask, feeling this ominous shadow creep over me. The ice cubes clink in my glass, and I realize my hand is shaking. Whatever I did out there, it really and truly messed me up. I'm not sure if I've ever felt this weak *and* this powerful, all at the same time.

"The Walrus and the Carpenter, their queen," Tee says on the end of an exhale, his amethyst eyes glittering with anger. "She can quite literally suck the magic out of anything and everything. She can't use it, but she can absorb it. It's why training with the Vorpal Blade, and with the Queenmaker, with North … why it's so important. If you're going to destroy her, you're not going to be able to use magic."

"Not that I can use magic now," I say on the end of an exhale, but my lids are already feeling heavy and I'm too tired to argue. Everything on me hurts, *everything.* I feel like I'm having period cramps in every part of my body, that's how bad it is. And ladies, you *know* that's real pain.

"We'll get there," North says, watching me as my eyelids slip closed. Dee reaches out at the last second and grabs my drink, sliding his fingers gently against mine just before I pass out. It's nice, having them all there.

Even after the crap-tastic day I've had, I'm starting to *like* it here.

What the fuck is wrong with me?

"Can I get sick every day that I'm here?" I ask as Dee places a tray on my lap the next morning. His wings are gone, and poor Tee never got to have his out yesterday. But that couldn't be helped: I slept through the afternoon, the night, and into the early rays of dawn. Once, when I opened my eyes, I could've sworn I saw Lar drawing some sort of magical symbol in the air in front of my face. Then again, there's also a good chance I hallucinated that, too. "Then I won't have to see the Hatter or the King. Frankly, I'd take about a hundred of those magical shocks to stay *out* of their company."

"I also brought you breakfast, if you prefer a raw food diet," Chesh interrupts as he drops an armload of rodents on my floor, most of them in various states of decapitation. Off with their heads, right? He grins at me, and then crawls up to sit on the top shelf of the carpeted cat tree in the corner. Pretty sure it was intended for him in cat form, but he doesn't seem to care, leaning his elbows on his leather covered thighs and peering at me curious gray eyes.

"Uh, thanks," I say, lifting the silver lid on my tray and finding porridge with edible flowers. I wonder if some of them were talking a few minutes prior to my meal? Oh well. They all seem like assholes anyway. It brings me some sadistic pleasure to crush their pretty petals between my teeth. "But as much as I enjoy cat-spit covered, dead rodents, I'll stick with the porridge."

"We'll need to continue with your training today," North says, standing with his arms crossed at the end of the bed. He seems awfully eager to get back into it. Maybe he just wants to rub his sweaty, muscular body all over me again? Perv. Or am the perv for looking forward to it? "You'll also need to learn about the quintrille."

"What the fuck is a *quintrille*?" I ask as I dig around in my food. The flowers have a bright, sharp sweet taste that melds perfectly with the strawberries and blueberries mixed into the porridge. Truth: I'm just making sure there aren't any insects hidden in there.

"It's like a quadrille, only different," Dee supplies, smiling brightly in my direction. I cock a brow at him.

"Thank you, oh so helpful seer. And a quadrille is … what, exactly?"

"It's a card game," he quips, teasing my arm with the tip of his wing. I like it too much to stop him.

"Or a dance," Tee adds.

"But never both at the same time." Dee crosses his

arms behind his head as he watches me eat. If I knew having this many boyfriends would essentially give me free slave labor, I'd have started my little harem up months ago. I wonder if they write scholarship essays, too? Because my parents used up Fred's college fund on his funeral, and mine and Edith's on a lawyer for Mom. If I want to go to college —maybe I don't anyway—then I'll need some serious help paying for it.

Then again, maybe I'd just rather stay in Underland for the rest of my life?

"And which version will I be learning?" I ask as I wonder where the White Rabbit and the Caterpillar are. Brennin Red the Royal Prick seems to 'need' their services on a regular basis. Not that I need or want them around anyway, but … what if I did, huh?

"The dance," Chesh purrs from his perch. "But certainly the Savage Duke won't be teaching you. He's a Hearts-awful dancer, aren't you, North?" The Duke ignores his cat, narrowing his gold eyes, his horns ridiculously tantalizing to my achy fingers, like they're just begging to be touched. If I ran my fingertips up the hard, curved lengths and touched the tips, would I bleed?

"Lar will teach her," Tee interjects with a small sigh, raking his fingers through his purple-streaked black hair.

"Why not you?" North asks, tilting his head quizzically. "You and Lar, you're the only ones who dance the quintrille with any skill or grace." He pauses for dramatic effect. "Well, besides, Red."

Red, huh?

'By the way, I prefer to be called Red, *rather than Brennin.'* Puh-lease.

"I've got errands to run today," Tee says, and I catch his gaze for just long enough to know he's talking about the Looking-Glass. He wants to find it for me, even as he's starting to believe I might be able to make a difference here. I don't stop him though, even if I'm beginning to believe the same thing. Having a steady, reliable way to get back and forth between Topside and Underland is vital. "Lar's a good teacher though. He'll make sure you know it well enough to dance at the ball."

"The Ball of Broken Hearts and Stolen Tarts," Dee singsongs with a sigh, folding some laundry and moving into the closet to put it away. He doesn't seem to be bothered that he went from prince to pauper in a relatively short period of time.

"The Ball of Broken Hearts and Stolen Tarts?" I ask, because what the *fuck* is wrong with that name? It's a rhetorical question, so nobody bothers to answer me. "What's the point of this thing anyway?"

"To introduce the Alice to the Court of Hearts," Tee says, exchanging a glance with the Duke. "Although I don't know how good of an idea this is. We'll need to be on top of security at all times. Assassination attempts are likely."

"Oh, well, great," I say with more than just a little sarcasm. Sunlight streams in through the massive windows on either side of my bed, casting gold bars across the thick furs covering my legs. There's a knock at the door, and I watch as Tee moves over to answer it. "Now I've got assassins chasing after me?"

"You had assassins chasing after you already," Rab says, sweeping in the door as Tee opens it. "Remember? *I* so gallantly protected you." He swipes his gloved hands down the front of his red and black striped vest and pulls out a watch from his front pocket. The white ears on the top of his head twitch. "The King of Clubs—the Carpenter—he sent that Rabbit after you."

Rab pauses near the refreshments table. It's always fully stocked with goodies although I never see anyone tend to it. I'm pretty sure it's the terrifying little card people, but frankly, I don't want to know. Maybe it's just Dee?

The White Rabbit pours himself a glass of lemon-infused sparkling water, and then makes his way over to stand near the bed. Having him this close to me, I can feel the tension between us, as taught as a bowstring. Let it snap and an arrow's bound to fly. The question is: exactly whose heart will be pierced by the wicked tip? "I'll be on patrol during the party, so don't worry." The look he flashes me is built of both confidence and violence as he taps a single tattooed finger against the side of his glass, lifting it carefully to his full, smirking lips for a drink.

"In bandersnatch form?" I ask, fishing for information. Supposedly, all Rabbits have three alternate forms, but I have yet to see more than one of Rab's. Considering Rabbits have to *eat* the meat of all their other forms, I just hope he doesn't turn into a kitten or a puppy. Shudder. Although I do suspect he can turn into a mouse. M.T. and the Gryphon basically said as much.

"We'll see," Rab says, his voice low and slow and dangerous. No wonder he's the King's personal go-to guy; he's terrifying. He blinks those red eyes at me, and I have to resist the urge to squirm as he snaps his pocket watch closed and tucks it into his pocket. His sleeves are rolled up, so I can see his tattoos, tick-tick-ticking away. "It depends on how … interesting the night gets."

"Hopefully not too interesting," Tee says with a small sigh. He takes a small step back, and when I reach for his hand, he takes another one, putting himself out of my reach. I raise an eyebrow. "Wings might … make my chores take longer today," he says, giving me another look. Ah. Gotcha. It's a bit harder to sneak around with a thirty-foot wingspan, huh? I nod and let him go, waiting until the door closes before I set my food aside. All of a sudden, I've got butterflies.

What if Tee comes back in an hour and says he's found the Looking-Glass? What will I do then? Take the twins with me and leave the others behind? Leave Underland to the King of Hearts and the Mad Hatter and the Anti-Alice?

Shit.

Since when did I grow a conscience?

"So," I start, swinging my legs out of bed and feeling this prickly rush of sensation race through me. "Should we get started with training?"

"Only if you think you're up for it," North says as I rise to my feet and close my eyes against a sudden wave of dizziness. I slept so hard and so long that I didn't realize it was morning when I first woke up; I still thought it was the previous afternoon. Fail.

"I'm up for it," I say, opening my eyes and locking gazes with the jabberwock. "Let's go downstairs, so you can kick my ass."

Or cup it, pound it, or otherwise touch it some way ... That part I only add inside my mind.

Yep, I am the pervy one here. No doubt about that.

♦ ♠ ♣ ♥ ♣ ♠ ♦

The Vorpal Blade reflects the light from the chandelier above my head, the one made of black and red glass in the shape of little hearts. It's quite beautiful, if out of place for a gym. But this is no regular gym. The floors are a sleek, shiny black, the walls are striped, and the ceiling is mirrored.

It's disconcerting, to see my own sweaty face staring at me when I'm flat on my back on the mat.

I wonder what else I could be doing on my back on this mat?

"Focus," the Duke growls, circling around me with quick steps. "The Anti-Alice will have trained her entire life for this moment. You … may get months at most, more likely weeks." He pauses and ruffles up his golden hair. "Hopefully not bloody days."

"Days?" I ask, feeling my throat get tight. I can't imagine fighting a combat trained woman in my current state. Whatever happened with that magic, it's still affecting me. I don't *feel* right, and I imagine it's going to be several days before I'm back to normal. But this ball bullshit, it's at the end of the week.

That doesn't give me a lot of time to prepare.

"What happens if I stab her with this?" I ask, flashing the blade. The Duke gives me a savage smile and steps close, bringing that warm, masculine scent with him. He reaches out one bronzed finger and traces it down the length of the blade, drawing blood.

"The Vorpal Blade is part of a Looking-Glass, pure magic. If you manage to penetrate the Anti-Alice with it, she'll try to absorb the power in it."

"And …" I start as blood drips down the length of the blade, hot and warm against my skin. I still don't understand who this Anti-Alice is exactly, and why she's called the Anti-Alice, but I'm learning as I go. It's hard to get a straight answer out of these people on the best of days anyway. If I were to sit down and ask them to lay everything out for me, they'd probably just confuse me with stupid riddles.

"Well, just as you can only channel so much magic without feeling the effects, it's the same with her. She'll pull endless amounts of energy through that blade … and she'll die."

"I've never killed anyone before," I say as North wraps his fingers around my bloody wrist and pulls me close, so close that my breasts brush against his chest when I breathe. His stare is so intense, I swear I can feel it cracking my soul in half.

"You'll do just fine," he says as Chesh moves up to stand beside us, flicking his fluffy, black and white striped tail. He's supposed to be my sparring partner while North corrects my form. So far the only thing he's done since coming down here is nap. "There are two sides to every coin; you can't always flip for heads."

"That doesn't make any sense," I say, stepping back from North. If I let myself, I could get all wrapped up in the

Savage Duke. Hell, I'd *love* to be wrapped up in the Savage Duke, tangled up in blankets, his hot, sweaty skin pressing against mine … Yeah, opening my sexual floodgate was maybe not the best idea. Now it feels like *all* I can think about is sex. "Not a lot does in this world."

"Maybe it's your world that makes no sense?" Chesh purrs, sheathing and unsheathing his claws. "Have you ever thought of it that way?" He circles around me like, well, a cat circling a mouse. Only, this bitch is no mouse.

North adjusts my grip on the Vorpal Blade's black hilt and then turns me to face the Cheshire Cat. He's wearing a loose leather vest over his bare, tattooed form, along with tight leather pants, and no shoes. I'm properly dressed in the full 'twin' outfit: black denim, button-up shirt, and boots. I started off in the coat, but I'm already soaked in sweat. I shed that shit a while ago. And yeah, there was no way I was wearing a skirt to train in. Can you imagine? It would get beyond carnal in here.

I did, however, put on Lory's corset with all the little hidden knives tucked into it. Figured that could very well come in handy.

"Put *him* on his bloody back," North growls, shaking himself out and then reaching up to tap at the pointed tip of one of his horns. "I already know you're good on yours."

"Oh fuck off," I snarl as I widen my legs in a fighting

stance … and Chesh yawns, stretching his arms up over his head. Clearly, he's not concerned. "Are you gonna fight me? Or you gonna lick your crotch again?"

"I'd much rather have *you* lick my crotch," Chesh says as he flashes a grin at me, showing off just enough fang to be cute. His eyes are wrapped in liner, and he's wearing a fucking collar. It even has tags on it—with *my* name on them. Well, Alice's name anyway. And I guess I am the Alice. Mistake or not, I'm the one that's here.

"Make me," I say, but Chesh just yawns and scratches at his fuzzy little kitty ears. Bastard.

"I'd rather just wait. That's what cats do, you know, stalk their prey. Don't you ever just sit and converse with your pussy?"

"Dinah doesn't exactly talk much," I say, ignoring his innuendo, and then I lunge forward, swinging the Vorpal Blade like North taught me. I hold it tight and low, thrusting forward as I pivot on my feet. I may as well have tried to shoot a slingshot at a fly.

Chesh leaps nimbly out of the way and lands in a crouch, smirking at me.

I shove my hair off my face, sending rainbow strands fluttering as I feign left and then sprint right. Chesh just flops onto his side and rolls out of the way, tail flicking as he laughs at me.

"Come at me, Alice," he purrs, all four limbs sporting

claws. He looks like Dinah does when she meets a new cat or dog, lying on her back with all five of her weapons exposed—two front paws, two back, and a mouth full of teeth. Dogs might be surrendering when they show their belly, but cats … they're getting ready to whoop some ass.

"You son of a bitch," I growl as North circles around us, watching Chesh twist up like an acrobat and land on his feet. When I come at him again, he grabs my wrist and uses my own momentum to flip me over and onto my back.

All I can say for myself is that I manage to keep the knife.

Using my left foot, I kick out at Chesh's right knee, and watch as he jumps and sails right over it, landing with a foot on either side of my pelvis. I see that he's going for a pin, and pull both legs back, doing this awkward somersault thing that gives Chesh the perfect moment to go for my throat.

His fingers dig into the back of my neck, claws drawing blood. I cry out, but I don't stop, using my full bodyweight to pull back. This time, I stumble, but I don't fall. Warm rivulets of blood drip down the sides of my neck as I fling my head back just in time to see Chesh coming at me again. Instead of throwing a punch, he shifts into his cat form, slips between my legs, and comes up behind me.

"In Underland, there's always another trick or two up your opponent's sleeve," he growls as he wraps an arm around the front of my neck, pulls back, and lifts me clear off my feet. Without thinking, I stab the Vorpal Blade down and back.

I really don't expect to hit him.

Blood explodes hot and warm around my fingers as Chesh screams and releases me with a hiss, stumbling back and collapsing to his knees. This time, he really does take the blade with him.

"Fuck!" I curse spinning and falling into a crouch next to Chesh. He's pulling the Vorpal Blade out with a snarl and tossing it aside. The mirrored weapon spins across the floor, leaving a trail of red in its wake as Chesh puts his hands over his wound and curls up in serious pain.

"Let me see it," North snaps, trying to pry his … uh, cat's … hands off the wound. There's blood everywhere, so much fucking blood. I feel woozy for a moment as I remember my brother, Fred, lying in a pool of the stuff. Dead. Cold. Gone forever.

My throat closes up, and I feel the hot, uneasy waves of panic washing over me.

"I didn't think I'd hit him," I choke as North forces Chesh's hands away from his stomach and takes a look at the injury. "I didn't know I *could* hit him."

"Never apologize for improvement," North says, but he's frowning *hard,* sweating, too. "Get the Mad Hatter," he tells me, flicking his gold gaze up in my direction. I look from his sweaty bronzed face to the Cheshire Cat's pale one, and I realize how much trouble we're really in.

Without hesitating, I stand up and take off for the door that leads back into the main hall. I have no idea where to find Raiden Walker, but I'll figure it out. I'll choke a dozen card servants if I have to.

Instead, I run into March.

He's waiting just outside the athletic facility doors, checking the cylinder of a revolver. Might be gold-plated, but I don't hold that against it. Everything in this world is deceiving.

"Where's Raiden?" I ask, and one brown rabbit ear swivels to face me. Or is it a hare's ear? I have no idea.

"He's in conference with the King," he says, noticing the blood on my hands, and reaching out to touch his fingers to mine. I jerk back, but all that does is make the asshole smile. "Why? Have you finally decided you can't live without him?"

"Just get him for me!" I scream, and I swear to God, the entire palace shakes around me. "Get him *please,*" I correct, but the March Hare is already smirking at me. He closes the cylinder on his revolver, slides it into a holster under his jacket, and nods briskly. "I live to serve," he drawls, but I get the idea that I'm being mocked. Doesn't matter, as long as he's getting the damn vampire mercenary asshole for me.

Well, it doesn't matter *right now.*

Later, I may very well punch him in the nuts.

March moves down the hallway, leading me to a small, quiet study at the opposite end of the palace. I swear, it takes forever for us to get there. I want to run or scream, but I have the feeling that if I do, he'll take longer, just to see me sweat.

When we finally do get to the room, the guards let us in without question, and I burst inside, all dramatic and shit.

"Hatter, I need you," I say, hating the words even as they come out of my mouth. They feel like sand, scraping past my tongue. When he lifts his head to look up at me, there's already blood on his mouth. And there's red on the King's neck. That bastard Brennin Red just *smiles* at me, like he doesn't care that I've just caught him red … uh, necked? No, that sounds too much like hillbillies. Red-throated? Fuck, red-*handed* it is then.

"You do?" Raiden asks, his dark hair feathering around his face. He looks like a metalcore star, some guy who screams onstage in a five-piece band and makes millions for doing drugs and banging chicks. I hate him. "That didn't take long, did it?"

"The Cheshire Cat," I start, and I swear to fuck, the King

actually smiles, like he looks *happy*. His crown slides forward on his head, obscuring one of his stupidly beautiful eyes. "I need you to heal him the way you did the Duke."

"The Cheshire Cat is dying?" Brennin asks, so interested it's almost creepy. The one eye of his that I can see is literally sparkling with magic. It really does look like a galaxy, filled with endless possibility and stars. At the same time, the expression on his face is most certainly malevolent. "Excellent. Let the little bastard bleed out."

"If you let him die," I start, curling my hands into fists, "you'll wish you'd never brought me back to your palace."

"Is that so?" Red asks, standing up from his massive desk and tilting his head to look at me. "And you have the power to back that up, *Alice*? Because yesterday, it seemed to have laid you flat."

I can feel those knives burning a hole in my corset. If this asshole keeps pushing …

"Hatter," I start again, focusing my attention on the man sitting at the King's right. He pulls a white handkerchief with red hearts on it out of his pocket and dabs at the blood on his lips. "Please."

"There's a price for every occasion, Alice," he says, standing up from his chair. From the shelves, I hear strange whispers, like the books are talking. I don't have time to deal with that shit right now, so I file it away for later. "What are you willing to pay?"

I'm shaking so bad right now that it feels like I'm having another seizure.

"Save the Cheshire Cat and prove to me you're not a complete waste of breath," I snarl as Raiden rises from his seat, picks up his cane, and makes his way over to stand beside me. His orange eyes are locked on mine. I feel trapped, like I can't look away. I wonder for a moment if he's trying to like, fucking hypnotize me or some shit. "And if you ask me to answer another riddle, I'll stab you with your own cane."

Turning away, I start back toward the doors, the Mad Hatter following along at my heels. The March Hare is waiting just outside for us, but doesn't bother to move as we pass him by.

"Leave the cat to die," Red says, moving into the hall behind us. "That's an order."

Without thinking, I spin around and stalk back toward him. The guards bristle a bit, but the King holds them off with a wave of his gloved hand. Guess he isn't afraid of me. He should be though. Tenacity goes a long way for making up for lack of physical strength.

I open my mouth to start off on a rampage, but the Mad Hatter beats me to it.

"If you think you can order me around—even on a good day—you've got another thing coming," Raiden says, reaching out and taking me by the wrist. The King is lucky, really. I might've stabbed him.

I can practically *feel* Brennin radiating anger from behind me as Raiden pulls me down the hallway, our boots loud against the marble floors.

"You're lucky, little Alice," the Mad Hatter says as we move in the direction of the athletic center. I'm so stressed right now that I can barely think straight. The thought of the Cheshire Cat dying at my hands is making me sick to my stomach. "Because I don't take orders from any king."

We step into the gym and move over to Chesh, lying on his back in a pool of blood. His face is ashen, and even the sturdy Duke looks concerned.

"What price is this going to come at?" North snarls as Raiden kneels down beside him, unconcerned by the blood soaking into the knees of his pants. I wonder what he was doing in there with the King, but I don't have time to analyze that at the moment. Another issue for future-Alice to tackle.

"Only your dignity," Raiden says as he bites hard on his wrist and opens his veins. Chesh is awake and breathing heavily, eyes half-lidded. "I just hope you'll remember this next time *I* need a favor."

"You're insufferable," Chesh manages to choke out before the Hatter puts his wrist to the man's lips. The cat laps it up with a grimace while I look on fascinated. There's something about all of this that interests me. Maybe it's because I've been a bookworm my whole life and now, I'm finally the character in the story. Isn't that what every reader wants? To discover their own adventure?

"Insufferably vital," Raiden purrs as Chesh reaches up and digs his claws into the Hatter's arm—with his claws out. The exchange only lasts a moment, but when Raiden pulls his arm back, Chesh's face is already warming up, pink returning to his cheeks. He sits up and adjusts his vest, giving me a sly look.

"Nice shot, Alice." He winks at me as he rises to his feet. There's blood literally everywhere, but nobody seems to mind. In fact, I'm pretty sure I'm the only one freaking out. Before my nervous heart can catch up with my brain, I'm flinging my arms around the cat's neck and giving him a massive hug.

He hesitates for a moment, but then his arms go around me. You can tell a lot about a man by the way he hugs. Chesh is strong, and he squeezes me tight, but not too tight. His breath feathers my hair near my ear, but he doesn't press his luck or turn the moment into anything weird.

As I pull back, I reach up and give him a pat on the head and a scratch behind the ear. He doesn't look offended by it;

I even get a little purr out of him.

"I'm really sorry," I say as North picks up the blade, swings it around in a circle with a single flick of his hand, and then offers it up to me. I hate to say it, but I'm pretty sure that look on his face is *relief.* "I let you both down."

"Down?" the cat asks, swishing his tail. "You just stabbed me. And if you can stab me, you can stab the Anti-Alice. I must say, I'm quite proud."

"If anything, it was my fault as your teacher," North says, and he's flicking his tail, too. They look like tail twins, these two men. It's kinda funny, really. "But now that I know you've moved past the *fatal flop* stage and onto a new level, I'll be more vigilant." North glances briefly in the Hatter's direction, sneers, and then grinds out a forced, "*thank you.*"

"Don't thank me, thank the King," the Hatter says, dipping a finger in the blood and lifting it to his lips. He sucks the red off while staring right at me, and then grins. "If I didn't hate him quite so much, your pussy here might just be dead."

He stands up and leaves the three of us staring after him.

"Grab a mop," North says, gesturing with his horned head in the direction of a supply closet. "Clean this up, and let's get going again. There's certainly no rest for the wicked."

♦ ♠ ♣ ♥ ♣ ♠ ♦

My next lesson of the day is with Lar in the ballroom.

I *thought* I was prepared to see the grandeur of that room.

I was nowhere near it.

As soon as I step into the domed room, I'm reminded of *Beauty and the Beast,* of Belle dancing under that chandelier in a yellow dress.

"Shocked shitless?" Dee asks, holding the door open for me. The ballroom is in the shape of a heart—no surprise there—but the architecture is to die for, reminiscent of gothic revival but ten times as intricate. There are arches carved with roses and faces of happy, dancing couples, their clothing flowing in a non-existent breeze. Above us, the ceiling is made entirely of glass, revealing the setting sun and washing the red walls with rays of gold. Several chandeliers drip from the ceiling, heavy with black and red crystals, giving off flickering light that adds to the ambience.

In the center of it all, Lar's waiting in a pale blue shirt that matches his eyes, his sky blue/blonde hair falling just below the level of his chin. When he brushes some loose strands back from his forehead, his sapphire earrings dance, and his ice-blue gaze locks onto my own.

"I hear there was drama with the Cheshire Cat," he says, his voice like a calm breeze. It's a refreshing change from North's savagery, Chesh's cattiness (pun intended), and Tee's direct honesty. I find myself exhaling for the first time in hours, reaching up to rub at my sweaty forehead. I tried to find time between training and dancing for a shower or bath, but Dee grabbed my elbow straight after lunch and brought me here.

"Yeah, well, I accidentally stabbed him in the kidney and almost killed him." I shrug my shoulders loosely as the scent of blueberries and fresh-cut flowers fills my nostrils. Jesus. Every dude in Underland smells good enough to eat and looks it, too. No wonder I can't keep my hands to myself. "Okay, so I don't know if I actually stabbed his kidney, but it sounds more dramatic that way, right?"

Dee chuckles beside me as Lar raises a pale brow, tilting his head to one side as he studies me.

"Getting the Hatter under your thumb so quickly, I'm impressed," Lar breathes, his white and gold jacket draped loosely over his shoulders. He folds his stained-glass wings together behind his back.

"Gossip travels quickly around here, doesn't it?" I ask, unable to pull my attention from Lar's gaze. As glorious as the ballroom is, it doesn't compare to the beauty of his face. He has high, fine cheekbones, a gloriously full lower lip, and long lashes framing his pale eyes. There's something about the way he holds his mouth, lips just slightly parted, that intrigues me. It's like he's always on the edge of asking a question, like there's a question mark resting on the tip of his tongue. "Although I'd dare say the March Hare is the one you should watch out for. Sometimes, he's not just the Hatter's right hand—he *is* the Hatter."

"He's …" I start, and then realize what Lar's saying. My eyes fly wide, and the Caterpillar chuckles softly, pulling out a small glass pipe in the shape of a toadstool. He snaps his fingers and then lifts his pointer finger in the air, a small flame dancing on the tip. He uses that to light his pipe, the grassy scent of marijuana quickly taking over the room. It's not quite right though, like pot mixed with a bit of rosewater, some crushed lavender, and just a hint of chai tea spice. "He *ate* some of Raiden's flesh?!"

"What do you think?" Lar replies in a low, cool tone that helps soothe away some of my anxiety. He takes a long drag before passing the pipe my way, exhaling beautiful blue smoke from between his lips. I'm about to tell him no, because as much as I want to get high, I have a feeling that could also get me killed in this palace of hell. "Just a little bit goes on a long way," he tells me, the edge of his mouth twitching in a smile. "I can't properly teach you to dance if you don't take any."

"What is this?" I ask as I glance over at Dee, but he's shaking his head and putting his hands up.

"Just a bit of *whiting*," Dee says as I raise an eyebrow. "But I can't have any. I have to keep both feet firmly on the ground, so I can play the piano for you."

"On the ground?" I ask as I glance back at Lar, and finally take the pipe from his outstretched fingers. Our fingertips brush together, and a warmth fills me, traveling down my arm and into my chest, making my heart beat. I jerk my hand back and cradle the pipe in my palm. "Isn't a whiting a type of fish? You know, like salmon or trout."

"Just like a quadrille can be a card game or a dance, so can a whiting be a fish or a magical plant." Lar taps the side of the glass pipe with a fingernail. "Take a hit, Sunshine, and I'll show you what it means to join the dance."

"Good luck," Dee says, leaning in to give me a kiss on the cheek. His mouth lingers, turning the relatively chaste moment into something so much more. His wing dips down and brushes along my bare arm, making me shiver, before he finally retreats, moving over to a massive red and white grand piano in the corner. Dee stretches his fingers *and* his wings out as he sits down to play.

"Good luck?" I ask Lar, turning back to him as I lift

the pipe to my mouth and inhale. I close my eyes as I do it, feeling the hot smoke curl its way into my lungs, the taste of lavender and chai clinging to my lips. As soon as I breathe out, I feel it hit me, this lightheaded, airy sensation that makes me feel like I'm floating. "What's he talking about?"

The Caterpillar just smiles at me, takes the pipe, and sets it on a small glass table next to a gramophone. When he holds out his hand, I hesitate to take it.

"I haven't forgotten about Raiden and March," I say, and Lar's smile turns into a confident smirk, like I've taken the bait. Exhaling sharply, I put my hand in his and watch his pale fingers curl around my own. It's enough to make a girl swoon—if I were the swooning type, that is. I am most definitely *not*.

"I mentioned that little tidbit all of two minutes ago," Lar says as he leads me into the center of the room. "I wouldn't have expected you to have forgotten already." I roll my eyes because he knows what I mean. What a dick.

As I pause beneath the largest of the five chandeliers in the room, I wish suddenly that I'd worn a dress. Dee suggested it, but nooooo, I had to be a rebel. Damn it.

"Sunshine," Lar says, releasing my hand, and then taking a bow. When he stands up, he whips his jacket off his shoulders, revealing a short-sleeved sky blue tunic underneath. He then shakes it out and tosses it behind him, spreading his wings briefly like he's trying to hide the garment from me. I never see it hit the floor; when Lar folds his wings together again, the jacket is gone. Magic. It's everywhere in Underland. "Tell me: do you know how to waltz?"

"I don't know how to dance for shit," I reply, feeling my cheeks warm slightly. I've never been much of a dancer, not even a social dancer. But I *have* read about a million books with characters who attend balls and dance their asses off with noble princes. Does that count?

Dee starts to play some sad, slow sort of song, his fingers dancing across the ivory keys as a card servant I hadn't noticed before begins to pluck at a harp with its too-human fingers. I can't look at its face, no freaking way. If I do, I'll get too creeped out and leave before my lesson has even begun.

"Just follow along and don't worry about it for now," Lar says, placing one warm hand on my hip and curling the fingers of the other through my own. I find myself licking my lips and avoiding any sort of eye contact. We're standing far too close for that. Besides, he smells like tobacco and blueberries, a toxic sort of combination that makes my heart flutter. "You're thinking too hard," he tells me as we start to sway, and I end up stepping on his foot.

"Oops, sorry," I say as I cringe and struggle with where to place my left hand. Lar sweeps his right up my side, making me shiver, and takes hold of it, placing it on his right shoulder. He just smiles at me, earrings swaying with the motion of our bodies. He holds his wings just high enough that the curled tips brush the ground. "I'm sort of a dance-virgin."

Lar smirks at me, his eyes going half-lidded as the chandeliers flare to life, brightening up the room before the sky is completely dark outside.

"Don't apologize for being inexperienced, only for refusing to learn. Seems to me like you're trying plenty hard." He spins me around as Dee picks up the pace on the piano, giving us a bouncier tune than I'd expected. I have no idea what one dances a quadrille or a quintrille to, but I suppose I'll soon figure that shit out.

"There's certainly a lot to, uh, take in," I say as Lar picks up our speed. He's right though: when I'm not focusing on what I'm doing, I have no problem keeping up. As soon as I let myself get laser-focused on his feet, and my feet, and that yummy smell of his … that's when shit gets fucked up.

"Don't think too hard," Lar whispers, moving his hand from my hip to tap at my chin. I lift my face up to look at him as we make our way around the dance floor. "And don't think too little, either. Just enough to point yourself in the right direction. Once you've done that, you have to learn to trust yourself."

"So you're a seer *and* a wiseman?" I ask as the

Caterpillar starts to guide my feet with his own, pushing me back with his shoe, or to the side, or beckoning me forward by hooking my ankle. It's a little unorthodox, I have to admit, but I'm not really thinking about dancing anymore. I'm just looking at him. He has big, round eyes, but they seem to be in a near perpetual half-lidded state. His mouth is generous and full, lips pink, skin pale, and that hair … it's blonde, but when you look at it just right, it tints blue. I wonder if he really is a faerie?

"I'm a slave," he says with a loose shrug of his shoulders, spinning me around again. If I had a dress on, the fabric would swish around my calves right now. Damn it. I should've just worn the fucking dress. That easy, fantastical high I felt when I took a drag on the pipe amplifies with each movement we make, promising that I'm in for a serious trip. "I'm whatever the King wants me to be."

"You're a prisoner, too, huh? Who isn't?"

"The damn cat," Lar says in a soft voice. It's not weak, just … quiet. Like he expects the world to shush up and listen to *him*. Considering his talents, I don't think that's much of a request. "And the Duke. I think he actually *likes* Red."

"Anyone else?" I ask, thinking of Tee and Dee. They are most certainly prisoners. Slaves, actually.

"You know Rab hasn't much of a choice either.

Although I think he likes his place in the palace now. There are bets out there to decide if he was crazy before or only after the King made him a Rabbit."

"Psychopath? Or sociopath?" I ask as the music slows, stops, and then starts up again. Lar doesn't skip a beat, keeping us moving before I can trip on my own feet.

"Both?" he asks with a lift of one, pale brow. There's something soothing about his hand on my hip, this guiding presence that makes me feel like I'm being taken care of. But, like, not in a creepy way. "Rab is an easy man to get along with, but a terrible man to cross."

"He shot my schoolmate in the face," I say, looking past Lar and feeling my eyes blur with the memory. God, that feels like it happened ages ago. When was it really? A week and a half ago? For fuck's sake.

A week and a half back home without me … Dad and Edith are probably frantic. I just hope they haven't told Mom. Being trapped in jail with no way to look for me, that very well might kill her.

"King's orders," Lar says simply, shrugging his shoulders. After meeting the royal prick, I guess I can see why they're so eager to do what he says: he's not insane, he's just evil.

Our steps get more elaborate as we go, until I feel like I'm really and truly dancing for the first time in my life. My hair billows out behind me in a blonde and rainbow wave as we make another turn on the dance floor.

"This is easier than I thought," I say, just before I trip over Lar's foot and end up stumbling into him. He catches me and helps me upright, my face ridiculously close to his. His breath is sweet, fanning against my lips. I have to swallow hard to get past the sudden lump in my throat.

"Nothing is so hard you couldn't figure it out, mighty Alice," Lar says, folding his wings together and then opening them slowly, like he's putting on a show. I'm not sure that he even realizes he's doing it though.

"Well, most things anyway," I say as I right myself, brush my sweaty palms down the front of my red button-up shirt, and take a deep breath. Lar and I get into position again as Dee starts up a new song, this fast-paced piano solo that makes me want to move.

"I've never met a problem I couldn't solve," he says as I cock an eyebrow.

"The King of Hearts?" I hazard, but Lar just shakes his head, long blue-blonde strands of hair falling across his forehead. His earrings catch the light as he moves, too, and I can't help but admire them. He has a fine-boned look to his face, this aristocratic air that begs attention. Jewelry suits him.

"He's not a problem," he says with a long sigh, blinking pale lashes at me. "The King of Hearts is the *best* ruler Underland has right now. Compared to the King of Spades, and the King of Clubs, he's practically a saint. I'll serve him without resistance," Lar starts, leaning in and putting his lips against my ear, his breath tickling my skin, "until I find someone better."

I feel weightless, with the Caterpillar this close to my face. It's quite obvious to my body right now that a slight turn of my face would put my lips to his. We could kiss right now. My tingling lips tell me it's the right thing to do, that I should try. After all, when am I ever going to feel like this again, like I'm floating across the dance floor?

Lar chuckles, like he can sense what I'm feeling. When I do turn my head and kiss him, it's with laughter dancing on both our lips. My mouth presses softly against his, and he doesn't press the moment, letting me come to him. My fingers squeeze his right shoulder, curl around his left hand. His tightens on my hip, letting me know that he's enjoying the moment as much as I am.

Barely spoke ten sentences to the guy, and you're shoving your tongue down his throat, my brain quips, but I'm not listening to her. When am I ever going to get this chance again? I'm surrounded by attractive men that want me, that think I'm the literal answer to all their prayers. Am I supposed to keep fighting this? Am I supposed to hate it?

I don't.

Lar teases the tip of my tongue with his own before

pulling back and leaving me breathless. My chest aches as his wings open wide, a gold, black, and blue backdrop to … the sky? I blink a few times and look down.

I shouldn't have looked down.

With a squeak, I realize we're floating far above the dance floor, our heads just a foot or so from the domed glass ceiling of the ballroom.

"Lar," I choke out, but he doesn't seem concerned, twirling me around as easily up here as he did on the marble floor below. My feet continue to follow his, mimicking the steps of the dance as best I can. I'm afraid to stop. What if I fall? "I have a thing about heights."

"Will you, won't you join the dance?" the Caterpillar whispers, tugging on one of his earrings. The blue jewel lights up, and then dozens of wall sconces burst into brilliant flame, casting beautiful shadows across the walls and floor. "When the King asks you that at the ball, you take a curtsy and reply '*What matters it how far we go?*'"

My eyes get caught on Lar's as we twirl through the air, dancing on the wind as easily as if it were the earth beneath our feet. Next time these people ask me to smoke a pipe, I won't question it. Prophetic visions and magical air dances? Sign me up.

As we move, Lar's wings sparkle, the colors in the center shifting and adjusting until I'm looking at something … *carnal.* There are two naked people in this image, playing out like a porno inside the confines of his beautiful wings. Just like last time, I can see, hear, smell, almost *taste* that vision. It's so real that I have to shake my head to remind myself that it isn't actually happening.

No, I'm just *watching* two people fuck.

"A prophecy," I start as I squint and … realize that the two figures in the image are me and Lar. I squeak and jerk back, slipping from Lar's arms. Almost immediately, I begin to fall, tumbling through the air like I'm on my way down the damn Rabbit-Hole again. Lar tucks his wings in tight, dives down, and snatches me from midair, setting us both gently down on the marble floor.

When our eyes meet, I feel my cheeks heat.

Lar looks at me for a long moment before raising his head and narrowing his eyes at something over my shoulder while Dee finishes up the music and turns on his bench seat to follow the other man's gaze. There's a tingling between my shoulder blades, and it takes me a moment to realize that's because there are eyes boring into my back. When I glance over my shoulder, I find Brennin Red watching me with cold, dark eyes.

"I'm starting to get the feeling you don't like me," I call out, putting my hands on my hips and staring the asshole down.

"You're a deplorable dancer; the court will notice." He

runs a finger absently along the scar at the corner of his lip. "Oh well. Nobody expects the Alice to be … cultured. I suppose it'll have to do. We don't have a lot of time."

"Is your stupid ball that important?" I ask, moving across the marble floors toward him. I get the idea that this is a guy that thrives on manipulation and intimidation, and I refuse to play into his hand.

"The Ball of Broken Hearts and Stolen Tarts is a send-off for my soldiers, the people who inhabit this world that means nothing to you. The Walrus and the Carpenter are mobilizing an army on our border. You wouldn't want to see what they'd do if given free rein to terrorize the kingdom. *You* might be interested in disappearing through the Looking-Glass, but the rest of us are stuck here, *Alice*."

"I'm not responsible for the pain of an entire world!" I shout as Brennin—or Red or whatever his stupid name is—turns and leaves the room with an entourage of guards swarming after him. The White Knight is with him, but at least *she* gives me a sympathetic look as she follows the King out. He's wearing that stupid suit again. I'm guessing it's his version of casual wear. Prick. He probably sleeps with a stick shoved up his ass.

"I don't think Red likes you, Allison-who-isn't-Alice," Dee says, moving up to stand beside me. He puts his hat back on and pulls it down firmly over his mussy hair. With Lar on one side and Dee on the other, their beautiful wings resting behind them, I feel pretty plain and boring. At home, I was the weirdo. Here, I'm the beige house with the white picket fence.

"Good, because *I* really don't like him," I say as Tee strides in the open door and makes his way straight over to us. He pauses for a moment as he glances at the Caterpillar.

"Continue your plotting," Lar drawls, reaching down to play with his gold bracelets. "I already know what you're up to. Don't worry: I won't tell."

Tee narrows his amethyst eyes before looking over at me. I can't believe I had sex with him. What was I thinking? Now I'm invested in what happens to the guy. Life must be a hell of a lot easier for assholes like the King and the Hatter.

"The Looking-Glass," he starts, giving Lar another skeptical look. With a scoff and a shake of his head, Tee turns back to me. "It's inside a Game."

"Fuuuuuuuck," Dee says, sliding his hands down either side of his face. "How the hell are we supposed to deal with that?!"

"Uhh, what's a Game?" I ask, crinkling my brows up. Lar is whistling, so I'm going to guess that this shit is bad. I've already flown over the forest hanging from a giant bat, so I don't think they're going to be able to say much to surprise me.

"It's enchanted by a curseworker," Tee says, putting his hands on his hips and looking at the floor.

"And what is *it*?" I ask as Dee runs the tip of one finger along the leather brim of his hat.

"A Game can be … a lot of things," he says with a loose shrug of his shoulders. "But in the King's case, it's probably chess." He lifts his blue eyes up to the glass ceiling above us as the giant bat passes by overhead with a screech that cuts straight into my brain. Speak of the devil …

Twinkle, twinkle little bat, my ass.

"A chess game with life-size pieces," the Caterpillar adds, looking at my mouth for much longer than is really appropriate. His stare makes my lips tingle, and I shift unconsciously, doing my best not to think about that vision in his wings, the one that just showed me making love to the guy. "And life-size appetites."

"In short, they're armed, alive, and very, very angry," Tee adds as I look between the three men.

"An entire set of aggressive, people-size chess pieces?" I ask as I raise my eyebrows. "And what idiot curseworker was responsible for that shit?"

"I was," a voice says from near the door. I look up and find a beautiful woman cloaked in flowing red robes with a big frilly white collar around her neck. The way she smiles at me, I can tell we're not going to be friends.

"Who's that?" I ask, feeling a small spark of fear. This is only the *second* woman I've spoken to since I got to Castle Heart.

And I don't like her.

Ugh, I'm trying not to act on my patriarchal-blessed internal misogyny, but all of a sudden, I'm nervous. Like, *really* fucking nervous. A bunch of alpha dude assholes, I can deal with. But women are smart, creative, and logical. That scares the crap outta me.

"The Knave of Hearts," Tee says, curling his hands into fists at his sides.

"A knave is a jack, right?" I ask, and I feel like I should get serious points for that. Doubt Edith would've known the answer. And Fred … I wonder if Fred could've been the Alice?

"She's like, a second-in-command, as Underland doesn't consider males intelligent or rational enough to run kingdoms, yet at the same time shuns anyone who isn't of royal blood," Dee adds. "All the kingdoms have male rulers now with no queens, so the Knaves act as backup. They can veto any decision the King makes."

Oh … dear.

The Knave sweeps into the room with a pair of men on either side of her. One is dressed in gold with a thick brown-gold beard, sideburns, and mustache, while the other has long white hair scooped into a bun on the back of his head.

He doesn't look old though, maybe thirty at most. They stick to her like glue as she makes her way across the empty marble dance floor toward us.

"Those are her husbands, the Lion and the Unicorn," Tee growls out, and I can already tell he doesn't like this woman any better than I do. I stare at her, her silky brunette hair hanging nearly to the floor, her spring green eyes focused on mine.

"Why are they called the Lion and the Unicorn?" I whisper, but then, I'm standing next to a dude named Caterpillar, and a pair of twins named Tweedledee and Tweedledum, soooo … Stupid question much?

"The Lion has all that facial hair," Dee says with a chuckle, catching my eye and winking, "and the Unicorn, well, it's not because his horn is on his forehead, if you catch my drift." I clamp a hand over my mouth to stifle a chuckle, and the Knave narrows her eyes on me. I'm wracking my brain trying to remember any of these characters from the original books.

The Knave … pretty sure he was accused of stealing the Queen of Hearts' freshly baked tarts. He was a minor character though. And the Lion and the Unicorn? They must be from *Through the Looking-Glass, and What Alice Found There*. I'll have to check in that copy Tee gave me. There's no such thing as being too prepared here.

"Aren't you pretty?" the Knave says as she pauses next to me, a good half a foot shorter than me *at least*. Her husbands, however, are huge. I have to look up to meet the cold, silver eyes of the Unicorn and the equally drab rust-red of the Lion. "These are my husbands, Rook and Knight." She gestures at the Lion first, and then the Unicorn. But considering the Mad Hatter's name is Raiden, the King is Brennin, and the freaking Duke's name is North, I'm not surprised. Normal names, weird nicknames. It works with the Underland vibe.

In fact … I sense a chess reference. Isn't the entire second Alice book just one big chess game? My chest feels tight suddenly, like a queen on a black and white board. Fuck. Is Tee sure the Looking-Glass is trapped in a Game? Because it feels like *I* am already one of the players.

"I could say the same for you," I reply, smiling tightly. I *could* say the same, but I'm not going to. I'm hoping the Knave will miss my play on words, but nobody here ever does, do they?

"The King doesn't seem to like you," the Knave quips bluntly, stepping back so she can look me over. "You are a bit scruffy, and awfully uncouth. Although it's not a surprise why the Hatter is interested."

"A mercenary powerful enough to topple kingdoms? That's an offensive thing to say," I blurt, knowing that I shouldn't start shit with a person I just met. Who knows?

Maybe we could be friends? Lord knows I don't have many back home. Before the Knave can speak again, I exhale and hold out a hand. "Name's Allison Liddell. And you are ..."

"Ines Fripon," she says, looking at my hand like it's diseased. She lifts her green eyes up to mine, and I see it right there in her beautiful irises: she's jealous of me. Guess it makes sense, considering I'm supposedly the next Queen of Hearts. I get this little mean girl thrill out of the moment, and then shove it down.

No, that's something Edith would do, use this woman's insecurities against her. I'm not like that; I don't want to be like that.

"Nice to meet you," I say, forcing a genuine smile. It almost hurts my mouth. Guess I'm still a cynical asshole at heart. Dee looks at me like I've sprouted a second head—something I feel could easily happen here in Underland—while Tee frowns hard. Lar brushes some of his pale hair behind one ear, showing off his silver hoops at the top of his ear. He appears contemplative, looking between the two of us like he's got money riding on our interaction.

"We came to see if you needed any further assistance with the quintrille? It's a very important dance, you know," the Unicorn, err *Knight*, says. Think that *I* might go mad trying to memorize all these fucking weird-ass names. "It's vital for building alliances and friendships within the court."

He smiles at me, and I swear, he's got big, horsey front teeth. Maybe *that's* why he got the nickname Unicorn? Just so long as he doesn't ask me to start believing in him, we're good.

"Allison is a quick learner," Lar says, lifting both brows. "I think she'll make a fine dance partner."

"Well, we'll see," the Knave of Hearts says with a little titter of a laugh. She looks over at Dee like she's just seeing him for the first time, and her lips curl up at the sight of his wings. As soon as he sees her looking, I notice his shoulders stiffening up. "Glad to see you and your brother are getting along now." Her sneer changes to a smile as she flicks her eyes up and down my boys. "Because I'd *hate* to see what I might do the second time around."

The Knave turns and leaves, gesturing for her husbands to follow after.

"Wait," I start, looking between the twins. "Is that …"

"The witch that cursed us?" Tee asks in a low voice. "Yes."

Oh.

Well.

No wonder I hated the cunt from moment one. Never mind all that shit I said about the benefit of the doubt and whatnot. Bitch is going *down*.

5

Tweedledee, Tweedledum, and the Alice's Harem

"You didn't think to tell me about the Knave?" I ask Tee and Dee as we sit on these ridiculously comfortable red chairs in a fitting room so draped in fabric, I feel like I'm crouching inside a tent. *Hoarders: Underland Edition,* anyone? There's so much fabric in here, I could easily drown in it.

"She's not important," Tee says, watching Rab as he checks his pocket watch for the thirtieth time.

"He's late," the White Rabbit grumbles, rolling his red eyes. His gaze comes to rest on March, and I see the corner of his mouth curl up into a sneer. "He's late, and you're not welcome. What do you want with a dress fitting anyhow, you stupid fuck?"

"Oh, I'm the stupid fuck, now am I?" March asks, reaching out to finger a pink dress on a headless mannequin. Heh. Hope that one's not for me. I am *not* a fan of the color pink. "I'm not the one who broke the FUCKING DRINK MEs and left the Alice behind. You know, if you hadn't done that, it's doubtful that Raiden and I would even be here."

Rab scowls, snapping his pocket watch closed with a finality that promises violence. So far as I know, all 'Rabbits', that is, servants to the Kings and Queens of Underland, have bandersnatch forms. That's what *makes* them Rabbits. As for their other two forms … I intend to ask March about his Raiden form at some point.

"It feels like you're here simply to irritate me," Rab grinds out, swiveling one ear back in March's direction. When he glances over his shoulder with those bloodred eyes of his, I get chills. "And you know I don't fucking like to be irritated."

"Are you going to fight me in here while the Alice watches?" March teases, his panty-melting accent dripping with disdain. "I'd bloody love to see you try."

The White Rabbit turns around slowly, this cool, calculating look tracing its way over his features. I would not want to be on the receiving end of that look. He glances down at his vest and then slowly, oh so slowly, unbuttons it. Once his bare chest is revealed, he seeks out a clock and taps his finger against the tattoo.

"Damn, it's not quite your time to die," he says with a false moue of disappointment. "Shame, that. I was looking forward to hastening your demise."

March just laughs and shrugs out of his velvet trench coat, tossing it onto the pink-dress wearing mannequin before striding forward in his massive combat boots. When he stands next to me, I realize how fucking tall the guy really is. I hear he's some sort of master thief, but how the fuck does he get any sneaking around done with that big, muscular body of his?

"If you'd like, *the Alice*, I could challenge Rab to a cock-race, and you could see which Rabbit fares best in a brawl."

"Thanks, but no thanks," I say, still feeling slightly lightheaded from my dance with the Caterpillar. I hate heights, but I have to say, that was one of the most miraculous things I've ever done. I'm suddenly desperate to do it again. How long do I have until the ball? A week? And I have lessons with Lar every day until then.

Fantastic.

My mind conjures up that moment when our mouths connected … and then dives straight into the dark, carnal delights of that vision.

I shake my head to clear it, and reach my fingers up to rub at my temples.

"After this, we'll go back to the room," Tee murmurs under his breath, giving March a dirty look, like he doesn't appreciate him standing so close. "I'll have dinner brought up."

"By one of those creepy card servants?" I say, because I still can't stop thinking about the King and how he killed one of them in cold blood. Nor can I possibly forget that he won a *kiss* from me—a kiss in front of the entire court.

I imagine he'll collect at the ball. Why wouldn't he? Fucking prick. I hate him.

"At least you know they're all given fair chance to defend themselves at the Trial," Dee says, lounging back in his chair and tapping his fingers against the red leather arm. I can see about two inches of the chair's actual fabric peeking out beneath the mounds of cloth draped over it. This entire place is just swimming.

"*The* Trial?" I ask as March leans against a decorative column, keeping his brown eyes locked on me. It feels like he's searching for something intangible, something I can't name, but want to keep hidden. Maybe I'm just imagining it? Does not hurt to be paranoid in a place like this. "Like, there's only one?"

"The King holds the Trial once a week," Rab says, pausing in front of me and smiling in that cruel way of his, a slash across the face, sharp as a knife. "The accusers are tested with magic to determine their, shall we say, *veracity*.

Some are selected for servitude … and others for execution. Rapists, murderers, traffickers, that sort of thing."

"I feel like you're trying to make me hate the King less. FYI, it's not working." I cross my arms over my chest and try not to sigh. Whoever this tailor person is, I'm getting mighty irritated. All I want to do is crawl up the stairs and flop into bed. Of course, now that I've fucked North, Tee, and Dee, it's like sex is on the plate with all of them—it's an option. I *could* go back to the room and invite them into bed with me.

Oh, it's tempting …

"I would never try to sway your opinion," Tee says, looking up from under the leather brim of his peaked cap. My mouth is aching to kiss his, to free those gorgeous wings from his back, but again, it feels weird to do it front of these other men. Not because I'm ashamed or embarrassed, but because it feels like special moments with Tee should be private. "I just want to reiterate: if any of those people were innocent, Dee and I would've made a stand a long time ago."

Exhaling, I lean back in my chair and close my eyes, crossing my legs at the ankle. With the twins around, I feel safe. Maybe I shouldn't, considering I *did* get kidnapped out of North's house, but I do anyway. Since the biggest, baddest mercenary in all the land is now supposedly engaged to my ass, I may as well relax.

The sound of a curtain swishing back draws my attention, and I crack my eyes to see Rab slipping out of his vest, and slipping into … another vest.

"What are you doing?" I ask him as he picks up a pair of wire-rimmed spectacles from a side table and perches them on the end of his nose, peering at me over the top of them.

"I've just received a text from the King," Rab says, shaking his phone in my direction. Every freaking time I see one of these weirdos holding what looks like the newest iPhone, I have a mini heart attack. It's just too weird to be sitting in a castle, being fitted for a ball, and seeing the King's servant holding something that looks like it could be browsing social media or looking up porn. "The tailor was executed this morning, so I'll be acting tailor until we can find a new one."

"Do you know anything at all about sewing clothes?" I ask as Rab buttons up his new brown leather vest and rolls up his sleeves to reveal a sea of glorious ink. It feels like every time I look at him, I notice something new. My eyes catch on a sea of ghosts drifting up from a graveyard toward a full moon. Very pretty, very me. I would totally get something like that tattooed on my body.

"I've sewn flesh before, does that count?" Rab asks, which is not a particularly comforting sentiment.

"Flesh?" I ask as he holds out a tattooed hand, gesturing

for me to step up on a round dais surrounded by mirrors. There are a lot of fucking mirrors here. I wonder if Brennin Red has one above his bed?

Aaaand, why am I thinking about Brennin Red's bed anyway?

"You know, battle wounds and all that," Rab replies, but his voice is too smooth and practiced. He's lying to me. And the sad part is, I don't actually want to know the truth anyway.

"Since when have you ever sewn up a wound, mate?" March asks, trailing along behind me as I stand up and head for the dais, shrugging out of my coat and boots. Reluctantly, I also set the Queenmaker and the Vorpal Blade aside. "Usually you're the one making them."

"I've been known to show compassion," Rab says as he grins at me, white ears twitching atop his head. I can smell him from here, this musty, earthy scent mixed with the copper reek of blood. I shouldn't find it appealing, but I do. My nipples pebble beneath my shirt, and I curse under my breath.

Great.

He's going to measure me, and I've got my headlights turned on bright.

Fan-fucking-tastic.

Tee and Dee flank either side of the dais, arms crossed over their chests in identical positions. One has wings, and one doesn’t. That makes me sad somehow.

"You? Compassion?" I ask as Rab slides a cloth measuring tape from a hook, winding it around his hand as he watches me with those red, red eyes of his. He manages to make the motion sexy, wrapping it around two fingers and suggestively licking his lower lip.

I roll my eyes.

Hey, I can't help it: I'm a fucking young adult. It's in our DNA to do annoying shit.

"Sorry, but I can't see it," I say as Rab steps closer and March circles around behind the dais, balancing a knife on the tip of his finger. "You being compassionate, I mean. Isn't that against the very nature of a sociopath?"

I'm smirking when Rab comes around in front of me, but that quickly dies when he leans in and wraps the measuring tape around my waist, tugging it tight and stealing my breath away. His mouth is disturbingly close to my nipple.

"Psychopath, you mean," Rab whispers, taking note of the numbers on the measuring tape and calling them out to March, of all people. The brown-eared Rabbit takes the knife in his hand and carves the measurements into the wooden stand of a dress form. "And you're right: I have no compassion. What was I thinking?"

He slides the measuring tape up in the back and then cocks a dark brow at me.

"Well? Do I have permission to touch the Alice's luscious

breasts?" Rab doesn't look ashamed to be asking. Nor does he look professional, as a tailor should. Instead, he's just … lascivious. I hate him. Okay, not really. I hate the King and the Hatter maybe, but not the White Rabbit, not even if he shot Brandon in the head right in front of me.

After all, it led me here.

And I'm starting to *like* it.

"Provided you act a gentleman," I say, lifting my chin as Rab pulls the measuring tape up and over my breasts … *riiiiiight* over the pert points of my nipples. It feels good, even through the shirt and the knife-filled corset underneath it.

"I never act a gentleman," Rab purrs, his voice like a frost-covered branch collapsing under the weight of fresh snow. It's like he's having as much trouble touching my boobs as I am having them touched.

"How long is this going to take?" Tee snaps, flicking his attention between March and Rab. Clearly, he's not much of a fan of either Rabbit.

"The more times you ask that, the longer it takes," Rab purrs, squeezing the measuring tape around my breasts and forcing a sharp exhale between my lips. I feel almost as lightheaded now as I did when I was dancing with Lar in the ballroom. But … at least my situation's a *why choose* moment, right? I can't imagine having to pick between these men. That'd kill me.

"The Alice needs her sleep," Tee grinds out, grabbing the lapels on his jacket and forcefully straightening out the fabric with a sharp snap. "So save your dirty flirtations for another day."

Rab ignores him, moving down to measure my ass next. I've never been measured for clothing before—ever heard of Target, anyone?—so I'm not sure how orthodox any of this, but I *like* it.

"Don't you dare cop a feel," I whisper, and Rab pauses to look up at me. He's so gloriously sexy, dripping in ink, his hair black as black, his eyes as vibrant and piercing as his tattoos. "You may measure my ass, but *be a gentleman.*"

"How boring," Rab drawls with a sigh, but even though he's a psycho murderer, he keeps it respectful as he wraps me in the measuring tape again. "Like I said, most definitely *not* a Mary Sue."

I almost smile, because I can hear the teasing note in his voice, and I like that, too. But then something occurs to me.

"How do you know what a Mary Sue is anyway? That's a term coined Topside." I like the way I refer to my own world as Topside now, like it's as easy as breathing. Something about that makes me happy. Clearly, I've gone mad.

"I spend a lot of time Topside, Sonny." Rab stands up and reaches for one of my arms, pushing my sleeves up and making my skin pebble with pleasure, like he's petting me or something. "I know what a Mary Sue is, I prefer Pepsi to Coke, and I do *looove* to read manga."

"Manga?" I ask as Rab measures my leg, my foot, my … ear? And then lastly, my head. I suppose that makes sense, seeing as I could be getting a custom hat. But my ear? Sigh. "You read manga, like Japanese comics?"

"Exactly that," Rab says as he finishes up and steps back, looking me up and down with a sly smile. "Surprised?"

"Honestly, no," I say, sensing that we're done, and hopping down from the dais. "It suits you." I pause and glance down at my button-up shirt, fingering the fabric as I narrow my eyes. "Wait a minute. When I got here, there was a closet full of clothes, all in my size. Actually, I've never had clothes that fit better than the ones that are in my room upstairs." I raise both eyebrows and glance between the four men. "So what is this fitting all about?"

"We're not measuring your body, you cheeky twat, just taking your mettle." March pauses next to me and grins, grabbing his velvet trench off the mannequin and fishing out a small note. "Here."

"What is this?" I ask, as he pulls out a small green vial, flashes me a sharp grin, and then tosses the small glass item on the floor to shatter. Smoke billows out, smelling like sour green apples and sugar, and when I blink through it, the March Hare is gone.

I unfold the note as Tee steps forward to explain.

"This isn't about body measurements—we need your *mettle*, that is, how resistant you are to magic. Your dress for the ball is going to have spells woven into it." I glance down at the note—there's a location and a time scribbled on it—and then back up at Tee.

"And who's going to cast those spells?" I ask, already fearing the answer.

"The Knave …" Tee says, and then pauses, glancing over at his brother. They both turn to look at me as Rab pockets his borrowed wire spectacles. "We're not happy about it either, but … King's orders."

"Well, clearly the King wants me dead because I don't trust the Knave for shit." I stare at the note again. *Tomorrow, same time. Ask where the dungeon is.*

Oh, the dungeon, huh? That sounds promising.

I crumple the note up and chuck it toward a half-full trash can. Tee intercepts it in mid-air, and opens it to read it, scowling as he goes about it.

"She cursed you both, and you want me to wear a dress with her magic in it? No way, no how." I cross my arms over my chest as Tee passes the note to Dee. The twins exchange a look.

"I'll be with you the whole time, Miss Alice," Rab says, grinning maniacally at me. "I wouldn't worry about the Knave. As much as she dislikes you, she quite likes the King

... and she also likes keeping her head. Besides, you'll have an ace in the pocket, so to speak." As I watch, Rab's ears shrink toward his head, becoming rounder the smaller they get. At the same time, his body folds inward, and bright white fur sprouts up over his skin and clothes.

Before my mind can even register what's happening, there's a tiny mouse clawing his way up my pants and clinging to the hem of my button-up shirt.

Wish I could say I was shocked. Instead, I just scoop the mouse up and hand him over to Tee, so I can put my jacket back on. As soon as I do, I pop the Rab-mouse into my pocket.

"I will be your eyes and ears at the ball," he says, tiny pink nose twitching. It's fucking weird as fuck, but the mouse-Rab has tattoos on his naked little rodent feet. One of them is tick-tick-ticking away. *"As well as your teeth and claws."*

Oddly enough, I do feel better.

"After the Knave spells your dress, Dee and I will check it out, don't worry." Tee reaches out and squeezes my hand, and I nod.

But I have a funny feeling about the Knave.

And a woman should always trust her instincts.

♦ ♠ ♣ ♥ ♣ ♠ ♦

Dinner is turtle soup which sort of creeps me the fuck

out.

"Beautiful soup, so rich and green, waiting in a hot tureen," Dee singsongs as he ladles me a bowl and passes it over. I take it, but only begrudgingly, and only because I'm starving and tired. Snatching a bit of cheese from the refreshments table, I pass it down to Rab who's been transferred from my jacket pocket to my pj's pocket.

Chesh watches him hungrily from his perch on the cat tree.

"Put the little mouse down, and we'll have some fun," he says, pupils dilated, tongue sliding across his lower lip. "Play a little game of cat and mouse."

"How about a little game of cat and bandersnatch?" Rab says, his icy voice the same in his mouse form as it is in his … human? is he a human? … anyway, same as in his human form. It's a tad disconcerting.

"That doesn't sound nearly as fun," Chesh purrs, stretching and then wincing slightly. He reaches down and touches his side. There's no blood there, just a phantom pain, but according to the Duke, it takes a while for the Vorpal Blade's magic to run its course. Poor Chesh really is still hurting, despite the Mad Hatter's intervention.

I sit down on the bed, and Tee moves forward to fluff my pillows for me.

"You don't have to do that, you know," I say, feeling a slight blush color my cheeks. And I am not a girl who blushes easily. It's not that I don't like being fawned over, but I just sort of feel bad when Tee does it. He's too princely, too regal.

"I don't have to; I want to," he whispers, making me comfortable before retreating to grab his own bowl.

My room is bustling, far from the quiet little sanctuary I thought it was going to be.

Every one of my wannabe lovers save Red, Raiden, and March are here.

"Was I dreaming or did you cast some sort of spell on me while I was sleeping?" I ask Lar, looking at the green soup on my spoon and seriously debating if I'd rather live off cupcakes and candied honeybees for the rest of my stay here. There's even a plate of brightly colored mushrooms that each taste like a different fruit. How desperate am I for a hot meal right now?

"I cast a spell," he says, eating his own soup in a way that's undeniably sexy. He puts the metal spoon into his mouth, sucks on it, twists it around, and pulls it out oh so slowly. "Just to give your body a small reprieve from the pain."

"You knocked me out?" I give him a look that says that sort of pisses me off. Although, to be fair, I'm glad I slept through most of the day yesterday. That agony I felt when I used my magic was almost incomprehensible.

"No, I cut a small hole in your natural aura, so the

extra magic would bleed out." Lar lets his wings hang loosely over the arms of the chair, like two glorious glittering tapestries.

"The Caterpillar isn't just a soothsayer," North purrs, lounging on the chaise at the end of the bed, black tail curled around the bedpost. "He's a fine curseworker in his own right."

"You flatter me," Lar says, putting his spoon down and setting his bowl aside. He crosses his legs and steeples his fingers atop his knee. Some men might look ridiculous in blue and white pinstriped pj's, but not him. He's a fucking enigma, and I love it. "But the Knave is better."

"Is there a difference between witches and curseworkers?" I ask, because I've heard the men use them interchangeably. Closing my eyes, I take a quick bite of my soup and pray to whatever goddesses rule over Underland that it won't taste so bad I puke.

Ohmyfuckinggod, that's good!

Turtle tastes like … veal.

And the broth is spicy and flavorful, a punch to the tongue that reminds me of Fred's favorite Indian restaurant. But then I swallow, and the yummy flavor leaves my mouth, making room for melancholy. When Fred was alive, we fought like cats and dogs. Now that he's gone, I miss him so much that I feel like I'm having period cramps even when I'm not.

I take another bite of soup to ward off the agony of missing my brother.

"Synonyms," Dee says, flopping down on the bed and somehow managing not to spill a single drop of soup. His wings are gone, disappeared in a flash at midnight, but since he's shirtless, I can see the beautiful tattoos they make along his back. Drool-worthy. "But the Knave is the highest ranking curseworker in the Kingdom of Hearts, which means she can throttle the power of other curseworkers." He takes a few bites of soup, blue-black hair falling across his forehead.

"She has you on a leash?" I ask, and I can see Lar's mouth tighten at the corners. Maybe that wasn't the best way to phrase things?

"Only the King holds my reins," the Caterpillar says, taking out a small pipe and fingering it for a moment. As soon as I see it, I'm reminded of his prophecy in the ballroom: we're supposedly going to have sex one day.

Wish I were shocked by that.

But then it's like he doesn't have the strength to see anything else today and pockets the pipe instead, pulling out a cigarette and smoking that while Rab's mousy nose twitches. Without thinking, I reach down and stroke the mouse's tiny head. *I'm stroking the tattooed asshole assassin,* I realize, but I don't stop doing it either.

"I'm just not *permitted* to use magic beyond a certain

extent," Lar says, flicking his tongue across his lower lip and gently fanning his wings. He taps his cigarette ash into a gold tray shaped like a mouth, and I swear to fuck, it *burps* afterward.

"So you can't spell my dress?" I ask, still unsure how I feel about the Knave putting her stupid cursing fingers on it. She messed with the twins, violated them in a way I'm not even sure I understand; she took away their wings. I'm not okay with any of that.

"No, but I'll check it over—we all will. Sunshine, we won't let anyone or anything rain on your parade." Lar flaps his wings hard, sending glitter and brilliant blue-gold dust into the room. In his place, there's a small butterfly that flits over to one of the flowers from Dee's bouquet and rests gently on a white petal.

I have a feeling that Lar is not a shifter like Rab; he's gone to his room or wherever else. The butterfly is just that, just a beautiful insect.

"I want to sleep in here tonight," Chesh purrs, melting into his cat form and giving me a very dramatic stretch with his tail straight up in the air.

"Agreed," North says as I pull the Rab-mouse from my pocket, and set him on the end of the bed. "I say, banish those that aren't in the Alice's harem and leave the rest of us."

"Right little bugger," Rab growls as he grows in size, his

fur sucking back into his skin, his ears elongating into a rabbit's, and his clothes falling neatly back into place. So Dee claims that North's clothes don't shift because he was cursed into becoming a jabberwock, while Rab was born a shifter and gets to keep his. Makes about as much sense as anything else I've learned here. "Nice trick, but the cat can't stay either, now can he?"

The White Rabbit slides off of my bed then turns to face me, looking down at me with a lascivious little smirk. He pushes his shirt sleeves up, flashing brightly colored tattoos.

"Tell me I'm a part of your harem, and I'll stay. I'll even fuck if you want."

I smile sweetly back at him.

"Get the hell out of my room," I sneer, and he grins, sliding the gold key from his pocket and heading for—surprise, surprise—the painting that features the infamous Tenniel image of the white rabbit checking his pocket watch.

I wait until he leaves before I take the last bite of my soup and set the bowl aside.

"Please tell me I can join your harem?" Chesh begs, padding across the air toward me, leaving little glowing paw prints floating behind him for a brief moment. He hops onto the bed and bats at my bare feet. "Ask your primary if I can join. I promise I'll be good." The

Cheshire cat climbs up my legs to sit in my lap, looking up at me with big, round gray eyes, like two full moons in a night sky.

"Go to your room," I tell him, whittling down the men in my bedchamber to the ones I've fucked. Not sure if that's a good idea or if I'm just crazy.

Chesh shifts into human form, still sitting in my lap, and all of a sudden, it's not so cute or cuddly anymore. The tags on his collar jingle as he leans in toward me, one tiny fang peeking up over the edge of his lip. He's glorious, covered in tattoos, his vest gaping open to reveal the hard muscles underneath.

"I'll purr for you," he says, putting his mouth close to my ear. Chesh curls his fingers around my upper arm, and then licks my ear. I reach up and give his silver hoops a tug. He has them on both his kitty ears and his human ears.

"I'm glad you're not dead," I tell him as he pulls back just enough that his mouth is near mine. I can smell sweet cream and cupcakes on his breath, and I wish I could kiss him. But I've already kissed one stranger today, and that's enough. "Go to sleep, and we'll talk later."

"About me joining your harem?" he presses, and I flick him in the ear. I'd be mad if I thought Chesh was pushing at me like a typical misogynistic a-hole. He's not though. He's just lonely. If he really is the last of his kind, I can't blame him.

"Bed, now," North says, waving his hand lazily in the direction of the jabberwock painting. There's another one next to it though, one with a big smiling Cheshire Cat on it. I open the nightstand drawer, take out a key, and hand it to Chesh.

He curls his fingers around it, and meets my eyes with a much more serious expression on his handsome face.

"Thank you, Allison."

It's the first time he's ever called me by my real name.

Chesh curls his tail around my wrist as he turns, sliding the silky fur across my skin before he wanders off, unlocks his door, and leaves the room.

There's a certain finality to it when it closes.

"If I'd … sucked Tee off and swallowed, would you have had to eat some of his jizz, too?" I blurt at Dee, and I really wonder why the fuck I chose that moment to ask that question. He blinks big blue eyes at me. "I mean, when we first met, and you wanted me to go through the garden door …"

Dee lays back in the pillows and laughs while Tee flushes and turns down the lights.

The look he throws North is not particularly pleasant.

"I wouldn't have sucked my brother off if that's what you're asking," Dee chortles, chest heaving with laughter. "Just a little lick or a taste would've worked fine. I could've kissed you after and gotten enough to make the change, I'd think."

"I could've just … tasted some and gotten small?" I ask, wondering how a blow job would work with these guys. If I got even a little bit of cum on my lips, I'd grow or shrink depending on the twin? Sounds inconvenient. Yep, I am definitely going to break this curse. "Still gross, and I wouldn't have done it," I say, wondering what might've happened if Rab hadn't broken those bottles. Where would I be now? Home? The thought makes me uncomfortable. Would I still be here, lying in a half-dark room with these three men? Or sitting alone in my parents' quiet, broken home? "But really?"

"You have to swallow a certain amount for it to work, but basically, yes." Tee collects the empty soup bowls and spoons, setting them all on the refreshments table where I assume a card servant will come to collect them.

I lay back in the pillows and try not to seriously love the way all the linens smell here, like sunshine and wind. Back home, I had to do my own laundry, so let's be honest: my sheets did not smell even half this good, more like old Victoria's secret perfume and sweat.

"Enough about angel jizz," North growls, peeping his head up over the footboard to stare at me from narrowed, gold eyes. "You wanted us in here for a reason."

"Maybe she wants to discuss the nine?" Tee asks with a sigh, picking up my jacket from the floor and hanging it on one of the creepy, moving hooks.

"Maybe she wants to hear the rest of the prophecy?" Dee inserts, humming a tune under his breath.

"But nine young suitors hurried up,
All eager for their treat:
Their hair was brushed, their faces washed,
Their clothes were clean and neat—
And this was good, because, you know,
To date the Alice was a feat."

He starts reciting it, but North cuts him off, growling out another verse as he waves his hand dismissively.

"For all the monsters followed her,
They craved her bloody corpse;
So thick and fast the hordes attacked,
Just more, and more, and more—
All hoping for a bite or two,
Her men must prevent gore."

"There, you've heard quite enough of that nonsense," he says, climbing up over the footboard and crouching like a beast on the end of the bed. Tee moves over and sits beside me, crossing his arms over his chest. "Let's talk *shop*."

"There is no shop," I snort. "My vagina is not an open garage."

"A garage?" North asks, thinking hard on the word. "I'm not sure I know what that is. What I do know is that I am particularly interested in your *vagina*, for lack of a better word."

With a groan, I flop back into the pillows and cover my eyes with my arm.

"Please don't say vagina," I moan, feeling awkward tingles trace over my skin. I'm hot and achy inside, and I don't know what to say or do. I'm totally flubbing this moment up. Wait, flubbing? Where did that word come from? "I just … want to let you guys know that I'm not planning on running out and leaving you here." I move my arm off my eyes and pick at the edge of my blanket as Dee leans in close to me, pushing some rainbow strands of hair back from my forehead.

"You want to stay?" he whispers, and I shrug loosely.

"I want to help you," I continue, "for as long as it takes. I might … even want to stay. That doesn't mean I don't need to go home." I look up and find Tee watching me. "Because I do, but I want to be able to go back and forth, like Rab."

"Do you want me to show you?" Tee asks, tucking his hands into the pockets of his black linen pajama pants. He's wearing a tank top that shows off the muscles in his arms, and the purple and black feathers on the back of them. I swear on some Underland goddess' tits that if Edith and I had been watching a movie with Tee and Dee in it, I would've ended the film with my chest covered in drool.

"The Looking-Glass?"

I glance between the three men, and then back to Tee; he nods.

"Oh bloody hell," North growls out, but he stands up, too. "If Red finds us slinking around the Looking-Glass, he'll be furious." He taps a clawed finger against his lips and then shrugs those massive shoulders of his. "Oh well, I suppose it can't be helped. Were he to act a gentleman, he'd have offered the Alice use of it already."

"I understand not wanting to leave the portal open for the Walrus and his ilk, but I agree." Tee looks into my eyes, and I feel a shiver trace down my spine. He's got an old soul, that one. "You deserve a chance to see your family."

"You never realize how important they are until you lose them," Dee chokes out, standing up from the bed and grabbing his peaked cap off the nightstand. He tucks it over his blue and black hair, and then spins it around with a finger on the brim. "Let's go see the Looking-Glass, Allison-who-isn't-Alice."

My heart thunders in my chest, and I realize suddenly that I'm afraid.

And not of the King or the Hatter, not even of the

Walrus and the Carpenter.

I'm afraid of going home.

Sometimes, our greatest fears are not our most obvious. Sometimes, our darkest terrors hide in plain sight.

"So," I whisper as we walk down the dark hallways, a shirtless dragon on my left, and twin fallen angel princes on my right. "Do the card servants …" I trail off and lick my lips. I understand that they're just cursed convicts, but they do bear an awful resemblance to the soldiers in Dee's vision-memory thing.

But then, I haven't told him that I saw that, so how do I even go about asking?

"They're just cursed souls, don't worry about them," Tee says while Dee grabs a torch off the wall as we pass. There are tapestries everywhere in here, and I swear to fuck, it feels like some of them are watching me.

"If the King can enchant them to be servants, then couldn't he make soldiers, too?" I hedge, hoping I'm not pushing too hard. I don't want to make the boys relive their trauma, but I'm dying to know.

"It's not the King that enchants them, though he could," Dee says, his face paling slightly as he taps a finger against the brim of his hat. He's trying to be casual, but I can see right through that facade to the pain underneath. "It's the Knave that spells them. And yes, when the previous King of Hearts ruled Underland, he did order her to create soldiers."

"But not anymore?" I ask, and the twins exchange a look.

"Brennin Red doesn't need or want those sorts of soldiers in his army," North growls, slamming his tail against the stone floor as we walk. "He's nothing like his father."

"So you say," Tee snaps back, raking his fingers through his hair. "And yet, we're still slaves. Underland stills suffers. The guillotine runs non-stop."

"He's *different*," North snarls back, and I start to wonder if I might have to insert myself between the two men. "And he's only been on the throne for three years. Try cutting him a break, hmm?"

"It would take two seconds for him to free us," Dee whispers, reaching over his shoulder to touch his tattoo. He looks over at North who grits his teeth.

"The Knave won't allow him to do it; he's tried."

"Bullshit," Tee quips, but then we're all standing before a massive red door in the shape of—you will never guess this shit—a *heart.* Le gasp.

"This is it?" I ask, glancing over my shoulder and down the long stone hallway we just traversed. A dozen hallways and who knows how many staircases later, and we're here. I was almost hoping we'd have to, I don't know, cross a moat or something. Some part of me wants the Looking-Glass as far away from me possible.

Who knew I had such trauma?

I clutch the front of my pj's in a fist as Tee pulls a chain out from beneath his shirt, a pair of keys hanging from the end of it. One of them is the key I gave him to access a Suit in my room, but the other is twice as big and made of solid iron.

"Keeps the pixies from pinching it," Dee explains with a sharp nod, like that makes all the sense in the world. Right. An iron key keeps magical flower-possessing pixies from stealing it. Sounds good.

Tee unlocks the door and steps inside, holding out a hand for mine. I take his in one, and Dee's in the other, moving slowly into the room and pausing on a ledge with a gold banister separating us from the rest of the room.

Down below … there's a giant chessboard in black and white.

"Holy butt waffles," I choke out, making Dee chuckle.

As we watch, one of the giant chess pieces—easily as tall as North if not taller—slides across the board into a new space. It's the red king, moving out of a "check" by the black knight.

The pieces seem to be made of some solid stone, like

granite or marble, their faces frozen and silent, but menacing nonetheless. What would happen if I went down there and joined the Game?

"To get through to the Looking-Glass, you'll have to win against the black pieces," Dee explains, leaning his elbows on the gold banister and waiting for red to make their move. The red queen slides across the board, and a shiver travels down my spine.

"Don't get too close to the edge," Tee says, reaching out to grab a handful of his brother's shirt. "You've seen what those things can do if you piss them off."

"If you're not standing on edge, then you're taking up too much space," North says, crossing his arms over his bare, bronzed chest, and watching the Game play out below us. On the other side of the room, there's a mirror leaning against the wall.

It doesn't appear to be anything but a mirror from over here. I can even see the reflection of the chessboard and pieces in its silver surface. That's not to say it isn't gorgeous—it really is—with big gilded gold edges, a filigreed pattern etched into the swirling bits of metal. The frame reminds me of a winter-dead tree, its spindly branches reaching out to the edge of the world. If I saw that online back home, I'd order it. If I could afford it, that is.

"That's the Looking-Glass?" I ask, and both Tee and

Dee reply at the same time.

"It is."

Curling my fingers around Tee's, I struggle to keep my feet in place.

I want to run.

Because going back home means facing all the unspoken issues I left behind. It means remembering that Dad is never home anymore, that Mom is *never* coming home, that Edith is drifting further and further away from the girl she used to be.

"If I win the Game, I can cross through the Looking-Glass?" I repeat, and North nods.

"But nobody has ever won the Game without the King's permission to play; it's rigged. You cannot win without Red's say-so." The jabberwock shifter glances over his shoulder at the sound of skittering feet out in the hallway. "Card servants," he explains before he looks back at us, "probably collecting information for the Knave. We should be going before she sends her ridiculous husbands after us."

"We'll figure out a way to get you home," Tee says, the conviction in his voice warming my insides. Before, I think he wanted to send me home for my own sake, but now I think he's just desperate to make sure I get a chance to reconnect with my family.

I love him for that.

Love him?!

Ew. No. No, I do not fucking love him. What is this, some young adult romance novel?! Gross.

"Let's go upstairs," I say, feeling that hot heat between my thighs start to pulse. Just the idea of taking the three of them to my room turns me on. It's persistent, that throbbing, desperate need, when I'm around these guys.

All three men turn to look at me.

Oh yes.

That invitation, it's as lascivious as it sounds.

♦ ♠ ♣ ♥ ♣ ♠ ♦

"Are there any lions or tigers about here?" I ask as Tee unlocks the door to my chambers and pushes it open just enough that I hear a rumble from inside.

"It's only the Red King snoring," Dee says with a chuckle, pushing the door open the rest of the way and revealing a dark bedroom bathed in moonlight and shadows from the dying fire.

"Isn't he a *lovely* sight?" Tee says with clenched teeth, moving into the room to stand beside my bed.

I couldn't say honestly that he is. He has a tall, red night-cap on, with a tassel, and he's lying crumpled into a sort of untidy heap, snoring loudly.

Wow.

Talk about … total shock.

This man looks about as far from the dignified

dickhead I've been dealing with as anything I've ever seen. He may as well have shape-shifted into a baby kitten.

"He's dreaming now," North says, cocking his head to one side. "What do you suppose he's dreaming about? The Alice's creamy thighs?"

"You're disgusting," I choke out, feeling like the King's just doused my hot, summer—wait, what season is it in Underland?—night in ice water. "What is he doing in my bed anyway?"

"That's an excellent question," Tee growls as Dee fills a small glass with water and moves over to stand next to Brennin Red's face. I notice that even in his sleep, he still wears gloves.

"If you try to wake him up by touching him …" Dee starts with a shrug, drawing his thumb across his throat. I get it: off with his head. So, much to my horror and chagrin, the younger twin tosses cold water onto the King's sleeping face.

He comes to like a wild animal disturbed in its den, eyes snapping open, one hand reaching for his glove. It's half off, and he's off the bed before I can even register what's going on. I catch a glimpse of a red palm before he realizes it's just us, and tucks his fingers back into the white fabric.

"A simple curseworker incantation can turn a person's hands red if they're guilty of murder." Tee's words ring in my head as I raise an eyebrow.

"What are you doing in my room?" I query, crossing my arms over my chest.

"And how did you even get in?" North asks, tilting his head to one side. His gold hair slides around his dark horns. "Only the Alice or one of her Suitors can let someone into the Suit of Hearts."

"Rab allowed me in," Brennin says, lifting his chin and still managing to look like some entitled asshole CEO with a bad attitude, even in his stupid night-cap. "I needed a place to rest my head tonight that might allow me to keep it." The way he says that, biting off the words, it sort of scares the shit out of me.

What the fuck does that even mean?

Is the King afraid in his own castle? If so, how the hell am I supposed to feel safe here?

"Don't you have your own chambers?" I snort, and Red narrows those ebon eyes on me.

"Nowhere in Castle Heart is as safe as the Alice's chambers. I was going to head to my own room, but my keys seem to have been misplaced." As Brennin talks, his teeth clench even tighter, and his jaw tightens to the point where I swear it may very well just fall off. "Rab let me in, and then I started to wonder where you all *went*." He gives North a look, like he's disappointed in him. "Sneaking around the castle in the middle of the night, tsk-tsk, *Savage Duke*."

"The Alice wants to use the Looking-Glass," North says, and Brennin scowls, tearing the cap off his head and tossing it aside. I swear to fuck, I see it glow. "She has a right, certainly, considering she hails from Topside."

"She has no right," Red snarls, giving me a look over his shoulder that could curdle milk. "Any use of the Looking-Glass leaves us open to assault from both Underland and Topside. It isn't happening, not until I get things under control." The King turns back to the window and watches the rain pour down the glass. "And then don't worry: I'll ship the Alice back to where she belongs."

"I don't—" Tee starts, but I put a hand on his chest to stop him, storming up to the King and getting in his face.

"You don't know anything about me, and you haven't bothered to try to learn. I don't want to go back home *forever*, I just want to see my family and let them know I'm alright. I'm committed to this shit now, okay? I'm in. For fuck's sake, if you're going to make accusations, at least get the facts straight first."

The King whirls on me, and I can see in his eyes that he's not used to being defied.

He raises a finger in my face.

"And you don't know *anything* about this world or its problems. You are not the savior, just a piece on a board to be moved. So, *Alice*, just go where I tell you and do what I say. And what I say is: don't bother wondering around the fucking castle unless you want to lose your head."

Brennin reaches down and into the pocket on my nightgown where I've stashed the keys to the Suits. I keep them on a ring with the master key when I leave the room, just in case. He takes one of the keys off, and then throws the others on the floor, moving to a painting of the King of Hearts, sitting on his throne and holding a heart-topped scepter.

That fucker ...

I follow after him because I'm not about to be disrespected like that. I let Liam treat me like shit for so long; I will never let another man walk all over me.

"Listen up, *buddy*," I snap as I step into the dark hallway, and the painting swings shut behind me, trapping me inside with the King. He turns around to look me, completely aghast that I've dared follow him.

Dickhead.

"You need to learn to control your temper." Brennin steps up close to me, but I'm not afraid of him. I've faced the worst in life; this is nothing. "If you want my help—no, if you need it, and I think you really do—then you have to tell me what's going on."

The King just stares down at me, a muscle in his jaw ticking as he clenches his teeth, his fists curled tight, his breathing coming in hard, angry pants. I'm breathing fast, too, and sweating profusely. My fight or flight instinct has kicked in, and I am so done with this man's shit.

"Just show up at the ball, and do what you're told," he snaps, and I reach up to grab the front of his robes without meaning to.

"Don't boss me around like I'm a fucking *dog*!" I shout, and then … something just snaps between us. One minute I'm grabbing the King and getting ready to shake him to death, and the next, my back is pressed to the stone wall, my arms are around his neck, and his mouth is on mine.

The first hot press of his tongue between my lips drags a groan from my throat that echoes down the dark stone hallway. The throbbing warmth between my thighs floods with wetness, and before I know it, I'm letting the King lift me up and press me against the wall. Our bodies grind together in this hot, sweaty tangle, our mouths feeding at one another. It's like for a split-second there, I'm not even human anymore.

With a gasp, I shove the King back, and he stumbles, dropping me to the floor. I manage to catch myself on the wall, my knees weak and shaky beneath me. My eyes are wide, and I'm just staring at the floor like I can't figure myself out.

"My Queen of Hearts," the King says, and there's this break in his voice that tells me all I need to know. I was right: I bruised his ego. He fucking wants me, doesn't he? "I told you that you were meant to be mine."

He takes off down the hall before I can figure out a retort.

Doesn't matter anyway, because all I can think to say is: *no, you were meant to be* mine.

♦ ♠ ♣ ♥ ♣ ♠ ♦

"I'm sorry about last night," I say as the twins walk me to the athletic center, one on either side. North and Chesh were gone when I woke up, but Rab and Lar joined me for breakfast. So did March, but I chose to ignore him. It's pretty obvious the Hatter is sending him to keep an eye on me.

I don't trust that fucker as far as I can throw him.

"You don't have to apologize," Tee says, but the way he keeps his eyes on the floor makes me wonder if I should. I wanted last night to get lascivious … and I suppose it did, just not with the right guy. Or guys, rather.

"The King has a powerful presence," Dee says, looking up at the ceiling. We pass by several empty sitting rooms as we head down the stairs, take a sharp right, and then another hard left. One more right to get the gym. At least it seems I'm starting to get the layout of Castle Heart down.

"I wanted to spend the night with you," I whisper, drawing both twins' attention my way. Dee opens his mouth to say something else, but when we come around the next corner, we stumble on the Knave and her creepy husbands. They're all dressed in black, with tiny pops of red hearts.

"Good morning, the Alice," the Knave says, looking me over and then flicking her eyes to either twin with this awful, smug sort of expression, probably enjoying the fact their wings are not out.

"It'd be a better morning if this curse were broken," I say, pointing opposite hands at either twin so that my arms make a cross in front of my chest. "We're all on the same side here, so what say you?"

"I say your friends still have a lot to learn," she says, her brunette hair swept into a perfect bun, her tiny crown sitting pretty on top of her head. Her green eyes bore into me, and I know for a fact that this fancy dress she's spelling for the ball, we'll have to check it very carefully. The Knave wants me gone; I can see that plain as day. "Once I feel they've learned their lesson, I'll remove the spell."

"You mean once we bow down and kiss both your feet, and the King's?" Tee snaps, curling his lip up in a snarl. "I'll keep the curse."

"Suit yourself," the Knave purrs, giving us a venomous little smile. "Your people were offered two choices: come to heel, or die. They chose the latter. I see stupidity runs in your veins. Now, if you'll excuse—"

"Are you looking for the King?" I ask, taking a step

closer to her and noticing that both the Unicorn and the Lion are watching me with predator's eyes. Fuck, I don't like a single person in the Knave's little family. "Because after he kissed me, and we nearly fucked last night, he went to bed in my chambers." I smile, but the Knave's expression doesn't change. I do see a bit of the skin around her eyes tightening though.

I've pissed her off.

"He might still be in bed." I smirk and then turn to Dee first, wrapping my arms around his neck and kissing him hard. His wings unfold from his back in glorious swathes of black and blue feathers, the chains falling to the stone floor with the loud clang of metal. I feel something else, too, something I never noticed before: an loosening, an unleashing, an unraveling of power that explodes from Dee's body along with his wings.

His magic.

Without giving the Knave and her men a chance to walk away, I turn to Tee and I kiss him hard and fast in front of them, freeing his wings and his power to the scoffing dismay of the witch.

"I'm shocked the King lets you get away with such behavior," Ines clucks as I lean back and look into Tee's eyes, the lust and want and need playing out there making my toes curl inside my boots. "I doubt the Court of Hearts will allow you such trivialities."

She pushes between me and Tee, her lackeys … I mean *husbands* trailing along behind her.

"Fucking"—I start, looking for an insult that isn't inherently misogynistic—"butt waffle nipple licking asswad."

Tee raises an eyebrow at me, and then folds his wings around my body, holding me close.

"That was a creative insult," he says as he Dee pushes his way between Tee's wings, and slides his arms around my waist from behind. Being sandwiched between the two boys is a serious fucking turn-on for me, and I feel myself struggling to swallow past a surge of emotion.

"She deserves a creative ass-kicking," I whisper as the twins step back just enough to give me some space. And yet, the last thing I want to do is move out from between them.

"She does indeed," Dee says.

"Indeed," Tee repeats, but the way he's looking at me, I'm pretty damn sure he isn't thinking about the Knave anymore. Fuck her, right? I'm the Alice, so I should be able to (eventually) break the curse on the twins by myself.

"Why is the Alice called … well, the Alice?" I whisper, doing my best to change the subject. If I focus too much on the twins, and their glorious wings, their jewel-tone eyes, or their shockingly different but still amazing personalities, I'll probably collapse into a puddle on the floor.

"Because …" Tee chokes a little and takes another step

back from me, like he doesn't know what might happen between us if he stands too close. "It stands for *All Living Individuals Can Escape*. You are their escape from Underland, from the madness, from the remnants of the Riving." He turns his head and looks away for a moment.

"And you are *the* only one. You are not just Alice, or an Alice, you are *the* Alice." Dee puts his hands on my shoulders and kneads my flesh, sending warm tingles throughout my body.

It's not just because his touch makes my heart thunder —it's because I feel like he's right. Edith could've been the Alice, maybe, but now I *am* the Alice. This is *my* job.

Leaning forward, I let my breasts press against Tee's chest, and thread my arms around his neck.

"Allison," he says, almost like he's trying to warn me.

"What's in that room right there?" I whisper, pointing to the door behind him. Dee doesn't waste a single second in hurrying over to open it, letting us into a small library filled with the scent of paper and ink, that delicious old book smell that could turn me on even if I were soaking wet and on my period.

Add in the gorgeous twins with their beautiful wings?

I'm a goner.

The sound of whispering fills the room as Dee heels the door shut behind us.

"Do the books talk?" I ask, and I can't help it: I

whisper, too. With my arms still threaded around Tee's neck, I lift my head up and gaze at the bookshelves soaring above us. They must be at least thirty feet tall, if not taller. The room we're in is small, and pentagonal, but there must be tens of thousands of books in here, at least.

"Don't judge a book by its cover," Dee says, picking one up and flipping it open. "Judge by its pitch."

"A tale of knights so bold, so brave, they not only looked death in the face, they bent him over and fucked him in the ass with their swords."

Dee snaps the book closed and smiles at me.

"Holy fuck," I breathe, blinking stupidly at him over my shoulder before I turn back to Tee. "I'd read that. How come my Alice book doesn't talk?"

"It came from your world," Tee explains. Ah, that's right. There's no magic Topside. Nothing there but pain and suffering and rapists who walk out of court with smirks on their faces.

I'm struggling to remember why I wanted to ever go home in the first place. I mean, besides briefly to see my family. I *have* to see my family, but once I let them know I'm okay, I may never leave Underland again.

"You've convinced me," I say, letting go of Tee just enough that I lean back into Dee when he slides up behind me again. Just in case I haven't made it clear, I repeat myself. "I want to stay, Dee. I want to change the world."

The sound he makes from behind me, it's fucking priceless.

Releasing Tee, I turn around and put my hands on either side of Dee's face, leaning up on my tiptoes to kiss him. He beats me to it, dropping his face until our mouths are brushing together, until I can smell his clean air scent, feel his breath on my lips.

Our kiss starts slow and easy, almost languorous, but it quickly picks up speed.

My fingers tangle in Dee's jacket, and I drag him over to the chaise lounge, pushing him down onto it, and straddling his lap. When I grind my hips against him, I can feel his erection through his slacks.

I've never been on birth control because, as a point, I don't feel it's all a woman's responsibility to take it. There are much easier ways to deal with that, without having synthetic hormones coursing through my body: condoms, pull-out method, *male* birth control (about half the side effects, people), etc. But at least here, I don't seem to need it, at least not with North, Tee, or Dee.

Thank fuck, right?

Dee tangles his fingers in my hair, and I do the same to him, kissing him with all the pent-up emotion that's been coursing through me for the past few days. I'm surrounded by gorgeous men, and I'm resisting them at every turn when what I really want is to give in and let myself get swept up in the fantasy that's become my reality.

"Tee," I whisper, reluctantly breaking from Dee's lips for a moment, the only noise in the room the whisper of the books and the combined sounds of our heavy breathing. I look up at the elder of the two twins, and see a book slide off the shelf and flutter around like a butterfly, leaving gold sparkles in its wake.

Talk about a turn-on.

For a second there, I think Tee's going to run, but then he takes a step forward. And another, and another.

Tee climbs onto the couch behind me, sliding his palms over my rib cage and making me groan. When his hands reach the front of my body, he slides them up, palming my breasts through the pale blue, ruffled button-up I picked out for today.

He squeezes them gently at first, and then firmly, like he's decided for sure that he's doing this.

I lean back into him as Dee takes me by the hips and encourages me to move, grinding our bodies together in a way that's ridiculously pleasant, even with our clothes still on. Sliding my palms over Dee's shoulders, I find his wings and give his glossy feathers a sharp tug as we kiss.

Tee continues to caress and squeeze my breasts, finding my nipples through the fabric and squeezing them until I stop making any sounds that are remotely human.

Why didn't I wear a skirt today?! I think as Tee's left

hand comes down and starts to unbutton my pants. He makes an awkward sexual necessity into something sensual and exciting, sliding his hand inside and teasing the front of my heart-patterned panties.

"Three lovers entwined together in a weird, weird world," one of the books whispers as it crashes to the floor and opens onto a lewd ink drawing of a threesome.

How appropriate.

Dee moves his hands to my shirt, tearing open the fabric and sending buttons flying. He goes for my breasts next, popping the full, round mounds over the top of my corset and sliding his thumbs over my aching nipples.

I do the same to him, tearing his shirt open and teasing *his* nipples, making him buck his hips up against me while Tee utilizes his wings to brush and tease my now bare shoulders. Dee sweeps his up and around his brother, trapping the three of us in a feather cocoon.

Our hands and mouths explore and tease, work our bodies into wild frenzies. I can feel Tee hard and wanting behind me, grinding his hips into my ass as he teases my clit with his fingers, making me squirm and groan.

A book flutters past me as I sit up and start to shimmy out of my pants. I just want them off *now.*

Tee and Dee help me out, removing one leg first, and then the other. It's not the most acrobatic or sensual thing, and I certainly don't belong in a porno, but my awkward fumble ends with my pants *and* my underwear on the floor, and me feeling a hell of a lot happier about my current situation.

I scoot back slightly and help Dee out of his black denim jeans, freeing his cock from the confines of the fabric and taking him into my hand. My fingers curl around his shaft as he bucks up into my grip.

"Allison," Tee says in my left ear, "how do you want us?"

I'm not sure if I've ever heard a sexier question in my whole life. North's *"Mate with me?"* comes pretty close, but that's the only thing in the running.

I have to think for a moment because I've never been in a position quite like this before.

Two beautiful men, two glorious shafts.

Just … what do I do with them?

I've only tried anal sex once, and I hated it, but that was with Liam. Tee and Dee are different—and not just because they're fallen angels. No, these are *real* men. They care about how I feel, what I want, how they can pleasure me and not just themselves.

"I'd like to try …" I start, licking my lower lip. *Oh hell, Allison, if you can't even say it, you don't deserve to be having it.* "Having both of you at once."

There's a sound that Tee makes that travels straight to my core and floods me with vibrant waves of lust. He can't make that sound in my ear and not expect me to go crazy.

I lift myself up on my knees and gasp when Tee takes my hips, helping me guide his brother to my opening. I'm moaning and crying with pleasure before I've even taken all of him, putting my face in the crook of Dee's neck and breathing in his scent. His wings sweep around us again, this cocoon of safety that I just can't get over. It's too much, too amazing to be held in their wings like this.

Behind me, Tee kisses his way down the side of my neck, pausing to nibble at my shoulder. I get the weirdest thought then, of how I'd like to get each of them tattooed on my arm, an entire sleeve of Underland's most beautiful men.

Ink dreams aside, I settle down until Dee is fully sheathed inside of me, filling up all that empty space in my heart at the same time he fills my body. I feel happy and complete here with him and Tee; I trust them implicitly.

I know I shouldn't because I've only known them for two short weeks, but that doesn't matter. I'm riding the sex high in that moment, and I'm getting these waves of affection and feeling toward them that I've never experienced before.

"Touch me," I whisper as my eyes water. I'm not actually crying, but it just feels so damn good that my eyes are tearing up. "All over." The boys comply as I stare into Dee's half-lidded sapphire eyes and see his lips curve up in a cocky little smile.

"Your wish is our command," he purrs out, his voice this mix of playful and confident that I find irresistible. He's one of those people who's so full of emotion, they need to be unpacked on a regular basis. I feel an empathetic pang as I lean down to kiss him again, and he caresses the back of my neck with his fingers.

"Ditto," Tee whispers, sweeping hair off the side of my throat, so he can kiss me there again.

"Ditto, ditto," Dee growls as his brother fumbles with something behind me. When I look back, I see that he has some sort of lube bottle in his pocket, and raise my eyebrow.

"I—" Tee stutters, flushing red and then flattening his mouth out into a severe line. The expression is much less intimidating than it should be, considering he's got his cock in his hand. "This isn't what you think."

"Sure it's not," I say, but I don't care where he got lubricant or why.

I turn back to Dee, kissing him until his brother is ready, teasing a lubed finger down my ass crack and then stroking my opening. He caresses and plays with me until I'm warmed up and writhing, biting Dee's lower lip and wishing Tee would just put it in already.

When he does, there's this tiny, brief moment of pain where I'm convinced this position isn't going to work. But

Tee is so gentle and so careful that he works me up again, going nice and slow as I slide up and down on Dee's shaft.

"More," I grind out, sweating all over the poor boys and wondering if I still look sexy with blonde and rainbow strands of hair stuck to my forehead and cheeks. Dee reaches up and carefully peels some of it away, cupping the side of my face in his hand.

He locks eyes with me as his brother introduces a second finger, teasing that wall of flesh between my ass and my cunt. It feels *so fucking good.* I can barely even breathe.

"Allison-who-isn't-Alice," Dee breathes out, running his thumb over my lip. "Beautiful girl to change the world."

"Intelligent woman to win the war," Tee singsongs back, pulling his fingers out and putting the head of his shaft up against me. I wiggle back into him, but both he and Dee hold me in place and force me to keep it slow.

"Glorious angels to defend the queen," I say, and they both make these noises of acknowledgement. We're a team now, we got this.

Tee presses up against me, and then eases his shaft into my ass as my back arches, and I struggle to keep myself together.

I'm breaking apart in the most beautiful way; I'm

coming unhinged in glorious madness.

And all I want is more. More, more, more.

Once Tee is settled, there's this moment of perfect peace where both boys are sheathed inside of me, their cocks pressed tightly together with the thin wall of my flesh between them, a glorious twin sandwich that reminds me of my favorite books: The Kit Davenport series by Tate James.

Kit gets a twin sandwich and now, so do I.

"Fuck me?" I ask, but the twins respond in unison in the most twin-ly way possible.

"Fuck us?" they repeat in unison.

My body begins to move, but the twins can't seem to help themselves. They quickly take over, their fingers intertwined over my hips, their own hips thrusting in unison. Their shafts press tight against that sensitive bit of flesh I didn't even really know I had. I mean, logically, I always knew it was there, but who knew that pressure on either side of my vaginal wall would feel as good as a clitoral orgasm?

Dee takes over my breasts, leaving Tee to guide our movements as a group, thrusting hard against me. I can feel the strength in his hands and arms as he holds me and fucks me at the same time. These boys might be young, but they are fucking *strong*—physically and metaphysically.

I can't wait to see them kick some ass.

Dee's wings spread up and back all of a sudden, jostling all three of us. He arches his back and groans, squeezing my breasts so hard I might get bruises, but I don't think he means it. No, he just comes hard and fast, groaning and writhing with the pleasure as he spills himself inside of me.

My pussy is throbbing, my nipples hurt, and my brain feels like it might just explode if I don't get some release. It's like Tee can sense what I need—he always seems to—and his fingers find my clit, rubbing and teasing it with both my wetness and his brother's, making me come just as violently beautiful as Dee.

My fingernails dig into Dee's shoulders as I throw my head back, both twins sweeping their wings around me until I'm wrapped up in feathers and bliss, orgasming with a scream that echoes around the quiet, whispering library. I even drag Tee with me, making him grunt and pound harder until he finishes inside of my still throbbing body, the aftershocks squeezing my muscles around both twins' shafts until they can't take it anymore.

Tee rolls off and onto the floor while Dee very gently pushes me off of him.

For several moments, we just lie there and breathe.

There's—for lack of a better word—*fluid* all over the place, running down my thighs when I stand up.

"Do you think North will forgive us for being late?" I ask, but at that moment, I'm too happy to care.

"I think he'll have no choice," Tee says, and even

though he's lying on his back on the floor, he looks haughty and sexy as fuck. "*I* am the primary, so he better get used to it."

I grin, and press a kiss to Dee's lips first, and then Tee's.

Bring on the training, bring on the Knave, bring on the ball.

I'm Allison Liddell, and I have fucking got this.

♦ ♠ ♣ ♥ ♣ ♠ ♦

"My mate," North mutters as he opens a pistol of his own and loads it up with a small metal ball. It looks like a Kingmaker to me. I love that it's smaller and less impressive than a Queenmaker. In the human world, anything labeled queen is usually smaller and less important than the king version: beds, chess pieces, etc.

Underland is weird as hell, but it's refreshing, too.

"Mine," he growls, tail thrashing as he grits his teeth and turns to me. The White Knight is there, too, and she gives him a very unimpressed look.

"Your strange jabberwock possessiveness is entirely unappealing," she says with a sniff, lifting her chin and then glancing over at me. "And this is why I don't keep husbands. Too much work."

"It's simply in my nature to want the Alice to be mine," North says, flicking blonde hair off his forehead in a very dramatic and Duke-ly way. He takes his station very seriously, prancing around with his nose in the air and his gold eyes full of disdain. I sort of love him for it.

"Well, get over it," Chesh purrs, lying on the rafter above us, one arm hanging down, his finger drawing glowing gold designs in the air that disappear like fireflies in the wind. "Everyone knows a cat owns everything he sees."

"I thought Underland men were supposed to be different than Topside men? You all belong to *me*," I say, aiming the Queenmaker at the targets in the far distance. We're standing just outside the athletic facility, the back doors wide open, facing a stretch of beautiful green field as far as the eye can see.

There's a floral border on either side of the grass, separating this part of the royal gardens from the rest of the grounds. I can hear the flowers bitching about me right now.

"As likely to blow 'er head off as the Carpenter's," one says, her accent reminding me of every generic peasant character I've ever seen in a cheap budget fantasy movie. *"Maybe she should aim for the Walrus', eh? At least he's got more to shoot at!"*

"Won't last a minute against the Anti-Alice," a lily replies, flicking her leaves in my direction. *"We're liable to lose the Kingdom of Hearts to the clubs."* I turn and

point the Queenmaker in her direction. I would blow us all to kingdom come if I were to shoot at this close a range, but at least I see the stupid flower quiver, and the pixie spirit jumps to a blossom several feet away from me.

Another one of the stupid things tries to pull my room key from my pocket, and I slap it away, watching its translucent wings as it flitters over to a daisy and slips inside. This is my first time actually seeing the pixies, and I'm surprised to find that they really do look like fucking Tinkerbell or some shit, albeit with brightly hued skin in every color of the rainbow.

They are also naked as fuck, and I swear I've seen enough pixie pussy in the last five minutes to last me a lifetime.

"The Queenmaker uses your magic," Tee explains as Chesh shifts into cat form and hops off the wooden beam under the awning and onto my head. About two hundred yards out, there are nine silver bowls gleaming in the sunlight. North and the twins claim they'll help absorb the blasts from the Queenmaker, so I don't destroy the entire castle while I'm still learning. "That's what makes it so powerful; it's more than just gunpowder and sulfur."

"How did I just randomly pick this off a shelf in the Rabbit-Hole?" I ask, but nobody bothers to answer me with actual words.

Instead, Dee claps his heels together, salutes, and recites

another verse from the prophecy that never ends. How many fucking stanzas is this thing?! My guess, based on personal experience here in Underland, is that it has eighteen, just like the original *The Walrus and the Carpenter* poem.

"The Gryphon and the Mock Turtle
Watched on from perches far,
And then they contemplated hell
On kingdoms so bizarre:
The Queenmaker their only hope
Against a ragged scar."

Dee finishes with a little bow, and a grin.

"Prophecy, Allison-who-isn't-Alice-but-whom-I-quite-adore." He winks at me as I flush and turn back to the targets, watching as the White Knight loads up a gun that matches her armor. It looks like a flintlock pistol as well, but it's all white, like it's been carved of marble or something.

Apparently, it's called a *Knightmaker*. Very creative, huh? I do appreciate the theme, however.

"So I was destined to hold this weapon in my hands?" I ask, teasing my fingers along the gold designs on the side. I lift my eyes to look up at Dee, and he smiles softly.

"You were destined," he says, but I don't fully believe him. I think people can create their own destinies. Then again, maybe there's magic at work here, as a guiding hand or something? I can't help but think how I was compelled to follow the White Rabbit down the hole, or how I keep saying things that are straight out of the original book without even meaning to. It's like there's some grand storyteller in the sky, trying to guide my fate.

If there is, she better fuck off, because I have ideas of my own.

"What's your name?" I ask the White Knight, because everyone here seems to have a nickname, even me. In fact, I have several: the Alice, Allison-who-isn't-Alice, Sonny, Sunshine, Miss Alice, Miss Liddell, and so on and so forth.

"My name?" the White Knight repeats, blinking pretty lavender eyes at me. She tosses some blonde hair over her shoulder, and it shimmers in the sunshine like it's spun gold. Seriously, she must be the most beautiful woman I've ever seen in my life. "Chevalier." She smiles at me like she thinks I have no idea what that means in French. It means *knight*, by the way. I took like two years of classes at my high school.

"Is your last name *Blanc*?" I question with a raised brow, and the White Knight grins. So the White Knight's name … is literally *Chevalier Blanc,* aka White Knight in French. Very creative, almost as creative as calling the Cheshire Cat,

Chesh.

"The King wants to make sure you're actually learning something down here," she states in crisp, clear tones, no judgement, just fact. "And he knows I'm the best woman for the job."

"You're an inventor?" I ask as North steps up close behind me, and makes me entire body tingle as he adjusts my grip on the gun, putting my fingers in the same place that Dee did. Having a second teacher repeat the same lessons I learned before is helpful in cementing them into my brain.

"That's right," the White Knight says, lifting up her gun with one hand and putting on a very dramatic sideways pose with her left arm outstretched. She fires off a shot that lobs up toward the sky and then falls perfectly down into the center of one of the metal bowls, slamming into the bull's-eye with a horrific wave of fire and heat. "Bam," she growls, lifting her pistol to her lips and blowing on it. "I'm a knight by day, inventor by night. Ironic, isn't it? It feels as if I should be a knight by night, and inventor by day perhaps?" She tilts her head to one side in that weird Underland way.

More nonsensical logic.

Fantastic.

"How are you enjoying your breastplate of courage?" she asks, making me feel a little warm and fuzzy inside.

You know when you read a book, and the female main character only has meaningful relationships with men, and you're left wondering why the fuck all her interactions with women are hateful and gross?

Yeah, I despise that shit.

I just want to … go get my nails done with the White Knight or something.

I *like* her.

"Breastplate of Courage?" I ask, lifting a brow as North steps to the right of me, takes aim and fires his own shot off. He, too, hits the silver target, but not the bull's-eye. The White Knight grins and he growls at her, thrashing his tail around wildly.

"I didn't just invent those easy-on/easy-off buckles," Chevalier declares proudly, tapping at her shoulders. "I imbued the armor with courage. If you put it on, you'll feel like a wolf amongst sheep."

"Huh," I say, taking aim with the Queenmaker and doing my best to hold her steady in both hands. "Do you think I can wear it to the ball over my dress? Because dragons that make my ears bleed and birds that shoot spider silk are okay, but dancing in front of other people sounds like pure hell."

"I think wearing it would be a great idea," Tee says, the warm sound of his voice making me tremble just enough that when I fire, the metal projectile goes wide, a miniature cannonball flinging through the air toward the row of flowers.

Pixies scream and flee their garden as North waves his hand, and with a bit of magic, sends the projectile into one of the targets where it explodes with enough force to singe the hairs on my arm.

Holy fucking hearts.

Dee moves over to a small table near the wall where a gramophone sits, spins the handle on the side, and then carefully removes a record from a sleeve sitting on a shelf full of others. He places the needle carefully onto it, and then steps back as it begins to crackle.

Some vintage, twenties sounding song starts to garble out.

One thing I would miss living here: fucking Spotify and iTunes.

I still have my cellphone … somewhere. I should dig it out and see if I can't get it to play some modern day music for these boys.

"Sorry, I was distracted," I say as Chesh weaves between my legs, rubbing on my ankles as the White Knight moves over to help me reload the Queenmaker.

"The sound of your lover's voice," she begins, and I blush. I'm still a tad sore downstairs, and every movement I make reminds me of my threesome with the twins. I won't soon forget. "Is nothing compared to the chaos that will ensue during battle."

The Cheshire cat shifts back into his human form beside me, as gloriously half-dressed as always, and stares at me from big, gray eyes.

"If you need to keep your calm during battle, simply repeat this mantra inside your head. It'll keep you focused," he purrs as Chevalier once again fixes my grip. I will get this, eventually. I'm not doing too shabby considering I've never shot a vintage, magical flintlock pistol before last week, right? "Ahem." The Cheshire cat clears his throat, licks his paw, and runs it over his dark hair and his striped ears, making the silver hoops in them jingle merrily. "As it goes:

'Twas brillig, and the slithy toves
Did gyre and gimble in the wabe:
All mimsy were the borogoves,
And the mome raths outgrabe."

Chesh pauses for a moment and smiles at me with that feral cat grin of his.

"Beware the Jabberwock, my girl!
The jaws that bite, the claws that catch!
Beware the Jubjub bird, and shun,
The frumious Bandersnatch!"

I raise my eyebrows as North growls from behind me, and I hear an icy voice at my back.

"Frumious?" Rab drawls, smoking a cigarette and swinging a pocket watch at his side. He's dressed in red and white today, no black. It makes his red eyes and dark hair pop even more. "How *daaare* you?"

Rab pauses next to me, and nods with his chin in the direction of the targets.

"You're already late for your dancing lessons with the Caterpillar," he says, that cold voice doing more to warm up my insides than it rightfully should. "So let's see what you can do with that thing and get going."

"I've barely gotten time to practice," I grumble, but I suppose that's my own fault. Mine and the twins', that is.

I glance over at Rab, his eyes ringed in dark liner, his smile a dangerous sort of pretty that kills happy hearts and makes them wish they had a million lives so they could die over and over again.

So not a guy I should be going after.

And yet …

Rab is so freaking distracting that I have to tear my eyes away from him and actually start to mumble the cat's stupid, catchy little *Jabberwocky* poem.

"Twas brillig, and the slithy toves," I grumble.

I smirk, take aim, and fire off a second shot.

This time, I hit the center target … *and* the bull's-eye.

When I leave the athletic facility and head for the ballroom, I realize that I'm actually looking forward to my lessons with Lar.

"I get an entourage today?" I ask, because Chesh, Rab, North, and the twins are all with me right now.

"You get an entourage the rest of the week," Rab says, glancing over at the Duke like they know something nobody else does. We pass under glass ceilings and glorious arches, past huge doorways that lead to Hearts only knows where. Card servants are everywhere, scurrying around like ants. I can barely stand to look at them, and based on the twins' reactions, I think they feel the same. "The castle is restless. Everyone wants to meet you. And, to be quite frank, several of them want to murder you. Personally, I'll settle for fucking you. What do you say?"

"I say … eat a dick?" I reply with saccharine sweetness as I flip him off.

When we head into the ballroom, the Caterpillar is already waiting for us, sitting on a big blue velvet pillow in the center of the room. He has his white jacket with the gold epaulettes resting on his shoulders, but there's no shirt underneath, showing off his glorious chest and those two key piercings through his nipples.

Don't think about the sex prophecy he showed you, I warn myself. *Don't think about it, Alice. Don't, don't, don't.*

Aaaaannddddd, now I'm thinking about it.

In detail.

Glorious, glorious detail.

"Welcome," Lar says, his eyes half-lidded, the color of a summer sky. He gestures for us to take seats on the colored pillows surrounding his, passing the hookah he's smoking over to me.

"Are we going to dance in the air again?" I ask, and I get this lazy, confident smile in return.

"We're going to dance the quintrille," he says, which is not really an answer to my question. "Although … we're a bit short on dancers."

I notice there are more pillows on the ground than people.

As in, say, ten total pillows including the one I'm sitting on.

Hmm.

The ballroom doors swing open, and I glance over my shoulder to find the Mad Hatter and the March Hare sauntering into the room with Dor on their heels.

"Oh *heeeeelllllll* no," I say, letting go of the hookah and standing up. The air is perfumed with the sweet scent of blueberries and tobacco, but as much as I want to experience that glorious feeling of floating and dancing, I will not put up with the Dormouse.

I mean, Raiden Walker and March are bad enough, but the Dormouse dick basically clobbered a chunk of North's skull out—and he'd happily do it again.

"I will not dance with him," I say as the big, ugly man scowls at me and scratches as his tiny, stupid mouse ears. They're so little and they blend in with his brown hair, I can't even remember if I've seen them before.

"Fortunately for you," the Mad Hatter says, whipping off his hat. A swarm of bats—yes, you heard me, a *swarm of bats*—explodes out from underneath, swirling in the air around him and then taking off for the domed glass ceiling, chittering as they go. "You won't be dancing with Dor tonight."

Raiden pulls his cane out, and taps it against the floor before replacing his hat and smiling at me with sharp, white vampire fangs. I'm too freaking dumbfounded to speak. Bats. Fucking bats. Now I really *have* seen it all.

"Then who's taking the place of this last pillow?" I ask indignantly, pointing down at the red velvet cushion on the floor.

"Me." The serene calm in that voice draws my attention over to Brennin Red, standing in the doorway to the ballroom with the White Knight on one side, and the Knave on the other. *Grrreeaaat,* exactly the woman I wanted to see.

She has her two weird husbands behind her, too, and I'm pretty sure all three of them are glaring at me.

Red walks his supreme asshole-ish-ness over to me, his dark eyes hard, his crown drooping lazily over his forehead. His white gloves squeak as he reaches up and adjusts the gold hook and eye clasp that holds his voluminous white and red robes in place.

"You'll be expected to dance with me at the ball, so we may as well see what clumsiness we can iron out today."

"I'd rather dance with Dor," I say, but I don't mean it. My palms are sweating, and I can't take my eyes off the King's. He makes my throat feel tight and sticky and sore, my heart thunder, my fingers twitch. I want him dead, but I also want to leap into bed with him. I've never been so confused about my own feelings before.

"Is that so?" Brennin asks coolly, eyeing me up and down like a steak served too well-done. He'd rather just send me back and get a new slab of fresh meat for his plate. "Well, too bad. That brainless thug isn't the ruler of an entire kingdom—*I am*. And as my future queen, the court will want to see you dance with me."

"I am not your future queen," I snap back, hating myself for having made out with this guy. Shit, more than made out: I practically fucked him. I turn away and run my fingers through my hair, making eye contact with

March.

He sucks on a very ... shall we say *phallic*-shaped lollipop, and gives me this dirty half-smile that promises awful, awful things.

"Lackey piece of shit," I grumble as I sit back down on the velvet pillow and take the hookah from Lar, letting his pale fingers tangle with mine, just so I can feel that little thrill between us. "Whatever. I don't have time to argue. Let's just get this over with, shall we? After the ball, we'll figure out how to deal with each other."

I can *feel* the King staring at me from behind. His eyes are like lasers, making me squirm with their heat. Fucker.

Deep down, there's some part of me that's *thrilled* at the idea of being the Queen of Hearts. What little girl wouldn't jump at the thought of not only visiting their favorite childhood storybook world, but *ruling it*.

"Maybe we can get married, and just not talk?" I glance over my shoulder and find Brennin Red still staring at me. The Knave's mouth is turned down at both corners, and I just know I'm going to trip and fall on my ass because she's here staring at me. Thus, the story of my life. "Then I can be the Queen of Hearts, your little prophecy will be fulfilled, and then we can just never speak again?"

"Mm," Lar murmurs, and when I glance over at him, I catch him watching me with that half-lidded stare. I get the feeling there's something he's not telling me. Another prophecy? I wouldn't be surprised.

"Your lack of interest in our glorious King of Hearts is disturbing to me," the Knave purrs, her voice like velvet and sandpaper. There's a painful softness to it that makes my teeth hurt. "And what's disturbing to me is disturbing to the court."

"That's quite enough of that," the King says, and when I glance over my shoulder again, I get caught in that ebon stare, and find it impossible to take another breath. "You were invited to observe, not to talk."

The look on the Knave's face is *priceless.* The Lion—I can't remember if he's Rook or Knight—takes a step forward, but Ines reaches out and puts a hand on his shoulder. The three of them move over to a seating area filled with tufted chairs in red and white, sitting their black-clad asses down on the cushions. They look like they're on their way to a freaking funeral.

I turn back to Lar and accept the hookah again, pulling in a long, smoky breath of tobacco and flowers, teased through with the fruity freshness of blueberries. Already, I can feel that lightness in my skull, as if I'm starting to float.

"Let's get to this, shall we?" March says, his accent thick and sexy as hell. He looks like a model, lounging there in an unbuttoned white shirt, the sleeves pushed up, a small top hat on his own head. He's still eating—do I ever see him *not* eating?—sucking the lollipop between his lips in a very suggestive sort of way. "The Alice and I have an appointment in the dungeon."

"And you're already late," Rab says, checking one of his tattoos. "I don't see how we're going to be ready for the ball. If everything went smoothly—and I mean *everything*—we'll be lucky to get out of there with a disdainful approval from the court. But I can hardly imagine getting through the evening without bloodshed and substantial crimson splatter."

"Why is it you sound so fucking excited about that?" I ask, passing the hookah around the circle. Brennin Red finally sits down on the side opposite the Hatter, two titans in one room. I have this feeling they're being civil for *now.* But their relationship is like a powder keg ready to explode. I'm desperate to know what they were up to in the study, with that blood on the King's neck and Raiden's mouth. Clearly, the vampire was drinking from the King, but why? And why did Red let him?

"Oh, I love blood and bones," Rab says, rolling his head in a circle and blinking those disturbingly beautiful eyes at me. "Snacking on assholes feeds my soul."

"You'll get a chance to eat at the ball, I'm most certain," the King says, his voice that disturbing eerie calm I was so awed by when we first met. I've seen his temper though, and it's mighty. I've also seen his self-control crumble away, when he pinned me to the wall and kissed the fuck out of me.

The way he's staring at the floor though, I get that there's something else going on inside these castle walls. Internal politics. Gross. I've never liked politics. As far as I'm concerned, republicans and democrats … douchebags and turd sandwiches.

"Well, I hope so," March says, drawing Rab's attention over to him. "Because it's been a while since I've popped someone's head from their shoulders. It comes right off, just like a bloody grape."

"Don't you dare steal my kills, or I shan't ever fucking forgive you," Rab says, as Tee rolls his eyes, meeting mine from across the circle.

"Can we get on with this?" Chesh purrs, sitting with one knee propped up, his elbow resting atop it. "I've got rodents to kill, a hairball to choke up, and an Alice to woo."

"Please don't put *hairball* and *woo* into the same sentence," I say as the hookah finally makes its way back to the Caterpillar.

"*Purrrr-lease* make me part of your harem, Alice?" Chesh yowls, flopping onto his side and pawing at the air with tattooed hands.

"Insufferable beast," the King grinds out, as North slaps his tail against the floor and then grabs Chesh by the collar, making him sit upright like the rest of us.

What a ragtag group of men, I think as I glance from Raiden Walker to Tweedledee. *What am I going to do with them all?*

"So," Lar says, his quiet, commanding voice drawing a close to all of the nonsense. "The quintrille. Alice, do you know why it's called that?"

"Uh, no clue," I say as he gives me this calm, easy sort of smile. He draws designs in the air with his fingers, and the blue-gray smoke from the hookah forms into a little, smiling crocodile.

"Because it requires five couples," he explains. "As opposed to the quadrille which requires four."

"Quint and quad, got it," I say, giving him a salute without even thinking about it. My cheeks flush and Dee grins at me from across the circle, his wings framing his beautiful face. I've been around the guy for a handful of weeks and already, I'm picking up his habits. "Five couples, ten people, the prophecy?" I continue, cocking a brow.

Everything in this damn world revolves around the prophecy.

"Ten people," Lar says, standing up and handing off the hookah to a card servant. There are a few of them scattered around the room, staring at us with dead, ink-drawn eyes. A few others approach as the men stand up, removing the pillows as Lar slowly unfolds his right arm, holding his hand out to me. "Five couples. Come, Sunshine, and we will dance."

I take his hand as the boys pair up around me.

Tee and Dee; Chesh and North; March and Raiden; the King and Rab.

Lar leads us into the center of the ballroom, positioning us over a gold medallion inscribed with small designs. They make a story around the circle, with a much larger design in the center. I don't have time to examine it at the moment, but it looks interesting.

The Caterpillar leans in, putting his mouth against my ear, overwhelming me with his scent.

"Pretend I'm the King," he says, but I'd rather not. I get that I'll be dancing with Brennin Red at the ball, but I'd much rather dance with Lar right now. "You'll start in the center of the room, with everyone else around you."

He places my hand on his shoulder, and curls his fingers around my other. We stand tall and straight and proud, staring into one another's eyes.

"The other couples will approach the circle, turn to one another, bow." Lar nods his chin, and one of the card servants starts up the gramophone. "And then they'll turn to their right, and bow again."

The music gurgles out of the old machine, a cheery marching band sort of sound with trumpets and a piano.

Lar and I wait, poised like statues as the King and Rab waltz forward to meet March and Raiden, weaving around us and clasping hands as they pass. When they get to the opposite side of the circle, the King puts his hand on Rab's lower back and they spin in a circle, coming to face us again. They do the same moves one more time before clasping arms and parading around us.

I'm happy standing right here, not doing any of the actual dancing.

"How long does this part take?" I whisper as the same two pairs move forward and switch partners; the Hatter ends up with the King, while March and Rab wind up together.

Oh.

The plot thickens.

"You'll see," Lar says, tilting his head to the side, his beautiful hair feathering across his face, his earrings dancing in that strange supernatural wind that seems to follow him around. He, too, has an aristocratic air, and I can't help but wonder if he's some sort of fae prince. It would only stand to reason, considering Tee and Dee. But who knows? In Underland, anything is possible.

The other two couples switch partners as well, and then repeat the first set of movements, doing what the King and Co. did in reverse.

"Now, we dance," the Caterpillar says, turning us in a circle, sliding his hand to my lower back, and then galloping us around the circle of men. I can feel all their eyes on me, watching me, studying me. I've never had so many guys interested in me before; it's fucking weird.

Some part of me can't be happy about it though, because it feels like most of them are after the Alice and most definitely *not* Allison.

Except … not the twins, or North, maybe not even the cat.

Lar, he's hard to read. I study his face as we weave in and out of the four other couples, our feet slowly rising off the ground as we go. My heart stutters a bit, half from fear, half from excitement as the ballroom slowly falls away.

My dance partner opens his wings, these two glorious glittering swathes of color and magic. They glow blue, the edges ruffling in the breeze. It jangles the bracelets on his arms, his earrings, teases his nipple piercings. The coat, despite not actually being on his arms, sits pretty on his shoulders, the gold fringe and epaulettes catching the wind.

God, I hate heights, but holy shit I love this, I think as we dance, Lar adjusting our arms until they're hooked at the elbow, and spinning us in a circle. What girl doesn't want to fly, after all.

The other men are floating, too, but not as high as we are, not until Lar spins me one more time and releases me. He pauses for a brief moment, wings flapping softly, as he adjusts my arms so that one is behind my back, the other held to the side, bent at the elbow, with my palm up.

He bows and sinks down a few feet, switching places with the Hatter.

Fantastic.

"Hello, *Alice*," he says, grabbing my outstretched hand and bringing it to his lips for a kiss. I shiver, but not in an unpleasant way, letting him parade me around in a circle.

The sky outside is darkening, but I do not miss that giant ass bat landing on an arch and peering in at us with eyes as dark as the King's.

"Your pet is staring at us," I say as Raiden raises an eyebrow and marches us around in the air. A small bat peeks out from under his hat and takes off, perching itself upside down from a decorative rose carved into the golden arches of the ballroom.

"Is that so?" he asks, not even bothering to look in the creature's direction. "Does she bother you?"

"No," I say, feeling far less comfortable all the way up here with Raiden than I did with Lar. Not only does the Caterpillar have wings, but he's just generally a much nicer guy. "I don't like heights, that's it. I don't have a problem with bats."

I stumble over my own foot, an odd sensation floating that high up in the air, but the Mad Hatter catches me and keeps me upright, his tattooed fingers curled around my arms. His marmalade colored eyes are so intense, all I want to do is look away. And yet, I can't bring myself to do it.

"How did you get here anyway?" I ask, licking my lower lip and trying my best to keep my gaze neutral and focused. "To Underland, I mean. You're from Topside, aren't you?"

"Not everyone that falls down the Rabbit-Hole is an Alice," he breathes, spinning me around and then stepping back. Before I get a chance to probe him further, the King is taking his place, and I groan.

"Try not to act so thrilled," Brennin grinds out, his stupid crown reflecting back the chandeliers' lights as they flicker and dance along with us.

"Don't worry: that shouldn't be hard," I quip as the music changes to this slow, strange drawling song with a heavy bass and a chorus of snapping fingers, like some jazz lounge special performance.

"What's all this talk of marriage?" he says, his eyes like shards of onyx. "I thought you wanted to go home?"

"You clearly don't listen to a damn thing I say: I want to be able to go home and come back at will. That's what I want. Free will. Ever heard of it?"

Brennin tightens his lips at my words, but he doesn't stop dancing. I realize that North and Tee were right: he's as good as Lar. Raiden was a decent dancer, but I had to think about the steps with him. With the King, it comes naturally.

We stop talking then, and with the arrival of silence comes that awful, aching tension.

My body *wants* the goddamn King, and I don't know how to make it stop.

"Your Majesty." A female voice rings out, and I glance down to find the Knave with her head tilted in our direction, the White Knight at her side. "We have a problem."

With a growl, Brennin Red scoops me up in his arms. I let out a small squeak, but I'm all the way up in the fucking air, so I thread my fingers together against the back of his neck as we drift toward the floor. Without meaning to, I play with the fine red hairs at the base of his scalp, and feel my heart skip a few beats.

"What is it?" he asks, setting me down and stepping away in a swirl of robes.

The White Knight cups her hand around the King's ear, and I see him stiffen.

He glances back at me, slides his eyes down my body and makes me feel like I've just been dipped in warm honey. When they flick back to my face, I know I'm in serious trouble.

This thing between Brennin Red and me, it's going to come to a head at some point.

"Continue with the lessons," Red says, snapping his fingers. The White Knight steps forward and offers me a cheeky smile and a little bow, stepping in to take the King's place. I wish I wasn't sorry to see him go.

But I am.

Fuck.

He moves across the marble floors with the Knave and her minions falling into step behind him.

"Interesting," Raiden purrs, exchanging a look with March. "Very interesting."

"Keep your filthy nose out of the King's business," North snarls, getting between the two mercenaries and his ruler's retreating back.

"The King's business?" Raiden asks, tapping the brim of his hat in thought. "But the King's business is now my business. We're soon-to-be husbands-at-arms."

"Over my dead body," I grumble, but I'm not about to get into it with them right now. I cross my arms over my chest as the Duke stares down the Hatter. Near the ballroom entrance, the Dormouse stirs, cracking his knuckles and stretching his neck from side to side in a particularly menacing way.

If he goes for North, I swear, I'll unleash some of my special Alice magic on his ass.

"Boys," I say, stepping between them before things can heat up. The last thing I need is a jabberwocky/vampire battle in the ballroom. "When am I going to start training to use my magic?"

"Once we've dealt with the Anti-Alice," North says,

but my change of subject isn't working. He's not even looking at me.

"After the Torrid Tea Party," the Mad Hatter says, finally turning to look at me. "I'll show you how to use your magic."

"The Torrid Tea Party?" I ask, blinking stupidly as the other men gather around us. "Is this one of the 'Hatter's famous parties'?" I make little quotes with my fingers.

I get a saucy vampire smile in response.

"Oh, most certainly."

"And when is this supposed party taking place?" I ask as March lifts up his top hat and extracts a new lollipop, this one in the shape of a knife.

"The night before the ball," Raiden says, smirking and looking stupidly delicious as he goes about it. Bad guys are not supposed to be attractive. They're supposed to wear dark robes, smell like old cheese, and cackle from the shadows. "I have to know who I can trust."

"And how would a tea party help with that?" I ask as Dor moves up to stand beside his boss in a very threatening sort of way. North reacts, black scaly wings exploding from his back as he takes a step forward.

I leap between the two of them and put my hands on the sides of his face, kissing him hard and fierce, a tangle of tongues that he accepts with carnal desperation. His hands are all over me, his wings wrapped around us, his tail squeezing my ankle.

"If I weren't a civilized monster …" he snarls against my mouth, and I find myself melting against him. "I'd throw you to the floor and fuck you right here in front of the rest of these morons."

"Oh god, don't say that," I breathe, my body throbbing in response to his words. "I might just take you up on that."

"When I get agitated, I need to mate," he growls, nuzzling at my hair. I wrap my arms around him and sigh, knowing that everyone else is staring at us. Frankly, I just don't give two fucks. "It calms me down."

"Oh, I see how it is," I whisper, but North tucks his wings back behind him and looks me over.

"I can wait though," he says with this devilish expression on his face, his big black horns curving wickedly up from his gold hair. "Tonight, we'll mate in the Suit of Hearts."

"Thank you for announcing that to the whole world," I say, feeling a blush color my cheeks as the White Knight chuckles at me, and the Dormouse scowls. I hope he gets hit by a brick and dies. Freak accidents happen, you know.

"Shall we continue?" Lar says, appearing beside us and holding out a hand.

"We shall," March replies from behind me. "Enjoy

your dancing, because in about, oh, an hour or so … I'm going to fucking poison you."

The dungeon is as clichéd as my future ball.

It's down a spiral stone staircase, and it's cold, damp, and scary as shit.

"This is beyond creepy," I say as the twins escort me past flickering torches and down into the bowels of Underland. The March Hare is walking just ahead of us, but I can see his brown ears swiveling to listen to our conversation.

"The former King of Hearts used to keep prisoners down here," Tee says, and there's something incredibly melancholic about the way he phrases that. I wonder if any angels were locked up here previously? "The current king just curses them into card servants or sends them to the guillotine."

Tee pushes purple-streaked black hair off his forehead and casts his jewel-toned eyes in my direction. I can't tell if he's relieved or upset by what he's just said.

"They say the stones have absorbed the screams of the wicked over the years," Dee whispers, keeping his wings tucked in close and refusing to touch the stone walls if he can help himself.

"Nonsense," Tee scoffs, and Dee rolls his eyes.

"Contrariwise, it makes perfect sense. Locations absorb trauma, that's common knowledge."

"It's common nonsense," his brother quips back, and I smile. I love their interactions. It makes me miss Fred a little, but in a good way, floods me with happy memories. Oh, Fred. Being here in Underland, that trauma seems so far away, but I know I'm not over it, not even close. Does a person ever really get over losing a loved one? Or does the pain just crouch deep inside the soul, waiting for the worst possible moment to pop out and shout *peekaboo!*

"I've set up a little *la-bohr-uh-tory* for myself down here," March drawls, stretching out the word laboratory while he sucks on his knife-shaped lollipop. He pushes open a door at the bottom of the stairs and welcomes us in with a flourish.

"What did you mean about poisoning me?" I ask as I step inside and notice the various jars filled with colored fluids, the beakers, the tiny pots with handwritten labels.

"I'm going to start you on a series of poison-pricks, so we can build your immunity to the most common ones." March moves over to a table covered in knives and picks through them, setting one aside. It has a purple edge that glows faintly, warming up the dark space with each pulse of light.

Creepy.

"I don't like this at all," Tee growls as Dee exhales and

rolls up his sleeves.

"Which is why I'm going to test the poison *first*," Dee says as his brother raises his brows. "Dear brother, you are the heir to our people's throne. And she"—he casts me a sly look—"she is the Alice. Please, allow me." Dee sits down on one of the stools as March shrugs out of his velvet trench coat, turning to face us. I can't help but stare at the bare expanse of mocha colored skin showing between the two unbuttoned sides of his white shirt.

He, too, rolls up his sleeves, revealing two, thick muscular arms.

Thief, poison expert, Hatter's lackey, shapeshifter.

That's all I know about the March Hare—stupid facts. I have no idea who he actually is as a person, and I'm not sure I care to. He and the Hatter are, for lack of a better word, dickheads.

"Eventually we'll move onto mixing poisons, but this'll do for now."

"What are your other forms?" I ask, crossing my arms over my chest and glancing around at the old prison cells on either side of us. They still have their rusted gates, separating off these tiny cubicles that I can't imagine could even fit a twin bed inside. The people that were kept here, they suffered—*greatly*. "If you're going to poke and prod and stab me, I have a right to know a little more about you."

"Oh, Alice-Doll," March says, his chocolate-colored hair

cut short into a neat, polished style, like a model. The longer hair on the top of his scalp is slicked back and hidden partially beneath his purple top hat. I notice he never wears a larger hat than his boss. "I imagine when we bed each other, it'll be a lot less violent than all that. Nobody wants to be poked or prodded or stabbed with a cock. It's all about the thrust."

"I meant the needles ," I snarl, narrowing my eyes as I point at the collection of shiny, sharp objects on the table beside me. Apparently, this is going to be like those allergy tests at the doctor, the ones where they poke your skin with tiny needles tipped in allergens. Hopefully, I don't die down here. That'd suck. "You know what I meant. I know you can shift into a bandersnatch. What else?"

"You're a pushy little Alice, aren't you?" he murmurs, his brown eyes twinkling.

"Can we just get this over with, so we can move on?" Tee snaps. "If the King hadn't personally ordered us down here, we wouldn't be here. And if anything—and I mean *anything*—happens to Allison, I'll kill you myself."

"Oh?" March asks, and then he throws back his head with a chortling laugh. His ears, on either side of his top hat, twitch. "Glorious. I'd love to see which of us would win in a fight. I might bet against myself, to be quite honest with you." March stands up and moves next to me, a good foot fucking taller. I have to crane my neck to look up at him. "Would you believe me if I told you I could shape-change into a *slithy tove*?"

"What the fuck is a *slithy tove*?'" I snort, vaguely recognizing the words from the original *Jabberwocky* poem, the one that Chesh recited for me earlier to keep my head calm. I've been sing-songing it in the back of my mind all day now. I'm not sure how calming it is, but it's certainly catchy.

"A tove is a … sort of like a Pegasus," Tee explains as my eyes open wide in disbelief.

"Okay, sure …" I start, but March is already laughing at me, and I can't decide if he's telling the truth or not. "So can you really turn into the Mad Hatter?"

Well, now, *that* stops him dead.

He pauses with his hands on a bottle marked … well, *Poison* before turning to look at me. He tries to hide his surprise with a smarmy smirk, but I can see it. I've well and truly shocked him.

"Where would you get a ridiculous idea like that?" he says, but his voice is too casual while his shoulders are too tense.

The Caterpillar was right.

I smirk back, because even if I have no idea if he's telling the truth above the *tove*, I know at least this much is true.

"None of your damn business," I ooze, enjoying my

temporary feeling of superiority and smugness. It’s not often one gets the jump on a mercenary bastard asshole. “How many poisons are we testing today?" I ask as I take a seat on the stool next to Dee; he immediately starts up a game of footsie with me. Cheeky bastard. It lightens the mood in that dreary dungeon with its long hallway, its straw-filled cells, and the light but persistent reek of sweat and urine.

"Just a handful," March says, dipping a tiny needle into the bottle, and then turning to face me. "Don't want to overwhelm your fragile system, Doll. Now, arm." He gestures with his fingers, and I sigh, removing my red and black military coat and pushing up the sleeve of my button-up.

The Vorpal Blade is strapped to my thigh, the Queenmaker is on my hip, and I'm wearing the corset filled with knives. I have to say, I feel like kind of a badass.

"Me first," Dee says, gesturing with his own arm.

March obliges him, cleaning Dee’s skin with alcohol, and then poking just the tiniest prick into the pale flesh of Dee's underarm. He tosses the needle and readies a new one while the twins and I wait in tense silence. I think we're all half-convinced that Dee's going to keel over at any given moment.

Fortunately, several pass and nothing happens.

"Oh give me some credit where credit is due," March says as Tee very carefully watches him poison a new needle. "Killing the Alice in the King's castle with two angels to face off against, knowing my boss is eventually going to hunt me down and kill me, while I've already pissed off the King of Clubs with no way to go running back. Must think I'm bloody daft, eh?"

He moves over to me, running his fingers up my arm. I swallow hard, but I refuse to let him see that he's having any effect on me. March carefully pushes my sleeve up a little further, running his thumb over the pulse in my elbow. He swabs my arm in slow, lazy circles with a cotton swab, the sharp sting of alcohol teasing my nostrils. And when I say alcohol, I don't mean rubbing alcohol—I mean, like, fucking *whiskey.*

"You look like Rob Evans," I blurt, and March raises an eyebrow just before he pricks me. There's something weirdly intimate about that moment that I don't like, and I jerk my arm out of his grip, cradling it against my chest.

"Who?" he quips, sounding a bit like an owl.

"A model from Topside," I murmur, rubbing at the sore spot. I feel a little tingle there, and start to panic, but it fades as quickly as it came. I've had worse wasp bites or bee stings.

"A model, huh?" he asks, as I refuse to look at how tight his pants are over his firm ass. Underland is turning me into a freaking nymphomaniac. "You think I'm that pretty, do you?" He grabs up a banana from a bowl of fruit, peels it, and stuffs half in his mouth while he readies the next needle.

"Hardly," I say, but I'm probably the only person in that room who believes what I'm saying. Even then, it's questionable.

"We're going to work our way through these poisons," March continues, flattening his rabbit ears against his skull as he struggles with a corked bottle. "And then I'm going to give you a test kit to keep with you. At any time you suspect something is poisoned—food, clothing, even a fucking handrail—you take the swab out and test it. If the liquid turns cloudy, it's poison." He turns back around and moves to prick Dee with a second needle.

"Cloudy, huh," I murmur, thinking how ingenious that would be, to poison say, a doorknob or a banister. Something innocuous and unexpected.

"It'll test for ninety of the most common poisons." March murmurs after he's finally sucked the rest of the banana into his mouth and eaten it all. Impressive. Bet he could give good blow jobs with that gag reflex. Speaking of … I've sort of been wondering if he has a thing with the Mad Hatter?

Wouldn't surprise me.

"And if you leave it for about a week," he continues,

taking care with what he's doing to Dee. That makes me happy, to see that he actually does give a shit about this poison stuff. It's the first time I've seen him really show off his own personality, aside from being the Mad Hatter's second-in-command. "You can test for another nine."

"Ninety-nine poisons, huh?" I ask as March steps up next to me again. When he gets close enough, the stale reek of the dungeon fades away, and I get a hint of gardenia and the musky bitterness of dark tea on the back of my tongue. He smells like a tea party in a garden, this giant dude with all the needles and knives. "Can we test the Knave's dress? I don't trust her for shit."

The March Hare smiles at me and looks up, meeting my eyes.

"Can I tell you a secret?" He leans in and puts his lips disturbingly close to my ear, stirring my hair against my overheated skin. "Neither do I."

I shiver as he grabs hold of my arm, rubbing my pulse with his thumb, and then pricks me—all while staring into my eyes. Those shifting flecks of color in his gaze remind me of fall again, of pumpkins and changing leaves and apple cider. The March Hare has all of the colors.

"You know what," he says, taking a step back, his eyes twinkling with mischief. "Take this." March reaches behind his back and pulls the glowing purple knife off the table, balancing the hilt on his fingertip for a moment before he flicks it up in the air, lets it spin, and then catches it again. He grabs a leather sheath off the table and slips it inside before offering it up to me. "Just don't stab yourself with it, love, or you are *f-u-c-k-e-d*. Up bloody shit creek with no paddle."

He winks at me as he hands over the knife, tangling our fingers together in a very purposeful way. I notice then that his fingers are covered in rings, and I have to wonder if it's just for looks … or for beating people up. Hmm. Considering the way he flanks Raiden Walker, like some movie bad boy bodyguard, I'm guessing the latter.

"Why?" I ask, sliding the knife out and gazing at the glowing poison. Not particularly subtle, but I don't think this is meant to be. No, a weapon like this is a *threat*, a warning, like a caterpillar patterned in bright colors. Fuck off, jubjub bird. "There's no antidote?"

"Just my cum," he says with a bright grin, and I swear on Hearts and Diamonds, I almost stab him with his own blade.

Why does everything in this world have to do with drinking semen?!

"Well, shit, if that isn't motivation to take care …" I use the leather straps on the back of my new sheath to hook it to my thigh holster, putting the poisoned weapon right next to the Vorpal Blade.

Look at me: I am a veritable freaking badass.

“If you get into any trouble at the ball,” March says, leaning his tight ass against the table and crossing his huge arms over his chest. His grin is cheeky as fuck, white-white teeth in a face cloaked in shadow. “Stab the cocksucker with that, and I’ll know exactly where you are.”

I glance over at Tee and Dee, both of them watching my interaction with March with interest.

I turn back to him and smile, touching my fingers to the knife.

“Thank you,” I tell him, and both brows go up. Pretty sure he expected some witty banter.

He’ll get that … later. For now, I’m just trying to be nice.

“You’re welcome?” he says, almost like it’s a question, tilting his head to one side as a single one of his ears flattens back against his skull. Aha. He doesn’t know quite what to make of me, and I love it. “Now, shall we prick you again, Doll?”

Doll.

Fantastic.

Another goddamn nickname.

North is naked on my bed when I get upstairs.

"Oh for fuck's sake," I whisper, but I'm actually seriously turned on when I find him there with nothing but a scrap of blanket over his erect dick. "Look at you, jumping the gun like that." I fill a plate with goodies from the refreshments table as Tee goes about preparing cups of chamomile tea for Dee and me. I've learned from conversations with the twins that it's boosted with a drug that makes you go to sleep fast, and sleep well. That, I can handle. It's just, like, melatonin or something.

"I'm just making myself available," the Duke drawls as I sit down on the bed and accept the cup of tea from the angel prince's fingers. Tee gives me a tight smile as he does the same for his brother, and then sits down at the desk to pull out his journal.

We both like to write down our thoughts, me and Tee. It makes me like him more. *If I do get to go back home, I should grab my diary while I'm there.* I'd even start a new one tonight if I felt I had the energy. But after the sex, the shooting, the dancing, and the poison … I have nothing left.

"If you're too tired to change into pajamas," the cat purrs, curled up in a black and white ball on his cat tree," you could certainly sleep in the nude."

I kick my boots off onto the floor and give him a look.

"Sorry, dude, not tonight. You're just going to have to use your imagination if you want to see my boobs." I give him a tight smile, flip him off, and then take a sip of my tea.

"Imagination is the only weapon in the war against reality," Chesh purrs, shifting into human form as he leaps off the cat tree and lands on all fours on my bed. His collar jangles as he slides up between North and me. "Jules de Gaultier."

"How do you know who Jules de Gaultier is?" I ask. I mean, you have to admit, it's weird as hell that the Cheshire Cat knows a quote from an obscure French philosopher.

"He used to live in Underland, before he traveled Topside after the Riving," Chesh says, grinning widely at me. "Don't you love how full of useless information I am? All cats are, you know. We're keepers of knowledge."

I snort in response, picking through the banana bread on my plate as I look for insects or flowers or whatever other weird shit might be in it. Working off a random thought, I pull one of the March Hare's test bottles from my pocket, unscrew the top, and swab my food. I put it back into the liquid, put the top back on, and shake it up as instructed.

"Not poisoned," I say as the liquid stays clear. March had said it would turn cloudy right away if there was even a trace of poison.

"Likely not," Chesh purrs, kneading the pillows next to me with his black painted fingernails. "The card servants test all your food before they put it down. If it were poisoned, you'd see their corpses littering the floor around the table."

"Thank you for that image," I say as I eat my food, smiling when Dee begins to snore.

"You're quite welcome," the cat replies, pillowing his head on his arms and swishing his tail as he closes his eyes.

The door to the room opens, and Lar and Rab walk in, completing our little evening routine. To be quite honest, I'm starting to enjoy it. I'm glad we have a few days before the ball. There's a weird feeling in my gut, like everything's going to change after that. So even though I know it won't last, I want to enjoy this peace for a few more days.

"Evening, Miss Alice," Rab says, taking off his shoes near the door and getting comfortable in one of my chairs. The Duke makes an annoyed sound, but he doesn't bother moving from his position on my bed to put any clothes on. I'm quite enjoying the bronze expanse of his chest, so I appreciate that.

Besides, I never said I'd changed my mind about, uh, *mating*.

"Sunshine," Lar says, sweeping his jacket off his shoulders and hanging it up.

"Evening to you both." I set my empty plate and cup aside, unstrapping the Vorpal Blade from my thigh and setting it on the nightstand. North had originally said the blade was owed to him. I wonder why? But that's a question for another day. I'm too tired to delve into it tonight.

"How was your appointment with the March Hare?" Lar asks, lips twitching as he spreads his wings open wide and stands with his back to the fire. Based on the cheeky expression on his face, I think he already knows.

"You dropped that information about his Raiden-form on purpose." I don't even phrase it as a question; I know it's true.

"He liked that, did he?" Lar pushes his hair back from his face and uses a gold hairband he pulls from his pocket to tie it back. "I know all sorts of things about the Mad Hatter and the March Hare that would, well, not drive them mad since they're already mad, but perhaps *madder* still."

"He told me his third form was a *slithy tove*," I say, and several of the men laugh. Tee ignores it all, scribbling things down in his journal. The clock strikes twelve as he's writing, and he gasps, his wings folding into his back and leaving the glossy sheen of feather tattoos on the backs of his arms.

Note to self: break that fucking curse!

I care about the twins now, and I want to see them freed. Plus, I'm a smug bitch. I would *love* to see the Knave's face after I fuck up her spell. That'd be priceless.

"He is a tove, I believe, yes," Lar replies, surprising me. "It's a useful form, I'd think."

"It's a throwaway," Rab growls, looking toward the

painting on the wall that depicts the March Hare sitting at a tea party. It has not escaped my knowledge that the nine men I'm now surrounded by are all featured in these paintings. Or that I find them all physically attractive, even if their attitudes stink.

Fucking prophecy.

"What's your final form?" I look Rab straight in the face when he turns to stare at me, his gaze as icy as his voice. I feel like I must be getting frost on the tips of my eyelashes.

"State secret," he says, and I groan in frustration, flopping back into the pillows.

If there's a polite way to ask the rest of the men in the room to vacate so I can fuck a dragon, please point me in the right direction because I don't know how to go about doing it.

"Come to my room," North whispers in my ear, making me shiver. Chesh lays between us, but he doesn't seem bothered much by North's naked body leaning over him. I guess as the Duke's pet, he's probably seen worse. I wonder how many women he's seen North take to his bed? For whatever reason, that thought pisses me the hell off. "I'll fuck you into my mattress, and make us both scream."

"Oh lord," I choke out, but I'm opening my eyes and sliding them over to look at the jabberwock painting on the wall.

"Go," Chesh says, nuzzling against my arm. "If he doesn't get mated, the Duke will be rather savage."

"I …" I start, but nobody is looking at me, nobody's judging. And I *am* curious as to what the Suits look like down those long hallways. "I'll at least go and take a look at your room."

Chesh chuckles, like he's calling my bluff and I smack him, standing up to follow North into his chambers. His bare bronze ass when he stands up is *glorious*.

Don't drool, Allison, I think as he pads over and unlocks the painting for me, letting it swing aside so I can step into the hallway. Gotta wonder where he was keeping that key though. Clenched between his firm, bronzed buttocks perhaps?

Buttocks.

I snort and then slap my hand over my mouth to cut off the sound.

"Do you know," the Duke continues as he follows along, the door swinging shut behind us. "That in a siege, your attackers must fight their way through all nine chambers before they get to yours. That main door is spelled; anyone without a key must be let in by someone inside."

"That's … pretty fucking cool actually," I say, sweat dripping down the back of my neck. It does not help me calm down much when North reaches out and tickles my skin with his claws. No, pretty sure my dripping sweat becomes a monsoon. It's like I'm nervous or something, a blushing virgin on her way to the honeymoon suite. Cue eyeroll.

I follow the hall to its natural end, pausing to glance into a glorious marble bathroom on the right before I step into the bedroom.

It's small, but cozy, shaped like a heart with a bed situated in the point opposite us. There's a dresser on either side of me, both of them wilting and wonky, like they're melting. The ceiling is draped with red fabric, the floor with rugs, and there are chaises and chairs scattered all around. Also, I'm pretty sure the Alice statue on the opposite side of the room just waved at me.

"My sweet mate," North growls into my hair, wrapping his arms around me from behind. "Every day that I don't touch you is torture."

"We fucked once; that doesn't make me your mate," I whisper, but the words sound weak, like even I don't believe them. That's been happening a lot to me lately; it's like maybe I don't know myself at all. Or maybe I just stopped trying after Fred died. I changed after everything that happened, and I changed into someone I didn't want to know. Perhaps it's time for me to try? If I do, I might find that I don't hate myself as much as I thought I did.

"That's what it means to me," North says, pushing me forward. I stumble a bit, putting my palms flat on the surface of the bed to catch myself. I'm fairly certain that's exactly the position he wants me in, bent over with my ass sticking out.

Instead, I stand up and spin around before he can grab me.

I look up and meet gold eyes shimmering with lust.

"Slow down, would you?" I say, putting my hands on his flat stomach. Liam was not sexy like this, not even close. He was a boy, and North is most certainly a man. It's like I'm not even sure where to put my hands; I just want to touch all of him.

"How can I slow down when all I want is to ravage you?" the Duke whispers back, his voice hoarse, his tail trashing. I reach up and give a tug on one of his horns. I could never take him back home; he wouldn't last a day in Topside. Of course, the horns and tail are dead giveaways. I imagine he can probably shift them off the way he does his wings, but his temper would eventually get the better of him.

"Ravage, huh?" I ask, sliding my fingers down his body. He's already sweaty, that musky, masculine scent of his driving me up the wall. "That's a strong word."

"I have strong emotions," he says, curling his tail around my waist and yanking me even closer to him, so close that his erect cock is trapped between our bodies. With a snap of his fingers, he lights the flickering candles in the room and dims the chandelier at the same time. Magic. I can't wait to be able to use my magic.

"I can see that," I whisper, pushing him back with my hands on his chest.

North obliges and moves back. Let's be honest: if he didn't want to move, I would not be able to make him. He's huge and built like a truck. Plus, you know, he can turn into a dragon. Maybe my Alice magic could blow him to bits if I really tried, but I'm sort of fond of the guy now.

Slowly, I drop to my knees with the Savage Duke standing above me.

When I look up and meet his gold eyes, they're practically molten, dripping with lust. His horns cast wicked shadows on the ceiling and walls, making him look like a monster. A beautiful monster, but a monster nonetheless.

I wrap the fingers of my right hand around his bronze shaft and give it a squeeze, just to test his sensitivity. North exhales, tangling clawed fingers in my hair. He's dominant, but not cruel, and a definite change of pace from the twins. Dee is loving and cheerful, Tee is reserved but intense, and North is … savage.

He's fucking *primal*.

Licking my lips, I put my mouth up to the head of his cock and gently kiss his hot flesh, working my way down his shaft to his balls. My tongue runs along that seam of flesh in the middle as my fingers tease the soft skin.

"Allison Liddell," he grinds out, his hips moving up to meet my face. "You're going to break my black, little heart, aren't you?"

I just smile and keep going, licking and teasing him until his breathing is ragged. Then I oblige his desires and put my mouth over the head of his cock, just enough that he can feel the warm, wet heat of my tongue, but gets no satisfaction from it.

My right hand works his dick like a corkscrew, twisting around his shaft and making him growl in frustration.

"I want to fuck your mouth right now," he snarls, but he doesn't move. He just sits there and lets me pleasure him, working salty pre-cum from the tip. *I can't believe I'm sucking off a dragon,* I think, and seeing as my jaw is already starting to ache, I know the prophecy is right about one thing.

Nine big cocks.

"Aren't you glad we're taking our time?" I whisper, making sure my lips move against his shaft when I speak. Once I've got him all lubed up with saliva, I breathe against the shiny wetness on his cock, and he snarls at me.

"I can't quite decide at this precise moment," he grinds

out, and I grin. I open my mouth and lightly tease him with my teeth before sliding my lips over the head, taking as much of him in as I can.

I slide my mouth up and down North's shaft like a porn star, and then hold him deep in my throat. That's when I start to hum. As soon as the sound vibrates from my mouth and into his shaft, the Savage Duke fucking loses it.

He slides his cock from my lips, picks me up off the floor, and tosses me onto the bed.

He's crawling on top of me before I can even catch my breath.

The Duke of Northumbria pins me to the black fur comforter on his bed, his strong hands holding my wrists with a firm but controlling intensity that makes my heart flutter. I both love it, and find that it scares me.

"I …" I start, thinking of Liam and his friends, struggling to pin me down. I don't want to have flashbacks like that with the Duke, but I can't help it. There's so much trauma inside my chest that I've never dealt with, and I can't keep pushing it back. I know that as soon as I cross that Looking-Glass, it'll come rushing back, a tsunami of pain and frustration. I'm from a world that doesn't care or respect me, and now I'm in one where everyone wants a piece.

I don't even know what to do with myself.

"Relax, Miss Liddell," North whispers, putting his mouth to the side of my neck and kissing me. "You're quite tense all of a sudden."

"I had something happen to me," I say, but I don't want to go into it. There's no point in ruining this moment. To be honest, I just want to get fucked by a dragon and not think about any of it. But maybe if I say it aloud, some of the pressure will go away?

North stiffens up, releasing his grip on my wrists. I put my palms up against his chest, over the hard points of his nipples.

"Someone hurt my mate?" he asks through gritted teeth, gold hair falling across his face and getting stuck to his sweaty brow. "I'll fucking tear their cocks off, and melt their faces with fire." He exhales and little puffs of smoke escape his nostrils. He leans down to rub against the side of my face.

"They didn't get to go through with what they were planning," I say, licking my lips and noticing that North sits up and takes notice, his eyes following the path of my tongue like a man possessed. "Although the incident did ruin my life. Is it wrong for me to want to start a new one?" He shakes his head and looks at me with this undeniable certainty.

"No."

Fucking kiss me then, I think, and either he's a mind

reader or else he's just good with body language.

The Duke drops his face to mine, capturing my lips with a delicious fervor that reignites the passion in my blood. Later, I'll tell him more about what happened. Right now, I just want him to touch me … all … fucking … over.

North cups the back of my head with one hand, cradling my skull in his huge palm while he kisses me, paying special attention to my lower lip. He sucks it in between his teeth and then nibbles on it, making me writhe. His musky male and sandalwood smell is like a perfumed cloud, taking over my body and drowning my senses, making it hard for me to believe there's anything else left in the universe.

He's so much taller than me, so much bigger, and I love it, especially when he uses his tail to reach up and unbutton my pants. The muscular tip slips inside and strokes my already damp panties, just before he uses it to start pulling my pants and underwear down.

"I want to be consumed by you," he growls, and I swear, even as my clothing comes off, I giggle.

"You just want me because I'm the Alice," I say with a roll of my eyes, and North goes completely still.

"Lies," he hisses, and there's literal fire on his breath. "It was your *scent* that got me. A jabberwock chooses its mate by scent. You smelled like mine from moment one."

"I thought female jabberwocky picked their mates?" I ask, suddenly breathless again, and North snarls, biting my lower lip.

"Sometimes they do, sometimes they rape the males, sometimes it's a mutual attraction. Allison Liddell, our attraction is mutual, is it not?"

He sits up and yanks my pants aside, chucking them onto the floor, and then tearing my shirt off next. The fabric rends as he tosses it away like it's somehow personally offended him, and then he goes for the corset next.

"It's mutual," I whisper as his bronze fingers slow, and he carefully undoes the hook and eye clasps, unwrapping my sweaty, aching body from the corset like he's just gotten the most amazing Christmas present.

"Look at how beautiful you are, *Allison*," he snarls, and then he flips me over and puts my ass in the air, holding onto my hips as he positions himself at my opening.

We're both naked, both sweaty, and I can tell this is going to be just as wild and animalistic as our first time.

"Fuck me, Savage Duke," I whisper, and that's all it takes. He drives himself into me hard, his pelvis hitting my ass with an audible smack. His hips move with a wild frenzy as I dig my fingers into the fuzzy bedspread and hold on for dear life.

There's something so freeing, so wild about that moment, and yet all I can think about is what he just said to me: *It was your* scent *that got me.*

My scent.

I find that wildly sexy.

North squeezes my pelvic bone with his fingers and curls his tail around my waist to help hold me in place as he pounds into me, his balls hitting my clit and teasing just the right spot to make me groan.

I don't feel like a lost, restless young idiot in that moment; there's something about taking control of my sexuality like this that makes me feel like a strong, capable adult. I know it's just fucking, but … I like it. And I like knowing that I do.

The Duke isn't gentle with me, taking me hard and fast, just like I wanted.

Surprisingly, he gets *me* to finish first, my body collapsing onto the bed, the only thing holding me in place his muscular tail.

My muscles spasm around him as he readjusts his pace, transitioning to slow, steady thrusts that make me feel like I'm sobbing. It almost feels *too* good, too intense. I don't even know where to begin.

North pulls out and flips me onto my back, holding his slick cock in his hand and staring down at me with his metallic eyes as he works himself with confident, sure strokes.

I bite my lower lip and wait, absorbing this moment

and filing it away for later. Surely, there will be some shitty times in my life, and this will be one of those split-seconds in time that I hold onto and dream about later.

The Duke lets his head fall back, his glorious golden hair feathering against his dark horns, and then he comes with a sharp buck of his hips, spilling his seed all over my belly.

When he collapses onto all fours, I think we're done, and I try to decide if we're going to snuggle in here or if I should shower and rejoin the twins or … or what. There is no Google here for me to look up *when in a polyamorous relationship, should I stay in bed with guy three while guys one and two are waiting back in my room?*

Wouldn't that be nice if there was an easy answer to that question?

But then North's mouth is on my belly, making my stomach muscles flutter as he kisses and licks the sticky semen from my skin. My fingers tangle in his hair and then slowly creep toward his shiny, black horns, taking hold of him and steering him to my aching clit.

His tongue finds the sensitive, swollen bit of flesh, swirling around it and working it into a stiff, desperate frenzy. It's that pleasure on the edge of pain, that line that both wants to be crossed and abhors it. It's that moment in the bedroom where you're not even sure you know your own body anymore.

I let mine take control, thrusting my hips up against

North's face as he takes hold of my pelvis, his claws pricking my skin, drawing tiny beads of blood. He licks these off, too, and then moves to my opening, loving me with his tongue before he uses his long black tail to slide into me.

I'm not sure at first if I love it … or hate it.

But then he crooks the tip and teases the sensitive flesh just inside my opening, and I'm done for yet again.

I yank the Duke up toward my face by tugging on his horns, and then I kiss him, tasting a mixture of his seed and my own on his lips.

"You've got the Duke on your side now, the Alice," he whispers, kissing his way along my jaw. "So tell me, what will you do with me?"

"Well," I whisper, panting and tingling and enjoying the aftershocks of my double orgasm, "I think … I'm going to turn Underland into Wonderland again."

6

In Which Allison Liddell Attends a Torrid Tea Party

"Lurid, sordid, a bacchanalian affair," Dee says, twirling his hat around on the top of his head. He's dressed in red and white today, like everyone else here. The uh, matchy-matchy thing is starting to get ridiculous. Although I do have to admit he looks damn good in the red military coat with the gold buttons, the tight red and white striped shirt, and the black slacks. "*That* is what a Torrid Tea Party is."

"This is a real thing?" I ask, squinting in his direction. "Like the cock-race? This is an actual *thang*?" I'm sitting at the edge of the training room with a spread of toadstool cupcakes, *actual* toadstools that glitter, and huge stacks of bread with butter. Tea is always served, and I always refuse, but this time there's also floral infused water with little edible blossoms floating on the surface.

There *is* a chance these things were alive and flipping people off not three hours ago, but I try my best not to think that. No point in it. The flowers are dickheads anyway.

I poke at one with my finger and try to bottle up some of this weird, gushing joy that's poisoning my body. There's no way happiness like this can be caged or contained. No, it always flutters away on broken wings.

"The Torrid Tea Party is a real event," Lar explains, his wings outstretched and drooping lazily on the floor. His key-shaped nipple rings keep catching the sunlight streaming through the glass ceiling panels, and I feel the urge to ask about them perching on the edge of my tongue. I saw the White Knight open the front gates with one, but why? Why is the most important key in the Kingdom of Hearts pierced through some guy's nipple? "The Mad Hatter is famous for it."

"So what makes this different than a *mad* tea party?" I ask, looking into Lar's blue eyes and thinking how much brighter they are than Dee's. The twin's eyes are an azure shadow, a rich jewel tone that gives his happy face a slightly darker note. Lar's eyes are almost Caribbean, light in color but heavy in saturation. In the sunlight, I'd almost call them *aqua* or *teal* or whatever the fuck that tropical blue-green color is. Sorry, but I played with black Sharpies instead of crayons as a kid. My parents were always too busy to remember to bring any when they took me to work with them. It was just me and Fred and yellow legal pads and Sharpies.

Fucking Fred …

"All tea parties are mad, of course," the cat says, slinking up beside me and putting his head in my lap—his very *human* head with the double lip piercing, the septum ring, and the silver stud in his eyebrow. Asswad. I shove him off, and he groans when his skull hits the red and white striped blanket underneath us.

Yeah, even picnic paraphernalia is themed here.

The King of Hearts has a big ego … among other things.

Piece of shit, I hate him, I think, even as I get this uncomfortable throbbing between my legs. Thinking about Brennin Red turns me on. And it shouldn't. And yet it undeniably does.

"All tea parties are mad?" I ask, trying to see if I can get clarification. It seems like, in Underland, that all of the nonsense really does have some sense to it which I suppose *makes* sense because the word sense is the root of the word nonsense. Sensibly, of course.

Oh God.

What the fuck did I just think?!

"All tea parties are mad, but there are even madder tea parties which is to say, that the Torrid Tea Party is really the maddest party of all," Dee starts, looking up toward the ceiling as he muses and taps a single finger against his chin. "Seems strange then, to wonder why it isn't simply called the Maddest Tea Party? Since it *is* mad, and the Mad Hatter is undeniably mad, and the March Hare may very well be the maddest of the mad—"

"Dee," I interrupt, reaching out to put my hand on the back of his. "Thank you." I force a smile that quickly turns real when he flashes one of his happy grins at me. I don't actually mind his riddling nonsense anymore. It's growing on me. Maybe it's growing on me like a tumor, but that's okay. I accept it.

"Why, thank you for such a glowing compliment," March says, snapping the end off a white chocolate bar with little red berries in it. See what I mean? All done up in the kingdom's colors yet again. I'm pretty sure he's always eating. In fact, I'd be hard-pressed to think of a single moment where he hasn't had *something* in his mouth.

Once again I can't help but wonder if he's had Raiden's *something* in his mouth, too. Like, are they lovers or just companions? And how does the Dormouse factor into all of this? I hope he's not at the Torrid Tea Party; he gives me the fucking heebie-jeebies.

"Explain to me exactly what goes on at these things again?" I continue, pushing some stray strands of hair off my sweaty face. The rest of it is gathered up in a high ponytail on the back of my head. North yanks on it during training, but I refuse to cut it off. Guess I do have some vanity, huh? Maybe the whole world does? Err, both worlds I mean.

"The room falls dark," Dee whispers, walking in a half-circle around us while he spreads his arms wide, palms out like he's miming the shape of this imaginary room. "The curtains are drawn, the candles are lit, and the tea is served piping hot." He squats down across from me, next to his brother, eyes glittering. "Tarts are served. Tarts are always served, preferably with gooseberries or cloudberries."

"And fresh cream," the Cheshire cat adds, still lying on his back and lifting a single black-nailed finger, his black and white striped ears twitching in his raven-dark hair.

"The tea is boosted with twice the usual magic," Tee says with a small sigh, pushing some of his purple-black hair away from his handsome face. The twins have such big, round eyes and long lashes, it feels impossible to look away from their faces sometimes. They're this perfect mix of pretty and masculine, this dichotomous contrast that makes my lady parts titter in the best way possible. "And steeped in truth herbs. Whoever it is that you're trying to vet—because a Torrid Tea Party is always about uncovering enemies or vetting allies—sits in a circle and drinks one cup per round."

"What's a round entail?" I ask, examining a glittering pink mushroom as North steps back in from the hallway, and my heart starts to skitter and jump. He's so … *much*. I mean, he must be exuding like alpha male beast pheromones or something because I don't act right when he's around. My cheeks flush with heat and I stuff the mushroom in my mouth. It's all crystalized with sugar, and it crunches when I chew. The taste of bubblegum fills my mouth, and I almost choke. Not because it's bad, but holy shit, that's weird as fuck.

"A round …" the Duke starts, making his way haughtily over to us and sitting cross-legged on my right, his chin raised defiantly. I'm starting to realize he's one of the *only* people in the kingdom that can or will stand up to the King of Hearts. I wonder what they were talking about out there? When Ol' Red popped his head into the training room and asked to play a quick round of croquet with the Duke, I figured something must be up. More internal politics maybe? "Consists of one question and one answer." He flicks his gold eyes over to mine and then sneaks his tail around my ankle. I let him do it, too, and I *like* it. Ugh, I really, really like it.

It's really starting to grow on me, this idea of being queen and dating all these guys. I mean, who wouldn't want that? The only obstacle is the King. Because he's a piece of shit and I hate him.

Oh and also … my family.

I can't leave my family with more questions than answers, especially not after Fred.

I lift my face up to meet Tee's gaze. It feels like he can sense when I'm thinking about my family. Maybe because he lost his, he's more empathetic or something? We stare at each other across the circle of food before I look away and pick up a toadstool cupcake. One bite and I can already tell I'm going to like it: it tastes like vanilla ice cream and hot fudge.

"One question and one answer?" I ask around a mouthful of cupcake. Oops. I have bad manners, sorry. Sometimes I talk while I chew. Guess we all have shit to work on, huh?

"Sometimes the question is a quest which is interesting because quest is the root of question," Chesh says, sitting up and stretching as he also surreptitiously goes to curl his tail around my other ankle. I grab it first, and give it a squeeze which turns his face into a leering grin.

"May as well just stroke my cock then?" he purrs, sitting up and then rubbing his cheek against my bare shoulder. He nips me and I yelp, causing a stir of chuckling around the circle. I'm still getting used to the idea of these guys *not* being jealous of one another.

"Get stuffed," I tell him, bringing the floral water to my

lips, so I don't have to say anything else. Because the idea of touching Chesh's cock is pretty enticing. It's like I'm sitting in front of more than just a food-laden smorgasbord. There's a buffet of men here for me to choose from, and I can have any one of them I want. Or all of them. And that's the best part. Why choose?

"So, a quest or a question?" I ask and then snap my fingers. "Truth or dare?"

"That's a silly name, isn't it?" Lar asks, blinking long blonde lashes in my direction. "Quest or question makes much more sense."

"And how do you figure that?" I ask as he shrugs his jacket off his bare shoulders and leaves his muscular arms open to investigation from my wandering gaze. And boy does it wander. Being eighteen and perpetually horny never looked or felt so damn good.

"Because a quest implies a goal while a dare implies nothing but cheekiness," Lar continues, looking at me like he's staring into my soul. I notice he's finished his cup of tea, and as I watch, he leans in and pokes around the tea leaves at the bottom of his chipped, wonky little mug. "This tea party tonight," he says with a nod of his head, blonde-blue hair falling over his forehead, "it'll give us answers." He lifts his face again and smiles in a way that promises there's something else that he's not saying.

And from the look of him? I'd say it was something truly lascivious.

"How humdrum dull and boring," Rab drawls as he rolls his red eyes. His right ear flops in half and he reaches up to straighten it. He's dressed in a black vest with his pocket watch chain hanging from one pocket. There's no undershirt this time, just rippling muscles dressed in tattoos. "Just pick a dress and be done with it. We're already late." He taps the clock on his right forearm and then saunters over to stand behind me.

When I glance back at him, I see that his slacks are hanging way too low again. There's this delicious strip of skin between his vest and his pants that's making it hard to concentrate. I wonder if he's finding it as difficult to focus with me wearing nothing but a pair of red lacy panties and a matching bra? Did I mention that there's a heart cutout on the back of the undies, flashing a delicious amount of crack?

"We could make it more interesting, however," he starts, his warm breath stirring my hair. It's interesting, how cold his voice is in contrast. He smells like the forest after a good rain, like wet earth and the softness of decaying leaves.

"And how might we do that?" I ask, digging though the massive closet and trying not to be creeped out that everything fits. Have you ever had that before, an entire closet of clothes *made* for you? Even stuff that doesn't look like it'll fit ends up stretching or laying just right. There are items in that closet that I never would've picked up before, big poof-y things that remind me of Edy's dress.

"I think *naked* is more interesting than *dressed-up*, don't you?" Rab comes around to stand in front of me, leaning against the wall near the door and looking me up and down with slow, decadent menace that turns my insides to mush. Asshole. He's a serious asshole. Most of these guys are. Maybe they have to be to survive in Underland? It's fucking brutal here.

"What makes you think you deserve to see me naked?" I ask as I flip through dress after dress after dress. This event has a dress code: black. And although my closet is made up of rainbow colors, it's a rainbow that's heavily skewed toward red and white.

"I'll fight in a cock-race for you," he whispers, red eyes focused on me, white ears twitching. When I look at him, I can't help but think of his bandersnatch form. But what is his third one? What other meat did he get forced down his throat at the Inaugural Feast? "I'll whip my dick out, and swordfight the King's prick if I have to."

"You'd fight the King?" I ask with a chuckle and a roll of my eyes. Imagining Rab and Brennin slapping their erect dicks together is about ninety-percent *hilarious* and maybe like ten percent sexy. Maybe eleven or twelve percent. "Please. You're his lackey, through and through." I pull a skintight black dress off the hook and hold it up to examine it. I would *never* wear anything like this back home. It's sort of ... grown-up and sexy, and I want it all over my body right now. Besides, it has bat shapes cut out of the midsection, leaving these sexy little gothic peepholes. The back is low-cut, and sewn to look like the top of a bat's wings. "King's orders," I mimic in Rab's cold voice, miming shooting a gun at Brandon's head.

Brandon.

Well, fuck.

Now that I've been here and I've seen what I've seen, I believe Rab. Which, of course, means that the Rabbit who was parading around as Brandon ... had to have *eaten* the real Brandon's flesh at some point.

Gross.

"You're still upset about me blowing your crush's brains out?" he asks, licking his lips as I step into the dress and wiggle it up my body. It has cap sleeves and a soft lining on the inside that makes my skin tingle. If I pair it with the black pirate boots I got from Lory, I will look fucking dope.

"It was a hard thing to witness," I admit, glancing at Rab and watching as his ears twitch like antennae on the top of his head. They're so expressive. I can see everything he's thinking. "But I … guess I'm glad it happened."

"Oh?" Rab asks as I scoot around him and pause for a moment in front of the mirrored dressing table to the right of my bed. It has little clawed feet on the bottom and I swear, it wiggles its toes every now and again. "You *like* it here, do you Miss Liddell? Fitting, since you'll be the ruler of Underland-turned-Wonderland for one hundred and twenty-seven years, give or take a decade or two."

"Nobody lives to be a hundred and twenty-seven," I start, and then pause. Or do they? After all, we don't have any angels or Rabbits or cat shifters back home.

"You will be, if you live long enough to save Underland. It's in one of Lar's prophecies."

"Well, don't believe everything you read in tea leaves, I always say," I joke as I lean over the table and apply red-red lipstick and too much black liner. The lipstick smells like berries, and the liner has a sweet, smoky sort of scent. Hey, I bet it's all natural, right? Probably organic. Most likely *not* vegan. This world is so fucked-up, I would not be surprised if my lip color was made from the blood of baby lambs or some shit.

"It was in his wings, I saw it," Rab growls, and there's something fiercely protective in his voice that draws me around to look at him. His reflection isn't enough; I need to see his face. He's looking down at me with this determined set to his features. I almost want to reach up and touch his cheek. Almost. Instead, I drop my arms to my sides and glance away, toward the door.

Everyone is already at the party. Even Tee and Dee went early to set it up. It's just me and Rab they're waiting for.

"We should go," I say, but when I try to move away, Rab reaches out and curls his fingers around my arm, drawing me close to him.

"There's only a thirty-five percent chance," he whispers, mouth slightly parted, red eyes ringed in liner and flooded with shadows, "but it's a chance worth fighting for." Rab touches the side of my face with his tattooed fingers, running his warm fingertips from my cheekbone to my chin, cradling my head in his hand.

We just look at each other for a long, quiet moment before Rab uses his other hand to brush the hair from my forehead.

"Can I kiss you, Alice?" he asks me, his voice like the quiet, cool shadows of a cave. I want to crawl into it and curl up, sleep in the circle of his muscular arms. *Eww, what the fuck?!* I must be getting soft.

"Yes." It's the only word that can make it past my already parted lips.

Rab slides his right hand back to cup my head, pulling me close and breathing against my mouth. I can already tell what his is going to taste like, this refreshing mix of peppermint and lavender that makes me wet my lips with anticipation.

The asshole takes his sweet time coming to me, teasing my bottom lip with his tongue, tasting me and making me groan. I rise up on my tiptoes and lean into him, pressing my breasts against his vest. It's not enough fabric to disguise the flat, chiseled expanse of muscles underneath, and my nipples pebble into hard points.

My right hand slides up and over his shoulder and doesn't stop until I'm running my fingers up the soft, fuzzy length of his ear.

"Oooh," he growls, moving his hand from my face so he can wrap an arm around me instead. "*Harder.*" He pushes his lips against mine, his tongue invading my mouth. It's the sort of first kiss you don't forget and yet, one where you can't remember all the details because it's nothing but a wild, ardent blur.

Rab lifts me up and sets me on the edge of the dressing table, knocking makeup and FUCKING DRINK ME bottles onto the floor. He presses in close, grinding our pelvises together and pushing my dress up in the process. I can feel him hard and wanting through his slacks as he presses against me, and I squeeze him tight between my thighs.

My hands play with his ears while one of his plays with my breasts, kneading and massaging the tender flesh until I'm breathless and wanting, near desperate for it. Rab drops his grip to my ass, squeezing me and pulling me even closer to him.

"If we didn't have an appointment with the King …" he growls against my mouth, and I turn my face away, these breathy gasps for air passing between my lips as I close my eyes and try to pull myself together.

"You said you'd fight the King for me," I whisper as Rab lowers his mouth to my neck and licks me, from shoulder to ear. My entire body flushes white-hot and I rub my pelvis against Rab's without meaning to.

"I can challenge him to a cock-race, if you want. But there'd be substantially more blood and substantially less cock than I might've promised." *He* is the one to break us up, stepping back and sighing as he smooths his palms down the front of his vest. He's still sporting a boner, but I don't think anyone in this nightmare fest gives a shit.

"No, I don't want that," I say with a sigh, running my fingers through my hair. "Besides, what would be the point? It's not like I'd fuck the King even if he *did* win." With a smirk, I hop off the dressing table and shove my skirt down my hips, heading for the door without waiting to see what the expression on Rab's face—or ears—is like.

Nope, I don't want to know.

And yet, my cheeks are warm and I know for a fact that there's a smile on my face I can't wipe off.

Allison and the Torrid Tea Party

The Torrid Tea Party is being held in a tower because like, of course it is, since this is a fairy tale on crack.

In the Disney version, there'd be a glittering pink wonderland in that tower where I'd wait for nine shining princes with white-toothed smiles and shimmery gold hair to come and save me.

In the Grimm version, I'd have a sleep spell cast on me and wake up giving birth after being raped. Yep. Did you know that's how the *real* Sleeping Beauty tale goes? Yeah, it's fucked-up beyond all reason.

In this version, there's a winding staircase with flickering torches and stone stairs worn down in the center to little dips that threaten to trip me with each step I take. At the top, there's a heavy wood door with a gold handle in the shape of a heart.

How shocking. More heart paraphernalia.

I reach out to open it, and the door swings inward on its own, propelled by the long, graceful fingers of the Mad Hatter.

"Hello Miss Alice," he whispers as he gives me a vampire grin and steps back to welcome me into the dark, hazy interior of the tower room. The incense is thick and smoky, and it smells like sandalwood and roses.

I can't see much of what's going on inside, but I can hear Dee chuckling from the shadows. I ignore Raiden and step into the darkness, feeling it close around me. It's not as stifling as I thought though, more like a warm blanket being wrapped around my shoulders. As I stand there, trying to take it all in, my eyes adjust to the flickering candles and I start to see familiar faces sitting at a table in the center of the room.

My eyes catch Tee's first, then Dee's, Chesh's, Lar's, North's … and the King's. I narrow my eyes on him, but he barely acknowledges me, leaning back in a black-on-black suit and looking like he's fucking bored out of his skull. On the opposite side of the table, March waits with a shiny *black* apple in his hand, yet another fairy-tale trope that scares the shit out of me. Sorry, but thanks, no thanks. He can keep it.

I sit down at the head of the table (or is it the foot?), so I can be next to Tee, staring at the other men across a small pile of warm rocks with a kettle resting above them. It has two spouts and no handle which is weird as shit, but I'm still all twisted up over my encounter with Rab. I'm like a soda bottle that's been shaken, all fizzy and threatening to bubble over the top.

Rab flops down on my left, purposely pushing his shoulder into mine as he passes.

"I can’t believe you’re letting these mercenary fucks put

us through the wringer," I tell the King, wondering what the hell his motivations are. I half-expect to see the Knave and her husbands lurking at the dark edges of the room with Dor. I'm pleasantly surprised to find them all absent.

"When one is entrenched in shadows, one doesn't simply turn on a light." The King sits up and stares at me from across the glowing embers. They cast strange shadows on his face, highlighting the perfection that is Brennin Red, the King of Hearts. He has high, defined cheekbones, and a mouth that won't quit. That little scar on the corner of his mouth just emphasizes how gorgeous he really is.

"What *does* one do?" I mimic, fluttering my hands near my face. "Trip on a pile of dirty clothes and break one's toe?"

"Speaking from experience?" Dee asks with a bright grin. His wings cast beautiful shadows on the wall behind him, and I have to hold back a malicious grin when I see Ol' Red cast a frustrated glance in the twins' direction.

"Maybe," I quip with a small shrug. "One of my toes is a little crooked. You make your own assumptions."

"Assumptions ..." Dee starts, but then pauses when he notices the dark-eyed gaze of the King sweeping over him. With a sneer, Brennin turns back to look at me as the Mad Hatter carries over a tray of chipped little tea cups.

"Aren't you a clever one?" Brennin purrs cruelly, tugging at the white gloves on his hands. It's driving me up the *wall* trying to figure out why he never takes them off. Like, maybe because he's a murderer with red palms? "Look at you with your puns, *Your Majesty*." The King sits up straight, crown sliding lazily across his bloodred hair. The heart-shaped jewels seems to glow in the ominous half-light. "I'm sure that'll make for exceptional pillow talk."

"Go eat a dick," I say smartly, smirking and flipping him off as I get comfortable and glance over at Rab. He's pulling a pipe from the pocket on his slacks and glancing over at me with eyes the color of a smoky moon. Last year, there were so many forest fires in California that the smoke tainted the sky for days, and the moon … the moon was as red as blood.

"You thought I was poking you with something else?" he asks as I snort and shake my head.

"If your pipe is capable of growing when aroused, and caps out at … six inches," I start with a loose shrug of my shoulders. I'm a little bit full of shit though because I'm pretty sure it was longer than that. His dick, I mean, not his pipe.

"Such a clever little Alice," Rab says, lighting up and holding the smoke in his lungs for an inordinate amount of time. When he exhales, it all comes out through his nose, like a dragon billowing smoke.

Speaking of dragons …

My eyes meet North's gold ones from across the circle, and he smiles at me, reaching up to slick some of his hair back. As he does, he runs his fingers over one of his horns. Pretty sure that's, like, a come-on. It's working, too.

"Welcome all," March says, waving his hands dramatically over the flames. He flicks water into the coals, and pink steam rises up from the warm rocks. I have no idea *why* the steam is pink, but at this point, if I asked questions about *every* little idiosyncrasy in Underland, I wouldn't get a single other word out. "To the Torrid Tea Party."

He stands up and claps his hands, casting a dark gaze around the table. There are sky-high silver trays filled with cookies, cakes, tarts, sliced fruit, and unidentifiable little pastries covered in raisins. Dee *and* March are already eating, so I just help myself.

"Before we begin," March says, adjusting his own top hat. It's not *quite* as top-hattish as the Mad Hatter's, but that's to be expected, isn't it? Clearly, we all know who the boss is here. "I'd just like to acknowledge a very merry un-birthday to both Alice and the King."

"Oh fuck my life," I groan, putting my face in one hand. "Here we go with the nonsense."

"So you can see they're a perfectly matched pair," March continues, whisking a teacup off the tray and spinning it in his hand. With a brisk flick of the wrist, he pushes it down the length of the table. It twirls and dances until it comes to a stop directly in front of me. At first I think he's given me three cups stacked together, but when I move to pull them apart, I realize it's all one piece.

"We mustn't waste China," Chesh purrs, tapping at the side of my cup with a nail. "It's on the other side of the world, you know. To get there, we must dig a very great hole." He winks at me, and I'm not sure if he knows how ridiculous that sounds. I'm about fifty-fifty on that one.

"Before I was so rudely interrupted," March continues, and Chesh puts his ears flat against his head.

"I was *un*-rudely interrupting," he corrects, and March pauses like that's actually a valid point.

"Righto, my apologies," he says, lifting his hat and pulling out another small tea cup. "I should pay more attention. I just get so … *excited* when we host these parties." At the word *excited*, March reaches down and cups his junk. I fling a pastry in his direction and he catches it with his *mouth*. "As I was saying, clearly the Alice and the King are meant to be together as they share the same un-birthday. What a coincidence."

"We *all* share the same un-birthday," I growl out because a girl can only take so much nonsense before she snaps. I grab another raisin-covered pastry and bite into it. The inside is savory and spicy, filled with some sort of meat and vegetable paste. It's actually fucking delicious, although the *source* of the meat is a questionable thing.

"So we do …" March continues in his drawling English accent. "Bloody brilliant observation. So, we all share the same un-birthday—except for Dor. Today *is* his actual birthday."

"And you've locked him out of the party?" I ask with a roll of my eyes. "Some friends you are." Although I'm seriously fucking thrilled that nutbag was not invited. I'd be more likely to put my life in the hands of the wisteria blossoms outside my bedroom window (although one of them did call me a whore today which is most certainly *not* appreciated) than trust the Dormouse.

"We are *not* friends," March says as Raiden leans back in his chair and crosses his booted feet at the ankle. "Friends are as rare as diamonds and twice as precious. The only person with a friend in this room is the goddamn Savage Duke."

"I have *three* friends," North growls, squeezing my ankle with his tail. "The Cheshire Cat, Brennin Red, and Sonny Liddell." He ticks the names off his fingers with a little growl. "I may very well be the richest man in the Kingdom of Hearts."

"Second richest, as I've just taken a large sum of your

money," Raiden corrects, pulling his top hat low and shading his orange eyes from view. He's unbelievably gorgeous, dressed in a black and white striped suit jacket with a frilly white undershirt and a big orange bow-tie. The only part of his face I can see right now is his smile, twisted to the side and sharp as the slash from a knife.

Good thing I remembered to strap *my* knives to my thigh before I left; I've got my trusty ol' Queenmaker on my hip, too. Allison Pleasance Liddell, totally rad badass extraordinaire … in training. Can't forget the in training part.

The Duke just growls as March spins a second tea cup over to his boss. I can *hear* the King's white-gloved hands curling into squeaky fists. I get a kick out of that and decide I don't *quite* hate the March Hare as much as I thought I did —although he does give Red his cup next.

"So it seems we're *all* celebrating a special day today," March continues, locking eyes with me as he passes out the Duke's cup, then his own, Rab's, Lar's, Chesh's … and then Dee's and *then* Tee's.

Clearly, he's the least favorite of the twins. This is not the first time I've noticed.

Tee clenches his hand tight around his mug, his nostrils flared, a muscle in his jaw ticking. I also notice he fluffs his wings dramatically, drawing the attention of the entire room.

"He's a prince, too," I say, looking into my cup. "They

both are."

"They're servants, little more than slaves," the King says, and I slam my cup down so hard that it breaks it half.

"They're *mine*, you gave them to me," I snarl, even as Tee reaches over to put a hand on my arm.

"Allison, don't," he whispers, voice tight and ragged.

"So I did. It doesn't change the fact that that's what they are." The King lifts his gaze to mine, and there's this unyielding defiance in them that makes me crazy. For the first time in my life, I want to *break* someone's spirit, watch them collapse into a heap on the floor covered in tears and snot.

I hate the King.

I fucking *hate* him.

"Your idiot father did this to them. He slaughtered an entire *race*." I stand up from my chair, knocking it to the floor. Brennin follows me up, leaning his palms on the table and *staring* at me like he's feeling the same damn way, like he wants to break me.

Well, all I have to say to that is *good fucking luck, buddy.*

"My *father*," the King says, sliding a gloved finger along the scar that bisects his throat. "Did *this* to me. My *father*," he continues, stepping back. I notice that he manages to keep his chair upright. "Murdered my mother and my sisters, and he tried to murder me." He comes around the table to lord the fuck over me, and I just curl the corner of my lip up in a snarl.

"So you're going to continue his legacy by treating the twins like garbage?" I ask, my voice low and dangerous. Swear to God, I am *this* close to stabbing the man with the Vorpal Blade. Wonder if I could do it?

"What do you suggest I do with them?" he growls out, and I lift my face to look into his.

"Let them go. Release their chains, remove their curse, and admit that *your* father made a mistake." I cross my arms over my chest as the King stares at me. He looks like he wants to strangle me. Instead, he turns away with a flutter of his black cloak, and returns to his seat—the biggest, nicest chair of the whole bunch. He might not be sitting at the head of the table, but he's damn well made sure we *all* know who he is.

"Continue, and let's get this nonsense over with," Brennin says with a wave of his hand.

I resist the urge to chuck my broken tea cup in his direction as Tee helps me right my chair, pushing me back in before he whispers in my ear.

"No one has ever stood up for us like that before," he whispers, curling his fingers around my upper arms and giving me a long, lingering kiss on the cheek. Dee is watching us, his mouth half-stuffed with cupcake. He stops chewing as he gazes in my direction. There's too much there, in Tee's whispered words and Dee's longing stare.

I glance away sharply.

What can I say? I have intimacy issues.

March lifts up his hat again, sliding it up and over his ears, so he can grab another tea cup. He gives it a little spin and sends it my way.

"Once I pour the tea, we all drink, and then we switch places," March says as he picks up one of the twenty-plus teapots on the table. This one is painted to look like a jabberwock's scales. I wonder if all jabberwocky are black? Seeing as I've only *seen* one, I have no idea.

"Why would we switch places?" I ask, and I get several *are you serious?* looks from the men.

"To have a clean cup, of course," March says as he walks around the table and starts by pouring me a steaming cup of black tea. He pours in the same order he passed out the cups, and I swear it takes a *massive* amount of effort for me to hold my tongue on this one.

Once March is seated again, he lifts his cup up for a toast and everyone else follows suit.

I'm the last one to raise mine up.

"To a very torrid tea party," March says, and the other men repeat after him.

"To a very torrid tea party," I say, lifting the cup to my nose for a sniff. I'm getting hints of molasses and a subtle milkiness, even though I've yet to add any cream. When I peer a little closer, it looks like the liquid inside my cup is redder than I first thought.

Oh, and also, there are little jars filled with *needles* on the table that I failed to notice before. The men each grab one and start pricking their fingers, kneading tiny drops of blood into their cups.

“To activate the magic,” North explains when he catches me staring at him.

Oh, well, of *course* we’d add blood to our tea. Nothing less would make sense. With a sigh, I do the same, wincing as I stab my finger and watch a tiny crimson drop well up. I shake it into my cup and try really hard not to think much more about it.

"What sort of tea is this?" I ask as a few of the men add varying amounts of sugar and cream to their cups.

"It's quite tippy," the Mad Hatter says, cocking his head to one side. I still can't see his eyes with the brim of his hat pulled so low. "Large golden buds, delicately twisted leaves. There's a copper finish to it, wouldn't you agree, March?"

"This here blend is a Golden Shower Black Tea," March says, sipping his cup with a single pinky outstretched. There's a pretty wicked looking ring on it, too, and I get the idea that maybe the motion isn't just for show.

"Pardon, what?" I ask, blinking stupidly through the shadows at him.

"Your pardon is granted," he says, but he doesn't bother to answer my question. I narrow my eyes at him and try to resist the urge to throw hot tea in his face. I'll show *him* what a scalding hot golden shower can do.

"Golden Shower means the tea was watered *only* by rain coming down when the sun is out." Tee adds two scoops of sugar with one dash of cream, staring at his drink like he's already dreading taking a sip.

"So what do they do the rest of the time when it rains?" I ask as Dee fills his cup with cream and about ten scoops of sugar.

"They cover the field with a tarp," he says, downing his own drink in a single gulp.

"A golden shower back home—" I start, when Rab interrupts me.

"Is hot piss in the face during sex? We know that, Alice." Rab smokes his cig, glances to his right and takes a good, long look at the Mad Hatter sitting next to him. "We're all moving one space to the left, am I right?"

"Most assuredly," Raiden growls, one sharp fang showing over the edge of his lip. He watches as Rab taps his cigarette ash into the tea cup. "How clever are you? Perhaps I'll leave a wad of warm jizz in your cup next time I serve you?"

"Wouldn't be anything I hadn't tasted before," Rab says as Lar extends his pale hand across the table and takes the cigarette from Rab's fingers. The light from the fireplace filters through the Caterpillar's wings, turning them into stained glass windows that paint the faces of the men on the right side of the table a brilliant blue.

"You've tasted jizz before?" I ask, but the Cheshire Cat is already tapping at my glass with the tip of his tail.

"Drink, Alice, drink," he says, his pupils dilated to the point that I can't even see his gray irises anymore. I can't tell if that's because of the dark … or the drugs. Maybe both. "You and your angel prince."

I look around and realize that Tee and I are the only ones yet to take a drink.

"Are you okay?" I ask him, noticing the tightness around his eyes and the hard lines next to his even harder frown. He takes his peaked cap off and rakes his fingers through his hair.

"Tee used to be a tea addict," Dee says, rhyming the words in that silly singsongy way of his. "He was drunk more often than he was sober."

"You don't have to do this if you don't want to," I say, but Tee is already shaking his head. I can see small beads of sweat on his forehead, and I pick my red cloth napkin up to wipe them away.

"He can't leave, not now," March says, twitching his brown ears. Rab's white ones seem to twitch in response, and the two men turn to glare at each other. They're both the same species, aren't they? And they're both cronies for corrupt kings. They're rivals when really, they should be besties.

"Why not?" I ask, narrowing my eyes and then tilting my head as I hear the lock on the door slide closed. My mouth drops open and I flick my eyes in that direction.

"Once a Torrid Tea Party's started, it's impossible to get out the door," March says with a shrug, and the Mad Hatter tsk-tsks, wagging a finger in his direction.

"Not impossible, simply *impassable*—nothing's impossible." He lifts his hat up and flashes those marmalade orange eyes in my direction.

"If he leaves, he's out," the King says, in that same bored, no-nonsense voice of his. "You cannot marry him." I flip Brennin off and turn to Tee, reaching out to put my hand across the back of his.

"If you don't drink, neither do I," I whisper, and he lifts his amethyst eyes to look into mine. There's a quiet pleading there, but also an inner strength that I feel resonating in the very depths of my soul. We're peas in a pod, me and Tweedledum. Heh. Tweedledum … I like his nickname better.

"I'll drink," he says, looking straight into my eyes, "for you."

He lifts his cup and downs the whole thing before I can even take another breath.

I watch his hands shake as he puts the cup down and runs his arm across his mouth, gasping as he shakes his head and yanks his cap back down on his head.

If Tee can do it, then so can I.

But also … I want to know more about his time as an addict later.

"Cheers," I mumble under my breath, and then down the sweet-smelling tea, feeling the hot liquid burn its way down my throat.

As soon as it hits my stomach, I can feel the effects.

"That was delicious," I blurt without meaning to.

"Truth herbs," Lar says, crossing one arm over his chest and resting his head in the hand of the other. "It makes you say and do things you never would otherwise."

"I want to fuck the Alice," the King says, and then he smirks at me and I get the idea that maybe that *wasn't* an accidental little quip.

"I want to kill the King," I say, crossing my arms over my chest and then shrugging, sticking my tongue out in a silly, stupid way, like Dee always does. "Oops. Guess the effects of the herbs are already setting in."

"I don't want to become an addict again," Tee whispers, and then closes his eyes and covers his mouth like he didn't mean to say that.

"Shall we begin the torrid bit of our illustrious tea party?" March asks, lifting his finger and motioning for us all to switch. Like we're playing a game of musical chairs, we all stand and shift places, moving one spot to the left. I get the idea that it'd be *really* easy to poison someone like this. I should've used one of my test kits. Epic fail.

"Has anyone poisoned these cups?" I ask, and I get several blurted *no's* in response.

From everyone but the King and the Hatter.

"Sadly, no," Raiden says after a moment. Spinning his top hat around on his head, he flicks his attention in the direction of the King of Hearts. "And you, dear friend?"

"He knows that if he poisoned you, I'd blow his head off," March clarifies as he gestures absently in Red's direction.

"I didn't poison anyone," Red says with a cruel smile that stretches the scar on the edge of his mouth. "If I wanted someone dead, I'd simply take their head." He adjusts his crown and then lifts his chin. "So *Your Majesty,* please pick a man and start the questioning."

"I start?" I ask and several of the men nod, like that's the obvious route. "Okay, then … Red." I turn to look at the King and try not to scowl. "Did you really bring me here with the sole purpose of showing the court how useless I am?"

"Yes," he answers without hesitating, sitting up and crossing his arms over his broad chest. I can hear Tee growling from beside me. "I don't like you, and I think you're a useless figment of the past. The Alice you might be, but I don't need your help to right Underland's wrongs."

"I suggest you watch your tongue when you speak to my bloody mate," North growls, skin rippling like he's having a physical reaction to watching me be disrespected. "You know I can't handle that."

"My turn," the King says, ignoring the Duke *and* the order in which March passed out the cups; he looks straight at me as Raiden snarls some very creative curse words in the background. Like I said, battle of the alpha titan assholes. "If I were to give you the key to the Looking-Glass right now, would you leave? Would you *run*?"

"I'd go, but I'd come back," I blurt, digging my nails into my thighs to stop myself from elaborating on that. But I guess those truth herbs are *really* fucking strong, and I can't seem to hold myself back. "I can't leave my family not knowing. I also don't think I can abandon Underland, not anymore."

The King's mouth flattens into a thin line.

"Sorry, not sorry to disappoint you," I spit out, and I don't even try to fight the herbs on that one.

"The Knave wants you dead," he says, and then he cringes slightly as I raise my brows.

Well.

Now I don't feel so bad about hating the bitch.

"Why would the Knave want the Alice dead?" North says, slapping his heavy, muscular tail against the stone floor in a rhythmic pattern. "She wants your dick, doesn't she, Red?"

"She wants to be the Queen of Hearts," the King says, which is virtually the same thing. "I'm not sure if she wants to kill me or fuck me."

"She can't be queen," North growls, his nails lengthening at the end of his fingertips. "She isn't the Alice. The prophecy most *specifically* mentions the Alice. And you, you should be ashamed of yourself for trying to get rid of her. Fucking wanker." The Duke leans back in his chair with the gilded gold frame. He just sort of *melts* into it, draping his body elegantly across the navy blue velvet cushions.

"I should have you beheaded," Red says, but then the truth herbs kick in and he adds, "but I never will."

"No, you shouldn't. I hear a jabberwock can still bite with its head cut off." North taps his nails against the table and then scowls. "And now the Mad Hatter may have one question."

"I have a quest, not a question," Raiden Walker says, his mouth curling into a cheeky little smile. "For the Alice."

"Shocker," I say with a roll of my eyes. "What do you want?"

"I want you to let me drink your blood—and I *dare* you to enjoy it." The Mad Hatter lets his smile eat up his entire face, shadows from the fireplace dancing across his pale skin.

"Those are two separate things," I mumble, but I can already feel my cheeks heating.

Avid reader, remember? Like I've never fantasized about what it would feel like to be bitten by a vampire … Fuck.

Fuck, fuck, fuck.

I'm going to enjoy this *too* damn much, aren't I?

"I'm only asking you to let me as a quest," Raiden says, running his tongue over his lower lip. "Whether you enjoy it or not, that's up to you."

"What happens if I refuse the dare—err, quest?" I ask, not because I really want to, but because I feel like I need to make *some* sort of motion to pretend I'm not as eager as I am.

"Then you're out," Lar explains, folding his wings behind him. "You don't get to ask anymore questions although you must answer them."

"And if I refuse to answer?" I ask, and several of the guys chuckle at me.

"The herbs won't let you refuse." Lar smiles, gold bangles dangling on his arms as he leans back in his chair.

"Well, there's no way in fuck I'm letting myself lose this game," I say, standing up from my seat, and throwing some rainbow and blonde hair back from my face. I move over to the Mad Hatter and sit down on his lap before I can stop myself.

And oh.

Holy shit, that feels nice.

He wraps his arms around me and pulls me closer, filling my nose with that metallic, bloody scent of his, making my heart flutter strangely in my chest. I reach up to take his top hat off and hear several of the men make sounds behind me. Guessing it's taboo to touch the Mad Hatter's hat?

Still, he lets me take it off. And the next one. And the next one. The fourth hat is a small white one with the name *Alice* in gold cursive on the tag. It has red hearts, a big black feather, and black lace on it.

It's unspoken that it's supposed to be mine.

"A gift," Raiden says as I take the top hat and put it on my head. I can almost feel it *sealing* to my skull and let out a little yelp. "A spell to keep it on your head," he explains as I experimentally lift it up and set it back down again. Weird, but useful, I suppose. "It's got a little extra magic in there, too, just in case."

He sweeps my hair over my shoulder with long fingers, making me shiver as I close my eyes tight.

"This might hurt, at first," he whispers, kissing the side of my neck and sending hot, excited little thrills zinging through my blood.

"This is sexual, Alice," Tee says, his voice rife with worry. "If you don't want him to touch you like that, just refuse the quest. I'll ask your questions for you." His offer makes me smile, but I'm not backing down from this.

Not only will my stubborn side not allow it, but it … feels really freaking good, too.

Raiden licks his way over to the throbbing pulse point in my throat, putting his lips to it and tasting me as I struggle to hold back a groan, wiggling on his lap and feeling his cock hardening beneath my ass.

His teeth graze my skin, lighting every nerve-ending I have on fire.

When Raiden bites me, sinking his fangs into my neck, there's this white-hot burst of pain behind my eyelids that makes me cringe. I'm about to shove him back and pull away when a delicious heat spreads through me, invading my blood, poisoning me from head to toe. I let out a little whimper and sag against him as his arms tighten around me, and he growls against my throat.

I swear there's a string between that bite and my clit, yanking and pulling on it, making it throb. Like I wasn't already hot and bothered from what happened between Rab and me. But this, this is overwhelming. I feel like I'm drowning in my own pleasure.

Raiden takes his sweet time, sucking and licking,

twirling his tongue around each of the teeth marks on my neck before he bites me again. And again. And again. Leaving his mark on my neck.

His arms tighten around me and I can't help but wiggle on his lap, eliciting a sharp groan from his throat. The sound weaves around and through me, almost like a drug, and I find myself melting into him.

"That's enough of that," the King says, and there's a strange tightness in his voice that's either jealousy or longing or *both.*

I pull away from Raiden, slamming into the table and knocking over several ceramic tea pots. One rolls to the floor and shatters, but I'm too dizzy and disoriented to care. My head is spinning and I'm not sure if it's from the bite or the tea or what.

"Holy crap," I groan, using the table to feel my way back toward my chair. I end up in Dee's lap instead, and he helps steady me. "Is that ... the bite or the tea?"

"Both," Raiden says, and he sounds ... *explosive.* Not at all like the cool, calm psychopath he's been presenting himself as. "It's fucking both."

He's panting heavily, a bit of blood smeared across his mouth. When I lift my fingers to touch the bite, it feels too good and I let out a small groan of pleasure. My fingers are stained with red when I stand up, smearing across the surface of the table as I do my best to make it back to my chair.

As soon as I slump into it, I know I'm not going to make it very long.

We have to drink a fresh cup of tea after each round? You've got to be fucking kidding me.

"North," the March Hare says, ears twitching as he grins, his teeth white in his dark face. "Your turn."

"My question is for the Cheshire Cat," he says, surprising me. I sort of figured almost all of the guys would go for me. Egotistical much? The Duke turns toward his friend and leans in close. Chesh does the same until they're nose to nose, tails twitching in a similar rhythm.

"Do you like the Alice? Or are you simply after her because she's my mate?" His accent flows over me like water and invades my brain. I am so high, y'all. Like, higher than a goddamn kite. My head lolls against the back of the chair as I blink through a foggy haze and start to sway to imaginary music.

"Maybe a little bit of both?" Chesh says, triangular ears swiveling on the top of his head. He flattens one back against his dark hair and then glances over at me. "She's growing on me, you know. And she seems to like princes. Must be part of the prophecy?"

"You're a prince, too?" I ask, just barely managing to swing my gaze over to him.

"I'm a *cat*," he says, flashing me pointed little kitty teeth.

"All cats are princes."

What a non-answer. But I'm too high to question it.

"Looks like I'm next," March says, rubbing his hands together and then plucking up a sugar cookie in the shape of a pink bat. He bites into it and then gestures at me. "Okay, Doll," he says, and even though I'm feeling out of it, I roll my eyes at that. "Are you afraid?"

"Am I afraid?" I ask, and the question gives me cold chills.

Because the answer … is yes.

After meeting the Mocking Turtle and the Gryphon, after seeing the King so callously kill one of his card servants, after hearing the Mad Hatter tell me he'd like the Duke to be raped and killed … How am I supposed to tell who the bad guys are anyway?

"Yes," I say, because I'm just an eighteen year old girl from nowhere … but the question is, am I destined for somewhere? Am I really meant to be something? Prophecy or no prophecy, it's really up to me, isn't it? Only I can decide.

"True fear is fine," March says as he looks at me with eyes the color of coffee with cream. I want to drink them up, savor them against my tongue. Aaaand how high did that shit sound just now? Jesus. "It's how brave you are in the face of it that matters."

"Excellent question," Rab says, smoking his cigarette

with this easiness that invades every action he takes. He's just so damn confident, but also a little bit scary. I think about him holding me over that pile of bones beneath the Rabbit-Hole, and I can hardly match the memory to my current reality. It’s no use going back to yesterday; I was a different person then. "But mine's better. Mine isn't simply a quest*ion* but a quest which is funny because question is actually longer than quest, but I suppose spelling doesn't much matter tonight?"

"Just get on with it," Tee grumbles, slipping out of his jacket and using his napkin to wipe sweat from his neck and chest.

"My quest is for you to *let me prick you, Miss Alice.*" Rab taps his cigarette ash onto the floor and then flicks the butt across the table and into the fireplace. Pretty impressive. But I'm still sitting there fucked off my ass on boosted tea and trying to figure out what he's *really* saying.

"You want to give me a tattoo?" I ask, because if he wanted to sleep with me, he'd just come out and say it. Well, I'm sure he *does* want to sleep with me, but I feel like there must be an unspoken rule *not* to ask for sex during the Torrid Tea Party. Although the word *torrid* means ardent or passionate, right?

"Exactly that," the White Rabbit says, leaning forward in his chair and steepling his fingers beneath his chin. "So do you accept my quest, Sonny Liddell?"

"I've always wanted a tattoo." The words burst from my lips before I can stop them. Fucking truth plants or whatever the hell they are. There must be a cooler name than *truth herbs,* right? Everything else here has weird names. "Okay."

"Allison," Tee says, and I get the idea that maybe I've agreed to something I don't quite understand.

"Come here," Rab says, leaning back and patting his knee. It takes a *lot* of effort for me to stand up, pushing my bat dress down my thighs because it keeps riding up. No wonder I only wear jeans at home. That's one thing I'm really starting to miss. Note to self: if I ever do go back through the Looking-Glass, I need to snatch my favorite denim to bring back with me.

Back with me?

Wow. Look at that. I've already committed myself to coming back to this crazy place.

Because … I can't just let Underland descend into madness, now can I?

Steadying myself with my palms on the table, I make my way over to Rab, using the backs of Tee's and Dee's chairs to keep myself upright until I reach him. And then I tumble right into his lap, same way I did to the Hatter.

"Where do you want me … I mean *it*, Miss Sonny Liddell," he whispers, tucking some loose hair behind my ear.

"Where do I want it?" I ask, looking down at my bare thighs. I tap the left one as the blood sloshes around in my head like waves in a storm. I'm so fucked up right now, but I also figure that I've always wanted a tattoo. How could I possibly regret this?

Sounds like something a drunk person would say, huh?

Rab reaches out and pulls one of the tea pots close to him, lifting the lid and … removing a tattoo machine full of gears and cogs?! What in the ever-loving fuck?

"Who puts a tattoo gun in a teapot?" I slur, even though I've been told by several different tattoo enthusiasts that it's rude to call it a gun. It's a *machine*.

"Someone who's mad," the White Rabbit says, setting the machine aside and then tapping his fingers against the sheathed Vorpal Blade. "May I borrow your knife, Sonny?" He whispers my nickname against my ear and I shiver.

"For what?" I ask, but Rab's already ripping the sheath open and sliding his fingers along my thigh. My breath catches, and I feel that pulsing heat between my legs like it's shouting at me via vagina-megaphone.

Rab slides the knife out and then tugs a small China creamer over. He empties the cream out into his empty tea cup then cuts his wrist, bleeding a profuse amount into the pink and white harlequin patterned China.

I watch mesmerized as he massages ruby red droplets from his wrist, grabbing yet another teapot and adding some steaming hot tea to his bloody concoction.

I'm weirded the fuck out, but nobody else seems bothered by what Rab's doing, so I just wait. I've seen a man turn into a cat, prophecies played out on faerie wings come to life, and a living card have its neck snapped. I may never be shocked by anything ever again.

"And a little sweetness, just for you, Sonny," Rab says, adding a bit of sugar to the mixture and stirring it up with a teaspoon. He sets it aside and goes for the Vorpal Blade again, stuffing a cloth napkin into his mouth and biting down on it before he lowers the blade to his arm … and starts to cut into his skin.

My lips part in shock, but it feels like I'm moving in slow motion when I reach out to stop him. The Mad Hatter leans over my shoulder and pulls my hands away.

"Let him finish," he whispers into my ear, and I wait as Rab filets his pocket watch tattoo off and peels his skin away from his arm. My tummy rumbles with nausea, and if I weren't high, I might make a fucking run for it.

"What the hell is going on?" I ask, my voice slurring like I've had way too many bottles of Dad's top-shelf brandy. He used to have a small glass every Friday, Saturday, and Sunday night, sitting in the living room with a fire blazing and some hard-boiled crime show on that he'd watch with Mom.

Guess he didn't realize he'd be starring in a real life version of one, huh?

Rab pulls the tattoo off his body as I shriek like a banshee. When he puts it on my leg, I almost faint.

"Can I get a heal?" he grinds out as he picks up the tattoo machine, and pulls a … a needle and fucking *thread* from the end of it?! It's a literal goddamn sewing needle and piece of string.

The Mad Hatter releases my hand and bites his wrist, lifting it up to Rab's mouth. The White Rabbit licks him as he makes eye contact with me, stirring my hormones into a frenzy. I can't stop myself from thinking about what I walked in on, with the Mad Hatter's mouth on the King's neck.

If drinking blood can be sexual then what the hell were they doing in there?

As I sit there and watch, Rab's arm heals over. The tattoo is gone, but his skin is unblemished and whole. I run my fingers over it, and he shudders.

Of course, there's still a bit of his skin sitting on my leg.

Rab takes the needle and thread, and then bites my earlobe, making me shiver.

"Hold still," he breathes in his bones-and-ice voice. He dips the needle into the blood and tea mixture, then threads it into my skin, making me yelp. As I sit there trembling, he 'sews' the edges of his tattoo to my skin. As he goes, not only does he tattoo a lacey design onto my flesh, but he melds his tattoo into my leg, to the point where I can't see where his skin ends and mine begins.

When I poke at the design with a fingernail, it hurts.

It's not Rab's skin anymore, it's *mine*.

When he finishes and removes the needle, snapping the thread with his teeth, the seconds hand on the clock begins to tick.

"What is this a countdown to?" I ask as I rub my thumbprint over the design. There's a tiny calendar on the open face of the pocket watch, and I can see that we've got quite some time until this one hits its target.

"This is a pivotal point," the White Rabbit says, wiping some of the blood from my leg. It hurts, but it's also riding that fine edge of pleasure and pain. "We probably won't know what it means until it happens. Could be this is the moment you either save Underland … or destroy it." Gently, he pushes me off of his lap and pulls his white ears down to cover his eyes. "Now get the fuck off my lap before I come in my slacks."

"Charming," I groan as I look down at my new tattoo and wonder how long I'm going to last before I pass out … or what I might think when I wake up. I manage to make it back to my chair, but just barely.

"Now," March says, grinning and then biting down hard on a pastry. Red filling squirts out of the end like blood, making me feel dizzy. My leg, it still hurts like hell, too. "My turn." He watches me for a moment, and then turns to the Mad Hatter. "My quest for you … is to kiss the King."

"Really?" Raiden says, looking irritated. He pops an elbow on the table, cradles his hand in it, and sighs. "I suppose if I must."

"Really." March shoves the rest of the pastry in his mouth and then delicately wipes off his fingers with a cloth napkin. "That's my quest: kiss the goddamn King on the *mouth*."

"As opposed to where?" Raiden asks, tilting his head to the side and giving March a pissy little look.

"I'm sorry, but … *if you must*?" Brennin drawls, looking bored out of his fucking skull. I'm not sure what March is up to with this game, but I'm intrigued to see how it plays out. That is, if I can keep my eyes open. Twice the boost, they say. More like ten times. I remember how I felt dancing at The Pool; it wasn't nearly as psychedelic as this. "You'd only be so lucky."

Raiden stands up and straightens his bowtie with a sigh, letting his gaze slide over to mine. Now I'm thinking about his mouth on the King's neck which, of course, makes my own neck tingle and throb. I put my fingers against it, smearing blood everywhere, and find myself letting out the most embarrassing fucking moan known to man.

I sound like a dying cow or a birthing giraffe, maybe

some combination thereof.

"Why were you sucking on the King the other day?" I drawl, flopped over my chair like one of Salvador Dalí's melting clocks.

"Royal blood has a certain ..." the Mad Hatter pauses and adjusts his velvet top hat. "*Je ne sais quoi.* The King knows how to win over a mercenary's shaky loyalty."

"What a non-answer," I drawl, rolling my eyes as Raiden makes a show of rounding the table. The King acts like a kiss with a blackmailing rival mercenary male means nothing to him, leaning back in his chair and waving a gloved hand around dismissively.

"Let's get this over with, shall we?" He scoots his chair back, and then gets this super fucking annoyed expression on his too-handsome face when Raiden steps between him and the table, leaning down and putting his palms on either of the chair's arms. The Mad Hatter is pinning the King of Hearts into his seat and getting ready to kiss him.

Somebody pinch me please.

"I knew you'd like this, the Alice," March drawls, eyes sparkling like maybe I'm not the only one who's enjoying the show. I can't decide if he's into the guy-on-guy thing or if he just likes teasing his boss and seeing the King suffer.

Raiden Walker stares Brennin Red down, his top hat

sliding forward to shield his eyes from view. Yet I can tell from here that they're both staring at one another. The Mad Hatter holds that position for an inordinate amount of time, letting the crackle of the fire be the only sound in the room.

"Well?" Red demands, reaching up to adjust his crown. He just sits there with his stupidly stoic face until the Mad Hatter finally grins, flashing fang. Raiden closes the distance between them slowly, languorously, his mouth hovering above the King's scowl for an uneasy moment. I almost wonder if Brennin is going to shove him away and put an end to the Torrid Tea Party.

Instead, at the last moment, Raiden walker rips his hat off—his *last* fucking hat!—and Brennin Red tilts his head slightly to the side. Their lips meet, and their mouths part. There is clearly tongue at play here.

My jaw drops, and I find myself leaning forward in my chair to gape at them.

The kiss doesn't last long—a few seconds maybe—but it's one of the most beautiful things I've ever seen. Not only do both men look like experts in the field of making out, they execute it with movie-style perfection, a single take that falls together in perfect unison.

When they part, there's this thin string of saliva that connects them for half a second before the King shoves his gloved hand across his mouth, and the Hatter lets out a raucous laugh.

"Now, that was fun, wasn't it?" he asks, standing back up and swiping his palms down the front of his jacket to straighten out imaginary wrinkles in the fabric. Of course, there are none because the Mad Hatter is perfection incarnate.

He returns to his seat, as the King sighs dramatically and rubs at his temples.

"White Rabbit, if you'd please. I have other business to attend to tonight."

"Well, don't let my torrid little party interfere with your busy work schedule," the Mad Hatter says, putting his fingers to his chest in a very mocking way. He rolls his marmalade colored eyes and replaces his hat.

"Is that an order to hurry my ass up?" Rab asks, checking his pocket watch and sighing dramatically. "Oh my ears and whiskers, how late it's getting." He tucks the watch into his vest and sighs. "What do you wish me to ask, Your Majesty?"

"Wait, what?" I snap, getting just a hint of mental clarity back. "It's your turn: you pick the quest or question."

"I live to serve," Rab drawls, propping his head on his knuckles and staring at the King with a rather disrespectful expression. Brennin ignores him, sitting up in his seat and raking his gloved fingers through his red hair.

"Ask the room if anyone has been involved with the tampering of our network as related to the King of Clubs." Brennin pours himself a cup of tea from a red pot—I'm assuming this is just regular boosted, drugged tea as opposed to truth herb tea—and takes a sip. Seems to me like he's throwing a bit of shade.

"We all heard the question," I mumble, but Rab repeats it anyway.

"Is anyone in this room involved with the tampering of our network as related to the King of Clubs?" Rab touches his fingertip to the flickering flame of a taper candle. His eyes shift around the circle, waiting for the truth herbs to kick in and kick our asses.

"No." There's perfect unison from the twins, a grin from the cat, and me rolling my eyes as I answer.

"Intriguing question and good use of our time," the Mad Hatter says, watching the King carefully. "Well-played. And no, no I am not involved."

"Nor me." March moves onto his third or fourth cupcake —I've lost count at this point—and flattens his ears against his head.

"I would never." Lar fans his wings softly and takes up smoking a cigarette on a long, decorative gold holder, blowing blue smoke rings into the hazy darkness.

"And we all know I'm clear. I kill things; I don't network." Rab smiles sharply and unbuttons his vest, like …

it's getting hot in here, so take off all your clothes sort of a thing.

"You'll ask the Mad Hatter and the March Hare how the Clubs knew the Alice was with us on such short notice," the King says, looking to Lar next. "I mean, unless it was pure unhappy coincidence that the Mocking Turtle and the Gryphon showed up like they were summoned."

"That's a low blow, coming from someone like you," Raiden says, but the way he's grinning at the King says he likes the way this is going. There's violence and sex in the air here, and I feel like I'm drowning in it.

My body likes it though. As if I weren't wet enough from my encounter with Rab, from the Mad Hatter's mouth on my neck, his kiss with Brennin Red, the drugs also seem to have an arduous effect on my cunt. My panties are soaked, and my nipples hurt from staying pebbled for so long.

"Where did the Clubs happen to come across information that might lead them to believe the Alice was in our care?" Lar repeats, leaning back in his chair and using his finger to draw dog-and-caterpillars in the air next to him. Ya know, bugs with cat and dog heads? I'm assuming they exist somewhere in this nightmare.

"I haven't the faintest idea," the Hatter says, glancing over at his right-hand man. "March?"

"My only guess is that they were keeping a pretty close eye on us, tracking our movements. I can't imagine the King of Clubs trusts us much. After all, we do have reputations, don't we Hatter?"

"Oh March, we most certainly do. And so undeserved, too!" Hatter replies, spinning his hat around on his head.

March winks at me from across the table, and I cock a brow. Right. Undeserved. I shift in my seat because my pussy is so damn swollen, it almost hurts. March notices. Like I said, eyes, ears, and nose of the operation.

The rest of us mutter our thoughts on the matter, or lack thereof. It's quite clear this is a chess match between the Hatter and the King. Nobody else matters much.

"And now it's the damn cat's turn," the King snarls. "Horrid beast. I found hairs all over my finest robes this morning. How do you think they got there? I don't keep *cats*; I prefer *dogs*."

"No accounting for taste," Chesh repeats, disappearing from view, and then reappearing as an upside down white smile. His grin is as big as his head. "Though I suppose with the truth herbs I can't outright lie to you. All I can say is that I quite enjoyed urinating in your shoes." The Cheshire cat laughs as I sway in my seat and notice that the darkness in the room has now begun to take on multi-colored hues. Oh dear. I'm quite high, aren't I? "For my turn, I'd like to offer up a quest for the Alice."

"Of course you do," I ooze, barely aware of my own lips moving. "And what's that? A blow job? Because I'm not into perpetuating rape culture. A little bit high over here."

"A blow job?" Chesh's smile asks, turning back around the proper way. "Not at all. I was going to ask if you might scratch me behind the ear?"

The King sets his mouth into an ugly snarl, and sneers at the poor cat in a way that makes me furious. I stand up so quickly, my chair almost topples over, and Tee has to reach out to steady my swaying ass.

"You, sir, are a *prick*," I say before I head over to Chesh's spot, throwing my arms around his neck before he even really has one. His human body fades into view and he starts to purr. I rub my cheek against his, feeling this white-hot heat flare between us. Oh, this is so much more than a simple pet; it feels like a mating ritual.

My fingers stroke over his silky black and white ears, teasing the silver hoops, and noticing that there's a very distinct bulge in his lap that was not there before. His tail hooks around my ankle, and he makes this growling/mewling sound that has my panties all twisted in a knot.

"We'll be explosive pussy partners, don't you think?" he asks as I stumble and end up falling into his lap. I don't bother to move because, well, is there a better seat in the house? That, and I'm not sure I'll make it back to my own chair.

"Piss in my shoes again and you'll see the meaning of explosive," the King snaps, looking up as I chuck a teacup in his direction. He knocks it aside at the last moment with a gloved hand, and it explodes in the fireplace, sending bits of China all over the old stone floors. "That was not a particularly smart decision, *Your Majesty*."

"The cat is mine; he belongs to me. Leave him alone." I rub my cheek against Chesh's as his grin grows to gargantuan proportions, like it may very well fall off of his face. "You're mine now, Cheshire Puss. I'll hug you and love you and snuggle you as if you were my very own Dinah."

"Oh dear," Dee says, gritting his teeth from beside me. "You are quite out of it, aren't you Allison-who-isn't-Alice?"

"She won't make it a second round," Tee says, but I'm barely listening. I'm too busy snuggling the Cheshire Cat. Never snuggled a cat with an eight inch erection in his leather pants, but hey, there's a first time for everything! "Dee, make this count."

The chipper angel prince nods his head and offers up a salute, shifting in his chair to look at me, the feathers on his wings rustling.

"Allison-who-isn't-Alice," he coos, reaching out to run a finger down the bridge of my nose. "I need to ask you a question, my little Mary Sue." I grin and try to smack his hand away, but it looks like it's flickering in about a million different colors, and I find myself simply staring. "Can you look at me?" He taps my chin, and I lift my gaze to those glorious blue eyes of his. Like oceans, I could swim in them.

We stare at each other for what feels like eons, and I know in that crazy drug-induced moment that it will never be long enough. I want to stare at Dee forever.

My hand lifts up and seems to cup the side of his face of its own accord; Dee leans into my touch.

"Allison," he says, using my real name for once, "what should I ask?"

I blink my eyes at him, and it takes a good twenty seconds for the question to sink in. Lar and Rab still defer to the King, but the twins … are mine.

"What's Rab's third form?" I blurt, which is really a waste of a question, but I'm entirely *wasted*, so what does it matter? I reach over the table and snag a cupcake from one of the tiered silver trays. It has a crystallized butterfly on the top, which I eat in one bite. It tastes like marmalade and butter on toast.

"Rab," Dee singsongs as the bandersnatch assassin rolls his red eyes, "what's your third form?"

"It is a literal state secret that I've sworn on my life not to reveal without the King's permission," Rab says, looking like he's about to choke on his tea. The Duke grins and passes over a jug of ice water with tiny flowers dancing on the top.

"Two magical oaths warring against one another," North says, smiling and teasing the tip of one of his horns with a finger. "Whatever shall you do?"

"Your Majesty?" Rab chokes out, giving the King a look. But Brennin simply sits stone-still and says nothing at all. "Fuck." Sweat pours down the sides of his face as he leans over and curls his fingertips into the wood of the table. "May I simply say that my third form is a royal and be done with it?" After the words leave his lips, there's a visible loosening of the tight skin around his eyes and forehead. "Oh for Heart's sake, that was awfully cruel."

Rab exhales and leans back in his chair, my curiosity peaked to high hell. A royal, huh? Perhaps his third form is the King, like March's is the Mad Hatter? It wouldn't surprise me.

"An intriguingly insightful question," North says, glancing over at the King. Brennin returns his look and they hold each other's gazes for the longest fucking time. Or maybe I'm just high on boosted tea? Either way, that look is sketch as fuck. Makes me wonder if Rab's third form is actually something worse? What … if he's got the King's father's form in him or something?

"Surprisingly so," Tee replies, narrowing his eyes slightly. He doesn't trust North, and I know it's because of the Duke's close relationship with the King. But I think—*think*—that North is on my side now, or at least leaning that direction. "I won't waste your time because I can see Allison isn't faring well. Lar." He turns to the Caterpillar who's still lazily smoking his cigarette. "In any of your visions, did you see us as being the Alice's nine?"

Oh.

Damn.

Tweedledum does not fuck around.

Lar smiles slow and easy, tilting his head to one side, earrings swaying with the motion. His jacket is black today, to match the dress code, but the epaulettes and fringe are still gold, rustling in that supernatural breeze of his. When he opens his mouth to speak, smoke escapes and begins to dance in the air with fantastical shapes.

"How doth the Alice prophesied
Improve her all-male harem,
She dates assassins, kings that bleed
princes, angels, dragons!

How cheerfully her kitty grins,
How neatly shifts her rabbit,
She welcomes winged seer men in
While dating thieves is habit!"

The Caterpillar fans his wings as he recites and then executes a very small bow from his seated position.

"That's about all I know," he replies cheekily, a saucy smile taking over his lips. "Make of it what you will."

"That's not at all subtle," I drone, trying to push up from Chesh's lap. I don't believe in destiny or prophecy anyway; if these guys are interested in being one of my nine, they better show me their true colors and let me decide if they're worthy of my time. "Is it time to drink and switches places again? I could very well use a clean cup." I try to grab a teacup half-filled with tea, but Dee extracts it from my wobbly grip.

"Nah ah, Allison-who-isn't-Alice, you must wait for the official pouring and the blood prick to drink."

"But I'm thirsty," I whine, throwing my arms around Dee's neck. I end up tumbling out of Chesh's lap and straight into his. He collects me in his arms and holds me close.

"No more extra tea for you," he starts and then pauses suddenly, like he's seen a ghost. Slowly, I crane my head around to see what he's looking at.

It's Lar, bent over his empty teacup with a severe frown in place on those perfect pink lips.

"Oh, dear," he says, as the King glances into the cup alongside him. "Well, this certainly isn't any good." Ah, he's reading the tea leaves. I'm both fascinated and terrified to find out what it is that's caught his interest—doubly so, considering my intoxicated state. "We need some whiting, and promptly."

Rab scrambles up and out of his seat, moving to a cabinet in a dark corner. All I can see of him as he digs around in it are his white ears. When he returns to the table, he has a hookah, and he quickly readies it to be smoked.

"What does it say?" the King asks, gesturing at the chipped tea cup in the Caterpillar's hands. "Don't be coy, Lar, spill the tea, please."

The Caterpillar sighs and tugs on one of his earrings.

"The cup spells danger, clear and immediate danger." Lar snaps his fingers and the White Rabbit passes over the hookah. He takes a drag, exhaling blue-gray smoke, and then passes it around the table, starting with the King.

We all take turns breathing in the sweet scents of tobacco and blueberries. The high hits me like a ton of bricks, compounding on the two cups of boosted fucking tea that I drank.

I hope I'm awake long enough to see Lar's premonition, let alone act on it.

He stands up and pushes his chair to the side, spreading his wings wide behind him. They're bigger than the fireplace, blocking out the flicker of flames, and turning into this hazy dreamland that I can't seem to look away from.

Images flicker to life within the black-gold edges, sucking me into the dark gardens of the castle and beyond the wall. It's like I'm inside the head of whatever's watching us, staring up at the tower from the safety of the woods.

There's a long moment of silence, broken only by the melodic sound of an insect that vaguely—and only vaguely—reminds me of a cricket. Vultures in every color of the rainbow sit perched on a heavy tree limb, watching and waiting.

"Oh, I do believe we're being spied on, old chap," the Gryphon says, lounging next to the vultures like he's one of them. Now that I think about it, his face does vaguely remind me of one of the ugly scavenger birds. His wings, too.

"I believe you're right," the Mocking Turtle says, smacking his pointed and deadly mouth with a grotesque, wet smack. "But no prophecies will be held here today. This is a warning to hand over the Alice, not a chance at espionage."

The Mocking Turtle glances up from his position at the base of the tree and waves his hand, cracking the vision in the Caterpillar's wings and making Lar cry out. Blue, gold, and black dust explodes outward, coating everything.

Lar collapses, but the King is there to catch him, hoisting the other man up and then laying him on the tabletop with the Duke's help. Cups and teapots scatter everywhere, rolling to the floor and cracking into pieces.

"We need to get out there," Rab snarls, and he doesn't wait for the King to give him an order of any kind. Instead, he shifts into the massive, hulking form of the bandersnatch, his thick white coat spotted with black, his tail fluffed, the hair along his spine raised. He noses open a set of black shutters I hadn't noticed before, so buried in the shadows were they.

Silver light from the double moons shines into the room in thick beams, ruining the Torrid Tea Party's ambiance. Tee moves up beside Rab and opens the massive windows for him, throwing them out and into the night air before he makes room for the angry bandersnatch.

I try to head for the window, too, but Dee holds me back.

"Oh hell no," he says, shaking his head and wrapping me up in his wings. "They're here because they want to see you—if not snatch you. You're not going out there."

"But I'm *the* Alice," I slur, drunk as fuck on boosted tea. I manage to somehow get the Queenmaker off my belt and into my hands, but Dee curls his fingers around my grip and shakes his head. "I'm the …" I stop and sit down heavily in Tee's vacated chair.

My head is *swimming*.

The King and North manage to tie Lar down by borrowing both the Hatter's and the Hare's belts, stuffing a cloth napkin between his lips to keep him from biting his own tongue. The fit he's having looks awfully similar to the one I had.

Magic is afoot again.

I stand up and put the palm of my hand against Lar's forehead, glancing over my shoulder to find that Tee has also disappeared from the room. The Mad Hatter and the March Hare are conferring in the corner, and the Duke is already on his way out.

"Kisses, love," he says, putting his mouth to my cheek. "I won't shift unless I have to, but if I do …" He winks at me as I blink big, stupid eyes up at him. "I'll be quite savage, and I'll need my mate." He tousles my hair and then heads for the window, climbing out onto the roof before shifting his jabberwock wings.

"Well, you wanted a part of my kingdom. Are you planning on defending it?" Brennin growls at the pair of mercenaries. Chesh simply shifts into cat form and hops onto my shoulders. I'm not sure how useful he is in a fight. I mean, he could very well throw up his hand, shout '*Moon prism power!'* and change into a magical girl for all I know. Anyway, he takes up residence on my shoulders, prepared to watch the power exchange taking place in front of us.

"That depends," Raiden says as March balances a butter

knife on his fingertip. "I want the Alice to tell me how she plans on weaseling out of our little marriage deal—while she's high on herbs. In fact, have her drink the second round cup and tell me."

"If she drinks another cup, she'll pass out," Dee snaps, losing his cheerful attitude to defend me. "Fuck you, vampire dick."

Raiden raises an eyebrow and shrugs his shoulders. I can hear shouting outside, the crash of stone, the crack of a tree limb. I race over to the window with Dee on my heels and peer out, finding Rab scrambling to his feet in a tangle of broken branches, blood dripping from his wolf-y jaws.

He flattens his rabbit ears against his skull and circles the pair of disturbingly calm men.

As if they can sense me, they both look up in unison and meet my eyes. A shock travels through me, and I stumble back and away from the open window again.

"Those are not Recitations," I whisper, feeling my body start to shake. It's involuntary, that shaking. I can't control my emotions right now; I can barely control my own feet. "They're really here."

"If they're willing to approach Castle Heart, they're not afraid," the King says, moving to stand beside me. "That's not good at all." I have the Queenmaker still clutched in my hand, but as I stand there, I find my fingers inching toward the Vorpal Blade. "Don't touch it," Red snaps, grabbing my wrist. The cat hisses at him and scratches out with a paw, but it's all for show. He knows better than to make the King bleed. "They're trying to get a read on your magic, so they can summon the Anti-Alice. The Vorpal Blade is power incarnate; activate it, and the Anti-Alice will come running. I can smell her out there in the woods, like dusty coffins and death."

My eyes widen, and I choke back a small sound of terror. This tea is making me paranoid *as fuck.*

"Can they get in?" I whisper, watching North stalk along the top of the wall. There's a huge fucking hole in it, but neither the Gryphon nor the Mocking Turtle seem inclined to cross that invisible barrier.

"*They shall not touch, with hands of hate, the pleasance of our Heart'd gate*," the King says, and clearly he's reciting some poem or prophecy or something. He turns ebon eyes to me, the silver moonlight turning his red hair into fire. "They can't get in, but the Anti-Alice can … *if* you fuck with the Vorpal Blade while the wall is down. And anyway, even if those two can't get in, it doesn't mean they can't hurt you, Allison Liddell. If I were you, I'd leave. Now."

"If you'd fucked Liam and his friends, your brother would still be alive," the Mocking Turtle calls out, and my entire body goes cold. I turn my head slowly to look at him and find those cold, dead eyes watching me with interest. I have a feeling he's not the only audience in that macabre stare; someone else is looking at me through his face.

And, if possible, they're even more terrifying than the Mocking Turtle himself.

"If you'd just relaxed and let it happen, your family would be whole. How does that make you feel?" I just stare at him because there's bile in my throat and a horrid, righteous anger clawing its way through my heart. If I lose my temper now, while drunk and confused, I'll regret it later.

So I say nothing.

Because there's nothing bullies hate more than being ignored.

I back up and leave the raucous outside to the men … for now.

One day, I'll kill those bastards.

Tonight is not that night.

"Here," Raiden says, handing me a teacup and a needle when I turn around. "Do me a favor, and I'll end the chaos outside." I look down at the tea and then up at his face. He really is gorgeous, like a movie star or something. His eyeliner is flawless, his lips full, his smirk just arrogant enough to be attractive.

But I don't need magic tea to deal with him.

"I won't fuck someone I don't love—not ever again. If you want to try to win my heart, go for it. Otherwise, I'll marry you as a political move and nothing more. You can have your slice of the kingdom I'm going to turn around." I push the teacup aside and lift my chin while Chesh nibbles my ear and lets out a wild purr. "So, help those men outside or don't. Your choice."

The Mad Hatter lets the teacup go, letting it crash to the floor in a sea of boiling liquid and shattered China. He looks at me for a long moment, smirks, and then reaches out to tap the brim of my new top hat.

"I knew I liked you, little Alice." With a jerk of his head, the Hatter moves toward the window with March trailing behind him. As his boss jumps out the window and into the garden, March turns back to look at me with eyes like wet earth, brown and endless and deep.

"Good choice, Alice-Doll. You make smart moves with your pieces." He wiggles his ringed-fingers, and then starts to shift into a bandersnatch, brown fur sprouting up through his clothes, the sides of his muscular body marbled like a Bengal cat.

The March Hare shakes out his coat, and then hops down next to the Mad Hatter.

"Party's over, my friends," Raiden says, slow-clapping as he approaches the wall. "Nothing to see here, move on."

"You, sir, are a right bloody traitor," the Gryphon replies, shifting his ragged, ugly wings as Rab pants and watches M.T. and the Gryphon like he'd rather enjoy biting their heads off. Tee is standing on the wall opposite North, flanking the giant hole in the stone.

In the distance, I hear the scream of a jabberwock and blood begins to trickle down my ears. North stiffens up, so I figure it's a female, but he's safe inside the castle walls, right? The King seemed to think the Anti-Alice's ability to get in was unique.

"What can I say?" the Hatter asks with a shrug as Dor makes his way out of the castle to stand beside his boss, on the side opposite the March Hare. The Dormouse crosses his arms like a Hollywood bodyguard, holding his wrists in front of his junk. "I received an offer I couldn't refuse. Send the King of Clubs my apologies. Oh, and let him know my army will be joining the King of Hearts' on the borders of this illustrious kingdom."

The Gryphon visibly bristles, but the Mocking Turtle does not take his eyes off of me.

"Untie me, please," Lar chokes out, and I whip my head around to find him lying there with his wings curled inward, like he's in a serious amount of pain. "You and me, Sunshine, we need to get out of here. You don't want to be on the end of the Mocking Turtle's stare."

"Why not?" I ask as Dee helps me stumble over to the table. He very gently pushes me into a chair while Chesh shifts back into human form and helps untie Lar. The Caterpillar sits up, chucking aside the saliva soaked red napkin he's just spit out.

"He can sense your mettle. That's something we want to keep as secret as possible." Lar stands up on shaky legs and holds his hand out for me.

"Let's get you back to your room," Dee says, peering into my eyes and brushing some hair from my forehead. "They've got this, I promise you. Nobody can cross onto the castle grounds without permission from the King." He pauses and grits his teeth. "Well, nobody but the Anti-Alice."

"Or the Knave?" I ask, but Dee shakes his head, and I let out a sigh of relief.

"Just the King," he says, and then pauses. "Or the Queen."

The way he looks at me, I know there's no doubt in his mind that one day, I *will* be the Queen of Hearts.

Dee tucks me into bed next to Lar when we get back, but try as I might, I cannot stay awake.

Guess I'm a boosted tea lightweight, huh?

The only time I wake up that night is to check on my men.

"Everyone's okay," Tee whispers, kneeling next to my bed and stroking hair from my forehead when I wake up in a blind panic, thrashing around and tangling the sheets up in the process. I have a full bed tonight, too, with the Caterpillar, the Cheshire Cat, the White Rabbit, Dee, and North.

The bed is plenty big, at least.

"You're sure?" I ask, panting and trying not to think about finding Fred in that dark alley, dead and bloody and alone. I'm not sure I'd survive that a second time.

"Positive," he says, bathed in yellow and orange from the dying fire. His journal is open on the desk, so I figure he probably came back, showered, and starting writing—all without waking me up. "They left; it's over."

"For now," I say, trying to figure out why those pieces of trash showed up in the first place. But my head is too full of sleep, and my hands are still shaky from my boosted tea. "But they must've come for a reason; they weren't just stopping in for tea."

"Definitely not." Tee smiles at me and then moves to close the gap between us, kissing me with this soft, gentle sweetness that curls my toes. His wings unfold from his back in glorious folds, the dark feathers catching the moonlight, the chains falling to the floor. Waking my prince at midnight. It'd be like a fairy tale, if everything weren't drenched in blood. "A distraction, maybe?"

He sighs as I lean back in the pillows and scoot to

make some room on the edge of the bed, patting the mattress to invite him to lie next to me.

After a second's hesitation, he climbs up, dressed in pajama pants and nothing else.

I'm still wearing my bat dress, but it's ridden up to my hips, and it only takes a minute to kick my panties off.

"What are you doing?" Tee whispers, but I just smile and roll onto my back, encouraging him to follow after me, so that he’s on top.

Before you can say *o frabjous day!*, he's sliding into me and we're making love by moonlight.

7

The Ball of Broken Hearts and Stolen Tarts

I wake the morning of the ball to find a pirate standing over my bed.

"Lory?" I choke out, scrambling to sit up and swiping the drool from my face. My increasingly bright rainbow hair is stuck to the corner of my mouth. Oh, I must *really* look like the future Queen of Hearts now, huh? I'm hungover, slightly confused as to where I am or what's going on, and now sporting a brand new tattoo on my freaking thigh—a tattoo made of *skin*. "What are you doing here?!"

"I invited her to the ball," Dee says, sitting up, his hair scruffy but somehow still cute. Wish I could wake up with a playful pink in my cheeks and a mischievous grin hovering around my full, delicious mouth … fuck. I've been up all of two seconds and I'm ogling Dee again. Before I forget, I lean over and give him a quick kiss on the lips, freeing his wings from their cursed prison. He grins at me as I sit back, refocusing on Lory and blinking to clear the sleepy cobwebs from my vision. "Anyone from the Kingdom of Hearts is allowed to attend anyway."

"They wouldn't give me a visa for Eaglet," Lory says with a loose shrug of her shoulders, and I remember vaguely the bandanna covered in diamonds he was wearing on The Long Tale. "Border control is tight right now." Lory adjusts her black tricorne hat—that's what a pirate hat is called, you know—and then plants her hands on her hips.

Tee is standing behind and to the right of her, so I figure he's the one that let her in. Stretching, I lift my arms above my head, and curl my toes against a soft, fuzzy pillow tucked under the blankets. Wait.

"Chesh!" I admonish, lifting up the covers to find the black and white striped cat purring and kneading the sheets near my toes. Before I can escape his reach, he flicks his little pink tongue out and licks my toes. "Shoo," I growl, pretending he's Dinah and grabbing his scruff. My little black asshole cat likes to sleep in my blankets and then attack me when I climb into bed. I'm used to this maneuver.

I pull Chesh out by the scruff, but he shifts back into

human form just as I'm dragging him from the blankets, landing on top of me with all of his beautiful muscles and that delicious fresh honey and black tea scent of his.

"What the ..." I start, but I find the words stuck in my throat, heart thundering like a herd of wild bandersnatch. That is, if bandersnatch even run in herds? I have no fucking clue. "Get off of me," I breathe, but the words don't come as bitchy or forceful as I intend them to. I haven't forgotten that I almost killed this guy a few days ago. Or that last night was a serious clusterfuck.

"Yes, mistress," he purrs, the tags on his collar jangling as he leans in and licks the side of my face.

"Should I go wait in the hall?" Lory asks, flicking some of her brunette braids over one shoulder. "You about to get it on in here?"

"No, no," I snarl, scrambling out of bed and rubbing at my sleepy face with the heel of one hand. Looking around, I notice most of the men are missing. It's just me, Chesh, and the twins left now. I suppose they're all out preparing for the ball. I'd almost forgotten that tonight's the night. "What time is it?"

"Time to be up and about," she declares, dressed in brown breeches, a red peasant blouse, and black boots. Reminds me ... I move over to my satchel, hanging on the hook near the door, and reluctantly pull out the outfit she lent me: corset and knives and all. "You lazy assholes better start getting ready. Guests are already arriving."

"Here," I offer up my borrowed clothes, but Lory waves them away with a hand covered in gold rings. They make a pretty contrast against her ebony skin.

"Keep 'em. We got paid handsomely by the King to bring the best tea in the kingdom down the river. I can afford new ones." She grins at me with white-white teeth. "Plus, I got an in with the Queen. That makes me pretty special, don't you think?"

"I'm not the Queen just yet. I won't ever be if I have to spend much time around Brennin Red. I'm as liable to murder as marry him," I start as Tee offers up a cup of coffee and a muffin. Our hands brush together and we exchange a look. It very clearly says *I know what you did in the dark*, and I smile. If I close my eyes, I can still feel him sliding inside of me last night. Other than that, the night is pretty much a blur.

"*Yet*," Lory repeats, turning, her long hair swaying against the backs of her calves. She moves over to the refreshments table and gets herself an EAT ME cookie, tucking it into her belt. There's a small wooden cabinet there as well that she opens, revealing several tiny glass bottles with FUCKING DRINK ME tags dangling off of them. Lory pockets two, and then turns back to face me, leaning her butt on the edge of the table. "You're not the Queen yet, but you will be."

"So you already know I'm the …" I stop talking and she throws her head back with a raucous laugh. It's nice though, to hear someone so free and unrestrained. Sitting in this palace, I'm starting to feel fucking stifled.

"The whole kingdom knows you're the Alice now," she says as Dee stumbles out of bed and knocks over a table with his wings. I don't think he's quite used to having them out all the time. Our eyes meet across the room as he flushes and does his best to fix it. Too bad the legs are broken into several pieces. I just smile, thinking of last night, the way he oh so carefully tucked me into bed.

Lory snaps her fingers in front of my face, and I groan. I'm doing it again, the stupid teenager daydreaming thing. After last night's nightmare, don't I deserve it though?

"Although I suspected when I first met you. Why do you think I had you come down to the ship so early? Coulda let y'all sleep in while we loaded cargo, but I wanted to get a good look at ya." She grins at me, pulls a knife from her belt, and promptly picks her teeth with it. "So, where's your dress then?"

"My dress?" I ask, because in the excitement of the last few days, I realize I haven't actually seen the damn thing. Got measured and fondled and caressed by Rab, but I never picked out fabric or anything. I don't even know what style of dress it is that I'll be getting. My bet is … that it's gonna be red which is fine by me. Just so long as it's not pink. "Good question."

"The dress will be delivered in …" Rab starts, stepping out of the painting on my right, the one with a white rabbit wearing a waistcoat. He's shirtless again, running his hands down his body in a way that just can't be accidental. He points to one of his clock tats. "About two minutes."

"Perfect," Lory says, settling herself into a wingback chair in the corner. "I'll wait and you can try it on for me."

"We'll have a fashion show," I say with a smile, sitting down on the bench at the end of the bed to eat my muffin and drink my coffee. "I'll show you mine; you show me yours."

"Bloody can't stand dresses," Lory says, shaking her head and sending her braids flying. "Makes me sick to my stomach; I'll be wearing my military uniform. You're more likely to see Dodo in a dress than me." She slides her knife back in its sheath and grabs a muffin. "Hear you lot got into trouble last night."

"And who's spreading that rumor?" Tee asks, hanging up a pair of identical outfits on a hook. Must be for him and his brother. Really, they're just nicer, more frilly versions of what they usually wear. Red military style coats, white button-ups, ruffled cravats, and black boots. The matching hats have giant red feathers sticking out of them.

"It's all over the castle. Nobody's stupid enough to miss the card servants scurrying to the hole in the back wall." Lory glances over at Rab as he lays out the stack of clothes draped over his arm on my rumpled bedspread. Chesh leans over to sniff the items and wrinkles his nose. He doesn't appear to have any intention of dressing up for the ball.

Fuck, I don't even know if he's invited.

Then again, he did practice dancing the quintrille with us, so maybe the King isn't as he stupid as pretends to be? If he excludes Chesh, I'll be pissed.

"Yes, well, we had some late-night visitors," Rab says, popping behind the bathroom curtain and stripping down. Lory barely glances his direction, grabbing an apple and peeling it with her knife. The motion of her hand on the blade reminds of me of March, of the two Rabbits shifting into bandersnatch form to face the enemy. "But that's been taken care of."

"The Knave looks to have her knickers in a wad this morning," Lory says as Dee picks candied insects off the pastry selection on the refreshments table. "Guess she's finally realized she's never getting Brennin Red's dick, eh?"

"That's about right," Dee says with a yawn, turning around to see me scratching at my new tattoo with a chipped fingernail. When Rab comes out from behind the curtain, running a gloved hand over his white ears and dark hair, he pauses and grins at me.

"You like what you see, Sonny?" he purrs, and I raise an eyebrow. This is some gorgeous ink, but I cannot get over how it came to be. I look at the empty spot on Rab's arm, and then back down at the lacey cameo of my new tattoo.

"Getting this … was one of the weirdest experiences of my life," I say, tapping my fingertips against the tattoo and making a mental note to myself: *during visits home, I need to cover my moving clock tattoo with pants or a long skirt.* Not sure how I'd explain this fresh ink to my father.

Not sure how I'll explain my two week long absence either.

My throat gets tight, and I push that thought aside. I just need to get through this stupid ball, and this stupid dance, and then I'll figure out how to get into the Looking-Glass. Lord knows I'm no chess champion. Fuck, I barely know the names of the damn pieces.

"I'm so glad you enjoyed yourself," Rab purrs as I stuff the rest of the muffin in my mouth. He moves over to stand beside me, cracks his knuckles, twitches his ears. His body starts to shrink, his ears get round, his nose flushes pink. Within a few seconds, Rab is sitting on the carpet in his mouse form, looking up at me with red eyes. *"I'll be with you the entire night,"* he promises, climbing up the leg of the bench to sit beside me.

"Oh, how delicious," Chesh purrs, clawing at the air above Rab's head. "I could just eat you right up."

"Do, and see what happens when I become a bandersnatch in your belly," Rab teases, whiskers twitching. I will not forget what he said last night, twisted up into a magic induced conundrum. Royal blood, huh? I need to know what this third form is; it's killing me.

"Put some nice clothes on; you're dancing the quintrille tonight in front of the whole court." Tee lays out an outfit for Chesh, too, and the cat's ears go back in frustration. He obliges, stripping down and changing right there in front of Lory. She raises her eyebrows but doesn't ogle. Guess she knows cat's don't give a shit about nudity; they will literally put their buttholes right in your face while asking for pets. Thankfully, Chesh hasn't done that to me … yet.

There's a knock on the door, and we all pause. Dee moves to open it, accepting a big red garment bag and four different sized boxes from a card servant's creepy human hands. He slams the door in its face, and spins around, the bag dangling from his fingers. He hands off the towering stack of boxes to his brother.

"Excited, Allison-who-isn't-Alice?" he asks, smiling from ear to ear.

"More like terrified out of my fucking mind." I put

my coffee aside and stand up, unzipping the bag and trying not to cringe at the amount of poof and lace that explodes out. "Oh dear," I mumble, pushing the garment bag back to get a good look at what's inside.

There's a dress, a short coat, and a corset. And from the looks of the boxes in Tee's arms, I would guess jewelry, hat, shoes, and … undergarments.

"Hmm." I pull the items out, handing the coat and corset to Chesh while I lift the dress up for examination.

It's a red ball gown with a satin bodice and a heavy skirt comprised of yards of flouncy, lacy fabric. It literally bounces when I shake it, and I narrow my eyes. I was hoping for something more modern, like the bat dress I wore last night.

"This is positively medieval," I murmur, and Dee chuckles. The dress has off-the-shoulder sleeves, a heart-shaped neckline, and a deep V where the satin bodice dips into the skirt. I hang it up on another hook, cringing a bit when the hook reaches out to assist me, scooping up the wooden hanger from my hands. I take the black and white striped corset with the gold buttons out next and hold it up, imagining it layered over the dress.

Things are starting to look up.

"Okay, I can work with this," I say as I take the velvet coat and add that to the ensemble. It has three-quarter length sleeves, epaulettes, fringe, and long coattails in the back.

The front of the jacket should hit me at about mid-waist.

Tee sets the boxes down on the bench and removes my coffee cup before it gets a chance to spill.

Dee's like a kid at Christmas, tearing open the top box and pulling out a garter belt and thigh-highs.

"Oh Hearts on a card," he groans, rubbing the garments against his cheek. I snatch them from his hand and sigh.

"I'm not wearing these," I say, chucking them onto the bed where Chesh bats at them playfully. "I'll wear plain cotton panties, thank you very much." I shove the lingerie box aside and check out the hat box instead.

Inside, there's a crown.

A fucking crown.

It looks like the King's, gold with big red diamonds, sharp points pricking my fingers as I run a fingertip along the top rim. The bottom is padded with white fur speckled with black spots, big roses—*real* roses—clustered on one side.

When I place it on my head, I feel it seal to my scalp the way the Mad Hatter's top hat did last night. A spell. Which reminds me …

I take the crown off and hand it over to Tee.

"Take a look at this," I tell him, wondering where Lar is. I could use his help checking over the spells in my new clothing. Like I said, I'm not stupid: I don't trust the

Knave for shit. Moving over to the nightstand on the left side of the bed, I pull out a wooden box filled with the March Hare's test kits.

I'm going to use every single one of them.

The door to the room opens and I feel a huge shock of relief when the Caterpillar waltzes in, dressed in red and looking fucking scrumptious in his new outfit. Of course, he's wearing a half-shirt under his red jacket which is a little weird, but I can see his beautifully taut stomach muscles, so I'm not complaining.

"You're here," I say, glad to see that Lar's recovered fairly well after last night. When the vision in his wings shattered, and that dust went floating everywhere … fuck, I was worried. He smiles at me from across the room, his red earrings catching the light.

"I wouldn't miss your dress delivery, Sunshine," he says, turning to the red monstrosity and drawing a sigil in glowing gold over it. I move up beside him and open the first kit. I'm going to test several spots on this damn thing, just to be sure. "How are you feeling this morning?"

"Like total crap. Yourself?" Lar smiles, but he doesn't respond for a minute, drawing the same sigil over the corset and then the jacket. Nothing happens, and he doesn't say anything, so I'm assuming there's nothing wrong with the outfit.

When my first few test kits come up clean, I start to get

annoyed.

I was almost hoping the idiot Knave would do something like poison or spell my dress, just so we could catch her embroiled in bullshit. My instincts are still screaming that something is wrong with that woman. You don't just lust after a position of power your whole life, and then roll over and take it when someone steals it from you.

No freaking way.

"Sleeping next to you, that revived me," Lar says, and I can't tell if he's joking, flirting, or being totally serious. He turns to glance at Lory, giving her a small nod of acknowledgement before he tests my new high-heeled boots, my jewelry, and even my stupid lingerie. "It's all clean," he says, but he defers to Tee for a moment. "Look it over yourself, too, see if there's anything I might've missed."

"Who are we distrustful of?" Lory asks as Tee touches the clothing with his fingers, rubbing the fabric together between like he's searching for residue or something. I don't know anything about angel powers, so I have to assume he knows what he's doing. Then again, assumptions make an ass out of you and shins, and …

Jesus Christ.

I'm mad, completely and utterly mad—and loving it.

"The Knave," I say with tight lips, and Lory nods her

head.

"Good on you. I wouldn't trust that crazy bitch for nothing. She was the one who vetoed the King when he wanted to send food down the river. She let whole cities starve and then burn."

Well.

That's new information.

I wait for Tee to finish his inspection, and then raise an eyebrow.

"Everything looks legitimate," he tells me, trying for a smile. "But that doesn't surprise me. The Knave is smart. If she were to try something, it'd be more subtle than tampering with your dress."

"You're probably right," I say with a sigh, rubbing at my forehead. "This world is just making me paranoid."

"This world makes everyone paranoid," Chesh purrs, lying on his back and looking at me from eyes the color of a wild storm. I take the dress off the hanger and give it a long, lingering look. "Well, I suppose I could do worse for my first official ball. I wore jeans and a wifebeater to junior prom. This'll be a new experience."

I whisk myself off into the bathroom to shower and change into my outfit—which, of course, just has to include the white breastplate gifted to me from the White Knight. It's supposed to give me courage, right? And tonight, I am going to need that shit in spades. Err, in hearts? Anyway, you know what I mean.

Tonight, Allison and the Alice, they'll be one in the same.

Wonder how the Knave will like *that*?

♦ ♠ ♣ ♥ ♣ ♠ ♦

The ballroom looks completely different with the double doors thrown open, hordes of people moving between the foyer and the dance floor. Their outfits create a sea of shimmering red, white, and black, the fabrics shining under the flickering flames of the chandeliers.

I feel completely fine with the way the day is going until I'm standing outside those doors, starting to notice the ripple in the crowd as people turn to stare at me. This breastplate is supposed to give me courage? I call bullshit. I feel like the Cowardly Lion.

"We've got you," Dee whispers, giving my hand a squeeze. He's got his elbow through mine while Tee takes up a similar position on my other side. The cat is on my shoulders, lounging and probably napping, while Rab-mouse sits in the pocket of my velvet jacket. My makeup is done thanks to Tee because I have little to no makeup skills of my own; my rainbow hair is coiffed, this time thanks to Dee because … well, you get the drift. Lar stands just behind and to the left of me, like I really am a Queen and in need an escort. Hell, maybe I do because the White Knight stands opposite him, flanking me.

Wonder if someone will try to kill me tonight?

My panties are dry, my weapons are strapped in place, and my heart is pounding like I've just run a triathlon.

"I can't do this," I whisper as my throat closes up and I find that my feet have ceased to move. "I don't want to do this."

"Do crowds frighten you so?" a cool voice asks from behind me.

I don't need to turn around to know that it's the King.

Fuck.

I steel myself and glance casually over my shoulder, like I just can't be bothered.

But oh. Oh. Ooooooh.

The King looks good, wearing his lazy crown, his red and white robes framing his lean but muscular frame, a decorative sword hanging at his hip. He's got a huge, furred cloak on, too, and I get the weirdest urge to wrap myself up in it. Or … let the King wrap me up in it. When he moves, I notice the pants beneath his robes are black and white striped, very matchy-matchy to the corset beneath my breastplate.

Ugh.

"I'm fine," I say, turning back to look at the sea of unfamiliar faces. "I just don't care for parties."

"Oh, you don't?" Red drawls, swaggering up to stand

beside me. "That's too bad. You'll just have to suffer through this one." He snaps his fingers and several very human guards clear the crowds away from the doors, unrolling a red runner and sprinkling it with bloodied rose petals.

Like, really?

We're going to do the whole song and dance routine?

A Rabbit wearing the Castle Heart emblem—a broken heart intersected by a sword—on his surcoat, runs up the aisle with a trumpet. When he puts it to his lips and blows, every single person in that room goes silent.

"I hope you weren't thinking to make an entrance without us?" Raiden asks, appearing on my other side. While the King is dressed in luscious red and white robes, Raiden is drenched in black, save the single rose decorating his massive, wilting velvet top hat. He's got on a pair of leather pants, a ruffled top, and a white tie covered in black bats. The March Hare is dressed similarly, except his tie has little brown rabbits all over it and his shirt is white. He's also wearing a much smaller hat … and eating a pear. Plus, he's got a whole series of glowing vials around his neck that I can only guess contain poison of some sort.

He flicks an ear in my direction as he takes a bite of the fruit, spattering his beautiful lips with juice.

I look away, toward the ballroom.

There's a set of steps that lead inside, and at the bottom of them, I see the Knave and her husbands waiting.

Fantastic.

Usually we enter the ballroom from the downstairs entrance, so I've never actually come in this way. Maybe that's why I never really noticed how fucking cavernous this place is? I mean, I knew it was big, but standing up at the top of these steps, it looks like a football stadium, full of judgmental courtiers and women dressed in military uniforms decorated in badges. Each of them is surrounded by clouds of men, and none of them look very happy to see me.

The general population, however, people like Dodo and Lory who are waving at me from the center of the room, seemed thrilled.

"I'm going to puke," I whisper, no longer giving a shit that the King is standing right next to Tee. The elder twin grudgingly steps aside, ruffling his feathers in annoyance, so that Brennin Red can take my arm, pulling me ahead of Dee and giving the cat a glare so intense, I swear it makes *me* sweat. Or maybe that's the three hundred pounds of lace and tulle I'm dragging around? Or perhaps it's the thousands upon thousands of stares from the Court of Hearts?

"Please wait until after the quintrille, then you can be sick all you want in the privacy of your own room." Brennin pauses as the Duke strides up to us, wearing red breeches, a white shirt with tiny heart buttons, and the most ridiculous hat known to man. When he pauses next to me, he sweeps the hat off from between his dark horns and takes a ridiculous bow, tail trashing behind him.

“My mate, the gorgeous Allison Pleasance Liddell, the Duke of Northumbria awaits to accompany you to the ball.” I smile as North stands up straight and replaces his stupid hat with the giant cluster of feathers. His gold eyes sparkle as he takes me in and licks his lips appreciatively. The King simply rolls his eyes at our exchange.

“Fashionably late, as usual, North,” he says, letting the Duke take up on my other side. “Thank you *so* fucking much for joining us.”

“Anytime, *Your Majesty,*” he purrs as the King parades us over to the top of the stairs where the trumpet-wielding Rabbit is waiting. He lifts the instrument to his lips, gives three sharp blasts, and then unrolls a parchment scroll to read from.

"His Majesty, the King of Hearts, would like to formally present his future Queen of Hearts, the Alice, to the court. Make your judgments, state your intents, and if you should protest, now’s the fucking time. For tonight only, all executions are stayed!"

The crowd cheers as I go pale and give the King a scathing look.

"Awfully presumptuous of you, isn't it?" I snarl.

"Introducing me as your queen already?"

"You said it yourself: marriage for political gain. I've accepted it." Brennin ignores me as we start down the stairs to cheers and whispers and gasps. I'm sure I've been the topic of polite conversation all week.

So what do these people think of me, this little blonde girl with rainbow streaks in her hair?

I feel like a fraud.

"Alice, you're going to change the whole world, aren't you?" Dee's words ring in my head, and I close my eyes, taking a deep breath and trying to gather my courage together.

I tumbled down the Rabbit-Hole, fired a flintlock pistol at a giant monster bird, haggled my way out of a kidnapping by Underland's most infamous mercenary, and learned to fight with my hands. I have magic, a sharp tongue, and the will to make things better. I … survived an abusive relationship, found my brother's body, watched my mom get convicted in court.

This crowd, or the Knave, or the Hatter or the King … how can I let them intimidate me now?

The answer is: I *won't*.

I open my eyes as we pause next to the Knave, the Lion, and the Unicorn.

"Good evening, Alice," she says, her strange voice ruffling my metaphorical feathers. A quick glance at Dee shows me she does quite literally ruffle his *actual* feathers.

"Ines," I reply coolly, using her name instead of her title on purpose. Now whose feathers are ruffled?

The King quickly sweeps us past her, taking us down a row of glittering aristocrats and military personnel. There's no way I'll remember any of their names, so I don't bother to try. Instead, I focus on keeping my chin up, my shoulders back, my steps slow and confident. The Duke takes care of all polite conversation for me, thank God.

We make several rounds through the ballroom before Brennin finally releases me, letting go of my arm and watching me like he thinks I'm going to make a run for it.

The only thing I make a run for is the table piled with food. What can I say? I'm a comfort eater.

It's all the usual weirdness I'm starting to love about Underland: candied flowers, bowls of crickets covered in chocolate sauce, slabs of purple meat, and salads that are as colorful as a spring rainbow. There are toadstools, cupcakes, lollipops, and plenty of tea.

So much fucking tea.

I pick through the food, reaching absently into my pocket to stroke Rab's tiny head.

"If you're going to eat something," March says from beside me, sliding a test kit from the pocket of his leather pants. "Please test it first."

"I tested my dress," I whisper as he moves up to stand shoulder to shoulder with me. Well, arm to shoulder, I guess. I’m not nearly tall enough to reach his. I'm not the only one people are staring at. The Mad Hatter and the March Hare have quite the audience as well. "There's no poison."

"Nothing that shows up immediately," he drawls which, of course, makes me paranoid.

"You're a dick," I say as the March Hare tests some fizzy grapefruit infused water, and then passes it over to me. "Are you sure I should drink this? Or am I going to drop dead later from one of the nine less common poisons?"

"Guess we'll know by next week if the vial changes color, won't we?" he drawls, giving me a saucy little look as I sip my drink.

"You're awfully concerned about poison," the King says, still standing far too close to me for comfort. I half-expected him to wander off into the crowd, but it looks like he plans on shadowing me instead. How lucky am I?

I grab a fruit tart off a tray. After all, this *is* the Ball of Broken Hearts and Stolen Tarts, right? In the original book, it was the Knave that was suspected of stealing the Queen's tarts. Tonight, the Knave isn't stealing anything from me, not if I can help it.

The music tonight is played by a live orchestra, situated in the corner of the room and made up entirely of card servants. They're quite good actually, and I have to wonder how it's possible that the King managed to find an entire orchestra worth of criminals to curse.

I glance over at the Knave, still watching me from across the room. She's not subtle about it either. It could've been her, couldn't it? She's the official curseworker for the Kingdom of Hearts, right? I would not put it past someone like that to frame a horde of musicians for her own amusement.

"I couldn't get a read on anything else regarding tonight," Lar whispers, and I'm not sure if he's talking to the King or to me. Maybe both of us? "The Mocking Turtle ripped me in half, metaphysically speaking. I'm still healing." He sets an empty teacup down hard on the table, and I notice the tea leaves sitting on the bottom. "You're on your own tonight, Your Majesty."

"No matter," Brennin says, but his dark eyes won't stop scanning the room. It's as if I'm not the only one looking for trouble tonight … He notices me watching him and lifts his chin haughtily, turning away in a swirl of robes.

"Sorry to say," I tell Chevalier as she stands guard beside me, "but your Breastplate of Courage doesn't seem to be working. I'm scared out of my mind." The White Knight just smiles at me, and I notice she's wearing her shark shields or whatever the fuck they're called. Maybe she is just a kook?

"It's working," she says, still smiling at me. I quirk an eyebrow, but I'm not about to argue. If it is working, then it's not working very well. I mean, I'm putting on a good show, but I'll be relieved as fuck when this is over. "Just give it time."

"Her inventions never work; she's a nutcase," North says with a sniff, and clearly, he's also on edge tonight. It's either because of last night, or because of whatever's been going on inside the castle. For the most part, these men, as nonsensical as they are, have been pretty open with me. The only thing they seem to be holding back on is who or what they're nervous of inside the palace walls.

I wonder why?

"You'll see," the White Knight repeats, entirely unaffected by the Duke's insult. She sweeps long, blonde hair over her shoulder and maintains vigil on the room.

Unfortunately, when the Knave approaches from behind, nobody stops her. After all, she's a good guy, right? About as pure and innocent as Jafar from the move *Aladdin*. I just hope she's not the King's 'most trusted advisor'.

"*The Queen of Hearts, she made some tarts, all on a summer day; the Knave of Hearts, she stole those tarts, and took them quite away!*" I turn around to meet the Knave's green-eyed stare as she chuckles politely with her hand over her mouth. I see that she's donned a gown of her own for the occasion, one that's made up of yards of black satin and lace. A half-veil covers her pretty face as she looks me over with disdain. "Have you heard that one before, the Alice?"

"What do you suppose *that* means?" I ask her as the twins move up close on either side of me. At least I know their wings are out, and that each rustle of those beautiful feathers is like a stab to her broken, shriveled little heart.

"I've never been much for interpreting prophecy," she says, glancing over at Lar for a moment. "What do you think, soothsayer, what does it mean?" The Caterpillar gives her a bored stare right back, removing a pipe from the pocket on his red coat and lighting up. He smokes it for a moment and then shrugs his shoulders.

"I only repeat prophecies; I don't claim to understand them."

The Knave's husbands remain behind her, as stoic as statues, their gazes focused on me. I have no idea what their purpose is in this game, but I get the idea that they haven't made their moves yet—not even close. This is a disaster waiting to happen.

"How … useful," she says, moving past Dee and purposely hitting him with her shoulder.

Very mature.

"I hope she trips and breaks her face," I grumble, and notice Lar smiling at me from behind his pipe. He passes it over to me, and I take a hit, recognizing the very distinct scent of the whiting, like lavender and chai tea. Aaaand, now I'm starting to wonder why I didn't follow my own advice and put on plain cotton knickers like I'd planned. When we start floating during the quintrille, the whole court's going to get an eyeful of my lingerie. I *knew* I shouldn't have worn it! Damn my weak, curious little heart.

"She'll get hers one day." The Duke waves his hand lazily before taking the pipe from me, looking far more excited than any sane person ought to at a function like this. I get the idea that he enjoys politics and intrigue. That's sort of his thing. "Besides, seeing us dance the quintrille is likely to ruin the rest of the evening for her. She's always dreamed of being center stage in court."

"It is?" I ask, perking up substantially. "She has?" The cat bats at one of my earrings with a furred paw, and I swat him away. "Shall we dance it now then?"

"It's generally polite to make conversation with the courtiers first," the King says, but I'm already rolling my eyes. I pull the Rab-mouse from my pocket and set him on the table. The Cheshire cat gets put on the floor, and I hook my arm with the King's. I notice the Knave watching me again, and throw her this horribly triumphant look. It stinks of smug, but I just can't seem to help myself. I'm petty sometimes, so sue me; we all have our faults.

Brennin's eyes widen in surprise as I drag him toward

the center of the room, and the gold medallion design on the floor that I was admiring the other day. This time, I can see it's the quintrille, laid out step by step around the outer circle. In the center, a King and Queen dance the night away. How fitting.

As soon as our feet hit that medallion, the music stops briefly and a hush falls over the crowd.

"This is entirely unorthodox; the quintrille requires an announcement." I put the King's hand on my hip, and his fingers tighten around me, making me gasp. His black eyes gaze down at me from that severe but handsome face of his. He's a dark horse, this King of Hearts.

"And you're the King. Try setting the rules instead of following them." His mouth twitches as the other men slowly gather around us, just like we practiced. The card servant orchestra starts up again with the dark, haunting notes of a cello. Above us, the lights dim until we've got nothing but moonlight to see by.

I put my hand on the King's shoulder, underneath the folds of his cloak, and I try not to notice how warm his body is, how intense his stare. If I let myself, I bet I could drown in his darkness. I would die with wetness in my lungs, but intrigue in my heart.

"Will you, won't you join the dance?" the King asks, his voice booming above the music, echoing around the ballroom. It's loud enough to project above the cello's desperate moans.

"What matters it how far we go?" I whisper, just before the other men begin to move, dancing around us, like river water around rocks.

There is nothing we have to say to one another, so the King and I simply stand there, staring at each other. There's an intensity to that stare, and it makes me want to fidget. Or run. Instead, I meet him dead-on, waiting for our turn.

As I'd thought, when we begin to move, my dress swishes around my legs, the fabric as bright as the King's hair, as red as blood.

Our feet begin to lift off the floor, carrying us above the crowd.

I swear though, I don't see anything but Brennin Red in that moment. It's as if he's put me under a spell. The way his hair falls over his brow, the slight gap in the buttons of his robes and the peek of his white shirt beneath them … I literally cannot stop staring. That is, until the pace of the music changes and he breaks his grip on my hand.

"You seem awfully interested," the Duke purrs as he switches places with the King, twirling me around in the air and teasing my ankle with his tail. I won't soon forget that he recently fucked me with it. Or that I loved it. Or that I'll do it again first chance I get. "Decided you like the King now?"

"I never said that," I whisper back as the music

intensifies, the viola singing her notes in a high-pitched wail that brings goose bumps up on my skin.

"No, you never did," the Duke replies, "but I can see it in your eyes."

"Bullshit," I snort, frowning as he kisses me on the cheek, finishing our round before he switches with the Mad Hatter. Of course, they're both good dancers, but they're nothing like Lar or the King. I decide to tell Raiden Walker that, and see what happens.

"The King's a better dancer," I tease as he holds me in strong arms and manages to catch me before I mess up one of the steps. "What do you think about that?"

"Credit where credit is due, I always say," he purrs, flashing fang. My neck throbs and aches, but I refuse to touch it. When I showered this morning and went to scrub some of the crusted blood off, I almost fucking came. "Such as last night, when you stood up to me. I liked that." He leans down and puts his mouth near my right ear. "Although I still plan on making you beg."

"Fat chance of that ever happening." I break away from him, falling into Rab's arms next and loving the way he tosses a challenging glance in the March Hare's direction. There's something about their rivalry that interests me. Two Rabbits, two sidekicks to two powerful men. But they're both much more than just sidekicks. It's not impossible for me to think of them overcoming the rulers they're supposed to serve.

"What are you all watching out for?" I ask as his cold hand embraces mine, sparking an intense heat.

"What ever do you mean?" Rab drawls, not even bothering to hide his wicked smile. "You don't think you're the only one who's worried about the Knave, do you?"

My mouth tightens into a thin line.

"If you're all so worried about her, why doesn't the King lock her up? Have her questioned at his famous weekly Trial?" I raise a brow, but the White Rabbit doesn't look like he has any intention of answering me, marching us in a circle around the other men and trading me off to my next partner.

The quintrille … it's a lot of fucking work.

"Well, hello there, Doll," March says, sweeping me rather close to him. Much closer than the steps in the dance call for. "Did you miss me?"

"How can I miss you when first off, I don't even like you. And second, you never go away?" The March Hare laughs at me, flattening his brown ears against his head and causing his small top hat to slide forward until it's leaning at a rather precarious angle.

"Admit it: you don't *want* me to leave." He smirks at me, but I'm not about to dignify that response with an answer. No point in it anyway because he's soon handing me off to Tee. This dance, when performed at its proper pace, is breakneck. I feel like I can barely breathe, like I'm as high as I was last night, the edges of the room flickering in psychedelically brilliant hues.

Our eyes lock as we come together in the center of the room, the literal freaking center of the room, halfway between the floor and the domed glass ceiling. In the silver moonlight, the purple streaks in Tee's hair are twice as bright. I reach up to finger a stray strand and he smiles at me.

"Wondering how I managed to move up from last place?" he asks as I lean into him, breathing in that fresh mountain air scent of his.

"You drew straws?"

I can feel Tee smile against my hair as he spreads his wings wide, letting the full thirty-foot length of his wingspan shine its glory for the entire crowd. And it is fucking *magnificent.* The purple feathers catch the light the same way his hair does. I can just imagine the Knave, standing down there in the crowd and fuming.

"We drew sugar cubes," Tee says, and I lift my head away from his chest to give him a questioning look. Of course, then we're switching partners yet again, and I end up with Dee, grinning his magnanimous grin at me.

"What does drawing sugar cubes entail?" I ask, and he laughs, throwing his head back. The sound echoes around the room, this joyously infectious chortle that makes me smile.

"You pick a cube from the sugar dish, and whoever has the most granules goes first. The person with the least goes last, and everyone else in between."

"How do you know how many granules are in each cube?" I ask, and Dee squints at me.

"You count them, silly." Oh, right, of course. Excuse me.

"Does the King have the power to investigate the Knave? Have her locked up or something?" Dee's smile fades slightly and he tucks his wings in tight, like just the mention of the cursed witch is upsetting to him.

"Not at all," he says, licking his lower lip and then looking away from me. "Not unless there's a Queen of Hearts on the throne who agrees to the same punishment. You'll have to have an official wedding ceremony with the King first, but we can only hold that once the Knave approves."

"Which will be never?" I manage to grind out between my teeth. This bitch is becoming a silent thorn in my side. I've barely spoken a handful of sentences to her and yet, she seems to be around every metaphorical corner I turn.

"She's only allowed to delay the King's proposed date twice, and even then only by sixty days. He, of course, proposed you get married either the day you arrived or the day after."

Shocker.

Dee smiles at me one last time and then spins me to face the Cheshire Cat, looking ridiculously debonair in the suit that Tee picked out for him. It's a full ensemble —coat, tie, cufflinks in the shape of paw prints. I'm surprised the angel prince actually convinced him to wear it. Since I first met the fucker, he's been shoeless, mostly shirtless, painted into leather pants.

"I look a fool, don't I?" he says, flattening his ears against his skull and stumbling over the steps of the dance twice as badly as I am. We must make quite a pair, me and him. Actually, I don't remember him being as bad of a dancer as this when we practiced. "I feel so constrained, like I can barely move."

I chuckle at his melancholy expression, remembering the last Halloween before Fred died, when we dressed Dinah up in a tiny hot dog costume. She collapsed to the floor and acted like she couldn't possibly walk around in it. Oh, cats sure are amusing creatures, aren't they?

"You look stupid handsome," I say, giving his collar a tug. He's still wearing it, along with the tag that has my name on it. He's got all his piercings in, too, which gives a nice contrast with the crispness of the suit. "If I found you as a stray, I'd most certainly take you home with me."

One black and white striped ear perks up, but then we both stumble again, and Lar is there to catch us. He steps in a few seconds early and helps correct my form, passing the cat off to the Duke to watch over.

His pale blue-blonde hair makes a nice contrast against the red of his suit jacket.

He's definitely the best dancer of the group, hands down, even when paired against the King.

"Keep your eyes out tonight," he whispers, putting his mouth against my ear and making me shiver. "The only prophecy I've seen since last night was a broken image in the bathtub. And it was of you, covered head to toe in blood."

Lar leans back and for just a split second, the confidence in his face is gone, replaced with concern and just a hint of fear.

No wonder everyone's acting so sketchy.

Before I can think of how to respond to that statement, Lar is cupping my face with his hand and leaning in toward me. He leaves the moment up to me, lets me decide if I want to close that gap or not. I decide to go for it, lifting up on my toes to kiss the Caterpillar's full mouth.

That asshole of a king interrupts me, cutting into our sequence far before it's his turn again.

"What the hell was that for?!" I ask, giving him a little shove and hoping like hell he tumbles out of the air and breaks a leg. Instead his hand tightens around mine, his fingers digging into my hip possessively. The look on his face is pure, carnal hell.

"I won a bet during our croquet game, remember?" he growls, and my cheeks flush with a mixture of frustration, embarrassment … and lust. The music comes to an end, and Brennin Red tucks his gloved fingers under my chin, lifting my face toward his. *I knew it! I just knew it! He would wait until this moment to collect, wouldn't he?!*

My eyes slide closed of their own accord, just before I feel the hot heat of his lips on mine. His tongue isn't far behind, invading my mouth and drawing a groan from me that echoes around the quiet ballroom. I'm not even sure if I'm still floating at that point, or if our feet have finally made contact with the floor.

The King does one better and sweeps me up in his arms, crushing me against his much larger frame, holding me like I really am his queen.

My arms go around his neck, and I find myself on my tiptoes, straining for more, desperate for it.

"So it's true: you're a whore in both worlds."

That voice … it shatters my blissful little cocoon, and I end up breaking away from the King and stumbling. I spin around, trying to find the source of the voice. It sounds like the Mocking Turtle, but it can't possibly be, right?

"What is it?" Brennin asks, and in less than a second

I'm literally surrounded by all nine men *and* the White Knight.

"If you'd just done what you did with the King, with Liam and his friends, your mother would be free. Your father wouldn't be broken. And your sister, Edith ... oh, what a delicious little tart she is."

"You leave my sister alone!" I snap, putting my hands on the sides of my heads. How can I hear the Mocking Turtle if he's not even here? He can't get inside the walls, remember?

"The Turtle," Tee says, taking one look at me and catching onto the problem. Perceptive, as usual. He would've made an amazing king to his own people. "You shouldn't have let her look at him so long."

"Me?" Dee asks, but he's busy looking around the room as the rest of the men whisper.

"He's not doing this on his own," March says, tapping a knife against the palm of one hand. "If she's hearing him in her head, then he's got an accomplice in here somewhere."

My eyes fall on the Knave, frowning at me from the edges of the crowd.

"I'm going to go after Edith, and I'm going to have a little taste—the same sort of taste that Liam wanted." I fucking snap when I hear that, shoving past Chesh and Lar and moving over to the Knave. I don't even bother to be nice about it. I just grab her by the front of her dress and get in her face.

"You're doing this, aren't you?" I choke out, feeling like my skull's about to explode. "You brought him in here somehow."

"I don't have the faintest idea what you're talking about," Ines says, lifting up a hand when her husbands move forward to disengage me. What she does do is smile, which only pisses me off more. "But please, continue. Show the entire court what a useless waste of life you are."

"Oh, please do. Then they'll lock you up, and Edith will be all mine to snack on." The Mocking Turtle's voice drives me up the bloody fucking wall, like nails on a chalkboard, that screeching sound trapped inside my skull where nobody else can hear, nobody else can take the burden off of his awful words.

Shoving my skirt up, I whip the Vorpal Blade out of its sheath and press the mirrored blade against the Knave's neck. It's at that point when she actually has the grace to look scared.

Whispers break out amongst the crowd as they all peer at my weapon in wonder.

The Lion is there an instant, swinging his fist right at my goddamn face. To be fair, I do have a knife to his wife's throat, but I honestly don't expect it. Brennin Red moves in the flash of an instant, getting between us, but he does end up taking a fist to the face.

The court lets out a collective gasp as blood drips from the King's mouth, and he reaches up white-gloved fingers to touch the blood, staring at his fingertips for a moment before he gives the Lion a look that the other man won't soon forget. Me, I'm still standing there holding the Vorpal Blade and wondering what it is that I've just gone and done.

"You fool," the King hisses, turning around and snatching my wrist before tearing the weapon from my hand. He slips the blade back into the sheath, yanks me in the direction of a small door, and charges forward as the crowd parts for him like the Red fucking Sea.

♦ ♠ ♣ ♥ ♣ ♠ ♦

The King of Hearts drags me down a hallway, his white-gloved hand squeezing too tightly on my tender wrist. He throws me against the wall and then slams his palm into the stones near my head.

"Are you an idiot?!" he snarls out, his teeth gritted in anger, a muscle ticking in his jaw. He's panting, his chest rising and falling, speckles of blood decorating his cheeks and lips. There's just enough light from a flickering torch for me to see the scar that runs from the right corner of his lip and down, slicing right across his throat.

His father ... he actively tried to behead him.

Those words echo in my mind as I swallow hard and

squeeze my left hand tighter around the hilt of the Vorpal Blade. I shouldn't have taken it out here; the King warned me as much last night. But I just … got so goddamn pissed. The Mocking Turtle is digging up my worst fears and spattering them around inside my skull like so much carnage. That, and last night was such a blur, it slipped my mind and …

"Do you want to meet the Anti-Alice today?" he growls, his ebon eyes flashing as he turns away from me with a scowl. It's awfully dark back here, and the King smells awfully good. I hate how much I like it, and I hate how I can even notice something like that at a time like this. But I know logically that the Mocking Turtle cannot get to Edith; she's safe on the other side of the Looking-Glass. I won't let his words get to me. "You just risked everything, and for what?"

"My pride and dignity," I grind out, sniffling and then reaching up with my left hand to rub away some of the King's blood from my face. I hadn't realized so much had spattered when he took that punch. "I figured at least *you* would understand that?"

"Some things are more important," he snaps at me, slamming his gloved palm into the wall again for emphasis. I'm just suddenly desperate to know what's under there. What's he hiding anyway? Brennin leans in and puts his mouth deliciously close to my ear, his breath warm against my skin. "Like the fate of Underland. Not that you give a *shit*."

"You don't know that!" I snap back at him, turning my face so fast that our mouths brush together.

There's this … weird, tense moment between us. It stretches hot and strange, our hatred boiling out and over, tainting the air with pretty poison.

Red's mouth slams into mine, his hands going to my waist and pushing me back against the wall. He crushes me to it with his body, his gloved hands squeezing my corseted waist tight as he slips them beneath my breastplate. With our matching clothes, and this frightening level of passion, it really does feel like I could be his Queen of Hearts.

He bites my lower lip, sucking it into his mouth, and stealing a groan from my throat at the same time. I think this man is a piece of human garbage, but oh my ears and whiskers, as Rab might say, this is too much. It feels too good, burns too hot, sears my inhibitions away along with my rationality.

The fingers of my right hand fist in his bloodred hair as our mouths work to fire up these sparks into a raging flame. I'm making sounds right now I didn't even know I was capable of, curling my left hand around the nape of the King's neck. He's already soaked in sweat, and I love it. Pretty sure his mouth is dripping blood all over my dress, but it's already red so who would know? Besides, in that moment, I can't find it in myself to care about anything but this ardent heat. I need to seek it out to its natural end.

Brennin Red tangles his hands in my full skirts, pushing them up and out of his way. His fingers brush the Vorpal Blade's sheath as he slides his palm up my inner thigh, over the thigh-highs and garter belt I said I wasn't going to wear but did anyway. When his fingers brush over the dampness on the front of my panties, my knees buckle and the King puts one of his between them to keep me standing upright.

My only wish right now … is that he keeps his fucking mouth shut.

I keep kissing him with the sole intention of making that happen. Yeah, uh, no, I'm not at all interested in kissing the bastard for any reason other than this. The stupid crown on my head tilts to one side, but doesn't fall off. Guess that is a useful spell, even if the Knave did cast it.

I move my right hand from Red's hair to the clasps on the front of his pants, buried underneath his robes. These are not freaking jeans, people. There are way too many buttons, so many that I end up tearing them just to get access to what's inside.

My fingers slip into Red's pants and … brush across a hard, metal object.

"The hell is …" I start, pushing him back just a bit so I can see what it is that I'm groping. I was aiming for dick and ended up with a bejeweled codpiece?! "What on earth …"

"These are in fashion," the King snaps at me, just before he rips his codpiece off and chucks it aside. In case you were wondering what, exactly, a codpiece is, I'll tell you. It's a fancy dick cup that was worn by men in the fifteenth and sixteenth centuries because ladies, dick measuring contests have been around since the dawn of time.

My next kiss cuts off whatever else he was going to say. Frankly, I don't care. If he keeps talking, I'll stop wanting to fuck him. And right now, that's all I want to do.

At least underneath the codpiece is nothing but warm, velvety skin. My fingers curl around the slick length of him, using his sweat as lube. Red growls against my mouth and kisses his way across my jaw and over to my ear, biting my lobe as he teases my clit through my panties. I want them inside now, but I also don't want to speed the moment along. No, I want to enjoy it. For just a minute, I want to pretend that I am going to marry the King of Hearts and be his Queen, take nine husbands and rule over Underland.

But … why can't I?

What's stopping me?

I can just let myself stay here, see if I can finally find out what happiness feels like, tastes like, fucks like.

But back home, I have Edy and Dad and Mom waiting

for me.

My heart stutters and cracks, and I open my mouth to ask the King about the Looking-Glass. If I can jump back and forth, then … then this could work. Surely, he'd be willing to compromise?

But then his gloved fingers slip under the fabric of my panties, pushing into the hot slickness of my core and teasing me with crooked motions. He knows all the right places to press to turn my body to jelly.

In response, I tighten my hand on Red's cock, squeezing hard enough that he makes some accidental noises of his own, too close to animal sounds to be faked. I love it. Running my thumb over the tip of his cock, I feel his hips buck against my hand.

The King moves his mouth back to mine, hovering his lips just out of reach. I try though, leaning up on my tiptoes for his kiss. Because he might be a total fucking prick, but he's an amazing kisser.

"My Queen," he says, thrusting his fingers deeper inside of me at the same moment he leans down and starts to kiss and lick and nip at my throat. Oh Hearts and Diamonds, I curse inside my own head. Because there's just no way in hell I can talk aloud right now. The only noises that seem able to escape past the torrid confines of my lips are groans, moans, and whimpers. "My Alice."

Brennin sucks on my skin hard enough that I just

know I'm going to have a major hickey, but also just hard enough that I don't give a shit. With my left arm, I pull him closer, encouraging him to push this up a notch, join our bodies, break this tension.

Guess the King of Hearts is no idiot because he gets the hint, removing his hand from my panties as I extract my own from his pants. He lifts me up against the wall with one arm, my legs automatically wrapping his waist. There's so much skirt fluff, but he shoves it out of our way with a growl, locking his ebon-dark eyes on my pale blue ones.

There's nothing to be said, so neither of us bothers.

Instead, the King uses his right hand to push aside my panties, and guides himself to the throbbing heat between my thighs.

Keeping our gazes locked, he thrusts inside of me so hard that I let out a small scream. It feels so good, but he's so big, and the sensation of him is so foreign. When I try to bury my face in his neck to stifle my sounds of pleasure, he cups my face with one gloved hand and forces me to keep looking at him, pumping his hips in a hard, fast, frenzy. It's so quiet down this hallway, with just the two of us, that all I can hear is the wet sound of our joining.

My eyes get half-lidded, and my mouth parts for his, letting him slide his tongue in against mine, letting him claim me and loving every second of it. This is so different from North's animal instincts, from Dee's loving nature,

Tee's reserved confidence. This is … probably seriously fucking unhealthy. And yet, I've never felt such a rush before.

I'm completely flooded by passionate hate, and craving ardent ire.

"I hate you so much," I manage to choke out, and the King makes a sound, kissing me hard enough to bruise. He fucks my ass into that wall so roughly that I know I'm going to be scratched and bruised, and yet, I find myself losing control, my muscles clamping down around him. I'm freaking coming before he does, wiggling and fighting against his movements as pleasure destroys me.

The King comes with this angry, frustrated sound that soon finds its way to this horrid superiority and triumph that I so desperately want to punch off of his face. He finishes inside of me and then collapses against the wall, crushing our bodies together.

What. The. Fuck. Have I just done?

"Your majesty," Tee says from the end of the hallway. As soon as I hear his voice, strained and tense, it's like a bucket of cold water's been thrown over my face. The King separates us and fixes his pants before setting me down.

I'm panting and soaked in sweat, but suddenly ice-cold.

I push my skirts down and turn to face Tee with guilt riding heavy on my shoulders. I'm supposed to ask the other members of my, uh, harem before taking a new guy, right? Did I just … cheat? God, I have no idea how this whole thing works.

"Yes?" the King asks, his voice that deep, annoying know-it-all baritone that made me want to stab him with the Vorpal Blade the first moment I met him. But the way he looks at Tee, it's not like a King looking at his servant. It's an alpha male sizing up a threat.

"We have two dead guards in the kitchen, and no idea what or who is in the castle with us. The White Rabbit says he doesn't sense anything else out of the ordinary, but clearly, something's going on." Tee bites this last part off the end of his tongue, flicking his amethyst eyes to one side. He's not mad at me … he's fucking terrified.

I listen for the Mocking Turtle's voice inside my head, but it's gone. At least for right now. Or maybe I just couldn't hear it over our furious grunting and groaning? Gross. A hot flush fills my face. There's a strange silence in the hallway, broken only by the music from the ballroom which is still playing. Surely, if something nefarious was going on, the music would stop?

"Bring me the Du—" Red starts, cutting off abruptly and yanking what I thought was a decorative sword from his belt. He spins just in time to intercept the Gryphon's blade, looking boss as hell even with his robes gaping open and several buttons missing on the front of his pants. The King raises a boot and kicks his opponent in the stomach, knocking him back several feet.

Tee's at my side, tearing out the Vorpal Blade and putting it back in my hand.

I give him a look, but he just shakes his head.

"It's too late now; come with me," he says, but the Gryphon is using the tight space to his advantage, filling the hallway with his wings and using the extra appendages to attack the King. Now, I'm not sure I even like the prick, but he's one of the few threads holding Underland together. Snap that, and everything falls apart.

I break away from Tee's grip and head for the battle, intending to step in with the Vorpal Blade … or maybe a little bit of magic, and turn the tide. But I'm not faster than a fallen angel prince. He cuts me off by thrusting one of his wings in front of me and yanking me back.

"We need to go now," he snaps, gritting his teeth and pleading at me with his eyes to listen. "Where do you think all the guards are? Clearly not on their way here. The Mocking Turtle must be in the castle somewhere." He yanks me back and I stumble, watching as he moves his black and blue feathers out of the way to reveal the King struggling in his fight with the Gryphon. It looks like the two men are pretty evenly matched. If this were to play out to the finish line, well, I wouldn't be making bets on a winner.

We need to get help for the King, but I see Tee's point.

If I die, there's not just a paltry thirty-five percent chance to save Underland … there's nothing at all.

I let Tee pull me down the hallway, but when we reach a T-shaped intersection, both sides are littered with the bodies of card servants, and the Mocking Turtle is waiting for us.

"Hello Alice," he says, whistling a tune under his breath as he leans against the wall, hands tucked into his pockets. He lifts his dark eyes to mine, their murky, swampy color making my stomach churn. "You really have saved a lot of lives today—we were going to slaughter everyone inside the ballroom to get to you. But popping down to the catacombs for a fuck? Brilliant."

Tee puts me behind him, spreading his wings to block off the hallway, as he removes his knife from his belt. I push his feathers out of my way, so I can see what's happening. Behind me, the King continues to struggle with the Gryphon, the clank of their blades echoing against the stone.

Whipping my attention back to M.T., I catch sight of his eyes flicking briefly up to the ceiling and then back down to Tee just a split-second before he launches an attack, yanking out a knife of his own.

But it's that quick flick of the eyes that saves me.

I spin around just in time to see a girl fall from the ceiling.

She doesn't come from a secret hatch in the wall though, no, it looks like she was simply clinging to the stone like a spider.

When she does land, she twists her body in a way that I just know isn't natural. If I were to move like that, my spine would break.

I adjust my grip on the Vorpal Blade and take a deep breath, waiting for the girl to lift her face and look at me. She smells like death, but not the sickly sweetness of fresh death, more like cobwebs and dust and forgotten tombs. When she lifts her head, I recognize her and almost choke.

"Edy?" I whisper, because for the briefest of moments, the woman—if you can even call her a woman—looks just like my little sister. Or me. Fuck, she looks like me. But this is no dark version of Allison Liddell; this is someone else entirely. And this is a someone else I feel I should recognize, but don't.

Her mouth is black, her skin gray, her hair as white as bones, but her eyes are as blue as my own.

I take a step back, an icy shiver working its way through my blood. Moments ago, I was gettin' hot and sweaty with the King of Hearts. Now, I'm staring at something that could very well be my own corpse.

The Anti-Alice.

This is the Anti-Alice.

I move my feet apart into a fighting stance. Because I know for fucking sure I'm going to have to fight right now; there's no way around it. All those lessons with North, I hold them close to my heart and take a deep breath. If I'm good at anything, it's reacting well to a stressful situation. Well, at least good at *reacting*. Like how I chased Rab after he shot Brandon. I mean, it's better than freezing up, right? Even if I do make mistakes.

The Anti-Alice is wearing a ratty pink bow on her head. It's rotted away at the ends and riddled with holes, but somehow seems important. It's the only thing on her entire body that's in color. She's literally a color study in black, gray, and white. And she's wearing a dress that's eerily similar to the one Edith gifted me, with a skirt that goes to the knees, short sleeves, and a dirty white apron. It's black and white striped, like an old prison uniform, but it's pretty, in a morbid dishabille sort of way.

Well, okay, so I lied about the pink ribbon being the only color on her body … that white apron is spattered in blood.

She stares me down for what feels like hours, but what I know can only be seconds.

There are wounds all over her body, rough and scarred over but clearly visible against the ashy gray of her skin. Her nails are black and chipped at the ends, but far too long and sharp for any normal person. I can't take my eyes off of them as they curl around a curved sickle blade that looks like it's made of bone.

She doesn't say anything, but the way she looks at me says it all: *I'm going to consume you, Alice.*

There's a—how should I put this—lack of energy in the air around her, like she's sucking the color from the world. I can feel her disturbing lack of power as strongly as I can sense the blood flowing through my veins. Whatever she … *it* … is, it isn't human.

When the girl runs her black tongue over her lower lip, I know I'm in trouble.

This is going to hurt, I think, seconds before she throws herself at me like a rag doll or a zombie, like she has no bones and exists as simply as ashes in the wind. I barely manage to stumble out of the way of her weapon. It crashes into the wall next to my face, shattering the stone into pieces. Shards rain down on the back of my head as I roll out of the way, narrowly avoiding a second blow that slams into the floor inches from my face. Some rainbow strands of hair flutter away as they're sliced off.

Holy shit, holy shit, holy shit, I think as I struggle and fail to get to my feet, slipping on the shards of debris and thanking whatever spirits or gods are listening that I'm wearing thick-soled boots instead of regular heels.

My skirts wrap around my legs as I fall on my ass

with a grunt, keeping my hand wrapped around the hilt of the Vorpal Blade only with serious effort on my part. All I have to do is stab her, but there's no chance for it. She's on top of me before I can even think about lifting up the blade. Her sickle sword comes down at me with a speed that'll probably sever my head from my neck.

I have just long enough to recognize that fact, but not enough time to do a damn thing about it.

The Mad Hatter's cane whips down and deflects the blade, sparing my head. Arms go under my pits and drag me to my feet—it's March—and then haul me out of harm's way, trading places with Raiden Walker.

He flips off his black top hat with his cane, and pulls out a revolver from underneath it, leveling it on the undead girl's face and pulling the trigger. Instead of sparks and gunpowder, the weapon releases a net that drags the Anti-Alice to the ground with a wicked screech. It's ten fucking times worse than the jabberwocky noises, and I feel hot crimson liquid draining from my ears.

"Let's go," March says, hoisting me up and holding me in his arms like a baby. Not my favorite position, but I'll take this over decapitation.

"Tee!" I scream because the Anti-Alice is already clawing her way out of the net, and the Hatter is already on his way back over to us, leaving the angel prince alone with two enemies instead of one.

The King is still fighting the Gryphon, but now there are men in black armor, decorated with clubs. Soldiers sent by the King of Clubs, aka the Carpenter. Fuck. Brennin's outnumbered almost ten to one.

"Oh, get on with it, would you, Your Majesty?" Raiden rumbles, but even he sounds stressed.

The vampire mercenary badass that the fucking dragon doesn't think he can beat … is nervous.

As I watch, the King rips off one of his gloves and reveals a palm as red as his outfit. He slams it into the chest of the nearest man. The effect is instantaneous. Blood begins to pour from the guard's mouth, nose, eyes, and ears. And his screams, they echo like nightmares in the skulls of the insane.

The guard's head twists around in a circle … and then his neck splits, decapitating him.

What. The. Fuck?!

Red does the same to the next guard, and the next, and the next.

There's so much fucking blood. No wonder his name is friggin' Red—he's painting the roses red, that's for sure.

"We have to save Tee," I scream, fighting my way from March's arms, so that I'm standing on the stone floor again. I'm penned in between him and the Hatter, and neither of them look all that interested in giving into my request.

Actually, they're not looking at me at all.

"Do we take her to the Looking-Glass?" Raiden asks, staring instead at the King. Red manages to take out the guards, but the Gryphon is another matter entirely. I notice Red doesn't even try his magic hand technique on his sparring partner.

"The entire palace is overrun with Clubs," March says, looking up. His ears twitch and he bares his teeth in a snarl. As if in response to his statement, the sounds of pounding boots echoes from overhead.

"Are they here?" the Hatter asks, his question sharp and jagged as it rolls off of his tongue. *They?* Who's they? The Gryphon and the Mocking Turtle are already here. He doesn't mean … the Walrus and the Carpenter, does he?

"If the Anti-Alice is here, it's safe to assume they're nearby," March says, turning at the sound of shattering stone behind us. The wall caves in from the right and a jabberwock head snakes through with a hiss.

And this jabberwock is not the Duke of Northumbria, I can tell you that.

The face is all wrong, and the eyes are black, not gold. It screams at us and continues to dig and scrabble at the stone. If we don't hurry, it'll block our way completely and we'll be trapped in here.

While Raiden and March are distracted, I turn and run in

Tee's direction.

The Anti-Alice is already coming at me, her skirts catching on her legs as she sprints full-tilt down the hallway, shattering the glass sconces on the wall as she passes. She doesn't even have to touch anything to bring destruction.

I stop suddenly, my full skirts billowing around me as I feel the tingle of my own magic. I can’t use it on her, but I can make an assist, right? Using what little power I can summon on short notice, I chuck the Vorpal Blade as hard as I can. It embeds itself in the Anti-Alice's throat, and she stops dead in her tracks, choking on blood. It pours out of her mouth and down her throat in a crimson waterfall. But I'm already running again, shoving past her and pulling out the knife March gave me. The poison sparkles on the edge like glitter.

"Tee!" I scream, but he's too locked up in the fight to turn and face me. Doesn't matter. I can't leave him here to die. There are Club soldiers streaming down the halls on both sides. Tee's holding his own against M.T., but it's only a matter of time before he's overrun.

I move up beside him and stab the small blade into the Mocking Turtle's shoulder. Because of their violent struggle, it's the only place I can aim for that I know I won't hit the angel, too.

The Mocking Turtle barely acknowledges that I've

stabbed him, not at first. But then I figure the poison must be setting in because he's shoving Tee away and stumbling back into the onslaught of soldiers.

I snatch Tee's hand and take off.

"What a stupid move," Raiden says, but he picks me up and throws me over his shoulder while Tee follows along behind us. On our way past the King, Raiden tosses his gun to March, and the man fires off another net, pinning the Gryphon just long enough for Brennin to join us.

I notice then that the Vorpal Blade is in March's other hand, and the Anti-Alice is nowhere to be seen. So where the fuck did she go?!

Now we're all running down the hallway, slipping past the jabberwock before she—because this just has to be a she—cuts off our exit completely.

Red leads the way, taking us up a set of narrow stairs and into what I'm assuming is a servant's hallway.

This is where Tee showed me the Looking-Glass, I think as we round the corner and run straight into Dee. He's holding his cell phone in his hand and smiling tightly.

"Thanks for the text," he says, blood spattered across the front of his new shirt. It's sticky and glossy, making the fabric cling to the hard planes of his chest. "I might've gone down the main hall and gotten myself killed."

Dee pushes past us, opens up the main screen on his phone … and hits the bomb icon.

With a whistle, he chucks it back in the direction we came. It lands on the floor with the sound of shattering glass, cogs and wheels scattering across the stones.

"Go!" Dee screams as our ragtag little group pushes around the corner seconds before the jabberwock scrambles up the hall behind us. There's the distinct smell of sulfur in the air and then … *boom.*

The phone explodes with so much force that we're thrown forward. The Mad Hatter manages to keep me in his arms as he rolls, shielding me from any injury. When he stands up, he sets me down and then steps aside for the King, watching as the man unlocks the door with a simple wave of his hand. He doesn't even *need* the key that Tee stole.

"What about North?" I ask, panting and choking on the smell of smoke. There are spatters of blood and gore on the walls behind us, the heat of the flames chasing along the tapestries and carpets in our direction. "Lar? Chesh? Rab?"

"Not our problem," Raiden grinds out as Brennin opens the door and steps aside to let us in.

"Not *your* problem, you mean," I scream, shoving him away from me, feeling this frantic energy clawing at the inside of my throat. I put my palm against my chest, feeling my heartbeat fighting to escape my skin. "The prophecy says the Alice has nine husbands, right? So what happens if four of them die here today?!"

Ugh, I'm overreaching like crazy, I think as the five men in the room stare at me like I've completely and utterly lost the plot, as North might say.

Sapphire, amethyst, ebon, chocolate, and marmalade. Those are the colors blinking back at me with disbelief and anger and frustration. And like, there's no way in hell I'm committing to all these guys, but I'm also too invested in them to let them die. Lory's in there, too, somewhere with Dodo and Eaglet, and if I can, I'll find her, too. Oh, fuck, and the White Knight! I can't leave them all behind.

I move to the leave the room, and the King steps in front of me, looking down at me with this wild expression on his face that both turns me on and infuriates me at the same time.

"Get in the Looking-Glass, Alice," he whispers, low and dangerous. I glare at him as the March Hare slides up beside me and forcibly curls my fingers around the hilt of the Vorpal Blade.

"Go to *hell*," I growl out, but Red is grabbing me by the arm so hard that I let out a small scream. He shoves me back and into Tee and Dee and *they* wrap their arms around either one of mine. "Fucking traitors!" I scream, thrashing against their grips.

With another wave of his red palm, the King orders the giant chess pieces aside as if they're as harmless as puppies.

"Take her Topside and don't come back until I send for you," Red says, moving toward the door and pausing to put his glove back on. Now that I know what he can do with his hands—in more ways than one—I'm even more terrified and turned-on by him. Not a healthy combination, is it?

As he moves away, he gives me a dark look, curses under his breath and slams the door behind him. I hear several locks slide into place.

Is he going back for the others?

There's no way to find out because the twins are turning me around and leaving me to face my own reflection. Now that the mirror's magic has been … enabled, or whatever, it's as wild as a storm. The silver surface stirs up my image, creating a disturbing mess of color that's supposed to be me.

The gold and silver nightmare leans against the wall, like a wonky melted caricature of a real mirror. The edges are inlaid with carvings of all four suits, and there's a single red heart at the top. It'd be a pretty mirror, if I had time to fucking admire such things.

As it were, Tee's putting his mouth close to my ear and whispering in a tense, low voice, "I'm sorry, Allison," and then he and Dee are shoving me forward and into my own messy reflection. There's no time for me to scream or wonder if this is going to work. I slip straight through the liquid silver, my hands and arms blurring to a bright silvery mist as I start to fall. Much like the Rabbit-Hole, there's this sense that I've reached a new reality, like I'll just be falling forever and ever and I should get used to it.

This fall, however, doesn't last nearly as long.

For a few seconds there, I'm suspended in a silver liquid, falling and drowning at the same time. In the next instant, I'm tumbling out of the mirror above the living room fireplace and landing in a messy heap on the carpet.

Dinah arches her back, hissing at me, while my little sister Edith rises to her feet … and starts to scream.

8

Looking-Glass House of Hell

Edith darts past me and grabs the metal poker from next to the fireplace. I'd be proud of her for defending herself is she hadn't started beating me with it.

"Fuck!" she screams randomly, hitting me in the legs with the weapon. I roll onto my back between swings and use my lessons with North to bring the Vorpal Blade up, connecting with her next blow. Our eyes meet and everything goes still—even Dinah stops hissing.

"Son … Sonny?" Edith whispers, her eyes widening as I lower the blade and wait for her to put her own weapon down. Instead, she just stands there with it hanging in the air above my head.

I'm too busy shaking and lying there in a pool of silver goo to do much but freak the fuck out inside.

I've been fighting to get home for *weeks* and now that I am home … I want to go back.

This isn't right, I think, sitting up suddenly and leaning my head over my bloodied skirts. I feel like I might throw up. I *just* had sex with the King, and now I'm sitting in Dad's living room?

The mundane normalcy of my old life crashes into me with the force of a freight train, and I find myself gagging. Mostly on the mirror goo, but also … I'm suddenly *desperate* for the wicked depravity of Underland and the crazy men that I said I hated but maybe actually liked.

"This can't be happening," I whisper as Edith drops the poker onto the floor and stumbles back, falling onto the smaller sofa like her bones have just turned to Jell-O. "This can't be happening," I say again, pushing up to my feet and stumbling into the fireplace. There's a roaring flame burning, and it singes the edges of my skirts, but I don't care. I'm too busy putting my palms on the surface of the mirror and choking on my own doubts and fears.

Did I imagine all of that? Surely not, right? I mean, I *am* still wearing a bloody ballgown and holding a knife.

The Rabbit-Hole. If I have to, I can just go back to that house we were at the night of the party …

"Allison, is that you?" Edy whispers from behind me. I

look at myself in the mirror, my ice-blue eyes so vibrant that even *I* have to wonder if I'm wearing contacts. The rainbow streaks in my hair have spread, their color twice ... no, *three* times as bright as it was the day I put it into my white-blonde hair. My lips are full and swollen from Red's kisses, and there is most definitely a hickey on the side of my pale throat.

Plus, there's blood *everywhere*.

I didn't imagine a damn thing.

"Edy," I start, turning to look at her just before my fingers slip into the warm, liquid softness of the mirror. My head whips around just in time to see Dee tumble from the glass and straight into me, knocking me on my back on the floor. He ends up straddling me which is kinda nice, but then Edith picks up her poker and whaps him in the back with it.

"Aren't *you* a lovely sight?" Dee grumbles, grabbing the poker and yanking it from my sister's hands before he looks back down at me with his beautiful sapphire eyes, three shades darker than mine and twice as pretty. If I were liable to cry, I'd weep until the whole house was flooded with tears. "Are you okay, Allison-who-isn't-Alice?" he asks me, and I just barely manage a nod. "Good," Dee says, rolling off of me and taking me with him.

We move out of the way about three seconds before

Tee slides through the Looking-Glass, landing on his boots like a boss, military jacket billowing out behind him. He steps aside and looks straight into my face.

"I'm so sorry Allison," he repeats, but my emotions are too twisted for me to process his words. I'm excited to see him, but now that he's here and my fears of Underland being a dream or a fit of madness are banished, I'm freaking out about the people we left behind.

"What's going to happen to the castle?" I ask, panting and holding the Vorpal Blade so tight that my fingers start to cramp. What I'm really asking is *what's going to happen to the ones we left?*

The Mad Hatter hops from the portal while Edith gapes at us like she's about to burst a blood vessel in her brain. Seeing her sitting there with her blonde hair in a braid, her pink Under Armour shirt with *Break the Ceiling* scribbled across it, I feel like *she* is the weird one in this room.

How twisted is that?

Once March arrives—also gracefully, so I guess Dee and I are the clumsy ones—he takes the mirror off the mantle, wraps it up in his velvet trench coat, and tucks it under his arm. His ears twitch as he glances down at my sister.

"Rob Evans?" she chokes which would be pretty funny if the circumstances were any different.

"Put that back!" I say, pushing past the twins to stand next to March. I'm still panting and sweating, and I wish I had time to lie back on a bed and daydream of my time with the King. Buuuut, I don't. "The others might be on their way soon."

"*If* they come through," he says, handing the Mad Hatter back his revolver, "then surely a coat won't be enough to stop them?" He shakes out his free hand, spattering the ground with goo. Not that it matters: we're all covered in it. "Do you happen to have a shower available in this hovel?"

"This is a *nice* five bed, three bath in a good neighborhood," I growl out at him, lifting up my skirts and tucking the Vorpal Blade away in my thigh sheath. I hold out my arms like I expect him to give me the Looking-Glass … and he does, plops it right down. I almost fucking drop it.

"If you break that, there's *no other way through*," March says, locking his brown eyes on mine. "Do you understand what I'm saying, Allison? If the Looking-Glass breaks"—he points at it for emphasis—"then Underland and Topside are parted forever."

"What about the Rabbit-Hole?" I ask. It only goes one way, but at least I could get back … well, not *home* but …

"The Rabbit-Hole is like a stream off a river," the Mad Hatter says, adjusting his top hat and glancing down at my sister like he's just seen her. She's shaking now, her eyes so wide they look liable to roll right out of her face. "This is the river," Raiden says, caressing the edge of the mirror suggestively.

He turns and looks around the living room like it's been a while. He's from Topside, right? *Did you just think of home as Topside?* I think, and I almost roll my eyes. If the situation were any less dire …

The mirror in my arms suddenly seems to weigh a ton, and I feel sick to my stomach.

If I drop this, it's all over.

"Here," Tee says, and when he offers to take the Looking-Glass, I pass it over. I trust him not to break it a hundred times more than I trust myself. "And don't worry about the others: they're all capable men, I promise."

"What about Lory and The Long Tale crew?" I ask, wringing my hands in the fluffy folds of my dress. I should probably address Edith, but … she feels like a stranger, sitting there on Dad's white couch. I don't even know what to say to her.

"They're pirates, remember," Tee says with a small smile, and I have to blink several times to adjust to the idea of him standing in my living room. It's surreal as *fuck*. "They'll be okay. Once the castle's secured, the King will send for us."

I nod, but I can't tell if Tee's just trying to humor me, or if he really means what he says.

"Who's this?" Dee asks, looking down at my little sister

with his hands on his hips. "Mini-Allison-who-isn't-Alice?"

"This is Edith," I say as I move over to the couch and sit down next to her in a puff of skirts. I'm probably getting blood everywhere, but it hardly matters now, does it? I'm also coated in mirror goo, just like everyone else.

"There *is* a shower, thank my paws and fucking whiskers," March growls, slamming the door to the downstairs bathroom closed. The sound of the water running in the guest bath blurs into the normal background noises of my childhood home: the running of the refrigerator, the clink of fresh ice from the ice maker, the bubbling of a coffee pot.

"Edith," I start, reaching out a hand to touch her knee. She jerks back from me and swallows hard, sitting like a deranged crab on the back corner of the couch. "Calm down for a sec and talk to me," I coo, doing my best to stay calm. I did just hate-fuck a king, fight an undead girl, and run from a dragon, so that's a wee bit difficult at the moment, but I'm trying. Fuck, I'm trying. But now my teenager-senses are kicking off and I'm thinking about the mess of silver goo on the floor, the spatters of blood on the couch, and … me.

Back home after two weeks.

With four strange men.

Two have wings. One has rabbit ears. And the other

has orange eyes and vampire teeth.

Oh I'm *sure* Dad is going to love this. Aaaaaaand, I doubt he's going to believe my story of a White Rabbit leading me down a magic hole. Oh no. I bet Brandon's murder was all over the news, connected with my disappearance. How am I going to explain any of this?!

"You … you … *you*," she chokes out, slipping her phone from her pocket and frantically hitting the emergency call button on the bottom. I snatch it from her hand and hold it out of reach. "You … you … you," she repeats, starting to shake.

Hey, I get it: her missing sister just fell out of the living room mirror followed by four incredibly hot but really weird guys. That, and this weird ass silver shit is on *everything*. It's like that shiny silver oil paint I used on my dresser last year. I dribbled a little on my carpet and ended up having to cut the fibers off. That shit would not come out.

I hope this isn't like that since it's on everything, including Mom's favorite rug.

Not that she'll ever get to see it again. She's in prison for life, remember?

"Where is Dad?" I ask, looking into her face. I need her to snap out of it and talk to me.

"You … where … I didn't drop any acid," she chokes out, reaching into her pocket and pulling out a blunt and a lighter. "I swear, I didn't."

"Edy, this isn't an acid trip," I growl, reaching out to snatch the pot paraphernalia from her hands. This time, she manages to dance out of my way, and then Tee grabs it from over her shoulder for me, making my sister scream.

"This isn't happening," she whispers, curling up into a ball and starting to sob.

Scratch what I thought before. Now that I'm sitting here and looking at her, I know for a fact that she could not have been the Alice.

"This *is* happening," I say, getting on the floor in front of her and taking her hands in mine, just like I did the night Fred died. I held her hands and I told her through the thickest of tears that it wasn't a dream or a nightmare —it was real. This is … surprisingly, much less stressful. "But I'm here, and I'm safe."

"Brandon's dead," she sobs, letting me hold her hands. "I found his body." Gritting my teeth, I squeeze her hands and curse Rab out in my head, while simultaneously wishing with every molecule in my body that he's still alive. "And you were … I saved your book." She sniffles and lifts her head up to look at me. Tears drag her eyeliner down her face in two dark stripes, and my heart stutters a little. If I stay in Underland, I'll be leaving Edith behind. Can I really do that?

"Hey," Dee says, kneeling down next to me. When I

look at him, I get a different sort of stutter in my chest, like my heart is doing happy somersaults in the hot, hot sun. Warm, wild, a little messy … "Are there cleaning supplies around? Tee and I will work on fixing this place up."

"I … uh, next to the fridge," I start and they both cock their heads in unison.

Ooookay.

Right.

They have cell phones and revolvers in Underland, but not refrigerators. Gotcha.

"In the kitchen," I say, pointing in that general direction and refocusing my attention on Edy. The Mad Hatter walks in a slow, lazy circle, pausing next to the front window to peep out the curtains. "How long have I been gone?" I ask, because although I'm pretty damn sure time works the same in both worlds, I have to check.

"Thirteen days, four hours, and eleven minutes from the last time I saw you," Edith whispers, looking at me with fresh tears dripping from her blue eyes. The fact that she's been counting down the literal minutes makes me feel like a shit sister. "Where …" she starts and then pushes her blonde braid over one shoulder, lifting her fake eyelashes to peer up at the Mad Hatter.

He's standing behind me now, arms crossed over his chest.

"Where the fuck were you?" she chokes out, swallowing

hard and running her tongue over too-red lips. Edith looks like she's about to go out to a bar. She's sixteen fucking years old.

"I was …" *Jesus, how do I respond to this?* "I'll explain later. You need to tell me where Dad is."

"Search party in the woods behind Brandon's house," she says, and I get goose bumps all over my skin. What if someone stumbles across the Rabbit-Hole? What then? "He'll be home in a few hours." She pauses and blinks stupidly at me. "Do you want me to call him?"

"No!" I snap, harsher and louder than I mean to. I'm just wound all the fuck up right now, rising to my feet and glancing back at Raiden. He meets my eyes with his orange ones, and smirks at me. "No, not yet. Are there police here?"

"There were for the first week. But … not anymore." Edith stands up and I realize she's wearing my leather jacket on her small shoulders. "Everyone thinks you were raped and killed, Allison. They've been trolling me on every social media platform known to man …" She trails off, and I wonder if she's just realized she's making this about herself—as usual. But then, I'm just happy to see that she's okay. "Sonny, what the fuck is going on?"

"It doesn't matter," I say as I stand up and look at the mess in the living room. There's silver goo all over the damn place. Plus, the broken bits of the coffee table I smashed into when I landed. That, and I've smeared blood on the edge of the couch. "Let's get everything cleaned up and—"

"It doesn't matter?!" Edith asks, standing up and breathing hard. "You've been missing for weeks! I thought you were dead, Sonny. So did Dad. And Mom … How could you do this to us?" she screams, like I had any choice in the matter.

I just look at her, and I'm at a complete loss for words. There's too much turmoil inside of me. I can't stop thinking about North, Chesh, Lar, Rab … the King. And then Lory and her men, the White Knight, all the innocent bystanders at the ball … I need to get back to Underland, but to do that, I have to smooth things over here first.

"You have the Liddell blood as well, do you?" the Mad Hatter asks, cocking his head to one side as he studies my sister. She jumps when she notices that it's her he's talking to, and then her cheeks get red. "Share some with me, would you? Your sister is *such* a tease." He moves up beside me as I curl my lip in a little snarl. "Did I mention she's my fiancée?"

"Wha … what?" Edith asks as I mentally stab the Mad Hatter with the Vorpal Blade.

Tee and Dee come back into the room with a mop and a broom and not much else. I don't blame them; cleaning supplies in Underland probably look a hell of a lot different than they do here.

"You were kidnapped … and then engaged … Or were you kidnapped?" Edith asks, trailing after me into the kitchen. I'm tempted to wrap her in a hug and tell her everything's going to be okay, but we've always had intimacy issues in our family, issues that only got *worse* after Fred passed away. "Some people said it was *you* who killed Brandon."

"Me?!" I choke as I grab paper towels, Windex, and garbage bags from under the sink. I stand up and turn around to look at Edith to see if she's fucking joking. There's no way any idiot in their right mind could think I shot Brandon. With what weapon? With what *motive*?! "Please tell me you don't believe that."

"I …" Edith steps toward me, lowering her voice to a husky whisper. "You just fell out of a mirror followed by four weird-ass looking dudes. What should I believe, Sonny? Hmm?" She trails along behind me as I dump the cleaning supplies on the floor and Dee lifts up the paper towel roll to his eyes like a telescope. It'd be cute and funny under different circumstances.

"We have to clean all of this up before my dad gets home." I shove rainbow and blonde strands of hair from my face as I use the dust pan to scoop up some of the silver goo. It's glittery and extremely viscous, like molasses or something. Or blood. Yeah, maybe it's more like blood, warm and sticky. "Our brother Fred was a big guy. And my parents haven't touched his room since he … passed. Go in there and change into some of his shit." I yank a huge clump of paper towels from the roll and go at the carpet with some fucking OxiClean. Of course, the stupid things flake all over the place and get caught in the fibers.

"You can't give them Fred's clothes!" Edy yells, standing way to close to me, her shoes stuck to the carpet. The twins both have their wings out, and I'm not quite sure *what* to do about that. Edith hasn't really said anything, but maybe she thinks they're fake? I have no clue. I just figure she's probably in as much shock as I was when I fell down the Rabbit-Hole. Maybe more. "Who the hell are these guys anyway? And what are—" She reaches out to grab Tee's wing, and his hand flies up, slapping my sister away.

"Please don't touch my wings," he says, folding them tightly against his back as my sister gapes in horror.

"They're not real though," she chokes out, stumbling back and sitting down hard on the edge of the couch at the same moment the bathroom door opens and March steps out in my father's black robe. "They're not real, they're not real, they're not real."

I ignore Edith for a moment and focus on March instead.

"It's doubtful you have any servants, in a house this small," he says, and I swear to God, I would punch him in the junk if I were close enough. Rab has servants and his house is about the same size. So what's that about? Being a dick for dick's sake. "So who does the washing?"

"A machine," I snap as I gesture with my chin toward the bathroom. "Raiden, you're next. I'll bring some clothes down in a minute." I scrub the carpet harder, almost furiously, my hands shaking.

I'm all shook up; I'm freaking out; I'm home and I feel like I'm on Mars.

"Why don't you go shower and get us all fresh clothes," Tee says, reaching out and taking my wrist. He rubs his thumb along the sensitive flesh, tracing a purple vein underneath. I can feel our pulses thumping against one another. "We'll get this cleaned up and then take our turns washing."

We look at each other over the shredded lump of paper towels, and I realize I just want to throw myself into his arms and have a hug. Maybe these weird dudes are helping with my intimacy issues just a little?

"Okay," I say, because I'm too tired to argue, and I just *need* a minute.

"Can I come, too?" Edith asks, and when I look over at her, her eyes are just a little too big and weepy for me to say no.

"You can sit on the toilet," I tell her as I stand up and look around at the mess in my living room.

I'm finally home.

And ironically enough, it's the last place in the world I want to be.

The stupid fish-patterned shower curtain is see-through, so I just know Edith is staring at me as I uncoil what's left of my fancy hairdo, and squeeze some of her hibiscus-bamboo shampoo into my hands.

I'd like to clean my *whole* body, if you catch my drift, but I can't very well wash off evidence of my tryst with the King while my little sister's eyes are on me.

"Could you stare at the wall or something?" I ask as I lather up and rinse, feeling all the bumps and bruises on my body. Suddenly, I'm just *tired*, and I can't think of anything better than a nap. It's doubtful I'll be getting one anytime soon.

"I just can't believe you're here," Edith says, wrapping her arms around herself and staring at the red and black heap of my dress and jacket on the floor. "Mom, Dad, and me ... we all thought you were dead."

My throat tightens up and I turn away, staring at a drip of water as it runs down the white plastic shower surround.

"You're not going to believe where I've been, but I hope you at least believe that I didn't run away by choice. And I came back as soon as I could." I grab the conditioner next, soaking my hair in it and rubbing a few colored strands between my fingers.

"Who are all those guys?" she asks me quietly, the bathroom fan almost drowning out the sound of her words. But I'm on hyper-alert right now. I feel like I could hear my sister from a thousand miles away if she screamed for me.

"Friends," I say, because I am *not* addressing that fiancée comment right now. Raiden Walker, that prick. "From … where I was staying."

"They're all cosplayers?" Edith asks, and I mean, that's as good a guess as any. "Those wings look so *real.* They must've cost a fortune." Swiping soap from my eyes, I glance over at her through the wavy plastic of the shower curtain and see her picking at the hole on the knee of her jeans. "Where did you guys come from? It … looked like you fell through the mirror."

"We … there's a secret door in the fireplace mantle," I say, which is so fucking stupid and lame that I can't believe I even said it aloud. But Edith's in shock, and she's never really been into fantasy—unless you count *Vampire Diaries*—so her mind isn't quite as open as my own.

She believes it as soon as I say it because it's the safe thing to believe, that somehow there's a useless door secretly hidden in the fireplace.

"We had some paint for our, uh, costumes," I continue, hating myself for lying and knowing I don't have a lot of other good options. If I were to tell her what really happened, she wouldn't believe me anyway. "I spilled it everywhere when I came in the door."

"How do you get in the door anyway?" she asks, her voice sounding tinny and far away. Yep, she's definitely in shock.

"The attic," I say, because she's never been up there in her life. Too scared of spiders.

"You were in the attic?" Edith continues, and I realize I'm about to get these questions and more from my dad, mom, and probably the police. I need to come up with a story about Brandon's murder and quick.

"I climbed the trellis in the back, snuck in my room, and went to the attic." I bite my tongue and shake my head. Such a stupid lie, but if she buys it, fine. "Just don't tell Dad about that. Let me tell my own story, okay?"

"Why were you cosplaying when you knew we'd be worried about you?" she whispers, and I feel my entire stupid story fall to pieces. I don't know what to do or say; there is no rule book for this shit. For the first time since I fell down the Rabbit-Hole, I feel my age. Eighteen-years young and shaking under the hot water blasting from the shower head.

"Edith, just … believe what I'm saying and let it go,

okay? I don't ask a lot out of you. But, just this once, *please*."

There's a long period of silence as I finish washing and then turn off the water, wrapping the fluffy pink towel around myself.

There's a knock on the door before it bursts inward, and I see Tee and Dee waiting in the hallway.

"We have a problem," he says, just before I hear my name shouted from downstairs.

It's my dad.

"Allison!" he screams, his voice so raw and shattered that I feel like I've just been dipped in a vat of broken glass.

I rush out of the bathroom, slamming the door in Edith's face. I don't mean to be rude, but I need a minute to get a handle on this situation. Grabbing the twins by their hands, I drag them to my room and lock us in.

"Is there a way to put your wings back?" I ask, looking between the two of them. "Reactivate the curse? Just for a little while," I correct when I see dual expressions of disappointment on both their faces.

"If you can control your magic, you can do anything," Tee says, and then before I can even ask, adds, "even here in Topside." He looks at me with such a genuine expression on his face that I feel weak in the knees again. The King brought about that emotion with passion, and

Tee … brings it out in affection. Without further explanation, he reaches out and cups the side of my face, bringing my lips to his for a kiss.

"We belong to you. There's nothing you can't see if you don't want to." Dee's words sound loudly inside my tired skull, and I put a palm up to Tee's chest the way I did to his brother's the first night we made love. Closing my eyes, I let myself flow into him, catching on the edge of a memory and pushing it away. If I get sucked down that Rabbit-Hole—pun intended—I won't have enough time to get the twins into proper shape to meet my dad.

Oh God.

It finally hits me.

The Mad Hatter is in the living room with my father.

I'm sure this'll turn out *great.*

Dad, meet my vampire boyfriend. He has a pet bat that's bigger than your SUV.

I shove those emotions aside, putting my hands on Tee's shoulders and kissing him with this theatrical reverence, rising up onto my toes. My towel falls off and he curls his arms around my naked body. We've been here, done this before. I'm more than happy to let him hold me, even if I get silver goo on my freshly washed skin.

With our tongues dancing together, I reach into Tee with my power and find the curse, that ugly black heart stamped onto his soul, sizzling and burning him with every thump of his pulse. One day, I'll crush it completely, dragging it kicking and screaming out of him and toss it right back at the witch-bitch who cast it in the first place. For now, I nudge it with my magic and feel it tugging on Tee's soul.

His lips break from mine, and with a groan, he collapses to his knees, taking me with him. His wings fold inward with a burst of black light and the sound of metal on metal.

"Allison!" I can hear my dad screaming from the top of the stairs now.

Fuck.

"Dee," I whisper as he squats next to me, his lips twisted in a soft smile.

"You've got this, Allison-who-isn't-Alice." When he leans in to kiss me, I realize that he tastes different than his brother. Tee tastes like rainwater and sunshine breaking through storm clouds. Dee tastes like blackberry honey and mint. I tangle my fingers in his hair and do the same to him as I did to his brother, feeling like a traitor all the while. But there's no way in fuck I can convince my dad these wings are fake the same way I did my sister, especially not if the cops get involved.

Dee's wings light up with that same eerie black light before collapsing inward like a telescope.

It's at that moment that my father kicks in my door, tearing off the locks, and finds me kneeling, naked, and kissing a boy covered in silver goo.

How the fuck am I going to explain this one?

9

The Garden of Lies and Cowards

Henry George Liddell stands in my doorway with his brown eyes wide, and his dark hair tousled and messy. He looks like he hasn't slept in days, and his glasses are crooked and sitting on the tip of his pointed nose. Edith and I both look like little Mom clones, while Fred was always a spitting image of dad.

Right now, however, he just looks like a demon risen from the depths of hell.

"Allison," he breathes as I gather up my towel and rise to my feet.

I have to admit, I'm terrified.

There are only three times in my life that I've been

more scared than I am right now.

The night I was almost raped.

The night Fred was killed.

The day my mother was sentenced in prison.

"Dad," I choke out as he puts his arm against the doorjamb and leans so heavily into it that he looks like he might collapse altogether. His eyes take me in like I'm the second coming of Jesus before he flicks them to Dee, and then Tee, and then back to me again.

"Allison," he repeats, stumbling into the room … and giving me a hug?

I haven't had a hug from my dad in months. Honestly, I was starting to wonder if he even gave two fucks about me at all anymore.

"I can't believe you're here," he whispers, and I feel hot, salty tears falling on my bare shoulder. It's weird, to hug my dad wearing nothing but a towel, and yet I can't seem to find it in myself to move away from him.

Edith watches from over his shoulders, arms folded across her chest, eyes watching me and Dad like this scene is as shocking—or even *more* shocking—than the five of us tumbling out of the Looking-Glass.

Dad pulls back and then levels this *look* on Tee and Dee that I haven't seen since the trial against Liam and his friends, the one where they were acquitted of Fred's murder.

"What the hell is going on?" he demands, wrinkling his nose up at the sight of the two nineteen-year olds covered in goo. If he only knew I'd just screwed a twenty-eight year old king against the wall of his castle. Of … what could easily be *my* castle.

I don't really feel like a queen though, standing in front of my much taller father dressed only in a pink towel and a cloak of shame. Not for the kissing or the sex or anything like that, but because I already know that in my heart, I've abandoned my family.

I want to go back to Underland. And Lord willing and the creek don't rise, I *will*.

"Give me a minute to get dressed," I start slowly, pitching my voice like I'm talking to a scared and cornered dog. Dad looks like he might either piss himself, or attack. Not really sure which would be worse. "I'll come down and—"

"Get out," he tells Tee and Dee, and I could almost swear there's smoke leaking from his nose. The boys exchange a look and then check with me. I give the briefest of nods and they remove themselves to the hallway with my father. He, on the other hand, sends Edith into my room. "I'll be waiting," Henry tells me, reluctantly closing the door. Well, *mostly* closing the door.

"What were you doing in here?" Edith asks me,

looking at the towel and then my face like she's never seen me before.

But … that's an excellent question.

I'm sure my dad will have a similar one.

Moving over to my dresser, I pull a drawer out and just … *stare*. It's been so long since I've worn my favorite jeans that I'm practically salivating. Ignoring Edith's penetrating stare, I drop my towel, yank on some cotton panties, and then slip into my jeans and a loose tank. I grab the Queenmaker and the Vorpal Blade next—I told Edith they were cosplay props and had her hide them in my nightstand drawer while I showered. But I need to hurry: if I leave my dad out there long enough, he might start shit with the boys.

Even though I know I'm going to catch crap for this, a girl can't be too careful. I strap the thigh sheath on as well as the gun holster, even as Edith stares at me like I'm a crazy person. Sorry, not sorry for trying to protect myself though. Besides, I have that mushroom flesh tucked in a side pocket that's strapped next to the Vorpal Blade. It's so small, and it's already attached to the thigh holster anyway, that I sometimes forget that it's there.

I slip my feet into fuzzy kitty slippers and can't help but think of the Cheshire Cat.

As much as I would hate to explain men popping out of mirrors to my dad, I'd like to see him. All of them. Fuck, I just want to know that Castle Heart is still standing.

"Come on, Edy," I mumble, moving past her and stepping into the most awkward moment of my life.

"Can we have … coffee downstairs?" I ask as I flick my gaze from my dad and over to Dee. His features, his smile, his eyes, they somehow seem more familiar to me than my own father's.

"Coffee …" Dad starts, like he's not even sure what that word means. "Right, right, coffee." He's looking at me like he's about ten seconds away from bursting into tears. And after all this horrid apathy he's been showering us with since Mom's sentencing? I don't even know what to make of it. "I should call your mother."

He turns away from me, shaking his head, and starts down the stairs. As he descends, he keeps casting glances over his shoulder, as if he's checking to make sure I'm really there.

The Mad Hatter and the March Hare—who must've shifted because he's sans ears—are sitting on the sofa side by side, watching us all descend like they're taking in their favorite scene from a play. They look bemused, interested, but not off their asses scared shitless like they could be.

They don't know the wrath of a parent.

Dad moves into the kitchen, but I notice that he scoots

the coffee pot over so he can stare at me through the doorway while he makes up our mugs.

"What do you want us to say or do?" Tee whispers.

"Because you know we're with you, through and through," Dee adds, and their stupid rhyming makes me smile.

Edy is watching us from across the room, but I don't think she can hear us. At least, I hope not.

"No clue," I whisper, because my mind is still churning and trying to figure out a way to explain what just happened to my dad.

"Let me do the talking," Tee says as Dad reappears with three steaming mugs. One's for me, one's for Edy, and one's for himself. No way in shit he's going to make any coffee for the four weird men I brought home with me.

"If he'll let you," I mumble as my dad sits in his favorite chair. I can see that his hands are shaking, and I figure he's probably in shock. Can't really blame him, now can I? He lost one son to murder already. With a sigh, I take a sip of my coffee and notice the old family portrait of my parents with Fred and … my older sister Rhoda. She only lived for five days outside of the hospital, and passed away years before I was born, so I forget about her sometimes. But my parents lost a child to SIDS. That's two of their four babies gone.

How the *fuck* could I have forgotten that?

A cold chill creeps down my spine, but I ignore it. Rhoda has nothing to do with any of this.

"Allison," my dad says, and the way his voice falls so softly, I know he's more than just angry, he's happy that I'm home. "Where have you been?"

Where have I been?

Well, let's see.

I fell down the Rabbit-Hole, watched a bandersnatch and a jabberwock fight a jubjub bird, played croquet with a king, learned to wield a sword, and used a mirror to travel between worlds. I've *been* in Underland. But I can't exactly tell him that.

"You wouldn't believe me if I told you," I start, and my dad's hand tightens around the handle on his mug. He lifts his brown eyes to mine, accusation glaring and hot bright, like a spotlight searing my skin and turning my flesh to ash.

"Allison, don't do this to me. If you have something to tell me, you can say it." He swallows hard and glances away sharply. "You're eighteen years old. You're an adult now." Dad seriously chokes on those words, like he can't believe he's even having to say them. "If there's something you've done, or somewhere you want to go, I can't stop you." He lifts his head to look at me, an emotional plea hanging on his gaze.

"I didn't kill Brandon," I say, because I can feel that accusation tainting the air in the living room. It's making it hard to breathe. "But I *did* follow the murderer; I chased him. And I ended up … somewhere I never could've imagined in my wildest dreams."

My dad opens his mouth to say something, pausing when a knock sounds at the door.

"Eureka police," a voice booms, and I feel my heart plummet to my feet.

"Police?" Dee asks, blinking a few times, like he's trying to put together what that means with reality.

"Well, damn," Raiden says, rising to his feet as my dad moves over to the door to answer it. There's a bit of mumbled conversation as my heart thunders in my chest and makes it hard to hear anything above the screaming of my rapid pulse.

Dad steps back to let the police enter, and I drop my mug on the carpet that Tee and Dee never got a chance to finish cleaning.

The Mocking Turtle and the Gryphon are standing on my fucking doorstep.

For a moment there, I question myself. They *look* like M.T. and the Gryphon, but they're missing all of their, how might you say, *idiosyncrasies*. The sharp lips, the toothless gums, the wings. But as I watch, they shift right back into place.

They're wearing uniforms, but their faces are unmistakable now.

"Allison!" Tee shouts, grabbing and throwing me out of the way as something explodes from the mirror in a wild, screaming mess.

It's a giant fucking cat, as big as a lion, with black and white striped fur, and eyes the color of rain clouds.

Chesh.

Dee barely has time to pull me out of the way before he crashes into one of the policemen, knocking Mom's side table to the floor and cracking both the legs in half. Edith starts to scream, but my dad, ever the cool and calm one in the family, manages to stand up and set his coffee aside. He doesn't spill a single goddamn drop.

"Alice, the Vorpal Blade!" a voice calls from behind me, just seconds before a shot goes off. I swing around to find the March Hare with a pair of twin revolvers pointed up at the ceiling.

At the Anti-Alice.

She drops from the ceiling in a flutter of skirts and comes up swinging, ignoring the blood dribbling down the front of her face from a set of gunshot wounds through her forehead. March's aim is dead-on.

Unfortunately, I think the Anti-Alice might be dead, too.

I leap back and drag the Vorpal Blade from my thigh sheath, throwing it up just in time to counteract the scythe she's swinging my way.

Her blade hits mine with a horrible fucking crack, and I realize with a burst of white-hot fear that that sound … is my *arm* breaking. Shock takes over, and I don't feel a damn thing. I also can't seem to keep my feet, falling on my ass and using my left hand to push the Vorpal Blade forward and defend myself. My right arm flops uselessly at my side, broken by the impact of the Anti-Alice's swing.

Holy. Shit.

And I thought I was ready after training with the Duke? I might be ten times stronger than I was when I fell through the Rabbit-Hole into Underland, I might be a hundred times stronger, but it's not enough. Not by a long shot.

"You're *the* Alice!" Dee screams at me from across the room, shoving Edy behind himself as he holds up his knife and just *barely* manages to avoid being cut in half by his opponent. The Gryphon is swinging that same sword I saw him use on the King, but without Dee's wings, the angel doesn't have much of a chance of standing up to him. "Use your *magic*."

The smell of rot and bone taints the air around me, making my nose burn and my throat close up tight. The

Anti-Alice has eyes like dark pools, the endless depths of forgotten wells. I feel like I could tumble right down them, and my body would never be found. Besides, I *can't* use my magic against her, right? Isn't that the whole point.

But then I remember how I threw the Vorpal Blade at her. I don't need to actually touch her with my powers; I just need to manipulate physical objects.

The Anti-Alice presses in hard, draining every ounce of physical energy that I have as I try to hold her back. With a sudden jerk, she pulls away and then swings again. I throw the Vorpal Blade up, but not with the intention of deflecting her blade, but with every ounce of power I have. It vibrates every molecule in my body, turns my soul into a restless mess.

Energy surges up and swirls around me, throwing furniture at the Anti-Alice, knocking her across the room and into my father's antique record player.

The Mad Hatter is there, helping me to my feet, and offering up his bloodied wrist at the same moment. Even though my dad's looking, and Edith's screaming, I take hold of it and drink as deeply as I can, the coppery sweet taste of his blood tainting my lips.

There's an immediate relief in my arm, but no relief in the battle.

Something *else* is coming through the Looking-Glass,

and it's not one of my boys.

Two thick arms claw their way through, followed by a bulbous body and a face with horns protruding from the lips. The thing crawls through and shakes its blubbery, brown body out.

Doesn't take a genius to recognize the Walrus.

He looks like a goddamn ogre, with a massive underbite and tiny, beady little eyes.

And here I was, thinking everyone in Underland was attractive. My bad.

"Alice, don't," the Mad Hatter says, grabbing and jerking me back before the man finds his feet and grins at me, tipping a tall, vinyl top hat in our direction.

"So we finally meet the Alice," he growls in this guttural Scottish accent. "Plucky little thing, ain't she? I'd like to throw her over my knee and give her a good spanking." He smacks his big lips at me as the Mad Hatter curses under his breath. "And you," he says as the sound of a struggle echoes from just outside the front door. When I glance over my shoulder, I don't see Tee, March, or the Mocking Turtle, and that scares the shit out of me. My head whips around as the Walrus takes a step toward us, smelling like the rotten crabs my mom bought for Christmas dinner one year and then forgot in the trunk of her car. Death, rot, and crusted sea salt. That's what the Walrus smells like. "You made a bargain with the King of Clubs, and you broke it. You won't get that chance again."

The Mad Hatter grabs me and moves me just in time to avoid the slither of a massive head through the Looking-Glass.

It's a jabberwock, but it *isn't* North.

No, and it's not alone either.

On top of its massive skull sits a man that's all skin and bones, with sunken cheeks, and a wooden leg. He has a fucking axe cradled in his scrawny arms.

The Carpenter.

"Oh shit," I whisper as the Mad Hatter inserts himself between me and the jabberwock. It seems to get stuck on the other side of the mirror, one arm in the living room, smashing furniture as it struggles to crawl through.

"Oh shit is right," Raiden says, his pupils dilating as the Carpenter climbs off the dragon's head, and it retreats back through Looking-Glass. I'm just standing there staring, and all I can think is *I need to get that mirror before something breaks it.* Because … because … if I get separated from Underland, I will break. I will shatter into nothing and float away on the wind.

The Anti-Alice is pushing to her feet, pink bow fluttering in the breeze from the open door. It's then that I see the photo hanging on the wall beside her, of Rhoda cradled in my mother's arms at the hospital. And … she's wearing a pink bow on her head.

Bile fills my mouth and I almost throw up.

The Anti-Alice … is my sister?!

I shove the Vorpal Blade inside its sheath at the same time that I dive forward to grab the Looking-Glass, struggling with its weight as I do my best to stand up and beat a hasty retreat.

I'm about ninety-nine percent certain I'd have died right there if the March Hare didn't lift the Looking-Glass up and over my head, and kick my legs out from under me at the same moment. The Anti-Alice's bone scythe lands, and buries itself in his chest as he stumbles back, blood spurting from the wound.

I struggle to stand up, slipping and sliding in the hot crimson flood as the Mad Hatter takes the Looking-Glass from March and carefully sets it in my father's favorite chair. In the same breath, he catches the March Hare as he falls, and thrusts his wrist against the Rabbit's mouth.

"Well, now, this looks like a whole heap of fun, wouldn't you say, brother?" the Walrus chortles, his blubber jiggling as he laughs, his whisker-covered cheeks reddening. "There's nothing I love more than blood, death, and a screaming woman trapped beneath me."

Swear to fuck, I puke a little. I don't mean to; it just

happens.

I back up next to the Mad Hatter and the March Hare as the latter finally seems to find his feet, standing up and shifting all in one breath. In the span of an instant, I have my hand on the bloody, furred flank of a bandersnatch.

Yet somehow, I'm still worried.

"Focus on the Anti-Alice, no matter what," Raiden says, his mouth twisted into a severe frown. I don't like that look. That look says *we might not win this*. Holy hearts and diamonds, what the fuck?!

"Rhoda?" my dad steps forward, forgotten and standing by the bay window. His expression is rife with pain as he moves toward the undead monster that used to be my sister. Without thinking, I snatch the Vorpal Blade up and move between the two of them.

I don't see Dee, Edith, or the Cheshire Cat anymore, and I'm starting to panic.

One thing at a time, Allison, I tell myself.

"Free up one of the twins for me," Raiden growls, and the March Hare goes trotting out the front door. My dad barely looks at the giant, fantastical beast in his living room. He only seems to have eyes for the Anti-Alice.

"You're going to face off against us alone?" the Walrus asks, glancing over at his brother. "Who knew this would be so bloody easy?" With a roar, the Walrus' body ripples, his fat ballooning until he's almost too big to fit inside the house. He has a tail instead of legs, and by some stretch of the imagination, I can see why he's nicknamed the Walrus. He almost, *almost*, looks like one

Another scream tears from his throat as he thunders toward the Mad Hatter, at stark contrast with the skinny, creepy little Carpenter who's still standing there and watching *me*. He reaches down and strokes the bulge in his pants, making me sick to my stomach.

We are outclassed, outmatched.

Without more help, we are *fucked*.

And yet, the Looking-Glass is quiet, the walls are spattered in blood, and I have no idea what I'm doing here.

We are so screwed.

Holy fucking hearts, please help me.

TO BE CONTINUED . . .

ALLISON SHATTERS THE LOOKING GLASS

HAREM OF HEARTS, BOOK #3

The Family Spells

THE FAMILY SPELLS, BOOK #1

PACK
OBSIDIAN GOLD

THE SEVEN MATES OF ZARA WOLF, BOOK #3

THE NINE

FOXFIRE BURNING, BOOK #1

SPIRITED

ACADEMY OF SPIRITS AND SHADOWS, BOOK #1

1

BRYNN

The instrument of my own destruction loomed above me, casting a long shadow in the bloodred rays of a dying sun. Its crumbling facade was decorated with a morbid metaphor of a face—soulless eyes, a gaping mouth, tangled green locks. Okay, so I was exaggerating the broken windows, the front entrance with its missing doors, and the cluster of wild blackberries that had morphed into a monster of their own making, but come on: the former Grandberg Manor was bust.

"This is the place?" I asked, hoisting my equipment

up on one shoulder and eyeing the crumbling old house with a raised brow. "It looks half-ready to collapse. You know me—if there's an even the slightest opportunity that I might trip, I will. Just be honest: am I going to fall straight through the floor?"

"Probably," Jasinda said, moving around me and over the twisted, rusted remains of the front gate. Once upon a time, this place was crawling with nobility from around the world, and its gardens … even the drawings were enough to make my mother's green thumb well, green with envy. "Air and I have a bet going on whether or not you'll make it out of here alive."

She thew a smirk over her shoulder at me and I pursed my lips.

Jasinda and Air were always making bets about me despite the fact that Air was the flubbing prince and shouldn't be making bets with anyone, let alone my handler. I had to admit though: if there was anyone around that was worth betting on, it was me.

First off, I was a half-angel which meant I could see spirits. And second, I was a half-human which meant those spirits actually deigned to communicate with me. A full-blooded angel was too haughty and highbrow to give any ghost the time of day, and a full-blooded human couldn't see one if they tried.

This special ability of mine did end up getting me into heaps of trouble. For example, there was that one time I followed a ghost straight into the queen's chambers and found her, um, indisposed with the head of the royal guard who, you know, also just happened to be my mother.

Then of course, there was the fact that I had the small, slight frame of my mother's desert dwelling ancestors but the wide, heavy span of wings from my father's side. Let's just be frank and say I toppled over a lot. Oh, and I ended up having long, in-depth conversations with people who weren't really people but were, in fact, very tricky ghosts. Even my first kiss had been with a spirit.

I took a deep breath of the cool, lavender scented air and followed after Jas, tripping and cursing in my own made up language.

"Go flub yourself," I growled at a thick tangle of blackberry that had gotten wrapped around my ankle. "You bleeding blatherer."

"Are you making words up again?" Jas said, parking her hands on her hips and sighing at me. "Can't you just say you bleeding bastard like everyone else? And don't even get me started on you using the work flub instead of fuc—"

"Hey!" I snapped, putting my palm over her lips with

one hand and pointing at myself with the other. "Half-angel over here. Just hearing somebody use a word with an extreme negative connotation makes me lose a feather."

"Oh, please," Jas said, pushing my hand away from her full red lips and smirking at me as I tried to rub her makeup off on my breeches. "That's a myth and you know it. Air told me that when you were kids, he used to chase you around the castle saying damn and bastard and the like, just to see if you'd lose any feathers—you didn't."

I narrowed my eyes on her as she turned and headed up what was once an impressive flight of marble steps, now cracked and chipped like an old beggar's teeth. I shivered and followed after her, examining the red stain on my palm that stunk like copperberries. A lot of women painted their mouths with the stuff, but to me that fragrant floral scent was tinged with a metallic sting, like copper. Like blood. Thus, the name—copperberries.

As I hurried up the steps, I kept my eyes on the decaying black facade of the manor, all its intricate moldings and details stripped away by time and rain, the harsh winds that curled across this part of the kingdom in summer.

"Let's do a quick walkthrough and see if you can't sense any residual energies," Jas suggested as I set my black leather satchel on the floor and knelt beside it. The ground around me was littered with debris—leaves, twigs, bits of crumbling plaster, a dead mouse.

"Oh, that's flubbing sick," I whispered as I caught sight of the creature's spirit hovering nearby, its furred sides almost completely translucent as it took long, heaving breaths. Of course, the mouse didn't need to breathe anymore, but it didn't know that.

I pulled a dagger from the sheath on my belt—please Goddess, don't actually ask me to use this thing in combat—and prodded at the mouse's body with the jeweled hilt.

Fresh blood stained the white leather pommel and made me shiver.

"Jas," I started, because a long dead carcass was one thing, but a fresh one? Hell's bells—since Hell was an actual place it didn't count as a curse word so no lost feathers for me—but I hoped it was just a cat that had taken the rodent's life and not … something else.

"Brynn, you need to see this!" Jas shouted and I sighed, wiping the mouse's blood on the already dirty leg of my breeches and tucking it away. Before I stood up, I clasped the silver star hanging around my neck with one hand and reached out to touch the mouse's spirt with the other. The poor thing was too scared to even shy away, its soul becoming briefly corporeal as my fingers made contact with its fur.

"Goddess-speed and happy endings," I whispered as

the image of the mouse morphed and shivered, turning as silver as a beam of moonlight and fading away until there was nothing there but the warped and rotted boards of the old floor.

I stood up, leaving my satchel where it was on the ground and rubbing my shoulder as I followed the sound of Jasinda's voice. The road up to the manor was riddled with broken cobblestones, weeds, and the skeletons of long abandoned carriages. It was too rough for any sort of pack animal to make the trek, so we'd had to carry ourselves on foot, lugging all the equipment that a spirit whisperer—that's me—might need to exorcise a ghost or two or ten.

"Jassy?" I asked as I moved past the formal foyer with its double staircases, and down a long receiving hall that would've been used by servants in times past. The wallpaper was peeling like old skin, leaving behind water stained walls and flaky plaster. At some point, thieves had come in and stripped the old place of its wood moldings, sconces and chandeliers; they'd left nothing but a skeleton behind.

"In here!" she called out, drawing me through an empty archway where a swinging door might've once stood and into the kitchen. As I moved, I was conscious of keeping my wings tucked tightly against my back. My clumsiness was not limited to my feet. I was notorious among the castle staff for breaking things with the feathered black wings that graced my back. As a kid, they used to call me Pigeon Girl because I caused ten times as much damage to the royal halls as the flying rats that plagued the old stone building.

"What is it?" I asked as I leaned against the wall outside a small servant's room—a tiny square that would've belonged to the head cook. "Jas, there was a mouse—"

"Flub mice," she said, only she didn't actually say flub but I wouldn't lose a feather even thinking about the F-word that famously rhymes with duck. As a half-angel, my powers were bound to the light goddess and she was a serious stickler for avoiding words with negative connotations. I supposed I couldn't blame her; the very words I spoke held power. The more positivity and light I imbued those words with, the more powerful I was. "Look at this, Brynn. There's a distinct spiritual signature written all over this room."

The room itself was so small that with the collapsed remains of a small bed and a sagging dresser, there wasn't space for us both. I waited for Jas to step out, pushing her long dark hair over her shoulder, sapphire blue eyes sparkling with a scholar's excitement.

"Brynn, this could be it," she said as I took a deep breath and stepped into the room. "Our big break."

Jas was always looking for that one case, that one unique spirit that we could exorcise that would prove our worth to the scholars at the Royal College. In just two weeks, I'd be turning twenty-one and that'd be it; that was the cut off date for acceptance into the prestigious training facility. It wasn't that Jas cared about the status of being a student there, or the potential for a high-ranking position after graduation, it was the library. Only students of the Royal College were permitted to use the vast, twisting hallways of the catacombs. There were books there that couldn't be found anywhere else—not to mention ancient artifacts, exemplary professors, and vast resources that could be used for research.

It was Jasinda's dream, even if it wasn't mine. I hoped she was right; I hoped this was it.

I stepped over a small hole in the floor and into the tiny windowless room.

As soon as I did, it hit me, the pressure of an angry spirit, bearing down on me with the cold burn of something long dead and waiting. Waves of icy winter chill tore across my skin like knives, despite the warm evening air that permeated the rest of the building. Whatever this was, it was powerful.

I grasped the silver star at my throat and closed my eyes.

“Haversey,” I whispered, invoking the name of the light

goddess.

If I were Jas, I knew what I'd be seeing: a girl shrouded in silver moonlight, her tanned skin pearlescent and shimmering, her hair as white as snow lifted in an unnatural breeze.

I opened my eyes slowly and bit back a gasp.

Every inch of the walls was covered in the word Hellim, the name of the dark god. What I had originally thought were decorative splotches on the wallpaper were actually his name, written in blood a thousand times over. It had been impossible to see in the dim half-light, but now that I had my second sight open, the letters glowed with a strong, angry spiritual signature.

I started to take a step back when my foot went through the hole in the floor, and the rotting boards around me creaked and toppled into a black pit below.

"Brynn!"

Jas screamed my name as I fell through cold shadow and frost, hitting the soggy wet earth with a grunt and a crack of pain in my shoulder that almost immediately went numb. That was bad, really bad. Pain was one thing, but numbness meant that what'd just happened to me could be really serious.

I tried to stand up, but my arm gave out and I found myself lying in a mound of decaying wet leaves and dirt, the scent of rot thick and cloying in the air.

As I blinked to try and orient myself to the darkness, I felt a cold hand on my shoulder and a gust of icy breath at my ear.

When I turned, I found myself looking into the face of a handsome—and very angry—spirit.

His lips curved up in a smile meant to disarm me.

"Boo," he whispered as he reached out and pushed my dislocated shoulder back into place.

White-hot pain crashed over my vision and I passed out.

SIGN UP FOR A C.M. STUNICH

newsletter

Sign up for an exclusive first look at the hottest new releases, contests, and exclusives from bestselling author C.M. Stunich and get *three free* eBooks as a thank you!

@

www.cmstunich.com

JOIN MY BOOK CLUB

the bookish bat cave

Want to discuss what you've just read? Get exclusive teasers or meet special guest authors? Join my online book club on Facebook!

@

www.facebook.com/groups/thebookishbatcave

Discover your next five star read

in C.M. Stunich's (aka Violet Blaze's) collection and discover more kick-ass heroines, smoking hot heroes, and stories filled with wit, humor, and heart.

C.M. STUNICH'S

stalking links

KEEP UP WITH ALL
THE FUN ... AND EARN SOME FREE BOOKS!

JOIN THE C.M. STUNICH NEWSLETTER – Get three free books just for signing up http://eepurl.com/DEsEf

TWEET ME ON TWITTER, BABE – Come sing the social media song with me https://twitter.com/CMStunich

SNAPCHAT WITH ME – Get exclusive behind the scenes looks at covers, blurbs, book signings and more http://www.snapchat.com/add/cmstunich

LISTEN TO MY BOOK PLAYLISTS – Share your fave music with me and I'll give you my playlists (I'm super active on here!) https://open.spotify.com/user/12101321503

FRIEND ME ON FACEBOOK – Okay, I'm actually at the 5,000 friend limit, but if you click the "follow" button on my profile page, you'll see way more of my killer posts https://facebook.com/cmstunich

LIKE ME ON FACEBOOK – Pretty please? I'll love you forever if you do! ;) https://facebook.com/cmstunichauthor & https://facebook.com/violetblazeauthor

CHECK OUT THE NEW SITE – (under construction) but it looks kick-a$$ so far, right? You can order signed books here! http://www.cmstunich.com

READ VIOLET BLAZE – Read the books from my hot as hellfire pen name, Violet Blaze http://www.violetblazebooks.com

SUBSCRIBE TO MY RSS FEED – Press that little orange button in the corner and copy that RSS feed so you can get all the latest updates http://www.cmstunich.com/blog

AMAZON, BABY – If you click the follow button here, you'll get an email each time I put out a new book. Pretty sweet, huh? http://amazon.com/author/cmstunich http://amazon.com/author/violetblaze

PINTEREST – Lots of hot half-naked men. Oh, and half-naked men. Plus, tattooed guys holding babies (who are half-naked) http://pinterest.com/cmstunich

INSTAGRAM – Cute cat pictures. And half-naked guys. Yep, that again. http://instagram.com/cmstunich

P.S. I heart the f*ck out of you! Thanks for reading! I love your faces.

<3 C.M. Stunich aka Violet Blaze

ABOUT C.M. STUNICH

C.M. Stunich is a self-admitted bibliophile with a love for exotic teas and a whole host of characters who live full time inside the strange, swirling vortex of her thoughts. Some folks might call this crazy, but Caitlin Morgan doesn't mind – especially considering she has to write biographies in the third person. Oh, and half the host of characters in her head are searing hot bad boys with dirty mouths and skillful hands (among other things). If being crazy means hanging out with them everyday, C.M. has decided to have herself committed.

She hates tapioca pudding, loves to binge on cheesy horror movies, and is a slave to many cats. When she's not vacuuming fur off of her couch, C.M. can be found with her nose buried in a book or her eyes glued to a computer screen. She's the author of over thirty novels – romance, new adult, fantasy, and young adult included. Please, come and join her inside her crazy. There's a heck of a lot to do there.

Oh, and Caitlin loves to chat (incessantly), so feel free to e-mail her, send her a Facebook message, or put up smoke signals. She's already looking forward to it.

Made in the USA
Columbia, SC
16 January 2024

30565764R00307